E.R. PUNS
DEATH COMES TO CAMBERS

Ernest Robertson Punshon was born in London in 1872.

At the age of fourteen he started life in an office. His employers soon informed him that he would never make a really satisfactory clerk, and he, agreeing, spent the next few years wandering about Canada and the United States, endeavouring without great success to earn a living in any occupation that offered. Returning home by way of working a passage on a cattle boat, he began to write. He contributed to many magazines and periodicals, wrote plays, and published nearly fifty novels, among which his detective stories proved the most popular and enduring.

He died in 1956.

Also by E.R. Punshon

Information Received
Death Among The Sunbathers
Crossword Mystery
Mystery Villa
Death of A Beauty Queen
The Bath Mysteries
Mystery of Mr. Jessop
The Dusky Hour
Dictator's Way

E.R. PUNSHON

DEATH COMES TO CAMBERS

With an introduction
by Curtis Evans

DEAN STREET PRESS

INTRODUCTION

During the Golden Age of detective fiction, British crime writers set myriad murder mysteries in imagined stately mansions of the landed aristocracy and gentry, yet as far as I have been able to determine very few of these writers themselves sprang from this privileged milieu. One of the most notable exceptions was E.R. Punshon's Detection Club contemporary Sir Henry-Lancelot Aubrey Fletcher (1887-1969), a baronet who between 1926 and 1957 wrote, under the pseudonym "Henry Wade," twenty crime novels, in many of which he portrays country house settings that are, contrary to the stereotype of books by Golden Age mystery authors, decidedly demystified, shorn of nostalgia's romantic trappings. Although E.R. Punshon's first full-dress essay at the aristocratic country house detective novel, *Death Comes to Cambers* (1935), is hardly told in so grimly realistic a vein as some of Henry Wade's mysteries, *Cambers* nevertheless boasts, in addition to its interesting characters and accomplished puzzle plot, a delightfully subversive take on English country house mysteries. In my view it is one of the finest tales of its kind produced during the Golden Age of detective fiction.

Unlike his series sleuth, Detective-Sergeant Bobby Owen, Punshon's own immediate ancestral background was non-aristocratic, both his paternal and maternal relatives having been strongly associated with trade, yet on his mother's side of the family he possessed remoter titled connections. Ernest Robertson Punshon was born in 1872 in Dulwich, London, to

Robert Punshon, a sugar broker and civil engineer, and Selina Webb Halket Punshon, the eldest daughter of David Halket, a Newcastle timber merchant and convict ship owner originally from Perth, Scotland. In 1855 Halket, who seems to have stuck his fingers in altogether too many financial pies, suffered bankruptcy; and two years before his death he was taken to court on behalf of his wife, Mary Webb Halket, and their children, it having been alleged that he had mishandled money with which he had been entrusted in his capacity as his father-in-law's executor—a sad comedown for a man descended from the Halketts, baronets of Pitfirrane Castle, Fife. E.R. Punshon derived the pseudonym "Robertson Halket," under which in the 1930s he published another two mysteries, from his middle name and his mother's surname, suggesting he took a certain pride in his Halket line, despite its having in this case come down in the world.

At the time of his 1866 marriage to David Halket's eldest daughter, Robert Punshon, a sugar broker descended from a long line of Punshons of Gateshead, County Durham (presumably William Morley Punshon, a prominent Victorian-era Methodist minister, was a distant relation), had two unmarried schoolteacher sisters, Sarah and Elizabeth, the latter of whom had served as governess to the wealthy industrialist Colbeck family at Whorlton Hall, near Newcastle. He later styled himself a civil engineer and in the 1870s he patented a series of inventions, including a process for treating gun-cotton with a sugar solution in order to better regulate the rapidity of explosions in firearms---—just the sort of technical know-how that might have helped inspire his future crime novelist son.

After their marriage Robert and Selina Punshon for six years resided in Newcastle, one of England's most important shipping and industrial centers, moving in 1872 to London, where Ernest, the second of their three sons, was born. The Punshons seem to have led, like the Halkets before them, an unstable economic existence, a state that would follow young Ernest into his adult life. In 1868, Robert Punshon, recalling his father-in-law, filed for bankruptcy and by the 1880s apparently lived apart from his family. By 1881 he lodged at a house in St. Pancras, London, while Selina and the children resided in Harrogate, Yorkshire, where she was employed as a teacher in a girls' school. (Selina's four younger sisters, known as the Misses Halket, ran their own girls' school, Melchet House, at Lytham, Lancashire.)

By 1888, Ernest was a railway clerk and lodging in London with his elder brother. Many years later, Punshon at the age of fifty recalled with mordant humor that he "went to work in the accounts office of a railroad at the age of sixteen [the year his mother died]. After a year or two my office superiors told me gently that they thought I was not without intelligence but that my intelligence and my work did not seem somehow to coincide. So I thanked them for the hint, gracefully accepted it, and departed to Canada..." There, on the "golden prairies" of Saskatchewan, Punshon launched a venture in wheat farming that sadly quickly succumbed to the ungentle pressures of market forces. (He would later use this experience in his early mainstream novel *Constance West*.)

Again undaunted by failure, Punshon traveled to Canada's Northwest Territories--where, he claimed, he once evaded pursuit by a pack of ravening wolves--and later drifted downward across the border to the United States, where he followed such diverse avocations as cow-punching out West and lumbering in Michigan. Returning to England not long before the death of Queen Victoria aboard the cargo liner *S.S. Armenian* (he worked his passage as a cattleman), Punshon settled in Liverpool, where he resided with his elderly retired schoolteacher aunt, Sarah Punshon, and took employment as a life assurance agent, all the while trying finally to make fame and fortune in the literary world, writing novels and countless shorter fiction pieces for magazines. In 1905 he married Sarah Houghton, and the couple returned to England's literary hub, London, where they would reside until his death a half-century later.

Punshon's closest immediate family connection to the country house life of the landed gentry appears to have come from an aged aunt who once had been employed by the Colbeck family as the governess at Whorlton Hall (and the Colbeck fortune was built not on the land but on what lay under it—i.e., coal mines). Yet in *Death Comes to Cambers* Punshon not only set his novel in a classic country house milieu, he for the first time provided readers with additional detail on the aristocratic background of his own series sleuth, Detective-Sergeant Bobby Owen. When the novel opens, Bobby actually is staying as a weekend guest at Cambers House, having been invited there by his grandmother, Lady Hirlpool, an old friend of Lady Cambers, whose strangled corpse is discovered out-of-doors in the opening pages of the novel. (Additionally, Lady Cambers' fabulous jewelry collection has been burgled.) Colonel Lawson, chief constable of the county, is shocked to learn that Bobby, a lowly sergeant in the Metropolitan Police, is a grandson of no less than a peeress of the realm ("One moment he permitted himself in which to regret those older and better days when a gentleman was a gentleman, and, if he had to provide for himself, at least never thought of adopting such a dull, plebeian method as work. All this Bolshevism, he reflected gloomily…."). However, the good colonel determines--most providentially as it turns out--to request of Scotland Yard that Bobby's services be retained for this case.

Potential suspects in the murder of Lady Cambers, a well-meaning but imperious individual, are numerous, including her absconded husband, Sir Albert; a neighbor, Mr. Bowman, whose sister is suspected of unseemly carryings-on with Sir Albert; Mr. Tyler, a wealthy American (is there any other kind in Golden Age British detective novels?) who was most desirous of obtaining Lady Camber's famous Cleopatra pearl; Farman, a butler who may be hiding something shady in his past; Eddy Dene, the village grocer's son turned amateur archaeologist and fierce evolutionist who is the latest protégé of Lady Cambers; Amy Emmers, Lady Cambers' enigmatic personal maid; Reverend Andrews, vicar of the parish, violently opposed to what he considers Darwinian heresy; Tim Sterling, Lady Cambers' impecunious nephew and heir; Ray Hardy, son of one of Lady Cambers' tenants; and a mysterious stranger from London, in the vicinity possibly on account of burglarious intentions.

In *Death Comes to Cambers* Punshon deftly balances an ingenious and fairly-clued puzzle plot with considerable character interest and amusing satire of English class conventions. Not only is Colonel Lawson nonplussed by Bobby's ambiguous social status, he is outraged when those he deems his clear inferiors, like Eddy Dene and Amy Emmers, step above their stations, as he sees them, as can be seen in this exchange between the colonel and Miss Emmers:

"Well, Emmers, I don't think we need keep you any longer. Emmers is your name, I think?"

"My name is Amy Margaret Emmers," she answered in her aloof, indifferent way as she rose to go. "I am generally called Miss Emmers."

In the same calm, distant way she went gently from the room, and the chief constable, staring after her, went slowly redder and redder in the face.

"I...I...I..." he stuttered at last. "I believe she meant that. I believe she meant I wasn't to call her Emmers."

As it was quite evident that that, indeed, was precisely what she had meant, neither Bobby nor Moulland ventured any comment.

The times they were changing in the Troubled Thirties even, contrary to still-prevalent popular belief, in the Golden Age British detective novel--particularly in those written by E.R. Punshon.

Curtis Evans

CHAPTER ONE

THE EMPTY ROOM

AT THE FOOT OF THE STAIRS, FARMAN, THE BUTLER, and Amy Emmers, Lady Cambers's maid, met each other. Amy was carrying a tray with the cup of tea and the tiny square of dry toast it was her duty first thing each morning to take to her mistress. She was looking a little flurried and disturbed. She said: 'Her room's empty. She's not there.'

Farman had no need to ask to whom the 'she' referred. In the language of domestic service, the unrelated personal feminine pronoun means always and invariably the mistress of the house. Farman knew, therefore, at once Amy meant that Lady Cambers was not in her room. But the fact did not make much impression on him. As was not unusual with him in the early morning, he was in a bad temper. Besides, he disliked Amy, who, he considered, was tending to secure much too influential a position in the household —one, indeed, incompatible with the unquestioned authority that in his opinion should be wielded by the butler. That was always the worst of a house where there was no master, and ever since things had come to an open breach between Sir Albert and Lady Cambers, and Sir Albert had departed to London, the influence of Amy, as her ladyship's personal maid and chief channel of communication between her and the rest of the staff, had been steadily increasing. A 'favourite', in fact, she was becoming, and Farman didn't like it, and liked it all the less that Amy was so plainly trying to be conciliatory and friendly to him and to the others. But both her own position, and also the keen interest in Eddy Dene, Amy's cousin and fiancé, and his archæological researches Lady Cambers had been showing of late, gave Amy a certain intimacy and consequent authority with the mistress of the house that the rest of the staff, egged on perhaps by Farman, were a little inclined to resent. So there had been a good deal of satisfaction and nodding of heads when rumour spread of a violent scene of mutual recrimination supposed recently to have taken place between the mistress and the maid. And all that the butler said now in response to Amy was an ill-tempered: 'Mind you don't let her tea go cold.'

The remark was hardly relevant, but it tended to put Amy in her place and to remind her of her duties, and, having made it, Farman was passing on his way—on his morning tour of supervision—when, in the same worried and bewildered tone, Amy added: 'Her bed's not been slept in.'

Farman only caught the words imperfectly, and paid them no attention. He went on along the passage to the garden door that according to routine he unlocked and unbolted. It was a lovely morning after the heavy rainstorm of the evening before, and, even in his present mood of sleepiness and bad temper, Farman felt something of its peace and beauty and of the soft loveliness of the early sunshine. A recollection of Amy's last remark stirred uneasily in his mind, as though in contrast to the scene without. He went back along the passage. Amy was still standing at the foot of the stairs with the tray in her hands, evidently not quite knowing what to do next. He said to her: 'What's that you said?'

'Her bed's not been slept in; her room's empty,' Amy repeated.

Farman considered this. His was not a very quick mind; its tendency was always to reject the unfamiliar, the unexpected. He said at last: 'Don't talk silly. She's not been sitting up all night, has she?'

'I don't know,' answered Amy helplessly.

'Well, she must be somewhere,' declared Farman. 'You had better find her,' he added. 'Her tea'll be cold.'

'It's cold already,' said Amy.

Farman sniffed, as if to indicate that from Amy he had

expected nothing better, and then, what she had told him beginning to sink into his mind, he so far departed from his usual routine of next unlocking and unbolting the front-door, as to proceed instead to the small morning-room that was Lady Cambers's favourite sitting-room—her 'den' she had been used to call it sometimes, in opposition to the library Sir Albert had appropriated to himself and his special pursuits and interests wherein books and reading had no place whatever. That, of course, had been before the final breach, but Lady Cambers had continued her habit of using this small room as her own special domain—it was snug and quiet, she said, and she liked it, and gradually a convention had been established that when she was sitting there she was not to be disturbed except for urgent cause. Farman, opening the door, had a vague expectation of finding her there now. He supposed she might have got up early for some reason and come downstairs to sit here. But the room was unoccupied. The morning light, strug-gling through the still shuttered and curtained windows, showed that, and showed, also, on the table a tray with an empty tumbler on it, and a plate on which were still some crumbs. Glancing over his shoulder, to remark to Amy that anyhow her ladyship wasn't there, Farman noticed with uninterested surprise that the girl's former expres-sion of bewilderment had given way to one that seemed to show uneasiness and alarm—even terror. Though what there could be to alarm her or anyone else in this un-occupied room, Farman had no idea. He left the problem unconsidered, and said: 'Well, she isn't here.'

'I'll clear those things away,' Amy said, advancing into the room, putting down the breakfast-tray she was still carrying, and making to pick up the one on the table before them.

Again Farman was vaguely puzzled by a certain haste and uneasiness her hurried nervous action seemed to show. But it was plainly her duty, since she was responsible for the room, to clear away this tray that had apparently been left from the night before.

'Ought to have been done before,' he said severely, and then sniffed at the glass from which a faint odour had reached his expert and practised nostrils. 'Brandy,' he exclaimed. 'Well, now, and I thought she never touched it. That young Eddy Dene was here last night, wasn't he? Been standing him a drink, I suppose.'

Amy did not reply. She picked up the tray and began to hurry away. But Farman stopped her. He was beginning to feel really puzzled and uneasy now.

'I'll attend to that,' he said. 'You go and see if she's in Lady Hirlpool's room. Very likely she's there all the time.'

'I'll take this into the kitchen first,' Amy said, still holding on to the tray.

'You do what you're told, my girl; and look slippy, too,' Farman ordered, taking it from her. 'It's a bit rummy, where she is.' When Amy still hesitated, he added sharply: 'Now then, what are you waiting for?'

She obeyed then, though still as if reluctant to leave the tray with him. When she had gone, Farman smelt the glass again.

'Stiff,' he commented to himself. 'There's been no drowning that little lot. Is the old girl taking to drink on the sly?' He shook his head gravely, pleased at the idea—which, however, he did not believe for a moment. 'Or is it Miss Amy Emmers having a go on the q.t., and is that why she didn't seem to like me seeing it?' Again he shook his head gravely, again pleased at this idea and thinking it more probable. 'Or has one or other of 'em been standing Mr. Eddy drinks?'

But against this last supposition was the fact that he himself had let Eddy Dene out the night before, and certainly, so far as he knew at least, no brandy—or, indeed, any other refreshment—had been served during his visit, prolonged as that had been.

In the hall he gave the tray to one of the maids—for now the usual round of domestic work was beginning—told her to take it into the kitchen, and then went on upstairs. He paused on the landing outside Lady Hirlpool's room. There was a murmur of voices within, and almost at once Amy came out.

'She's not there,' she said. 'Lady Hirlpool's not seen her.'

They looked at each other helplessly, and there emerged from the room Amy had just left a little old sharp-featured lady, wearing her dressing-gown over her pyjamas, for, if she was over sixty and a grandmother of grown-up grandchildren, none the less she was as up-to-date as the most up-to-date young miss who ever let to-morrow toil after her in vain.

'What's all this fuss about?' she demanded. 'Lady Cambers has most likely just gone out for a stroll before breakfast—it's a lovely morning after the rain.'

'Yes, m'lady,' agreed Farman, 'but she never does, m'lady; and then all the doors were locked.'

'Her bed's not been slept in,' Amy said.

Lady Hirlpool looked as if she didn't believe it.

'But that's . . .' she began, and then, without specifying what it was, she marched across the landing and along the passage to Lady Cambers's room. She went in, and came out again almost at once.

'No, it hasn't been,' she confirmed, and stood still in the doorway, looking at them and apparently expecting them to say something.

By this time a certain uneasiness, a vague alarm, had begun to spread itself through the house. The maid who had taken the tray into the kitchen had reported that 'Mr. Farman looked that upset'; the chauffeur, coming into the kitchen for his early-morning cup of tea, had smelt at the glass on the tray on the kitchen table, and inquired, with jocular envy, who had been swigging brandy already;

the parlourmaid had reported that Amy had left Lady Cambers's early-morning tray in the morning-room for her tea to grow cold. All the domestic staff—parlourmaid, housemaids, senior and junior, the tweeny, cook, kitchen-maid, chauffeur—were now hovering doubtfully on the frontier-line that cut off the family rooms from the staff apartments, and then cook, strong in the knowledge of a dignity that enabled her to hold her own even with Mr. Farman himself, came resolutely through the hall and up the stairs.

'Is it burglars?' she demanded, voicing her perennial fear. 'And me thinking we were safe for once, with a young police gentleman in the house.'

Lady Hirlpool had vanished into Lady Cambers's room again, but now once more emerged. She somehow gave an impression of having just made a swift and careful search in every corner, in every drawer, behind every chair or curtain. She said: 'It's most extraordinary. She must be somewhere.' She paused to see if anyone contradicted this. No one did, and finding it was a proposition generally accepted, but not carrying the matter much further, she asked: 'Have you told Mr. Owen? If you haven't, you had better.'

The Mr. Owen she referred to was the young police-man on whose mere presence in the house the cook had so greatly relied. A grandson of Lady Hirlpool's, he had chosen the police for a career, and by good luck and a certain stolid persistence of endeavour that never let him abandon any clue, however slight, had attained some success and promotion to the rank of sergeant in the C.I.D. It was through his grandmother, Lady Hirlpool, an old friend of Lady Cambers, that he had come to spend the week-end here, partly because his grandmother wanted to show him off to her friend, but ostensibly to advise Lady Cambers on precautions to be taken against the burglary whereof she shared her cook's perennial dread that certain recent occurrences had much increased. His room was on the same floor, not far away, and when Farman entered he found the young man standing at the window, already fully dressed. He glanced round as the butler came in, and said to him: 'Isn't that field over there the one where Eddy Dene is doing his digging? Seems to be something up; there's a bit of a crowd and people running about. Looks as if they had found the Missing Link all right.'

But this jesting allusion to the archæological investigations that were being carried on brought no response from Farman. He came to the window, too, and looked out. He said abruptly: 'We can't find Lady Cambers. She's not in the house. Her bed's not been slept in.'

CHAPTER TWO

DISCOVERIES

FOR A MOMENT OR TWO THEY REMAINED STANDING in silence, the young detective and the butler, staring from the window at the little group assembled there in the sunshine in the distant field. Then Bobby said: 'I think we had better see what's up.' He added: 'Are you sure Lady Cambers isn't in the house?'

'We've looked everywhere,' Farman answered. 'Her maid says her bed hasn't been slept in.'

It was a piece of information that made Bobby look graver even than before.

'Any doors or windows open this morning?' he asked.

'No; they were all locked and bolted same as usual,' Farman answered.

'Well, then, how did she get out?' Bobby asked, and, when Farman only shook his head and looked bewildered, he went on: 'Are you sure she was in the house when you locked up? I suppose you see to that?'

'Last thing,' Farman answered. 'About eleven it was; and her ladyship wouldn't be out at that time of night, would she?'

They left the room together, and, on the landing outside, Bobby said to Lady Hirlpool, who was still standing there with Amy: 'We're going to have a look round outside. I expect she's just gone out for a stroll before breakfast.'

'No, you don't; and don't tell lies to your grandmother,' retorted Lady Hirlpool. 'Lotty never went for a walk before breakfast in her life. There's something wrong, and you know it.'

'We won't be longer than we can help,' Bobby answered. 'Anyhow, there's no sense in jumping to conclusions.'

Followed by Farman he went into the hall, where the indoor servants had now gathered in a whispering, excited group.

'May as well get on with the work,' Bobby said to them. 'If Lady Cambers has gone out for some reason, she'll want breakfast when she gets back. Miller,' he added, to the chauffeur, 'better see that the car's ready. It may be wanted.'

'Her bed hasn't been slept in,' called out the parlour-maid. 'I've looked myself and so it hasn't.'

'See that nothing in the room is touched till we know what has happened,' Bobby directed. 'Don't touch or disturb anything in the house if you can possibly avoid it. Understand?'

They said they did, and were plainly sufficiently frightened and impressed to make it likely they would try to obey, though sad experience had long ago convinced Bobby that always the important pieces of evidence get thrown away, because at first it seems so inconceivable they can be of any value, while irrelevant trifles are religiously preserved. Lady Hirlpool had come down the stairs now, and she and the maid, Amy, joined the little group of women-servants, while Miller retired to get the car ready in case of need, and Bobby, followed by Farman, went out by the front-door and round the side of the house, towards where, north of the building, was gathered the distant group they had observed from the window of Bobby's room.

Hurrying past the rose-garden and through the shrubbery above the tennis-lawns, they came soon to the boundary-fence of the grounds, where a small gate opened on a footpath leading to the village. On the other side of this path were fields sloping to the bed of a tiny stream, and then, sloping upwards again to a smooth rounded crest of grassy land known locally as The Mounts, the farm of which it formed part, going by the name of Mounts Farm. To the casual glance all this district might have seemed somewhat flat, dull, and uninspiring, but the trained geologist would have found it full of interest, such plain evidence did it show of slow rise and slower subsidence, of a time when The Mounts had been, in fact, a considerable range of hills, almost deserving the name of mountains, and when, in the place of the tiny streamlet of to-day, a great river had covered most of the valley, presently to flow into the Thames on its way to join the Rhine at some spot where now the North Sea ebbs and flows.

Leaving the footpath that ran in an easterly direction towards the village, Bobby and his companion hurried across the fields, and saw running quickly towards them a figure that had detached itself from the group on the other side of the stream.

'It's Ray Hardy—Mr. Hardy's son,' Farman said uneasily. 'He's in a hurry about something.'

Instinctively they paused. It was as though a sense of coming tragedy impinged upon their consciousness and held them still.

'Who is Mr. Hardy?' Bobby asked, his eyes fixed upon that coming, running figure.

'Mr. Hardy's the farmer here,' Farman answered. 'That's his son, Ralph. Ray, they call him. What's he running that way for? Some of the land's Mr. Hardy's own, but most he rents from her ladyship.'

Ray Hardy was quite close now. Though the long damp grass that still held much of the previous night's soaking rain hampered his progress, he came at speed. He called out pantingly: 'It's Lady Cambers. She's dead. In Frost Field. Mr. Bowman saw her. He told us.'

It seemed to both Bobby and to Farman that they had already known this.

'Well, now then, now then, now then,' Farman muttered, and he would have gone on muttering those two words over and over again to himself if Bobby had not stopped him with a gesture for silence.

Yet Bobby himself was almost as much affected by the bewildering suddenness with which this horror had leaped upon them. For a moment he had a brief vision of Lady Cambers as he had known her—brisk, energetic, authoritative—directing everybody and everything the way they should go, arranging all things to her taste, full of confidence in herself and in life. And now it seemed there had fallen upon her, without warning, a strange and dreadful doom. Recovering himself with an effort, reminding himself there was much that must need doing, he said: 'How ... I mean ... what's happened ... is there anything to show ...?'

Young Ray Hardy sank his voice to a whisper. It seemed he was afraid of his own voice, of his own words. He said: 'It's murder ... murder all right. ... I don't know who did it ... none of us knew anything, not till Mr. Bowman came and told us.'

'You've seen yourself ... you're sure ...?' Bobby asked.

'I helped carry her to Eddy Dene's shed over there,' answered Ray. 'Looks she's been throttled—strangled.' He gulped. 'I know nothing about it, but murder that would be—murder.'

'It was burglars she was afraid of,' Farman interrupted, in a queer, high-pitched voice. 'Burglars. If it's murder —well, who did it?'

'Yes, that's it. Who did it?' Ray repeated. 'That's what they're all saying, and no one knows. God knows I don't!'

He was evidently badly shaken, and that perhaps was little wonder. There was a heavy sweat on his forehead, and he wiped it away with the sleeve of his coat. Bobby, looking at him with close attention, did not find himself very favourably impressed. His eyes were bloodshot and heavy, his mouth loose, his chin seemed to run away from it. A weak face, Bobby thought, and with a suggestion in those bloodshot eyes of too great a fondness for beer and for strong ale; no lad of his apparent age should have eyes like that. But one had to make allowance for the shock of such a happening, and he continued in the same hurried, jerky voice: 'It's our field, but we didn't know, none of us, till Mr. Bowman came running and shouting to us to come and help. Awful he looked, and running like all, he was, and you've only to look at her to see it must be murder. Jordan says so, too. He's sent to Hirlpool for help. Dad says it did ought to be Scotland Yard up in London by rights, but Jordan says it's Hirlpool first and Scotland Yard afterwards as required. Dad said he had a good mind to ring up Scotland Yard himself, only Jordan's police, and he ought to know. It's our field where she was, but none of us knew a thing about it till Mr. Bowman came running and calling across the turnips.'

All this came tumbling out in one breathless spate of words. It was how the boy's terror and excitement found relief. That Jordan was the name of the local sergeant of police, Bobby already knew. With one constable, a man named Norris, to help him, he guarded the King's peace in this part of the country, and as a rule had nothing much more serious to deal with than the theft of a stray hen or the disputes of two quarrelsome neighbours. Bobby knew, too, that Hirlpool was the county town and the head-quarters of the county police, of which the head was a Colonel Lawson. It was quite recently that Colonel Lawson had been appointed to his position by a Watch Committee convinced that discipline and organization were the chief things to consider in police work, and, though Bobby recognized that there was much to be said for that belief, he also thought that probably the newly appointed chief constable was not likely to have done much as yet to improve a detective department known to be somewhat old-fashioned in its methods and ideas, or, indeed, even so far to have realized that that task was of any great or pressing importance. Nor was he altogether sure how the county police authorities would be likely to regard any action he himself might take in this emergency. But he was on the spot; he was a sworn officer of police; he felt he could not divest himself of responsibility. He said to Farman: 'I think you had better go back. Let them know what has happened. Better ring up Sir Albert, too. Lock the door of Lady Cambers's room; make sure, if you can, nothing has been touched. Look after her sitting-room, too; see that's locked as well. And don't let anyone move about in the gardens. There may be footprints.'

Farman, used to obeying orders, returned accordingly to carry out these he had just received, and Bobby, telling young Hardy to come with him, hurried on towards the scene of the discovery.

At one point the little stream running down the centre of the valley was crossed by a rough bridge of wooden logs, though, indeed, in most places one could easily have stepped across it. Here, too, was a gate in the wire fence that followed the bed of the stream and divided the different fields. Through this Bobby and his companion passed, though not till Bobby had given a moment or two to a close examination of the logs forming the bridge, without, however, being able to find that they showed anything of interest.

'Anyhow, she almost certainly came this way,' he thought. 'And most likely her murderer was waiting for her over there. Only what brought her out so late at night?'

The field Bobby and young Hardy now entered was laid down in pasture, as was that they had just traversed. In its centre there stood a small shed, apparently of recent construction. At various other points near-by, digging had evidently been going on—as though for some reason it had been desired to sink a number of wells or possibly shallow-depth mining shafts. Beyond was a road leading to the main London highway, a mile or two on the further side of the village. Near the shed a number of people were clustered, or going in and out, and others were hurrying towards it from the direction of the village. Bobby said to his companion: 'Who did you say found her?'

'Mr. Bowman,' Ray repeated. 'He lives over there with Miss Bowman, only she's gone now.' As he spoke he pointed vaguely to where, above the shoulder of the rising ground, the chimneys of a house or two were visible. 'He goes to get the train for Hirlpool every morning, and he saw her. He said first he thought it was someone sleeping out, and then he thought it was funny, so he went to look. It's a wonder he saw her. I never did, only it just happens there's a gap in the fence right in line where he was, and he saw her through it, lying there, and so he went to look.'

'Do you mean you had been that way this morning?' Bobby asked.

'Yes, along the top of the field by the road over there, but I never saw her. You wouldn't unless you looked, and I never did. Why should I?'

'You were out early,' Bobby commented.

'You've got to on a farm,' the other retorted. 'We aren't townsfolk. And I do a bit of rabbiting, too, on our land, so I go round the traps as often as I can—seeing the fuss that's made by some if they're heard crying out, as can't be helped always. Of course, I'm particular to keep to our own land, and we never knew, none of us, what had happened, till Mr. Bowman came running like I told you. Dead-white he was, and father sent at once for Jordan, and the doctor, too. Like dead himself Mr. Bowman looked—upset all right. Shock, you know—the shock did it. Look, that's where she was lying,' he added, pointing.

The spot indicated was about half-way between stream and shed, in a direct line from the gate in the fence by the rough bridge over the stream to the shed, and just about where the long, slow rise in the land to the grassy crest ahead first became noticeable. A glance told Bobby that much trampling and running to and fro had already quite certainly destroyed all chance of finding any helpful or significant tracks. He asked Ray to point out the exact spot where the body had lain, but evidently the young man's idea of precision resembled that of most other people, and for him meant merely 'there or thereabouts'. Then, too, when Bobby tried to question him he grew confused, and presently pronounced for another spot nearly three yards away from that he had first pointed out. It was only too certain that the exact spot, in the sense in which Bobby understood 'exact', was not to be discovered from him, though the point was of less importance in that the long, damp grass preserved few signs, and even those it might otherwise have shown had been confused by so much trampling and running to and fro.

'She was lying on her back, straight out,' Ray said, 'but Mr. Bowman said she was on her face when he found her, and he turned her over and she was so stiff and cold she must have been lying there all the night.'

He went on to give a few more words of description

that showed the characteristic signs of strangulation had been present, but added that Mr. Bowman had been very clear that no piece of cord, or anything else that could have been used by the murderer to effect his purpose with, had been left on the spot. Bobby, looking round about carefully himself, decided the whole field would have to be thoroughly searched to make sure of this. His shoes and trouser-ends got very wet in the long grass the previous night's rain had so thoroughly soaked, and Ray made some passing reference to the storm and how glad he had been, as he lay in bed and heard the rain coming down, that he was not out in it. He was very amused, too, when Bobby presently discovered a match-stalk. It was of the kind called 'book' matches, and printed on the flat stalk were the words: 'Hotel Henry VIII'. Bobby knew the name for that of an hotel recently opened with a great flourish of trumpets in the Mayfair district of London. The thing might be of importance or might not, and he put it carefully away, again to the amusement of his companion. One of the party, Ray explained, had been a good deal affected by the unfortunate woman's appearance and had lighted a cigarette to steady his nerves.

'That was Mr. Bowman—him that found her,' Ray explained. 'Miss Bowman's his sister. Funny like it should be him found her.'

'Why?' Bobby asked quickly, remembering that this was the second time Mr. Bowman's sister had been mentioned.

'They say it's on account of her Sir Albert left her ladyship,' the young man answered; and Bobby remembered that his grandmother had talked vaguely about some unfortunate dispute between husband and wife, though she had not mentioned any names, and Bobby had not been greatly interested at the time.

But now he thought it might be as well to bear the fact in mind, even though very likely it was only one of hundreds having no connection with what had happened. Also he was beginning to think that Ray Hardy was showing even more distress and excitement than even so dreadful a tragedy would appear to warrant—as well as a somewhat odd desire to emphasize that neither he nor anyone on the farm knew anything of what had happened till Mr. Bowman came to tell them. Since there was no reason to suppose they had had any means of being aware of it, why was the young man so eager to protest their ignorance? But no doubt allowance had to be made for the excitement and general disturbance produced in him by such an event; very likely the shock had made him loquacious and his flow of talk was merely his way of reacting to it.

On the point of moving on again, Bobby gave this patch of ground one final glance as he thought how he would have measured, mapped, described it in every detail down to the last tuft of grass, the last buttercup or daisy, had the case been his, and then in one of those tufts of long lank damp grass he caught sight of something black and shining. He stepped forward quickly, and, seeing that it was a fountain-pen, looked at it attentively, without at first touching it. Then with extreme care, using his handkerchief so as to avoid leaving finger-prints himself and so confusing any that might be already on its polished surface, he picked it up. It was of a well-known and expensive make, and it was mounted in gold, as if intended for purchase as a Christmas or birthday gift.

'Someone must have dropped it,' observed Ray, much more impressed than he had been by the discovered match-stalk, and even a little envious that such a find had not been made by him. 'I wonder who?'

Bobby wondered, too, as he busied himself hurriedly building up a tiny pyramid of small stones to mark the exact spot where the pen had lain.

CHAPTER THREE

PRIEST AND SCIENTIST

ROUND THE SHED IN THE MIDDLE OF THE FIELD, A TEM-porary wooden building with a corrugated-iron roof, a small crowd had collected, for already the news of a tragedy so startling, so incredible indeed, had spread through the neighbourhood, as the tale of an accident that has happened will run up and down a crowded street. From all sides people were hurrying to hear and see for themselves, to gape and gossip and deny and wonder. Among them, following a converging path to that which Bobby and Ray Hardy were pursuing, was a tall, thin, long-legged, long-armed personage in clerical attire, with a large, round, almost perfectly bald head that gave him an odd, and even slightly grotesque, appearance.

'There's vicar,' Ray said. 'He'll call it a judgement, same as he said in his sermon there would be.'

'Mr. Andrews?' Bobby asked, for though he had not attended the church during his stay, and had never chanced to meet the vicar, he had heard a good deal about him and knew his name. It was, indeed, a name that had acquired some notoriety, for more than once the Anglo-Catholic fervour of its bearer had carried it into the papers—as, for example, when he had attempted to exclude from his church any woman not obeying St. Paul's injunction to keep the head covered, or when he had wished to refuse communion to other women guilty of any kind of 'make-up'.

Then, too, he had quarrelled with the bishop of the diocese over some question of vestments, and in the same connection had publicly identified the diocesan chancellor with Antichrist, though this he had subsequently been persuaded to withdraw on the ground, not of inaccuracy, but of Christian charity. But if this fanaticism of his was more than a little embarrassing to his ecclesiastical superiors, and if at times it excited general ridicule, none the less his sincerity and the austerity of his life made him universally respected, even by those who found his zeal most trying. There were even, probably unfounded, stories current that he kept a private scourge for not infrequent use, and that he always wore a hair shirt—an article not too easy, perhaps, to procure in these days; and it was certainly true that he smoked even to excess four days a week, and on three days, Sundays, Wednesdays and Fridays, abstained entirely—on Sundays because he hadn't the time, on Wednesdays and Fridays because they were fast-days. It was, he explained, his way of taming the natural man by encouraging him to take full liberty and licence and then checking him abruptly.

'If I never touched tobacco,' he would explain, 'I should never miss it. I encourage the habit till it thinks it has a complete hold, and then I break off short. Then I know I am master, and I know I am depriving myself of something I really miss.'

It was with interest, then, that Bobby watched the quaint, ungainly figure running towards them—the long arms flapping, as it were, in the air; the long shambling legs, equally out of proportion to the short squat body; the big hairless face and head thrust forward on a long thin neck. Bobby found himself oddly reminded of a vulture flapping its way along the ground, and half expected to see the priest soar into the air in sudden flight. As they drew nearer to each other he was able to note, too, how little fleshiness that round face showed, how tightly drawn was the skin over the bony framework, how brightly shone and glittered the prominent eyes. To Ray Bobby said, as they slackened pace to allow the new-comer to overtake them: 'A judgement? Why a judgement? What for?'

'It was in his sermon,' Ray explained. 'He thought Eddy Dene was trying to prove the Bible wrong, and that was blasphemy and suchlike. He's preached about it before, only not so strong; and Lady Cambers was there, and sat all through, just listening. A judgement he said, and looked straight at her, and she just listened, quiet as you like.'

The vicar was close to them now, those long shambling legs of his carrying him over the ground at an astonishing rate. In one hand he held a small leather case. He made no pause as he overtook them, but rushed whirling by, calling out, but without waiting for an answer, as he fled past: 'Is there time still?'

'What's he mean?' Bobby asked, and Ray explained: 'Holy Communion. He's got it with him; he always has it ready in case. Anything he'll do rather than let you die without. One winter he ran miles through the snow, when it was too deep for a car, so he could get to Hicks's, just because he heard Mrs. Hicks was dying—and she wasn't neither, only just the flu and a drop more gin than usual. Eddy Dene says he's cracked. Eddy Dene says truth's truth, and if truth and the Bible don't hit it, so much the worse for the Bible. So vicar—he excommunicated him.' Ray chuckled. 'A fat lot Eddy cared, never having been near church since they christened him—and then he squalled his hardest all the time. But some said vicar meant to excommunicate Lady Cambers too, and she was fair upset about it.'

Bobby made no comment. He had heard before, in a vague, confused sort of way, that the archæological investigations being carried out by young Eddy Dene, with the encouragement and under the patronage of Lady Cambers, had much disturbed the worthy vicar, and had been roundly denounced by him from the pulpit. He wondered if by any bizarre possibility this dispute was connected with the terrible tragedy that had just occurred.

They had reached the shed now. At the door stood Jordan, the local sergeant of police, his uniform evidently somewhat hastily assumed, using all his endeavour for the moment to keep people from crowding into the shed. But his deference to local notabilities, the frequent distracting calls on his attention, his own state of general bewilderment and confusion, so that even yet he could hardly believe what had happened, prevented this endeavour from being very successful. The interior of the shed was, indeed, crowded almost to suffocation with people who had little other excuse than curiosity for their presence.

The latest addition to the group was Mr. Andrews, for Sergeant Jordan, who had sung in a choir, man and boy, for thirty years, would never have dreamed of trying to exclude the vicar of the parish. Now Jordan was endeavouring to make up for what he felt had been a certain laxity by vehemently exhorting those still without to take forthwith their departure.

'What do you want?' he was demanding. 'None of you got any work to do to-day? Trespassers, you are, all of you—trespassing and trapesing. Now then, be off, all of you.'

But no one took much notice, and Bobby, pushing through the little crowd of spectators, said to him: 'I've been staying the week-end at Lady Cambers's place. They've only just found out she wasn't in her room. Her bed's not been slept in.' He added: 'My name's Owen. I'm a sergeant in the Metropolitan Police, attached to the C.I.D., Scotland Yard.'

He offered his card as he spoke, and Jordan studied it with interest, still more bewildered at finding that one of the guests at the big house he had from earliest youth regarded with deepest awe and reverence and respect was also a brother-sergeant of police. A confusing world it had become, he reflected sadly; and aloud he said: 'Well, now then, pleased to meet you, I'm sure. I've sent for Colonel Lawson and doctor, too, but they aren't here yet, either of 'em.'

'If there's anything I can do to help,' Bobby suggested, 'I'd be only too glad.'

'Better wait till the Colonel gets here, and then you could ask him,' Jordan answered, and Bobby nodded and said that would be best no doubt, and walked past into the shed with such an air of being, so to say, one of the force, that Jordan never even thought of trying to stop him, but resumed instead his ineffective exhortations to the rapidly swelling crowd outside to be gone about their own affairs they all thought so much less interesting than what was happening here.

Within the shed the body of the murdered woman lay on a table in the middle of the room. Someone, with some idea of doing it reverence, had covered it with a large cloth that had been lying about. A collection of what Bobby recognized as flint implements of the early stone age had been hurriedly tumbled from the table, on which they had been carefully ranged in ordered sequence, to the floor to make room for the body. Mingled with them, in the same untidy heap, were a number of fossils, all pushed together out of the way. The only other furniture of the room, besides this table, consisted of a small oil stove, a couple of chairs, one or two packing-cases, some rough shelving round the walls. On these shelves stood, not too tidily, a few pieces of crockery, various tools, a camera and other photographic apparatus, and a few similar objects. Evidently a workroom, Bobby told himself. Lying on one of the packing-cases was Lady Cambers's hand-bag, which he recognized at once. It had been picked up near her body, and contained her handkerchief, glasses, a pencil, a small mirror, and various other trifling objects of everyday use, including a few shillings in small change. On the same packing-case lay a small suit-case that Bobby recognized as also her property. It had her initials on it, and Bobby wondered why she should have taken it with her on this strange midnight expedition that had ended so tragically. He went across to it, and saw that it was quite empty, and again he wondered what object it had been meant to serve.

One of the bystanders, seeing him looking at it, said: 'It was just by her—empty like that.'

'Wasn't there anything in it?' asked another bystander, either for confirmation or for want of something to say.

'Empty just as it is now,' repeated the other.

Near-by, bending over the confused heap of fossils, flints, and so on that had been tumbled so unceremoniously from the table, was a smooth-faced youngster, apparently about twenty-two or three. He said ruefully: 'It's going to be a job to get them straight again.'

From the other side of the room someone said loudly: 'You've no call to be thinking of that, Eddy Dene, with her ladyship lying there and all.'

The vicar, who had been engaged in silent devotion over the dead body, took up the rebuke.

'No, indeed, Dene,' he said sharply, 'this is no time to be thinking of such things.'

Dene straightened himself, and from half-shut eyes looked round with a gentle, deprecatory smile. He was not a good-looking lad, for his features were irregular and even insignificant, though he had a fine lofty forehead, and against a fair complexion, with little trace as yet of beard or moustache, and under fair eyebrows, a pair of dark and flashing eyes glowed with unexpected and unusual fire. There was a certain chubbiness, too, about his features, a suggestion of youthfulness and inexperience, that again made curious contrast with the haughty and dominating gaze now veiled beneath his half-closed eyes. In height he was below the average, but of a strong, sturdy build, with long arms terminating in somewhat disproportionately small hands that had slender, sensitive-looking fingers. Looking at the lower part of his face, one might have been inclined to dismiss him as a commonplace, rather spoilt, and petulant youth. That broad forehead and those darkly brilliant eyes suggested another and a different personality. He said to Mr. Andrews, a little in the manner of one offering excuses though not much used to such an exercise: 'Oh, well, it's my work, you know. I've got to think of my work, and thinking of it won't hurt her now, poor soul, will it?'

'Your work, as you call it, had an evil aim—a blasphemous aim,' the vicar retorted, loudly and harshly, so that the low murmur of other voices in the shed was hushed. 'A judgement has been given.' The priest's eyes lighted up fiercely, the intense emotion of the man, his enormous conviction, lent to them fire, and to his voice a vibrant, penetrating quality. 'It was a blasphemy you planned,' he said, 'and here's the end.'

Eddy Dene moved forward. He looked quite good-humoured still, his easy assurance an odd contrast to the other's intense, emotional fervour. As well as the crowded condition of the room permitted, the rest of those present drew back, so as to allow the chubby-faced Eddy Dene, the emaciated priest, to face each other. Dene said slowly, his broad brow puckered now as with a certain anxiety: 'I dare say that's right about this being the end. I don't know where the money's to come from now. That may put a stopper to the whole show. Only, why a judgement? Judgement? Why? Whose judgement?' he asked with a sudden, unexpected emphasis that was in curious contrast to his former easy assurance.

Into Bobby's mind there flashed the thought that the tone and phrasing were almost those of an accusation, and he even had the impression that to others in the room the same idea had occurred. Surely it could not be possible that Dene suspected the vicar of this atrocious and apparently purposeless murder? Yet it was almost in an attitude, and with an air, of mutual accusation that the two men faced each other. And then Bobby told himself that that was absurd, that it was only their mutual dislike and suspicion breaking out: the age-long conflict of the priest and the scientist, both right and both wrong, the one mistrusting too much reason, and daring to doubt where truth may lead, the other mistrusting too much faith, and daring to doubt where love might go; both so tremendously right, so presumptuously wrong.

But then Eddy's expression changed. He shrugged his shoulders as if dismissing an idea that had indeed crossed his mind for an instant, but that he now clearly saw to be merely foolish.

'Oh, well,' he said, 'that sermon of yours has turned out quite prophetic, and, if it is a judgement, it's done for me all right. Looks like the end of my job here.'

'Hard luck, Eddy,' someone called.

'I hoped a lot from it,' Eddy said musingly. 'It might have meant a lot if I could have gone through with it. And now I shan't even stand a show with the American bloke, either—done in all round, I am.' He looked again at the stern-faced vicar. 'Oh, it's a judgement all right,' he said, 'but don't go saying it was one on her—that's a dirty thing to say.'

'In the presence of the dead, cut off without warning,' began the vicar, 'it is not seemly . . .'

But then the door opened, and a tall military-looking man came in, followed by two or three others. Though he had never seen him before, Bobby guessed at once that this new-comer was Colonel Lawson, head of the county police.

'What are all these people doing here?' demanded the colonel angrily. 'Good Lord, it might be a public meeting. Sergeant, don't you know better than to let this crowd in? Clear everyone out immediately.'

CHAPTER FOUR

THE TIME QUESTION

THE AUTHORITATIVE MANNER, THE EMPHATIC VOICE, of Colonel Lawson had immediate effect, and those who had a little before crowded so eagerly into the shed began now almost as eagerly to file out again, sternly watched by Sergeant Jordan, who tried to atone for his previous laxity by endeavouring to look as fierce as the colonel and by calling loudly, in the best imitation of the military voice he could manage: 'Pass along there, please. Pass along now.'

The vicar seemed at first inclined to linger. There were duties he thought should be performed, rites to be carried out. But Colonel Lawson, though careful to show the punctilious respect due from one official force to another, soon got rid of him, and then turned sharply upon Eddy Dene, who had again become absorbed in his collection of stone implements and fossils in their confusion on the floor.

'Now, you, sir,' the colonel rasped out. 'You heard what I said?'

Eddy looked up mildly.

'Well, it's my shed, you know,' he remarked. 'They've made hay of my stuff, as it is.'

'Your shed? I thought this was Mr. Hardy's land?' the colonel said sharply.

'But my shed,' Eddy answered. 'Lady Cambers got a lease of it in my name so we shouldn't run any risk of being disturbed. Lord knows what'll happen now, or where any more money for research is to come from!' He added: 'It'll be a week's work at least to get my stuff straight again.'

'You're young Dene, then?' the colonel asked. 'I've heard about you. Your father's the grocer here, isn't he?'

'Yes, that's right,' Eddy answered, and, Bobby fancied, with a touch of resentment in his tone and manner as if he had not much appreciated this loud-voiced reference to the paternal shop. Not that there had been anything offensive or patronizing in the colonel's tone, he had merely made the observation as stating a fact that helped to establish name, place, and residence. He went on: 'Well, Dene, I'm sorry, but you'll have to let us take possession for a time. We won't interfere with your things any more than we can help. If there's any information I want from you at any time, I will let you know, Sergeant.'

Jordan flung open the door.

'Now, Mr. Dene,' he rasped out, just like the colonel himself, and Eddy obeyed meekly, while the colonel swung round upon Bobby, now the only other person left of all the crowd who had been there before.

'You heard what I said?' the colonel demanded. 'What are you waiting for?'

Bobby offered his card.

'I was spending the week-end with Lady Cambers,' he said. 'I have some information I think I ought to offer you.'

Colonel Lawson looked from the card to Bobby and then back from Bobby to the card. The card proclaimed the young man a detective-sergeant of the Metropolitan Police, attached to Scotland Yard, and yet at the same time he declared himself a week-end guest of Lady Cambers. A puzzling world, the chief constable knew it had become, and one in which the old, simple, clear-cut distinctions no longer existed. Why, it was hardly even safe any longer to judge a man by the tie he wore! And once a tie had been so clear a guide through the social grades! Now here was a sergeant of police claiming to have been a week-end guest of a woman in Lady Cambers's position. But then a possible solution of the anomaly occurred to him. Possibly the young man meant he had been staying there as a friend of the butler or of the cook. He said quite brightly: 'How was that? Anyone there you know?'

But the poor colonel got a worse shock.

'Lady Hirlpool is my grandmother,' Bobby explained, 'and she's a very old friend of Lady Cambers. Lady Cambers was nervous about burglars. I believe all her jewellery is kept in the house, and there has been some sort of talk about suspicious characters being seen hanging about recently. My grandmother told her I could put her up to the best way to make things safe.'

Colonel Lawson blinked. A sergeant of police claiming, in a casual sort of way, a peeress of the realm for his grandmother! Hardly suitable, he thought! One moment he permitted himself in which to regret those older and better days when a gentleman was a gentleman, and, if he had to provide for himself, at least never thought of adopting such a dull, plebeian method as work. All this Bolshevism, he reflected gloomily, and was about once more, and even more emphatically, to invite Bobby's departure, when that young man produced the fountain-pen and match-stalk he had picked up near where the murdered woman's body had been found.

'I dare say they aren't of any importance,' he remarked. 'Very likely someone who helped to move the body dropped them. But I thought you ought to see them.'

'Certainly, certainly,' the chief constable agreed, examining them closely.

Bobby had very carefully wrapped up the fountain-pen in his handkerchief. Colonel Lawson commented on this. Bobby explained: 'In case there might be any finger-prints.' He added: 'It's an expensive-looking thing, mounted in gold like that. I should think it cost two or three pounds, so it's hardly likely to have belonged to any of the people in the village. It may have belonged to Lady Cambers, perhaps, if she ever used a fountain-pen, though it looks more like a man's to me. Or there is Mr. Bowman, who saw the body first. I think he is a business man, and it might be his. If not . . .'

'You mean it may have belonged to the murderer?' Colonel Lawson observed.

'It occurred to me, sir,' Bobby answered.

The chief constable turned to one of his companions,

who had been listening in grave silence to all this.

'You look after the thing, Moulland,' he said. To Bobby, he added: 'Superintendent Moulland will have charge of the case. Now, what about this match-stalk? It's marked, "Hotel Henry VIII". That's a London hotel, isn't it?'

'Yes, sir,' Bobby answered. 'Mayfair Lane. Just opened. Very good class, but not too expensive. Probably they give away thousands of their little books of matches every week—they are in every public room in the hotel, and on every table in the restaurant. But it may prove useful, if only as an indication.'

'Quite so,' agreed Lawson. 'Quite so. You seem to know how to use your eyes. Are you on leave?'

'Only week-end leave,' Bobby answered, a trembling hope dawning in his soul. 'I'm due to report for duty at two this afternoon.'

'I wonder if they would spare you for a little longer, as you were on the spot,' the chief constable said, and then turned to Moulland. 'What do you think, Moulland? The young man's presence might be useful, eh?'

'Yes, sir,' agreed the superintendent. 'He was staying at the house; there's a good deal he may be able to tell us.'

'I was Lady Cambers's guest,' Bobby said, in a low voice. 'If I can do anything to help . . .'

'I'll ring the Yard up and ask,' Lawson said decidedly.

'Thank you, sir,' murmured Bobby.

One of those who had accompanied Colonel Lawson, and had since been busy at the table where lay the body of the dead woman, spoke now. He said: 'The cause of death is plain enough. Strangling. With a cord—bit of washing-line, very likely. Sort of thing Dene sells by the dozen yards. Every house and cottage in the village has it. Probably slipped over her head from behind, and pulled tight. Simple. Efficacious. Silent. Never knew anything about it, most likely.'

The speaker was a Dr. Ball, a general practitioner in the neighbourhood.

'Ought to be a post-mortem, though,' he added. 'Might be something else as well.'

'Yes, that would be best,' Lawson agreed. He turned to his superintendent again. 'Moulland,' he said, 'look after that, and have a search made to see if any piece of washing-line can be found. It's a clue worth following up—somebody may know something in the village.' He turned back to the doctor. 'Can you say what time death occurred?'

'Probably about eight hours ago. I should say a little before midnight. Very heavy rain about eleven. She wasn't in that. Clothing only a little damp, and quite dry next the skin. I've noted the rectal temperature. Best guide. Of course, I'm assuming she was murdered where they found her. Bit different if body had been kept in warm, dry room. But not much different. Rectal temperature is pretty safe, taken with other indications.'

'I think Dene was with Lady Cambers till half-past ten or thereabouts,' Bobby volunteered. 'I remember hearing Farman saying he would be nicely caught in that heavy rain there was last night.'

'Who is Farman?' Colonel Lawson asked.

'Lady Cambers's butler,' Bobby answered.

'I suppose Lady Cambers did not accompany Dene—there's no suggestion that she went out with him, or followed later on?'

'I hardly think so,' Bobby answered. 'I was playing bezique with my grandmother. Lady Cambers had been in her own sitting-room with Dene since soon after dinner. When we finished our bezique, about eleven, my grandmother said she would go to bed, but first she would say good night to Lady Cambers. I think she was a little curious to know why they had been talking so long. She came back to get her glasses, and she remarked to me that Lady

Cambers seemed very agitated and upset, but wouldn't say what the matter was. She went to bed then, and I sat reading till nearly half-past eleven. Then I went to bed, too.'

'You didn't see Lady Cambers again, hear anything unusual, or hear her go out?'

'No,' Bobby answered. 'But there is a garden door only a little way down the passage from her sitting-room. She could easily have slipped out without anyone being the wiser, if she had wished to. I believe Farman found all the doors and windows fastened as usual this morning.'

'Then, apparently, except for Lady Hirlpool, when she went to say good night, Dene is the last person who saw Lady Cambers alive?'

'Except the murderer,' Bobby answered gravely.

CHAPTER FIVE

FIRST SUSPICIONS

FROM THE SHED, COLONEL LAWSON AND HIS PARTY, TO which Bobby had now, unostentatiously but firmly, attached himself, proceeded across the fields towards Cambers House, where the chief constable meant to continue the investigation. On the way they had to pass the spot where the murdered woman's body had been found, and to the colonel's intense indignation most of those he had expelled from the shed, together with a number of newcomers, had gathered here, to begin again gazing, arguing, gossiping. But heated arguments as to exactly where and how the body had lain the colonel interrupted with a flow of pungent eloquence beneath which the crowd melted somewhat sulkily away.

'Every inch of ground trampled over and over,' complained Moulland, and neither he nor his chief were much comforted by Bobby's assurance that every track or trace or useful sign had long before been obliterated by the restless feet of the first-comers to the scene.

Even the precaution Bobby had taken of piling some stones on top of one another in a tiny pyramid to mark the precise tuft of grass in which he had found the fountain-pen had been rendered nugatory by someone who, noticing the stones in their careful pyramid, had promptly yielded to humanity's profound destructive instinct and amused himself by kicking them away.

'You should have stopped here yourself to see nothing of the sort happened,' frowned the chief constable, who had a lively sense of the duty laid upon him to point out the shortcomings of his subordinates, and Bobby supposed, ruefully, that in fact he ought to have done something of the kind.

'Who saw the body first?' Colonel Lawson demanded next. 'Farman was the name, wasn't it?'

'No, sir,' answered Bobby. 'Farman is Lady Cambers's butler. It was Mr. Bowman saw the body, from the road. He went to tell Mr. Hardy, who is the farmer, and it was they who moved the body to the shed up there.'

'Know anything about Mr. Bowman?'

'I understand he is in business in Hirlpool. I think he was on his way to catch the early train there,' Bobby answered. 'I'm told there is a sister, a Miss Bowman.'

It was because he remembered the story Ray Hardy had repeated that Bobby mentioned her name, and he fancied from his manner, but was not sure, that the chief constable, too, had heard the gossip evidently current in the neighbourhood.

'Oh, yes,' he said. 'Yes.' Then, rather with the air of deliberately changing the subject, he turned to Moulland, and asked: 'Do you know this Mr. Bowman? Was he one of that crowd?'

'Couldn't say, sir,' Moulland answered. 'Don't know him by sight, sir, only by name. Can inquire.'

'I was told it was a great shock to him, and he went straight home after helping to move the body,' Bobby said. 'Apparently he said he felt sick, and lighted a cigarette to calm his nerves, he said. So that match-stalk may be his.'

'Try to get hold of him,' Lawson said, to his superintendent. 'We had better hear what he has to say before his imagination gets to work on the details. If he went straight back home, he may be there still. I suppose he lives near?'

'I think in one of those houses over there—you can just see the chimneys,' Bobby said, pointing to the chimneys Ray Hardy had indicated as those of Mr. Bowman's house.

'Send and find out if he's there,' the chief constable ordered again. 'If he is, get him along to Cambers House. We shall have plenty to see about to keep us there for the rest of the day. But most likely every bit of useful information has been lost or destroyed already.'

'I told Farman,' interposed Bobby, anxious to retrieve some of the kudos he had lost over the failure of the precaution he had taken to identify the fountain-pen tuft of grass, 'to lock the door of Lady Cambers's bedroom and sitting-room, and to see that as little was disturbed as possible.'

The chief constable received this information with a non-committal grunt. His theory of discipline was that blame should plentifully fall, like rain from heaven, upon both the just and the unjust, but that, as the old saw says, 'praise to the face is open disgrace'.

So Bobby got no comfort, and, as they went on towards the house, he fell back a step or two to walk by Moulland's side. The superintendent was a tall, heavily built man with a heavy moustache, a somewhat wooden expression, and large, light-blue eyes that seemed to look out upon the world with a gravely puzzled expression, as though feeling that it, and most things in it, entirely evaded explanation.

Bobby summed him up as a man who could very efficiently and patiently and carefully carry out instructions, but who always required instructions to act on.

'There seems to be some sort of talk about this Miss Bowman, sir, isn't there?' he asked cautiously.

'There's some say,' Moulland answered, 'it was on account of her Lady Cambers wanted a divorce—only the vicar here, Mr. Andrews, wouldn't hear of it. He's all against divorce, and there was many thought her ladyship would have been glad enough to get Sir Albert back.'

'Does Miss Bowman live with her brother?'

'Did. She kept house for him, but now she's gone off— London, they say. There was a good deal of talk going on, and very likely she didn't find things too comfortable. Now the talk is, she's followed Sir Albert.'

'If there is anything really serious in it,' Bobby remarked thoughtfully, 'I suppose, now Lady Cambers is dead, there is nothing to prevent their getting married?'

Moulland pondered this for some time in silence, and the puzzled look in his eyes grew still more marked. Finally he said, as if at last coming to a conclusion: 'No, I don't suppose as there is—if so be they still want it.'

Bobby nodded. He knew well enough that this sort of intrigue is often dropped quickly enough; especially when an obstacle that had seemed to make the affair as deliciously safe as deliciously daring, disappears suddenly. But then, also, there are cases in which passion overwhelms every other consideration, every scruple, too. He said presently: 'Do you know anything about Mr. Bowman? If he is in a good position and so on?'

'There's nothing against him,' Moulland answered. 'Always well spoken of. Accountant and estate-agent. Not in a big way; only a girl and an office-boy for staff. I suppose it might mean a good deal to him in the way of standing and connection if his sister became Lady Cambers, if that's what you are getting at.'

'It was in my mind,' Bobby admitted. 'Nothing to it, most likely.'

'It was him found the body,' reflected Moulland. 'Must have been pretty quick to see it from the road—of course, if he knew it was there . . . I'll just mention it to the chief.'

By now they had reached the gates that admitted to the Cambers House grounds from the footpath that made a short-cut between village and house. Colonel Lawson, who had been walking on alone, evidently deep in thought, paused here to let the others overtake him. To Bobby, he said: 'You said something about Lady Cambers being more nervous of burglars lately. Was there any reason?'

'I understand a stranger had been seen hanging about the house and grounds in a suspicious way, or what she thought was a suspicious way,' Bobby answered. 'He had been trying to pump some of the servants, too, and then she heard he had been asking a lot of questions in the village. She kept all her jewellery in the house—in a safe in her room—and she got the idea that perhaps it was some advance agent, so to say, spying out the ground for a gang of burglars.'

'Well, they do that sometimes,' admitted the chief constable, and called Jordan, who was following in the rear. 'Know anything, sergeant,' he asked, 'of any suspicious-looking stranger about here?'

'There's a London business gentleman staying at the Cambers Arms, sir,' Jordan answered. 'Retired gent. Sold his business in London, and looking for a small house, with a bit of land attached, for fruit and poultry. Made a lot of inquiries to see what he could find to suit.'

'Better look him up, Moulland,' the chief constable directed. 'Have you seen him, Jordan? What is he like?'

'I've only seen him once or twice, sir,' Jordan answered, 'and I didn't pay any particular attention—seemed no call to. Very chatty and friendly, I've heard. A.1 at darts, but no class at all at shove-halfpenny. Big-made man—about my height; spends his money freely enough. Fond of a glass, but never takes too much. Writes to his wife and family twice a week regular. Long letters, and always takes them into Hirlpool to post. Quite the gentleman always, but not what you would call a gentleman, or anywhere near it.'

The chief constable nodded as if he understood this somewhat cryptic remark.

'Yes, decidedly, he's got to be looked up,' he said. 'You'll see to that, Moulland. Though I don't understand how preparations for a burglary, if there were any, would explain her going out alone at that time of night—without saying a word to anyone, apparently.'

'She seems to have taken a suit-case with her, too, sir,' Bobby remarked. 'That seems curious, I think.'

'Yes, I know. It was empty,' Colonel Lawson said. 'I looked at it. Nothing to show what had been in it.' He added slowly: 'If we knew that, we should know a lot more.'

Bobby's sense of discipline was too acute to allow him to criticize this remark. He did glance at Moulland, but saw the superintendent nodding a grave agreement.

'Yes, sir,' Moulland said. 'If we knew that . . . Have to concentrate on finding out what that suit-case held.'

Bobby thought otherwise, but thought, also, that very likely he was wrong and they were right. By now they had passed the shrubbery and were near the house. In front of it, on the other side of the broad gravel drive by which the building was approached, and near to a large flourishing clump of rhododendrons growing there, stood three men, talking eagerly and excitedly together. They were: Farman, the butler, in his sober black; Miller, the chauffeur, in shirt-sleeves, fresh from the garage where he had been getting out the car; and O'Hara, the gardener. At the front-door the women of the household were standing in a group, talking together excitedly and watching the three men.

Colonel Lawson said: 'Looks as if they had found something over there.'

With the other two following him, he walked across to where the three men stood by the rhododendron-bush. Both the butler and the chauffeur knew who he was, and Farman said: 'There's been someone hiding here, sir. There's matches and cigarette-ends.'

'Soon as I came along,' explained the gardener, O'Hara, 'I saw someone had been at the rhododendrons—and no stray dog nor cat, neither. You can see for yourself, sir. It's as plain as the nose on your face there's been someone hiding there—all night long, in my humble opinion.'

In fact, a clearly defined depression in the soft mould provided sufficient evidence that someone had been lying there, concealed, for a considerable time. A number of matches and cigarette-ends were lying about, and their condition, and that of the ground, showed plainly that position had been taken up after, and not before, the heavy rain of the previous night. But careful search failed to reveal anything else of significance.

'Looks like burglary. Looks like someone watching for a chance to get inside,' Colonel Lawson remarked. 'One of the gang, hiding and waiting here. Another of them commits the murder and bolts. First fellow waits here till he gets tired, and then clears off, too. Only, what made Lady Cambers go out, and what had she in her suit-case?'

Bobby thought this obsession about what the suit-case had contained was unfortunate and more likely to confuse than help. But still he supposed he might be all wrong in holding that belief. He had been examining the cigarette-ends, and now he said: 'Bulgarian Tempo, sir. There's one here only half smoked, with the name quite plain on it. Expensive things; not the sort a burglar would be likely to smoke—not unless he was very flush. And then he wouldn't be out on a fresh job.'

'I don't think that follows,' observed Colonel Lawson.

'I suppose big jobs are often planned months ahead; it doesn't follow a job is taken on because of being hard-up. Or expensive cigarettes might come from some other burglary—part of the loot.' He turned to Farman: 'You don't know anyone here who smokes that brand of cigarette, do you?' he asked.

'No, sir; not that I ever noticed, sir,' Farman answered, his face so wooden and expressionless Bobby felt certain that he lied.

CHAPTER SIX

THE MISSING JEWELLERY

FOR A LITTLE TIME LONGER THEY ALL LINGERED, STARing, wondering, guessing, all oddly affected by this idea of the unknown watcher who had stayed in hiding here, watching and waiting after murder had been committed elsewhere.

'Did he know?' Colonel Lawson said, half to himself. 'If he knew, why did he stay? If he didn't know, why did he come?'

But these were questions to which none of those present knew the answer.

Except for the scattered match-stalks, the numerous cigarette-ends, the depression in the damp mould so clearly marked as to prove that the person making it had been lying there some considerable time, and for one or two plainly defined footprints, there was nothing to suggest who that personage had been, or what the object and intention of so prolonged a vigil. And footprints in these days of the mass-production of boots and shoes are seldom of much value, nor did these present any characteristic likely to be of use in tracing their owner.

'Number eight size, I think,' Bobby remarked. 'No hobnails or anything like that. But that doesn't go for much. Every farm-labourer to-day has his heavy boots he wears at work and his light shoes for afterwards.'

'There had better be plaster casts taken,' Colonel Lawson said.

Jordan was left on guard to see that nothing was disturbed, and the chief constable, accompanied now only by Moulland and by Bobby, so freely had he been obliged to shed his retinue, went on to the house, where, at the front-door, all its inmates were gathered to await him.

For the discovery that some unknown person had for some unknown reason been hiding among the rhododendrons had completed their disarray. Only Lady Hirlpool, upheld by a sense of responsibility, and Amy Emmers, Lady Cambers's own maid, upheld by her own strength of character, retained their self-control. The cook was in tears; the kitchenmaid in flight; the parlourmaid in something like hysterics; the first and second housemaids in each other's arms; the tweeny in a chair, hovering between an instinct to faint and a presentiment that no one would take any notice if she did. The arrival of the chief constable and his two followers did little to reassure them. Apparently the least they anticipated was immediate arrest, and not until they had all been shepherded back into their own special domain, behind the green-baize service door, could Colonel Lawson begin his task.

'All lost their heads,' he grumbled, 'except that tall girl. Who is she?'

'Amy Emmers,' Lady Hirlpool explained. 'She was poor dear Lotty's own maid; and of course they've lost their heads. Their mistress has lost her life.'

'Oh, yes, well,' conceded Lawson, admitting, as it were, that possibly a murder in a quiet country house is more disturbing, and even terrifying, than it appears to the calm official mind.

'Besides,' Lady Hirlpool went on, pressing her advantage, 'it's simply awful to think of poor Lotty's murderer hiding in the rhododendrons, waiting for her to go out. I feel like screaming, myself, when I think of it.'

'Yes, yes,' agreed the chief constable, somewhat hurriedly, for he was by no means sure that the threatened screams were not on the point of production.

Indeed that very nearly happened, for Lady Hirlpool, upheld before the household staff by a certain sense of responsibility, had lost that feeling in this official presence. What saved the situation before she finally yielded and let herself go was that Bobby moved forward and whispered ferociously into her ear: 'Buck up, grandmother. Buck up, I tell you.'

'Yes, Bobby, I'll try,' she answered, as meekly as though never had she applied her slipper to the appropriate portion of his anatomy, and with a sigh of relief for the crisis he saw averted, Colonel Lawson went on: 'Puzzling feature of the case, that is. Looks as if the fellow had been there nearly all night. Yet it seems the murder was committed somewhere before midnight—soon after that heavy rain there was. If he was the murderer, what was he waiting for? And if he was someone else, what was the motive?'

'Waiting to get into the house,' explained Lady Hirlpool, 'and then, most likely, he would have murdered us all.' She caught her grandson's stern warning eye and gulped down the trembling sob of fear she had not quite been able to repress. 'Poor Lotty kept all her jewellery in the house. I told her it wasn't safe,' she added.

'Nothing's been disturbed, I hope?' Lawson asked. 'I want to examine her rooms very carefully.'

'Oh, no, nobody's touched anything,' Lady Hirlpool assured him. 'Nobody would have, even without Bobby's message. Everyone was too frightened. Bobby's my grandson, you know. He's at Scotland Yard. It's so lucky he's here. He'll be able to tell you just what you ought to do.'

'Oh, yes, yes, quite so,' agreed the chief constable, with a baleful glance at the unlucky Bobby, on whom, too, Superintendent Moulland fixed a cold, menacing gaze, so that shivers ran up and down that young man's back as he miserably drooped and wished with ardour that grandmothers were both less partial and less outspoken.

But Lady Hirlpool beamed on him, quite sure that now she had retrieved her position in his eyes she knew her near approach to a breakdown had slightly compromised.

'But he needn't have worried about anything being touched,' she went on. 'After we knew what had happened, none of us dared move. We all just held each other's hands and tried to think it wasn't true—all except Emmers. She's braver. And then O'Hara called Farman outside, because he had found that someone had been hiding in the rhododendrons. After that,' said her ladyship frankly, 'we all made up our minds we were all going to have our throats cut immediately. Even Emmers, too.'

'Could you take us to Lady Cambers's room?' Lawson asked, just as, more than a little to the relief of Lady Hirlpool, Farman appeared in the doorway.

'Oh, here's Farman. He'll show you everything,' she said. 'I'll go and sit with the maids. They won't be so frightened if I'm with them. Bobby can come and tell me if you want anything more.'

As no objection was made, she vanished through the baize door with some precipitation, and probably it was not only the maids who found themselves less afraid in company. The chief constable beckoned to Farman.

'Which is Lady Cambers's room?' he asked. 'I understand there is one sitting-room she used more than the rest.'

'Yes, sir. This way, sir,' Farman answered, and led them down the passage leading from the hall to the garden door out of which opened the room required. The door was closed but not locked, and for that Farman apologized.

'The bedroom door I locked myself, sir,' he explained, 'but I hadn't the key for this. Lady Cambers kept it herself. She used to lock the door sometimes when she was busy with letters or business. But I told the staff no one was to touch anything, and I'm sure none of them did.

None of them moved out of the hall, I think, sir. Very upset, sir. Naturally, sir, if I may say so.'

'Where did Lady Cambers keep her keys?' Lawson asked.

'In her hand-bag. She was very particular about them,' answered the butler.

The chief constable turned to Moulland and Bobby.

'I can't remember there were any keys found on her,' he remarked.

Neither Bobby nor Moulland had seen any keys, though it was Sergeant Jordan who, while waiting the arrival of his superior officers, had checked the possessions of the dead woman.

They all entered the room. It was of only moderate size, comfortably and plainly furnished, in good taste, and with touches of daintiness and refinement, but also with a show of severity that proclaimed its use for the business of the estate. By the window stood a writing-table; on it a blotting-book, pens, and ink. There was a larger table in the middle of the room, with two chairs drawn up between it and the fire-place, as if two persons had been sitting there and talking. In one corner was a small safe, built into the thick outer wall of the old house. Lawson went across to the writing-table, looked at the leather-bound blotting-book lying there, opened it with some vague idea of finding important information on the blotting-paper, observed that it was quite clean and new except for a row of figures that did not interest him, and then began to open in turn the drawers of the table. Bobby took the opportunity of saying to Farman: 'Do you know if Lady Cambers ever used a fountain-pen? I don't think I ever saw her with one.'

'I don't think so,' Farman answered. 'Not that I know of.'

Moulland had been putting down on the writing-table various objects he had been carrying. Among them was the fountain-pen Bobby had found on the scene of the murder. While Moulland was saying something to the chief constable, Bobby turned down the handkerchief in which it was still enveloped and showed it to Farman.

'This wasn't hers, was it?'

'Oh, no, sir. That's Eddy Dene's,' the butler answered at once. 'A present from her ladyship, I believe.'

His tone as he said this was so markedly non-committal that Bobby glanced at him sharply, but, before he could say anything, Colonel Lawson turned round.

'What's that?' he asked. 'The pen—belongs to young Dene, you say?'

'Well, sir, I couldn't be sure, sir,' Farman answered. 'But it looks very like it, sir—very like it indeed; very much like one her ladyship gave him herself, sir, for a present.'

His tone was still so markedly non-committal that both Lawson and Moulland seemed to notice it. They exchanged glances, and Lawson, after a moment's hesitation, said: 'We'll go into that later. I would like to hear what you know, first, of what happened last night.'

It was not much Farman had to tell. He had locked up after Eddy Dene left at half-past ten. He was quite clear that he had securely locked and bolted every door. He had finished his task a little after eleven. He was quite sure Lady Cambers was then in her room, and he had seen her go up to bed about eleven, while the rain was still falling heavily. She had commented on the downpour to him, as she passed him in the hall, and he thought, now, she seemed a little worried or bothered over its being so unusually heavy. After that he had not seen her again. He had gone to his own room on the ground floor, next the pantry. Lady Cambers liked him to sleep there, as a kind of safeguard for the silver against burglars. He had not gone to bed at once. He had sat at his open window, reading the paper and smoking his pipe, till quite late—one o'clock perhaps. He wasn't sure. He hadn't noticed the time. But he had neither seen nor heard anything out-of-the-way, and when he had gone to bed he had gone to sleep at once, and not wakened till his usual time in the morning. It had all been a tremendous shock to him, and he couldn't understand it in the least.

Lawson asked one or two questions, and inquired about Lady Cambers's keys. Did she always keep them herself, or did she ever trust them to anyone else?

Farman was quite clear and emphatic in his assertion that his mistress was always most careful with them and never let them out of her possession. If they had not been found in her hand-bag, he could not imagine what had become of them. The chief constable opened a drawer of the writing-table, and took a bunch of keys that he had seen lying just within.

'What about these?' he asked.

Apparently very much surprised, Farman came nearer to look at them more closely.

'That's them, sir, all right,' he declared, blinking at them in the same surprised manner. 'I don't know what they are doing there, sir.'

Bobby, too, drew closer to look, and thought that he also recognized them as those of Lady Cambers he himself had noticed she was always careful to keep in her own possession. He remembered that string or column of figures that had caught Colonel Lawson's attention, and, going across to the safe, had a look at the combination lock. Farman was still expressing surprise over the keys.

'Her ladyship was always most careful and particular about them, sir,' he was saying. 'I've never known her put them in a drawer—never.'

'It seems she did this time, for some reason,' Lawson remarked. 'Do you know which is the key of the safe? Or the combination? It's a combination lock in figures, I think, not letters.'

Farman seemed equally uninstructed on both points.

'Key no good unless we know the right combination,' observed Lawson, and Bobby ventured to make a suggestion, indicating the leather-bound blotting-book as he did so.

'There's a row of figures someone jotted down there,' he said. 'Always five figures, and all struck out except the last. I was wondering if they could be the numbers of the combination Lady Cambers put down in case she forgot?'

'It's just a chance, we might try,' agreed Lawson, and Farman remarked: 'There was a difficulty, sir, about a year ago, when her ladyship did forget. We had to get a man down from the makers, and I remember her ladyship saying, afterwards, she would always make a note of the number when she changed the combination.'

'Just like a woman trying to be businesslike,' commented the chief constable, with considerable injustice. 'Gets a first-class safe and sets the lock all right, and then leaves the key and a note of the combination all handy.'

'I never knew her leave her keys about before, sir,' Farman said again. 'Her ladyship was always most particular.'

'Well, she did this time,' repeated Lawson, impatiently, fitting the keys one after the other to the lock of the safe till he found the right one. 'The jewellery is kept here, I understand?'

'Yes, sir. Her ladyship liked to have it where she could get it when she wanted.'

'Was it valuable?'

'I understood it was worth twenty or thirty thousand pounds, sir,' the butler answered cautiously. 'Especially the Cleopatra pearl there was so much talk about.'

The chief constable whistled softly as, having by now hit on the right key, he opened the safe. Within he found a good many papers and documents of one kind and another, a cash-box, containing twenty or thirty pounds in notes and change, but no sign of any jewels.

'Are you sure the jewellery was kept here?' Lawson asked the butler.

'Yes, sir. It was always understood so, sir. Everyone knew that was where it was kept,' Farman answered. He was looking over the chief constable's shoulder. It seemed he could not believe his eyes. He muttered, half to himself: 'Now then . . . now then . . . it's been took.'

With a touch of animation in his generally somewhat stolid manner, Moulland exclaimed: 'That's what the suit-case was for. That's why it was empty when it was found.'

'Yes,' said Lawson. 'Yes. Yes. Only we can't be sure . . . dashed odd.'

'What for should she take all her jewels out in a suit-case at that time of night?' Farman burst out suddenly.

'Well, if they aren't here, and if they were here, same as you say, where are they?' retorted Moulland.

'May have something to do with that fellow in the rhododendrons,' mused Colonel Lawson. 'Suggests the motive for the murder, of course, only how . . . who . . . why . . .?'

He was looking hard at the butler as he spoke, and it was easy to see what suspicions were running in his mind. Farman, more obviously agitated and disturbed even than before, was beginning to perspire gently. He said: 'Begging your pardon, sir, I think I ought to say I came, when Emmers told me she couldn't find her ladyship, to see if she was here, and she wasn't, and there was a tray on the table with a plate and glass, as if someone had been partaking of refreshment. The glass smelt of brandy, which her ladyship never took, so at first I thought perhaps Eddy Dene had had some, only, if he had, her ladyship must have served him herself, which isn't likely, and, besides, she would have had to go and find the brandy. If I may say so, sir, it looks to me as if someone else was here late, and her ladyship let him in and let him out again herself, without any of us knowing.'

They all listened with interest. It was evident this was a new fact of importance. Lawson said quickly: 'Have you the tray and glass? Can you find them?'

'I'll see, sir,' Farman answered. 'I gave them to one of

the maids to take into the kitchen. Emmers wanted to herself, but I told her to see if she could find her ladyship, knowing nothing then.'

'Better go with him, Moulland,' the chief constable said. 'There may be finger-prints.'

Moulland and Farman went off together, leaving Bobby alone with Colonel Lawson. After a pause, Lawson said: 'Do you know anything about this jewellery? Looks bad, if it's really missing.'

'I understood it was valuable,' Bobby answered, 'and that it was kept in the safe here, and that was why Lady Cambers was nervous when she heard a stranger was in the village asking a lot of questions and mooching about here, trying to make friends with the maids.'

'That'll have to be looked into,' Lawson said. 'Did he get on friendly terms with any of them, do you know?'

'I don't think so, sir. I don't think they liked his looks very much. He may have met the gardener or the chauffeur in the pub here. I believe Miller—that's the chauffeur—is a kind of local darts champion, and this man I'm speaking of used to play darts a lot. He was supposed to be looking for a cottage and land to buy, but I don't think many people believed that.'

'It'll have to be looked into,' the chief constable repeated. 'Sounds a bit queer. Only, I don't see how it hangs together. What made Lady Cambers go out so late without letting anyone know? How was it all the doors were locked in the morning?—that is, if the butler is telling the truth. Then, who was hiding in the rhododendrons long after the murder had been committed—and why? And who was Lady Cambers giving brandy to after Dene left her? Or was it Lady Cambers having a drink herself, to screw up her courage before she went out? If there are any finger-prints on the tray or glass, they may help us.'

Moulland and Farman came back without tray or glass or plate.

'All washed up and put away,' Moulland reported. 'One of the maids, Amy Emmers, says she remembers doing it. Says she thought they ought to be got out of the way. Farman says it wasn't her work to wash anything up, and he never remembers her doing anything of the kind before.'

CHAPTER SEVEN

STORY OF A QUARREL

THERE WAS A LITTLE PAUSE THEN, AS IF THEY WERE ALL considering the implications of this piece of information. Colonel Lawson scowled and frowned and breathed heavily, unwonted mental exertion betraying itself in evident physical signs. Superintendent Moulland took out an enormous pocket-book and made a careful entry in it, and Bobby read over slowly and attentively the full shorthand note he was taking. A little with the air of an actor repeating a gesture that has already won much applause, Farman said: 'I think I perhaps ought to mention there was a scene between her ladyship and Emmers, Wednesday last week. Something Emmers had done must have greatly annoyed her ladyship. It was after breakfast. One of the maids came and told me. She said she could hear Lady Cambers shouting at Emmers and Emmers answering back, and there must be something wrong. I told her at once it was no business of hers and she had best get on with her work, and'—Farman hesitated for a moment, and then continued —'I felt it was my duty, me being responsible for the discipline of the staff, to be on hand if required. So I proceeded towards this room where Robins—the maid who told me about it—said they were, and certainly you could hear them both distinctly—not what they were saying exactly, you understand, gentlemen.' Again Farman paused, this time to allow his features to express horror and disgust at the mere thought of even involuntary eavesdropping. 'Besides, they were both speaking at once—fair shouting at each other, and then Emmers rushed out and up to her own room as fast as she could, so we all thought she was packing to leave. But after a time there she was down again, going on with her work just as usual, and inclined to be insolent when asked what was the matter.'

'Do you think it likely she had been given notice?' the chief constable asked.

'I couldn't say, sir, I'm sure,' Farman answered. 'Everything seemed to go on just the same. Everyone noticed how Emmers had been crying, but, as cook said to me, she only bit your head off if you said anything. Of course, it wasn't my place to inquire, her ladyship not saying a word.'

'You are sure you didn't catch anything that was said; even a single word or phrase might be useful?' Lawson asked.

'No, sir,' the butler repeated, with visible regret. 'Shouting they were, and both at the same time, and Emmers giving as good as she got, if you ask me. Most disrespectful Emmers sounded. I made sure—we all did—her ladyship would pack her off at once. But it all seemed to blow over.'

'I think we must hear what she has to say herself,' the chief constable decided. 'But first we might have a word with the maid who told you about it.'

'The first housemaid, Robins, sir,' Farman answered. 'Shall I tell her you want her, sir?'

'Yes, tell her we would like to see her at once,' Lawson said, and for the life of him, discipline or no discipline, Bobby could not help putting down his note-book, and saying: 'Shall I go, sir? You meant me?'

'Yes, all right, you go and find her,' Lawson agreed, and whether he thought it a matter of indifference who went to find the girl, or whether he had taken the hint and realized it would be better to hear the girl's story before Farman had any opportunity of influencing her one way or another, involuntarily or otherwise, Bobby never knew.

At any rate, Bobby was through the door and outside before Farman had even begun to move, and as the door closed behind him Bobby heard Colonel Lawson again addressing to the butler some question that did not sound very important.

'Good,' Bobby thought, knowing as he did how easily people's memories and ideas are affected by those of others. 'That'll keep him out of the way till I've got hold of this Robins girl.'

He found his way to the servants' hall, discovered the first housemaid, and brought her back with him. Farman, warned not to say anything to Amy Emmers, was thereupon dismissed, and Miss Robins was asked if she remembered anything to indicate any dissatisfaction with Amy Emmers on the part of Lady Cambers.

'They had a fair old set-to last Wednesday,' the girl answered at once. 'You could have heard them half over the house. Regular going for each other, they were. We all thought Amy would get the sack after that—wages in lieu of notice, and no reference either. But it all blew over—or seemed to.'

'You don't know what it was all about?' Lawson asked.

'You couldn't hear nothing to make out plain,' Miss Robins answered, with what was in her case, also, an evidently sincere regret. 'But they were going for each other, hammer and tongs. I got so scared I went and told Mr. Farman, I thought they would be pulling each other's hair out next. You could have knocked us all down with a feather when everything went on just the same.'

'Amy didn't explain what the trouble had been about?'

'No. I did ask her. I said: "What's up, Amy?" Her eyes were that red and swollen you could see how she had been crying. She never said a word—just walked away. Even when cook herself said to her: "Why, Amy, whatever have you been crying about like that?" All my lady said was: "My own affairs," and not another word. Very uppish she's always been, not what I call friendly and open.'

A few more questions were asked, from which no more was gathered than that Amy Emmers had got the name of being a 'favourite', that this favouritism had been specially marked since the breach between Lady Cambers and her husband, and that as a result of this favour shown to her by her mistress Amy had very definitely lost any she had previously enjoyed with the other servants.

'Like having two mistresses in the house,' Miss Robins complained, 'as Mr. Farman said himself, what with her giving the orders and all.'

Miss Robins was warmly thanked, told that presently she would be asked to sign the statement she had made when it had been written out, and Bobby proceeded to find Amy Emmers, with whom he returned.

'A bad business this,' he remarked to her, as they came through the hall together. 'You must be feeling it dreadfully.'

Amy said nothing, and Bobby was aware of an impression that she was a young person with a quite unusual capacity for saying nothing—and that is as rare a gift as any. She was a tall girl, nearly a head taller than the other women of the household, and she was well made, with a quick graceful bearing. Bobby thought her very good-looking too, with her almost perfectly oval face and well-shaped, regular features, though both mouth and chin were a little on the large side, with the teeth also a little large and slightly irregular. But the eyes were magnificent—soft and bright, and veiled behind long drooping lashes that seemed to lend to them a dark mysterious melancholy. A striking young woman, Bobby decided, and one of many possibilities, not likely to occupy for long the humble and subordinate position of a maid, even a personal and favourite maid.

Colonel Lawson, too, and his superintendent, Moulland, were both visibly impressed by the girl's looks and personality, and the chief constable, generally exceedingly conscious of the great gulf that marked him off from his social or official inferiors, began to put his questions to her in a tone that was at first almost deferential. She gave her name and age—this last with a slight haughty lifting of the eyebrows as if she did not see the relevance of the question but would pass it over this once—and explained that she had been brought up by her uncle and aunt, Mr. and Mrs. Dene, who kept the village grocery-shop and were the parents of Eddy Dene, who was their assistant in the shop and archæologist in his spare time. As there was hardly enough business in the shop to keep her occupied, and as she had no taste for the work, she had left it to enter Lady Cambers's service. She had been with Lady Cambers, as her personal maid, for about a year, and it was partly through her that her mistress's interest had been aroused in Eddy, and in certain theories and beliefs of his.

She answered all the questions put to her quite freely and with apparent frankness, and yet there still remained about her a curious air of reticence, as though there were many things on many subjects that she would never tell. One had the impression that her inner life was a secret she guarded well, and Bobby, beginning now to remember something he had heard vaguely in talk by Lady Cambers and paid no attention to at the time, took advantage of an interval in the questioning to tear a page from the notebook he was using, and write on it a few words which he passed to Colonel Lawson. The chief constable read it, crumpled it up, and remarked: 'Oh, by the way, I believe you are engaged to young Dene, aren't you?'

For the first time Amy hesitated before answering, and for the first time seemed to become aware of the presence of Bobby as an actual personality. Her glance swept over him, disapproved of him, found him impertinent, forgot him, and Bobby decided that for some reason this reference to her engagement was unwelcome. She said, in her quiet way: 'It has always been the wish of my uncle and aunt.'

'But not yours, perhaps?' suggested Colonel Lawson.

Amy let the question pass unanswered. She had the air of not having heard it, and Colonel Lawson found himself flushing slightly. It was quite ridiculously as if he had been put in his place—a chief constable by a lady's maid! Possibly the question was not quite relevant to the inquiry, and at any rate she plainly considered it an intrusion into her private affairs she did not intend to encourage. Lawson left the point, and went on to question her about the alleged dispute or quarrel with her mistress.

'Oh, yes,' she said at once, 'I remember—Lady Cambers was dreadfully angry. You see, it was most awfully stupid of me, but I had put all her stockings away without mending them. I can't think how it happened. Every time she got a pair out to change, there was a hole in them. She nearly threw them at me, and the more I tried to say how sorry I was, the angrier she got. I just ran straight upstairs and had a good cry.'

It was the longest answer she had given yet, the most fluent, the most apparently candid. Colonel Lawson and Superintendent Moulland looked at each other. Bobby sucked the end of his pencil, and looked at her. She sat quiet and still and unconcerned, her dark mysterious eyes fixed upon the wall opposite as though there she saw and communed with secret things.

Of course, the explanation she offered was a quite reasonable one.

'Your voices were so loud you were heard in the hall, apparently,' the chief constable remarked.

'Yes, sir,' Amy agreed. 'It's surprising how far voices can be heard—if you're listening.'

There was the faintest, least, tiniest emphasis on that last word, and again Lawson flushed a little. Was the wretched girl presuming once more? Was she actually wishing to remind him that eavesdropping is—well, eavesdropping?

'I'm told it sounded as if you were shouting at each other,' he said.

Miss Emmers removed the dark mystery of her eyes from the wall-paper and fastened it upon the chief constable.

'Lady Cambers never shouted,' she assured him, gently rebuking such an idea. 'And I'm sure I never shouted at her—her ladyship would never have permitted it.'

'She was very angry, though?' Lawson asked.

'Oh, yes,' Amy admitted, as frankly as before. 'So annoying to find holes in all your stockings. Most uncomfortable if there's a hole and one of your toes comes right through. They were all such big holes, too,' she added pensively.

The chief constable gave it up, and began to ask if she had heard anything in the night. She had not. She had gone to bed at the usual time. One of the other maids had knocked at her door to borrow some binding. A little after eleven. She had given it her. After getting into bed she had fallen asleep at once, and only wakened when the tweeny brought her her early cup of tea—signal for her to get up and prepare, in her turn, one for Lady Cambers. It had been a great shock to find Lady Cambers was not in her room. She could not understand it, or account for it at all. She remembered perfectly the tray, glass, and plate Farman had mentioned. She had not thought much about it. Why should she? There was no reason why Lady Cambers should not have a little refreshment last thing at night if she wished to. No, it was not usual, perhaps, but it had not struck her as in any way remarkable. It was quite true that Lady Cambers very seldom took wine or spirits, except for a glass of sherry or claret at dinner. If Mr. Farman said there had been brandy in the glass, no doubt he was right, but she had not noticed it herself. She believed Mr. Miller, the chauffeur, had made the same remark, but Mr. Farman was wrong in saying Lady Cambers would have had to go to his pantry to get any brandy. There was a flask of brandy in her bedroom, in one of the drawers. Lady Cambers always took brandy with her when going on a sea voyage. At this the flask was duly sent for and produced, and proved to be about a quarter full, but Amy was quite unable to say whether any of the contents had been taken recently. It was always kept in the drawer where it had been found, but she had never troubled to notice whether it was full or empty. Lady Cambers had great faith in brandy as a medicine. No, she had made no complaint of feeling unwell recently, and certainly there was no reason that Amy knew of why she should have taken any last night. Of course, all this upset about Sir Albert had disturbed Lady Cambers terribly. She had never been really well since.

'I'm told you washed up the plate and glass,' the chief constable asked next. 'Why did you do that?'

'So as to put them away, sir,' answered Amy, mildly surprised at the question.

'Was it your work?' demanded Lawson.

Amy considered the point.

'I suppose not,' she conceded. 'But I do try not to be too silly about that. Some of the others haven't quite liked it because Lady Cambers got to leave a lot to me, especially since Sir Albert went away. So I've made rather a point of doing any little odd job no one else seemed to be looking after.'

'Wasn't this a little odd job that could quite well have waited?'

'Oh, yes, sir,' agreed Amy cheerfully, 'ever so easily, but with such dreadful things happening, and everyone so excited, you can't tell what a comfort it seemed to have just an ordinary everyday little thing to do. If you understand what I mean, sir, it made everything seem—well, less like a horrible nightmare.'

The dark mystery of her eyes seemed now to melt into a limpid frankness. Simple, natural, candid, they sought out Lawson as in mutual appeal, they confided in Moulland, they swept to Bobby—and swept away again, somewhat hurriedly, for he, indeed, was staring at her with a fixity, an intentness, a questioning deep intentness that seemed to demand of her whether what she had said was the truth and all the truth.

He was thinking to himself that women are good liars—especially good women. The better the woman, the better the liar.

Those stockings with the holes in the toes, for instance. Was not that explanation just a little too simple, a little too natural? And her explanation of her action in washing up the plate and glass? Almost too unchallengeable, too reasonable.

Colonel Lawson said abruptly: 'What can you tell us about Lady Cambers's jewellery? Where did she keep it, and where did she keep her keys?'

CHAPTER EIGHT

MORE STATEMENTS

TO THESE QUESTIONS AMY'S ANSWER WAS PROMPT: 'THE jewellery is in the safe in the corner there. Lady Cambers kept her keys in her bag. She was always very careful with them.'

Colonel Lawson and Moulland exchanged whispered comments. Bobby ventured to make a suggestion, and Lawson, adopting it, turned back to Amy and continued: 'No doubt sometimes the keys would be put in a drawer, either here or upstairs—at night, for instance?'

'Oh, no,' Amy answered promptly. 'At night she always had her bag on the table near the bed, and I've never known her put the keys anywhere but in her bag.'

Lawson consulted the other two again. Amy seemed to become once more lost in her own distant thoughts. Lawson said sharply: 'You are sure about that?'

Amy seemed to be considering, not whether she was sure, but what possible reason these people could have for asking her if she were sure of a statement when once she had made it. Finally, as if by way of a concession, she said: 'Oh, yes. If you like to ask the others, they will all tell you the same.'

'What about the combination number?' Lawson asked. 'Of the lock of the safe, I mean? The butler tells us it was forgotten once and the makers had to be sent for.'

'That was a long time ago,' Amy answered slowly. 'I forget how long exactly. Afterwards, when the lock was set to a fresh number, Lady Cambers generally told me what it was. She thought we wouldn't both forget. But I used to make a note of it, in case.'

'Where?'

'On a piece of paper,' Amy answered patiently, very much in the manner of one answering the persistent questions of a troublesome child one does not, however, wish to discourage.

Colonel Lawson was looking all he felt. Moulland was looking even more so. Bobby contented himself with looking at Amy, who on her part appeared again to have forgotten their existence and once more to be fixing her far-off gaze upon the wall-paper above their heads as though there alone was anything to interest her.

'And, pray,' demanded Colonel Lawson with an immense irony and a still more immense self-control, 'what did you do with the piece of paper?'

'I think generally I put it in my purse,' Amy answered; 'or somewhere safe,' she added; and the chief constable snorted indignantly at this last word. 'Sometimes Lady Cambers didn't tell me if she didn't think of it or I wasn't there. Then she generally made a note herself.'

'Where? On a piece of paper, I suppose?'

'Yes. Or in her blotting-book. I remember she told me to look there once for the right number when the key wouldn't turn.'

'What it comes to,' observed the chief constable, 'is that the number of the combination might be lying about on any bit of paper, or in the blotting-book where anyone could see it.'

'If they did, they wouldn't have the key,' Amy pointed out gently, 'so it was quite all right really. She was always most careful about her keys. So was I. If I had them for any reason I always gave them back to her immediately, and if I forgot she always asked for them.'

'And last night?'

'Last night,' Amy answered, 'the keys were in her bag on the table in her bedroom as usual. She asked me for something from her bag, and I remember taking the keys out to get it and then putting them back just before I said good night.'

'Then how,' demanded Lawson, 'do you account for their being in this drawer of the writing-table where I found them a few moments ago?'

He pulled open the drawer in question as he spoke by way of demonstration, but Amy shook her head.

'Oh, no, they wouldn't be there,' she declared; 'they couldn't be.'

It took some time to persuade her that the fact was really so. Then all she could say was that she could neither understand nor explain. Lady Cambers had always been most careful about her keys; she never left them lying about, never allowed them out of her possession except on rare and brief occasions; never kept them anywhere but in her bag. Most certainly she had them, as usual, with her in her room the previous night after retiring to bed, since Amy, as she had already testified, had herself seen them there, taken them out of the hand-bag, replaced them in it again.

'Then,' said Lawson, 'that means she must either have put the keys in the drawer for safety before she left the house, or else her murderer brought them back, used them to open the safe and secure the jewellery, and then left them behind in the drawer here. If it was like that, he could have got in easily enough, since Lady Cambers must have left a door open to return by, but how did he get out again, if all the doors and windows were locked on the inside this morning? Unless he had an accomplice in the house. Or was he an inmate of it himself?'

Amy said nothing. She was looking now at her hands folded in her lap, and had again her air of being wrapped in deep and somewhat aloof meditation. Lawson stared at her mistrustfully and began to fidget with some notes he had been making, though it was Bobby who was taking all this down in careful shorthand. Presently Lawson said: 'Let's try to get the times more accurately. Lady Cambers went to bed about eleven. Can you say exactly when? Was that her usual time?'

'Yes, but she was often a little earlier or later. Last night I was sitting in her room waiting for her. I can't be sure to a minute or two, but it was soon after eleven, during that very heavy rain. She put on her dressing-gown and said she didn't want me any more and I could go to bed. It wasn't more than five minutes after she came upstairs. I think the rain was just stopping; it stopped nearly as suddenly as it began.'

'She didn't say anything about going out again?'

'Oh, no.'

'You can't throw any light on that, or why she took her suit-case with her?'

Amy shook her head, somehow managing to put into that slight gesture a wealth of passionate denial, of dread, of horror of the unknown; and again Lawson looked at her very doubtfully and Bobby with intense and questioning interest.

'About the jewellery,' Lawson said, leaving the question of the time of Lady Cambers's retirement. 'I understand it was worth a great deal of money? Thirty thousand pounds?'

'I don't know exactly what it was worth,' Amy replied.

'A lot of money, I suppose, but I don't know. It was very lovely. There was one pearl—the Cleopatra pearl—the loveliest thing that I have ever seen,' she added with a kind of grave, impersonal delight.

'There was something about it in one of the papers a week or two ago, wasn't there?' Bobby asked.

'No,' answered Amy, 'that was the other one. There are two. They are supposed to have belonged to Cleopatra; she is said to have worn them as ear-rings—that is why they are called the Cleopatra pearls. Lady Cambers had one and Mr. Tyler has the other. He is a gentleman from America. He wanted to buy Lady Cambers's, so that he could have them both for Mrs. Tyler to wear as ear-rings, too, but Lady Cambers wouldn't agree. He came to see her about it a month ago, and she showed him hers but she wouldn't sell it, and he went off in a temper; he wouldn't even have a cup of tea, he was so angry. He said he had offered more than twice what it was worth.'

'And now it's gone, and all the rest as well,' Lawson mused, and looked again at the safe as if he would force it to reveal its secret, and breathed harder than ever. He said: 'Could the jewellery have been removed without your knowledge?'

'I suppose so,' Amy answered doubtfully. 'I think I should have known, though, unless Lady Cambers took a lot of trouble for me not to, and why should she? It was there last Wednesday, because I remember we had it out that morning. Why?'

'Why had you it out?' countered Lawson, ignoring her question.

'Lady Cambers liked to look at it sometimes,' Amy explained. 'That was why she didn't want to put it in the bank, where she could never see it. It is very beautiful,' Amy added, with a kind of slow appreciation that, in Bobby's mind at least, called up a picture of the two women sitting there with the jewellery outspread before them, both of them loving the sheer beauty of the glittering toys.

He found himself wondering if anyone else had by any chance been a spectator of that scene.

'Well, seems it's gone,' Lawson said abruptly. 'There's no sign of any jewellery in the safe now.'

'It's always there,' Amy persisted gently, and, when Lawson shook his head, she said: 'But it must be. Let me look.'

It was plain she thought they had not looked in the right place. Lawson gave her the keys. She picked out the right one at once, went across to the safe, set the combination, and opened it. After a moment she turned round, her expression less tranquil now, her voice a little breathless as she said: 'It's not there ... it's gone. ... I don't understand.'

'Lady Cambers took a small suit-case with her when she went out last night,' Lawson told her.

'Yes, I know; I heard,' Amy said.

'Could she have had the jewellery with her in it?' Lawson asked.

Amy did not answer at first. She looked from her questioner to the safe and back again. Presently she said: 'You don't mean you think she put all the jewellery in a suit-case and took it out with her alone at that time of night?'

'We have to consider every possibility,' Lawson answered, a little irritably. 'We have to consider the facts. There's the suit-case, empty now, but presumably there was something in it or why did she take it with her? There's the safe, empty now, but containing the jewels before. There's the fact that the keys were left here, in a drawer, as if they didn't matter much, as they wouldn't if the safe had been emptied of everything of value. Those are facts. We've got to interpret them.'

'If the jewellery's been stolen, that may be the motive for the murder,' suggested Moulland.

'Is there any list of it, any inventory?' Lawson asked.

'There was an inventory,' Amy answered, 'but I think

Sir Albert took it away with him when he left home.'

'How was that?'

'There was a disagreement about it,' Amy explained. 'Sir Albert lost a very great deal of money a little while ago. It was something about pepper. I don't know exactly. I suppose the lawyers could tell you. The entail was broken, and Lady Cambers bought the estate from Sir Albert with her own money, so that he could pay what he owed about the pepper. Lady Cambers wanted her nephew, Mr. Sterling, to be her heir and have the estate, as they had no children themselves. I think Sir Albert wanted it to go to a cousin of his, so it could stop in the family. Of course, after Lady Cambers bought the estate she could have left it to anyone else, if she quarrelled with her nephew. Sir Albert might easily have had his own way in the end if he had waited and they had come to make things up again between themselves.'

'About the jewellery,' Lawson asked. 'Was there any quarrel about it in especial, did you mean?'

'Lady Cambers thought it was her own to do what she liked with. Sir Albert said some of it was heirloom and went with the entail, and now the entail was broken it was his, as it hadn't been sold with the estate—or, at any rate, some of it that he said he had never actually given her. Lady Cambers said he should never have it. I think she thought he really wanted to give it to someone else. She was very upset about it. I expect it was all a misunderstanding because they were so angry with each other.'

'Was the jewellery insured, do you know?'

'I don't think so. I remember Lady Cambers saying the insurance company asked such a lot.'

'Yet she was nervous about burglars?'

'Only after Sir Albert went away and after we heard there was a strange man in the village asking a lot of questions and hanging about the place. She never seemed nervous before.'

The chief constable subsided into moody silence. Lady Cambers murdered; her jewellery gone; her keys where they had never been before, in a drawer of her writing-table in the same room with the empty safe; a hint of bitter domestic disputes in the background; no explanation of the solitary midnight expedition that had ended so tragically —the chief constable saw no line to follow likely to lead to a solution through so tangled a labyrinth. Moulland sat upright, waiting for instructions. To Bobby it seemed that half a dozen lines of inquiry presented themselves, simply asking to be followed up. He could hardly bear to sit still upon his chair when there was so much to be done. As for Amy, she seemed to have relapsed again into her habitual solitude of mind, and there to be once more communing alone with her own thoughts. When Lawson spoke again, she had again the air of having been called back from a remote and distant place.

'Mr. Sterling?' she repeated. 'His first name is Timothy; Lady Cambers always called him Tim. She promised to make him her heir, but she seemed to think he wasn't grateful enough. I think he didn't want to count upon it. She could have changed her mind, and perhaps he thought she might. He has a small factory where they make wireless things.'

'I wonder if there's a will and if he does inherit?' observed Colonel Lawson. 'Well, Emmers, I don't think we need keep you any longer. Emmers is your name, I think?'

'My name is Amy Margaret Emmers,' she answered in her aloof, indifferent way as she rose to go. 'I am generally called Miss Emmers.'

In the same calm, distant way she went gently from the room, and the chief constable, staring after her, went slowly redder and redder in the face.

'I . . . I . . . I . . .' he stuttered at last. 'I believe she meant that. I believe she meant I wasn't to call her Emmers.'

As it was quite evident that that, indeed, was precisely

what she had meant, neither Bobby nor Moulland ventured any comment. The chief constable went on growing red and looking bewildered, for such a thing as a lady's maid rebuking a colonel had never yet entered into his conception of the scheme of things. With a certain courage Moulland made a plunge.

'In my humble opinion, sir,' he said, 'that girl knows a good deal more than she's told.'

'Then she'll have to be made to tell,' declared Lawson very fiercely.

'Yes, sir,' agreed Moulland, in a tone that seemed to hint he saw difficulties in the way.

'She's given a lot of information,' Bobby ventured to remark. 'About the quarrel, and about the nephew, Mr. Sterling. And she was quite clear and emphatic about the keys.'

A knock came at the door, and Farman appeared.

'Mr. Bowman is here, sir. He says he understands you would like to see him. And Mr. Sterling, her ladyship's nephew, is here too, sir.'

'We'll see Mr. Bowman first,' Lawson decided. 'Ask Mr. Sterling to wait. There's this man we keep hearing about, too—the stranger Lady Cambers seems to have been nervous about. We had better get him along and see what he has to say. You had better see to that, Moulland.'

Farman coughed—a butler's discreet, informatory cough.

'Well?' said Lawson, understanding its significance.

'I'm told, sir,' Farman informed him, 'that the person left hurriedly this morning. He paid his bill and went immediately on hearing what had happened. He said he might return, and would let them know if he did. He appeared in a great hurry.'

The chief constable scowled and frowned, trying to think whom he could blame for action not having been taken more promptly.

'Looks odd,' he said. 'Ought to have been seen to, Moulland. We shall have to trace him. Very likely there's no connection, but it will have to be looked into. Ask Mr. Bowman to come in,' he added to Farman.

The butler retired and Mr. Bowman appeared. He was a short, round, fair man, who looked as if he did himself well and who was now in a not unnatural state of agitation and distress.

'Dreadful business,' he kept saying. 'Greatest shock of my life. I couldn't believe it when I saw who it was.'

His account of his discovery was simple and coherent. It was now his custom to take the early train to Hirlpool, where he was in business as an accountant and estate-agent. He had no car, as he had recently sold it, and he had not yet bought a new one, so he went by train. He walked to the station at this end. On his way, when he noticed the figure lying in the field, he thought at first it was a tramp sleeping out. But there seemed something unnatural in the figure's attitude, and a tramp would most likely have sought the shelter of a bush or a haystack. He had gone to look, and he was quite unable to describe his surprise and horror when he realized who it was. It was then about twenty past seven, he supposed, though he had not looked at his watch. But the train he was on his way to catch left at a quarter to eight, and the station was about twenty minutes' walk or so.

'The body was on its face,' he went on. 'I turned it over. It was quite stiff. She must have been dead some time. I ran to Mr. Hardy's place and told them, and they came at once. We took the body to that shed of young Dene's. Hardy said he would tell the police and get a doctor—not that a doctor could do anything for her, poor soul. I went straight back home. I felt too upset and ill to be able to do any work. I rang up the office after a time to tell them what had happened and that I shouldn't be coming. But I think I'll go on now, if there's nothing I can do to help. There are several things I ought to attend to.'

The chief constable did not think there was anything Mr.

Bowman could do just at present. Accordingly he departed, and Mr. Sterling was introduced.

He proved a good-looking young man, with a thin, dark face, about twenty-three or four years old, tall and of vigorous appearance. He, too, was in a nervous, agitated state. The news of his aunt's death had been a dreadful shock to him. He had heard of it at Hirlpool, where he had spent the night. Already everyone in Hirlpool was talking about it—the most sensational murder the district had ever known. He had started out from home the night before to visit his aunt, leaving his rooms on the outskirts of London, near his place of work, in quite good time. But the journey had been a series of misadventures. His motor-cycle had broken down repeatedly, and the more often he got it going the more certain it was to break down again. The ignition was all wrong. He began to enter into technical details that interested Bobby enormously, but that Colonel Lawson, who thought motor-cycles slightly vulgar, promptly checked. So Sterling apologized, and added that he had lost his way in the dark, and been caught in the rain, and had a skid and a tumble, and finally had reached Hirlpool somewhere in the small hours and then had knocked up a pub and secured shelter. It jolly well wouldn't have done, he explained, to disturb his aunt and her household at such an hour. Of course, if he had known what had been happening, he added moodily, it would have been different. But who could have dreamed of such a tragedy?

CHAPTER NINE

TEN SUSPECTS—THREE QUESTIONS

THIS WAS ALL STERLING HAD TO SAY, SO HIS EXAMINA-tion did not last long. As he himself explained, he had only arrived on the scene that morning. But one point of importance did emerge at the end of the interview.

'I think that's all we have to ask you at present,' Colonel Lawson had said, and then, remembering, added: 'Oh, by the way, yes. I understand you are your aunt's heir?'

'I don't know. She told me once she intended to make her will in my favour,' Sterling answered slowly. 'I have no idea whether she did or not. Of course, even if she did, she might have altered it again.'

'Had you any reason to think she might do that?' the chief constable asked.

'Oh, I don't know; she rather seemed to think it gave her a right to tell me what I had to do. She got a bit shirty if you didn't do just what she thought you ought,' answered the young man. 'Of course, it was awfully good of her, thinking of leaving me everything, and I was very grateful and all that, but I wasn't going to do the tame-lap-dog act all the same. There are limits.'

'Was there any special point you disagreed upon?'

Sterling hesitated, flushed, looked as if he would refuse to answer, changed his mind and said: 'Oh, well, I suppose it was that she rather wanted to pick out a girl for me to marry, and I didn't see it. I dare say we both got a bit ratty.'

'When was this?'

'Oh, I don't know exactly. Quite recently. She was always bringing it up.'

'Did she actually say anything about changing her will?'

'No. Yes. Well, in a way. I thought once she was hinting she would, and I told her straight out when I married I should please myself. It wasn't only that. I knew jolly well she wanted Uncle Albert to come back. She was very bitter about him and very keen on him at the same time. I knew he only had to make it plain he was turning down the Bowman girl for good and all, and aunt would have jumped at the chance of making it up with him. Then, of course, she would have had to make her will over again. Well, that's all right, of course, but I didn't see her making me marry some bally girl I knew nothing about just so she could fix it up with Uncle Albert again.'

'How? In what way? I don't follow that quite,' Lawson said.

'Oh, well, it's like this. The girl she wanted me to marry is one of the Cambers family, only another branch. Had the same ancestor somewhere about the Wars of the Roses or thereabouts. Uncle Albert had some sort of sentimental idea of perpetuating the family name by passing on the estate here to these other Cambers. Aunt thought she could kill several birds with the same stone: work a reconciliation with Uncle Albert, get me safely married, settle the destination of both the family estates and her own private money, all together. I did see the girl once. Quite a kid. We bored each other stiff at first sight. I told my aunt right out I wasn't having any.'

'Was that what you had come to see her about?'

'Oh, no. I was just running down to see how she was and all that.'

Colonel Lawson consulted his notes, asked one or two more quite unimportant questions, and then the young man was allowed to depart. But he was asked to remain in the vicinity for the present, and at any rate not to leave without letting his intention to do so be known.

'What about this young Dene?' the chief constable asked next, but had to be told that all efforts to find him had proved unavailing so far.

Apparently he was neither at his father's shop nor anywhere else in the village. No one had seen him, and the chief constable scowled and frowned very much on receiving this information. Then Farman appeared, to report that Sir Albert Cambers had rung through to say he was on the way and would arrive shortly. The news of the tragedy had reached him while he was in bed with an attack of influenza, but he got up at once and would have started before, only that he had been obliged to wait so long for the car he had ordered from the Jubilee Garage. Then, too, a message had been received from Scotland Yard agreeing to Detective-Sergeant Owen's services being placed for the time at the disposal of Chief Constable Lawson, in accordance with the request made. Colonel Lawson was very pleased on receiving this message, and beamed approval on Bobby. No one now could blame him for not calling in the help of Scotland Yard and yet the direction of the case would remain entirely in his own—as he felt—very capable hands: because to Colonel Lawson a sergeant was a person who stood to attention and waited for orders, not moving an inch till he got them.

'Better make a fair copy of your notes, sergeant,' he said to Bobby.

'Very good, sir,' said Bobby. 'I was wondering, sir,' he added carelessly, 'if I might potter about the village a little first and see if I can pick up any gossip. They all know I was staying here, so they'll think it natural enough, and they may talk more freely to me than they would to you, sir, or to Mr. Moulland.'

'Oh, by all means,' agreed Colonel Lawson, thinking no harm of 'pottering', 'and see if you can get any hint of what's likely to have become of that young Dene fellow. I dare say there's no connection, but it seems curious that two people should vanish immediately like this—Dene and the man reported as having roused suspicions by asking questions in the village.' He paused, hesitated, and added: 'There's one thing perhaps you ought to know, but you understand it is for information solely; it is not to be taken into account or allowed to prejudice the inquiry in any way.'

'Yes, sir; no, sir,' said Bobby, wondering what this meant.

Instead of speaking, the chief constable glanced at his superintendent, who cleared his throat and said: 'We have it on record that Farman served three years' penal servitude for robbing his employer just before the war. He was in prison when the war broke out, was released earlier than usual in order to join up, served till the armistice, and has had a good character ever since.'

'I understand, sir,' said Bobby. 'I won't let it influence me in any way.' And, indeed, it hardly seemed likely to him that this twenty-year-old story was of any importance.

He departed, therefore, and when he had gone the chief constable added to Moulland: 'What's the betting young Dene's bolted?'

'You think he's guilty, sir?' Moulland asked.

'Looks like it. Great mistake to take up a young fellow of that class. Gives them ideas. Puts notions in their heads. Did you notice that, after the butler let Dene out, no one seems to have seen Lady Cambers alive? What about this for a working theory? Dene knows all about the jewellery. He strangles the poor woman, opens the safe with her keys he takes from her hand-bag, where he knows she keeps them, pushes the body through the window in order to conceal it later, and fills his pockets with the jewellery. He himself rings the bell for the butler to let him out, goes off without any suspicion being raised, and, instead of going home, slips round the house to recover the body. He carries it as far as where it was found, but then it gets too much for him and he abandons it there. He drops his pen by accident at the same time; he hides the jewellery and goes off to recover his nerve and wait for the discovery to be made. That accounts for all doors and windows being found fast in the morning, as they were apparently.'

'Yes, sir,' agreed Moulland dutifully but a trifle doubtfully. 'The maid says she was with Lady Cambers in her bedroom after Dene left.'

'She's Dene's sweetheart,' the chief constable pointed out. 'If a girl's in love with a man she'll say anything to save him. She may have been in it from the first, for that matter. There's something I don't understand about that girl, and that I don't like.'

'Yes, sir,' said Moulland, who, indeed, had reached his present eminence in the county police force chiefly through the zeal, fervour, and frequency with which, all through his career, he had said, 'Yes, sir.'

But Bobby, well on his way by now to the village, was considering many other theories and possibilities, and presently, perched on a five-barred gate, he produced his pocket-book and began to make a list of the points that seemed to him to require special attention.

There was Mr. Bowman, for instance, to begin with.

Was there anything in the various hints and rumours that his sister was the cause, knowing or unknowing, of the recent breach between Lady Cambers and her husband? At any rate, it would be interesting to find out, if possible, how far Sir Albert was seriously entangled with Miss Bowman. A man infatuated with a girl might do strange things to rid himself of the wife who stood between.

What was Mr. Bowman's financial position? (He had recently sold his car and had not bought a new one.)

Was there anything about his discovery of the body to suggest he had seen it because he knew already it was there? (There was a high hedge, and the field sloped, and young Ray Hardy had apparently gone close-by without noticing anything. But, then, he might have been more absorbed with his own affairs and Mr. Bowman might have sharp eyes.)

Was his apparent nervous collapse after the discovery genuine or assumed? It had been so marked that he had felt able neither to stay on the spot nor go on to business, but had been obliged to return straight home. If it was genuine, was it a result of guilty knowledge? If it was assumed, why?

'Plenty there to keep a fellow busy,' Bobby told himself.

Then there was Eddy Dene.

How did his pen come to be on the scene of the murder?

An obvious clue, certainly, but perhaps a little too obvious. Still, obvious clues were sometimes good clues, too. There was that case in Chicago, for instance, where two young degenerates planned the perfect crime, and then one of them proceeded to leave his spectacle-case on the scene of the murder.

Was it significant that Dene had had so prolonged an interview with Lady Cambers so short a time before the murder? But, then, she was his friend and patron on whom apparently he depended for obtaining the money for carrying on his archæological researches—and there had been something about an American millionaire, an introduction to whom she had apparently promised. One does not usually kick down the ladder by which one is climbing upwards.

And then the girl he was engaged to—Lady Cambers's maid, Amy Emmers—who had explained away with such gentle assurance the story of the quarrel with her mistress. Certainly there was something about her that was hard to understand, and one of the deepest instincts of human nature is to regard with marked suspicion all that is not easily understood. Then, of course, she had every opportunity of securing the missing jewellery, so far as that went. How suavely and easily, too, she had explained the washing-up of the glass and plate whereon such valuable finger-prints might have been found—or might not. After all, the girl's action could easily have been quite innocent, and in that morning's excited, overwrought, slightly hysterical atmosphere it was conceivable she had found it a relief to perform an ordinary piece of commonplace household routine.

His thoughts turned to the vicar of the parish, Mr. Andrews. Far-fetched, perhaps, to suspect him, a clergyman of blameless life; but Bobby had seen his eyes of the fanatic, and he had threatened judgement and judgement had arrived. Bobby found himself reflecting that prophets have been known occasionally to take steps to make their prophecies come true.

Perhaps, of all those concerned, young Tim Sterling had the most obvious motive. He inherited his aunt's fortune, which by common rumour was substantial, and he was aware that the will whereby he benefited was subject to alteration at any moment. Then, too, pressure he evidently strongly resented was being brought on him to marry where his inclinations did not lie; and what had brought him down so late this Sunday night to visit his aunt? A week-end visit would have been more easily comprehensible than this dash down from town late on Sunday, complicated by his failure to reach his destination and the spending of the night at a Hirlpool inn.

There rose before Bobby a memory of Sterling's thin, dark, vivid face, a face, Bobby thought, of one of strong emotions, of many possibilities. Nor was Bobby altogether satisfied that Sterling's manner under examination had been quite normal. There had been, he thought, a hint of restraint, of carefulness not altogether natural in one of so vivid and eager a personality. But then, again, one had to remember the circumstances that perhaps made such an attitude not so much natural as inevitable.

Bobby shook his head impatiently, hoped he was not growing fanciful, and turned to the next on his list of suspects—Sir Albert Cambers himself—for Bobby felt he deserved not to be forgotten. There was not only the complication with Miss Bowman to be considered, but also the fact that there had undoubtedly been serious disputes over money matters. It sounded as if his losses in the City had given his wife the opportunity to take a high hand with him, and that she had succeeded in securing full control of the family estates. Then there had been a quarrel about the missing jewellery, Sir Albert claiming at any rate some of it as his own, and Lady Cambers insisting that it was all her property.

Could it be possible that he had attempted to enforce his claim with violence that had had tragic results? It would be necessary, Bobby thought, to inquire very closely into the movements of Sir Albert Cambers on this Sunday night.

Also there was the unknown visitor to the village about whom no one seemed to know anything but about whom everyone had something to say. Was it of any significance that with the news of the murder he had vanished in such haste?

Yet, if he had been guilty of the murder, would he not have vanished sooner? A disappearance after it had become generally known suggested dismay and fear rather than previous guilty knowledge.

It had to be remembered, though, that he had managed to get himself suspected of burglary by the marked interest he had shown in Cambers House, and that now the Cambers jewellery had disappeared!

There jerked into Bobby's memory the story Amy Emmers had told of the disappointment and anger of the American millionaire, Mr. Tyler, at Lady Cambers's refusal to part with her Cleopatra pearl. Did the truth lie somewhere there—in an attempt by an agent of Mr. Tyler to secure by theft the desired pearl—and had it resulted more tragically than had ever been contemplated? Another suspect, then, to be added to the list. For collectors have been known to go very far indeed in their efforts to secure the objects they have set their hearts on.

Finally there was the butler, Farman, and this story of the old far-off conviction, that should now have passed into oblivion after so many years of honest war and domestic service. But now it had to be remembered, Bobby supposed, only he would be very careful not to give it too much importance.

A complicated affair, it seemed, and carefully Bobby set down in order the names of the chief suspects, and the motive that it seemed might have urged them to the crime.

1. *Sir Albert Cambers.*

   Motive: Freedom to marry Miss Bowman. Money disputes. Rival claims to possession of the missing jewellery. (N.B.: Check movements on Sunday night.)

2. *Mr. Bowman.*

   Motive: Financial (reported hard-up), and wish to see his sister married to Sir Albert, with consequent advantages to his own business and social position.

3. *Mr. Tyler.*

   Motive: The Cleopatra pearl.

4. *Farman.*

   Motive: Doubtful; might be theft of jewellery on own account or to secure the Cleopatra pearl for Mr. Tyler.

5. *The Stranger from London (suspected of burglarious intentions).*

   Possibly in Mr. Tyler's pay. Must be traced.

6. *Eddy Dene.*

   Motive: Doubtful. Apparently a protégé of Lady Cambers, but then protégés and their patrons sometimes quarrel. Apparently a young man of unusual character, known to have been in Lady Cambers's company late on the Sunday night. The pen found on the scene of the murder now identified as his.

7. *Amy Emmers, Lady Cambers's personal maid.*

   Motive: If any, probably a desire to help or shield someone else. Engaged to Eddy Dene, a fact to remember, but apparently no great keenness on either side.

   Note: Almost certainly knows more than she has told. Various small suspicious circumstances observed.

8. *The vicar of the parish, Mr. Andrews.*

   Motive: Objection to Dene's archæological investigations, and fear of conclusions that might be drawn from them. Threats used from pulpit and now materialized.

9. *Tim Sterling.*
   Motive: His aunt's heir, but position precarious. Resentment at attempt to force a wife on him.
   Note: His visit so late on Sunday curious in the extreme, especially as he didn't reach his destination.

10. *Ray Hardy (hardly worth including).*
    Motive: None apparent.
    Note: His behaviour seemed vaguely suspicious. Was out early that morning and passed near body without seeing it. Nothing much in that, and behaviour to be quite easily accounted for in the circumstances.

With considerable distaste, Bobby surveyed this long list. It seemed to him almost certain the murderer's name was there. Only how to identify it?

By careful, painstaking work it might be possible to eliminate the names one by one till only one was left, and then it would be fairly certain that that one was the murderer's.

In the meantime he supposed there were three special points to clear up:

First: Why had Lady Cambers gone out alone so late at night without warning anyone, and why had she taken a suit-case with her?

Secondly: Who had lain and watched so long that night in the rhododendron-bushes, and for what object, since the watch must have continued long after the murder had been committed?

Thirdly: Who was it who had been served with refreshments in Lady Cambers's business room? And by whom?

CHAPTER TEN

LANDLADY'S PHILOSOPHY

HAVING CONCLUDED THIS SURVEY OF THE CASE, IDENTI-
fied his long list of suspects, decided on the first three points
to aim at, Bobby descended from his seat on the five-
barred gate, brushed his trousers, put his note-book back
in his pocket, and felt depressed.

It began to seem to him that in the dark and complicated
background to the tragedy must lie the secret of its cause
and perpetration. The murder of Lady Cambers was, he
felt, no isolated occurrence, but the perhaps inevitable
and, so to say, destined, outcome of a long series of events,
of passionate emotions that in the end had broken loose,
of deep conflicting interests in which love and ambition
and greed of money and position were all inextricably
confused.

But how to find the path that through such a labyrinth
would lead to the truth, how to discover with what degree
of passion and intensity these ten different people had
pursued their various aims so that, in one instance at
least, there had supervened so black a crime?

And then in the background the enigmatic figure of
Amy Emmers, with her aloof and proud indifference, her
gentle, ready explanations?

To Bobby it seemed clear that the truth was to be found
almost certainly, in this case at least, in a study of character
rather than in an examination of fact. Once the detective
had grasped character and motive, then he would know
'why' and, once the 'why' was understood, then it was
comparatively simple to follow out the 'how'. One might
easily have, so to speak, all the facts in one's hand, and yet
fail entirely to read their message for lack of comprehen-
sion of the motives that had inspired them. Whereas once
those motives were understood, then the most puzzling
facts would fall quickly and easily into place and present

themselves in one coherent story of simple and straight-forward reading.

It was a theory of detection—to concentrate more on spiritual motive than on material fact—Bobby had learned in part from his immediate superior at the Yard, Super-intendent Mitchell, in part from the writing of Mr. G. K. Chesterton.

A microscope, infra-red rays, supra-violet rays and their effects, finger-prints and footprints—all had their valuable, and, indeed, essential, part to play, but they could only be interpreted correctly in the light of character and motive. And to do so is a task both more difficult and less spec-tacular than to analyse a speck of dust from the pocket of a suspect and draw therefrom scientific conclusions.

Bobby shook off these somewhat depressing thoughts to find he had now reached the village. It was easy to see at the first glance how profoundly the small community had been stirred by what had happened. The women, their household tasks forgotten, were gathered in little groups, talking in subdued, frightened whispers. The men, if they could not always leave their work so easily, were none the less talking just as hard and much more loudly. Bobby's appearance as he walked up the street produced first a pause and then a renewed gush of talk, for they all knew both that he was connected with the London police and that he had been staying at Cambers House as a guest. From all parts of the straggling, sunny street curious eyes were turned in his direction, and one could almost feel the ache of the longing to question him.

At one spot the postman and the milkman were ex-changing condolences. Both had just been getting into trouble with their clients for being so late upon their rounds, and both had been protesting that they could not help it. People would insist on asking them a mort of questions, and they couldn't get away without being downright rude.

'Look at Mrs. Roberts—her that's cook up at Bowmans',' complained the milkman. 'I know I was over an hour late getting there; nine it was striking when I knocked, instead of half-past seven and a good twenty minutes before I got away again, all along of her wanting to know what was up, and having heard nothing about it. And just as I was telling her, there was Mr. Bowman himself came walking in at the gate; gave us both a turn, and cook and all thinking him in his office, for like a ghost he looked —white as a sheet.'

Bobby, who had overheard this, and who had previously chatted with both men, with one while delivering the letters, the other the milk, at Cambers House, thought this conversation sounded promising. So he joined in, and soon, since he had made up his mind it would be well to try to find out all he could about the stranger from London said to have been staying in the village and to have vanished that morning with a somewhat suspicious speed, he was inquiring about him. But the milkman knew nothing, and, remembering waiting customers, departed, and the postman did not seem inclined to be very communicative.

'The gent that was stopping at the Cambers Arms?' he asked. 'Jones was his name—Samuel Jones. Left this morning, they say, but there's no letters for him.'

Bobby tried to pursue the subject further, but the post-man grew suddenly official. It was forbidden to give any information about the mail without special authority. If any more letters came for Mr. Jones they would have to be dealt with in the ordinary way, and authority to hand correspondence over would have to be obtained from headquarters. As a matter of fact the good man had been telling in full detail everything he knew to everyone he met all the morning long, and had most thoroughly enjoyed doing so. But it was a different matter altogether to talk to a detective who had behind him all the mysterious powers of Scotland Yard. So he grew suddenly silent, and Bobby tactfully applauded this official discretion, felt fairly confident that, so recognized, it would in time easily dissolve in a pint or two of good ale, and moved on to the Cambers Arms, where all morning, during that generally mournful period when the licensing laws forbid the sale of 'wine, beer, or spirits', the consumption of lemonade and 'minerals' had touched unprecedented heights.

It was luncheon-time now, and, indeed, past it, and in the bar and the cosy sheltered dining-room the talk was largely about mysterious Mr. Samuel Jones and his equally mysterious disappearance. Most of the company appeared convinced he was the murderer, and, with various glances Bobbywards, wondered he had not already been found and arrested. But the landlady pointed out that he had always paid regularly and had settled his bill before he departed, which, as she justly observed, was more than could have been expected from a murderer.

But it seemed that neither she nor anyone else had much real information about him. He had appeared abruptly in the village, and at first everyone had accepted his story that he was on the look-out for a cottage, with a bit of land attached, whereon to settle down on his retirement from business. This had seemed to explain the many questions he asked, until it began to be noticed that the questions increased in number and detail in proportion as the prospective purchase grew vaguer and vaguer.

Still, he had made himself fairly popular; he had won a good many pints and half-pints at darts, and lost others at shove-halfpenny; he had received several letters with typewritten address, and those he had written himself, it had been noticed, he never seemed to care to post in the village. For that purpose he had invariably gone to Hirlpool or elsewhere, and he had taken pains to explain that his wife was very anxious to know how the search for a new home progressed.

All this seemed interesting to Bobby, and after luncheon

he managed to get the landlady aside. From her he learnt the further fact that Mr. Jones had been very fond of smoking a late pipe out-of-doors—so much so that finally he had been given a key of the side-door in order that he might let himself in when he was late without making anyone wait up for him. There were also hints that these late strolls had a way of taking him in the direction of Cambers House, but the landlady was quite clear that on the night of the murder the heavy rainstorm had brought him in fairly early and wet through—and that he had not gone out again, but had proceeded straight to bed.

If this were so, and could be confirmed, it provided, of course, a complete alibi so far as the actual murder was concerned, but of one thing Bobby felt convinced: that Mr. Jones's assumption of the character of a retired business man seeking a country home was an invention to conceal his real purpose, whatever that might have been— burglarious or otherwise.

Bobby got permission to see the room he had occupied, but close examination showed nothing of interest. Nor had Mr. Jones left anything behind. His room was on the first floor, so that exit from it during the night without attracting attention would have been easy enough, especially as there was a convenient gutter-pipe adjacent. As for his address, he had given it simply as 'Cromwell Road, London', which struck Bobby as about as helpful as 'Everywhere, Anywhere', since, indeed, there are probably few parts of London into which the Cromwell Road does not extend its interminable length. However, Bobby got as full a description as possible of his personal appearance, and a promise that the room should not be disturbed until a finger-print expert had visited it. If good impressions could be obtained from any of the furniture, and if Mr. Jones happened to be a gentleman who had had previous commerce with the police of the country, his identity would be very quickly established.

One thing that came out in further talk was that Mr. Jones had seemed specially interested in Eddy Dene and his archæological researches in Frost Field, on Mr. Hardy's farm. He had explained to the landlady that he himself had studied the subject, and was extraordinarily interested in old castles, cathedrals, and so on—that, in fact, he, so to speak, 'collected' them—and it took Bobby some time to deduce that in Mr. Jones's mind there probably existed a slight confusion between archæology and architecture. This interest displayed by Mr. Jones had not, however, much surprised the landlady, for, she explained, Eddy Dene was by way of being famous, and had even had his picture in the papers. And when once a gentleman came from Oxford to see him, Eddy had conducted the conversation as man to man, 'just as it might be you and me,' said the landlady, suitably impressed by Oxford, its accent, its general affability.

'Not that I hold with this proving we all come from monkeys,' the landlady went on, 'as those can believe who like, and, if it's true, what's the sense of raking up the past?'

As an answer was evidently expected, Bobby said meekly that he didn't know, and asked if Mr. Dene wasn't engaged to one of the maids at Cambers House.

The landlady shrugged her ample shoulders and opined that no self-respecting girl would put up with a boy who hardly ever took any notice of her.

'I wouldn't be taken for granted the way he takes her,' declared the landlady. 'It's all been the old people's doing. They brought Amy up, and they always had it fixed she and Eddy were to marry, but there's nothing he thinks of but his bones and stones and things, though I don't hold with all vicar says, because if it's a judgement, why's it fallen on her, poor lady, instead of him? But mark my words, there'll be a bigger congregation at church next Sunday than there's been for long enough.'

'Mr. Andrews felt strongly about it, then?' Bobby asked. 'I don't see why.'

'If Eddy Dene proved we were all apes before we were made,' explained the landlady, 'then the Bible's all wrong, isn't it? And if Bible's wrong, where's church? And church is vicar's living, isn't it? Why, my old man himself heard Eddy and vicar telling each other off proper, and vicar saying how God would speak, and Eddy saying he hoped, anyhow, God wouldn't speak with a sniffle like vicar's, him having a cold, poor man—which,' said the landlady, lowering her voice reverently, 'God wouldn't —and vicar tearing straight off to talk to Lady Cambers and how she was imperilling her mortal soul and all of ours as well, because of us being apes perhaps and so having none. But what I say is,' concluded the landlady, a little breathless, 'don't go raking up anyone's past, but see dinner's cooked and ready on time and the floors swept proper.'

CHAPTER ELEVEN

EDDY DENE'S ROOM

FROM THE INN, BOBBY WENT ON TO THE SHOP KEPT BY Eddy Dene's parents—theoretically a grocery establishment, but stocking many other things as well, from hardware to stationery, from cigarettes to aspirin. At the moment it was full of customers, most of whom, however, seemed less occupied in making purchases than in general converse. Even that Draconian law which forbids one commercial traveller to enter a shop while another of the fraternity is present there, seemed to have been abrogated for the time, since a gentleman who sought orders for paper bags was talking quite amiably to another who had for mission to establish a market in an entirely new brand of ink for fountain-pens, neatly named the 'Perennial', in the hope that a simple-minded public would accept the implication that it 'flowed for ever'. His instructions were to give away one sample bottle and one only—'one only' much emphasized and strictly observed—in each neighbourhood, so that the great opening day of the sales campaign might arrive to the accompaniment of the slogan, 'Every Retailer has Tried It Himself.' But though conversation in the shop was both general and animated, on one detail none touched. What had in fact brought all these people hither was the story spread already through the village that the police wished to question Eddy Dene, but were unable to find him. Even the fountain-pen-ink merchant had delayed his departure from a locality in which he had completed all his business the previous weekend in order to discover for himself whether there was or was not any truth in the story. For, oddly enough, the state of a traveller's order-book depends very largely on whether he has the latest funny story to relate, the latest bit of local gossip to recount. Unfortunately the attitude of Eddy's parents had not been of a nature to encourage much inquiry concerning his present whereabouts.

Mr. Dene, a small, withered, anxious-looking man, nervous and even excitable in manner, but plainly used to keeping himself well in hand, as befits a good tradesman whose motto has to be that the customer is always right, was behind the counter, making occasional, distracted, and not very successful, efforts to lead the conversation from the recent tragedy to current needs. Mrs. Dene, large, plump, and comfortable-looking, hovered in the background, occasionally vanishing into the parlour behind the shop, and then again emerging to listen to, or join in, one of the many discussions going on.

Bobby's entrance caused a sudden hush, for most of those present knew who he was. And since everyone was looking hard at him, and was on the evident tiptoe of expectation, he thought it best to ask at once for Eddy, and, on being told with a certain hesitation that he was out, to go on to request a few moments' talk with Mr. and Mrs. Dene.

Mr. Dene looked more worried than ever, paused to sell a frying-pan to a customer who didn't want it but could think of no other excuse for presence in the shop, remarked that he had enough to do to mind his own business, bad as business was with things the way they were and the motor-buses taking people to Hirlpool, where they seemed to like paying more than others nearer home charged for exactly the same thing. As for Eddy, Eddy looked after his own affairs, and little enough he cared about the business; and Mrs. Dene interposed with the remark that Eddy was so upset by what had happened it was no wonder he felt he couldn't face company, but if the gentleman cared to step into the parlour and wait, most likely he wouldn't be long, and then the gentleman could ask him any questions he wanted to, not that there was anything Eddy knew more than others.

It was an unpopular suggestion with the customers in the shop, who did not at all like this manner of ravishing from their ken one into whose every word could be read according to taste a meaning and a significance for general retailing and discussion. But Bobby accepted it at once, and in the little parlour Mrs. Dene set herself instantly to explain how terrible a shock it had been to them all, and in especial to her boy.

That she was vaguely uneasy and more or less on the defensive was perfectly plain, though with her this unease took the form of nervous chattering just as with her husband it took the form of an equally nervous restraint. She was bitter about the rush of customers to the shop, and especially bitter about the two commercial travellers. With some detail she explained that one had finished his business in that district and should have left before this for another, and that the second traveller, the paper-bag gentleman, had left a district he had not even begun to work in order to visit this one.

'Gossip, that's all they want,' she said indignantly. 'Just something to talk your head off, and then push an order-form under your nose before you even know what it's for.'

Bobby agreed that commercial travellers were undoubtedly the pest of all the ages, and gently brought the conversation back to Eddy. Mrs. Dene had evidently no idea where he was or what had become of him, but thought it no wonder he wished to be by himself, away from everyone.

'It's terrible for him,' she explained. 'Everything he owed to her ladyship, and wrapped up in his work so nothing else counted; and now, very like, it'll all have to stop with no more help coming from her, and even his chance of a situation with the American gentleman will be gone now, most likely.'

'What American gentleman is that?' Bobby asked.

Mrs. Dene was a little vague. All she was sure about was a magnificent opening had been as good as promised, through the good offices of Lady Cambers, with an American gentleman of enormous wealth. Now, most likely, no more would be heard of it. Misfortunes never came singly.

She went on to relate that as usual Eddy had been up early. A good hard-working boy he was, even if it was his own mother said it. But everyone would say the same. It was his habit to work in the shop in the mornings. After dinner, at noon, he would go on to his diggings at Frost Field—or, rather, to examine and check the results of the morning's work done there by the two workmen whose wages Lady Cambers paid. After tea, he would help in the shop again as a rule, unless business was slack, and then as soon as the shutters were up occupy himself again with his studies.

A busy, hard, laborious life, it seemed by Mrs. Dene's account, divided between the daily business of the shop and the archæological researches in Frost Field. Concerning these, Mrs. Dene was torn between pride and dislike—dislike because they took Eddy away from his work in the shop, pride that such learned pursuits should be followed by a son of hers. And it was fairly plain, too, that both she and her husband stood in considerable awe of the strange fledgeling they had so unexpectedly hatched out. Bobby gathered, indeed, that Eddy had not been suffered to go his own way without considerable opposition, and, indeed, scenes of some violence.

'Frets and worries and then flares up, that's him,' Mrs. Dene said, of her husband, 'and Eddy takes after him; but if he goes his own way, no one can deny he's a good son and does his duty by the business—shame as it is that with his learning he should have to think of such things.'

'He is engaged to Miss Emmers, isn't he?' Bobby asked.

'Settled ever since they were babies together,' Mrs. Dene assured him. 'He never shows it much, but she's all the world to him; only, a man always has to remember his work, too—it's not like it is with a woman; a woman's man is her work.'

'Is the marriage likely to be soon?' Bobby asked.

'Well, you see, it's like this,' explained Mrs. Dene, with a certain hesitation, 'and times being so bad and all. But if poor Lady Cambers had got Eddy a post with the American gentleman, then, as her ladyship said herself, there wouldn't have been any cause to wait not another moment. But how things will turn out now her ladyship's gone, there's no telling.'

'It will be a great disappointment,' Bobby observed. 'They must have found it very trying having to wait so long.'

Mrs. Dene agreed, but with a certain lack of enthusiasm still apparent in her voice, and went on to talk vaguely about young people in these days being in no hurry to settle down. It was different when she was young, she said. Bobby found himself forming the impression that it was partly in order to avoid being hurried into matrimony that Amy had left the shop for domestic service with Lady Cambers.

Lady Cambers too, then, had been urging on the marriage between her maid and her protégé, and the impression of her character Bobby had formed was strengthened. A busy, benevolent, managing woman, she had been, apparently, one always anxious to do what seemed to her best for others. Evidently she had been doing a great deal to help Eddy, had been anxious to do still more, and specially anxious to see the young couple settled down together for life.

'Most like Eddy will have to give up his studying and digging and suchlike,' Mrs. Dene said, with a mingling of satisfaction at the prospect and of dread of its possible effect on him, 'now it don't seem there'll be any more money to help pay for it with her ladyship gone, poor soul. And, likely enough, there'll be Amy coming home with no more call for her to stay at Cambers House—and that'll mean the four of us for the business to keep.'

Of the capacity of the business to perform that feat she was evidently by no means convinced, and Bobby asked: 'Perhaps your son will be able to get help from someone else?'

Mrs. Dene didn't think that likely, and evidently didn't much welcome the idea. She explained that two or three very learned gentlemen had come to see what Eddy was doing. But Eddy had not been very communicative, and they had not been very enthusiastic. He had told her afterwards that they had wanted him to explain his theories, and he had refused to do so, preferring to keep them to himself till he was able to produce proof he was right. Only Lady Cambers herself knew his real purpose. Bobby gathered that the 'learned gentlemen' had attempted to patronize

93

Eddy, and that Eddy had not been grateful. With mingled pride and terror, for it was easy to see Mrs. Dene was as scared of her formidable son as she was proud of him, she related the encounter, and told of a further encounter with the vicar, who apparently had managed to get Lady Cambers to tell him something of the theories Eddy was trying to establish, and had viewed them with much disfavour.

'Eddy flared up, same as his father does when you're least expecting it,' Mrs. Dene said, 'and told vicar right out he would dig proof out of Frost Field to show all Bible was wrong, and vicar said the Lord would judge. Next week he excommunicated him.'

'Who? Your son?' Bobby asked, and when Mrs. Dene nodded and looked more scared than ever at the recollection, he asked: 'Did he care?'

'He just laughed,' Mrs. Dene admitted. 'He never was one for church. And some said vicar hadn't the right, only the Pope in Rome, and even he couldn't, not in England, only in foreign parts, so there was talk of writing to the bishop himself about it. But Eddy wouldn't hear of it; said it wasn't worth the stamp. But there was talk Lady Cambers was real upset for fear it might be her next time.'

'To be excommunicated?'

'Yes, and now she's dead, poor lady, and that's worse.'

Bobby agreed that it was—more permanent, too. All this seemed to establish that the vicar had strongly objected to whatever work or aims Eddy Dene had in view, and that Lady Cambers's death had brought all that to an end. But it seemed impossible to suppose any casual connection between those two facts.

He glanced at his watch. Time was getting on, and still no sign of Eddy. He wondered if Eddy had in fact run for it, but thought that little likely. He asked one or two more questions, and learnt that Mr. Samuel Jones had made various small purchases in the shop, and had displayed a taste for conversation and thirst for information she and her husband had done their best not to gratify.

'We didn't either of us like his looks or his ways, or his manner of asking and asking all the time,' Mrs. Dene explained. 'If I was you, it's him I should be looking for, wanting to ask him questions that he was so fond of asking others.'

'Oh, I expect we shall try to get in touch with him,' Bobby answered. 'Early days yet, you know.'

In answer to another question, Mrs. Dene agreed at once that Eddy had possessed a very fine fountain-pen, mounted in gold, a present to him from Lady Cambers. He had been very pleased with it, and he always carried it with him. Quite certainly he would have it with him in his pocket now. Of that Mrs. Dene had no doubt. But she had no idea why Eddy had visited Lady Cambers the night before. He wouldn't be likely to say when he was going to see her, or why. He wasn't one to talk about his work, as even the gentlemen from Oxford had found out, and been proper vexed, too. But he not infrequently went to report progress to Lady Cambers, as was only natural since she was paying for all the excavations taking place. He had spent the whole day over his archæological work, as was generally the case on Sundays, though this Lady Cambers was not supposed to know, as she disapproved of Sunday work, and after a late tea had gone out again without saying, as he rarely did say, where he was going, or why.

'Would it be with the idea of seeing Miss Emmers that he went to Cambers House?' Bobby asked.

Mrs. Dene looked somewhat taken aback at the suggestion, and then agreed that it was a very likely one, but evidently did not really think so in the least. Bobby's impression that these had been no ardent lovers was strengthened, and he wondered if either of them was interested in anyone else, or whether it was just that they had come to take for granted an engagement that apparently dated from childhood.

'It was always his fossils and stones and suchlike came first with him,' Mrs. Dene explained. 'If it isn't one thing with a man, it's another, and better fossils than beer and betting, as many a time I've said to Amy.'

Bobby agreed, and went on to ask more questions about the visit to Cambers House. But Mrs. Dene knew nothing about it, except that Eddy had got wet through on his way home, and that it had brought on an attack of toothache, as almost always happened when he got a chill.

'And then there's no speaking to him or going near him till it's over,' she added. 'His father's just like that, too—if his rheumatism comes on, then he seems to think it's your fault, and it's best just to leave him to it.'

Of course, this time the rain had been exceptionally heavy—what the papers called a 'cloud-burst'—and Eddy had arrived home soaked to the skin, through and through. He had gone straight to bed, and all his clothing—coat, trousers, under-garments, everything—she had put in the kitchen to dry, banking up the fire before she went to bed so that it would last as long as possible. In the morning she had been up early, to iron them out, and assure herself they were perfectly dry before he put them on again.

Bobby thought it a pity Eddy's Sunday suit had been spoiled, as he supposed it must have been by such a drenching, and Mrs. Dene explained with simple, heartfelt gratitude that Eddy had been wearing his weekday things. Apart from his working clothes he had only two suits; one, his very best, kept for extra-special occasions, and preserved by Mrs. Dene in the company of many camphor-balls in the big chest in her own room, and his weekday suit. His working clothes it was a part of Mrs. Dene's regular Sunday task to patch, mend, and renovate for the trials of the following week. This time a torn elbow and a gaping knee had required prolonged treatment, and she had, in fact, only completed the task that morning.

There was not here, of course, a complete alibi, but certainly his mother's story did seem to indicate that Eddy had been in his room at the time of the commission of the murder, and that none of his clothing was available, one suit being before the kitchen fire to dry, one put away in another room, and his working clothes under repair. Much the same seemed to apply to his under-garments, either drying in the kitchen or under repair or put safely away, and of one thing Bobby found himself convinced—that Mrs. Dene was quite incapable of imagining or inventing anything. She might perhaps, like other people, lie at a pinch and for good reason, but her lies would be easy to detect.

Plainly with little idea that what she was saying was of any special importance, Mrs. Dene went on to talk about the attack of toothache Eddy's drenching in the rain had brought on. Nearly all night long she had heard him shuffling about the room in his old carpet-slippers. She had even ventured, in spite of her knowledge and experience of his general temper in toothache, to knock at his door and ask if he wouldn't let her apply a hot fomentation. But though the weary shuffling of the carpet-slippers up and down the floor had ceased, he had not even answered. Not until much later, in reply to another timid inquiry, had he replied, through the door, that he was all right now, and didn't want to be bothered with hot fomentations or anything else. But, said Mrs. Dene, the way his poor face was swollen in the morning, and the state of his temper, too!

'It always takes him that way, just as it does with father,' she explained again. 'Nearly bit Mrs. Unwin's head off when she mentioned his face just casual like.'

Mrs. Unwin was apparently a woman who came every day to help with the house-work, and even in the shop at moments of special emergency, and Mrs. Dene agreed there was no reason why the gentleman should not see Eddy's room, if he wished to.

It was a very ordinary apartment, very small and cramped, holding little beyond a truckle-bed, a chair, a table, and, against the walls, several home-made shelves laden with books, chiefly standard works on archæology and on the descent and antiquity of man. Bobby noticed that those by Sir Arthur Keith seemed special favourites. There was no washstand—the pump in the yard took its place in summer and the scullery in winter—and no chest-of-drawers or any wardrobe. Apparently all Eddy's stock of clothing Mrs. Dene kept in her own charge. Curtains, furniture, bed-clothes, all looked neat and clean, but very old and worn, though in odd contrast the linoleum covering the floor was of good quality, brand-new, and polished to perfection.

Mrs. Dene, noticing that Bobby was looking at it and admiring a shine and polish in which you could almost see yourself reflected, explained that Eddy had bought it himself only a little time ago—almost the first time his astonished mother had ever known him buy anything not absolutely necessary and not required for his archæological researches. But now he had bought something for the house, Mrs. Dene hoped he would continue, and what did Bobby think of the way he kept it polished so you could almost skate on it?

'I brought our Amy up to see it,' the good woman explained, with pride, 'just to show her Eddy could be house-proud, too, just like another, for all his brains and learning.'

Bobby agreed that the polishing of that linoleum was veritably a work of art. Glancing round, he noticed that the primitive night-shirt still held its own in the Dene household, and he observed, further, that the carpet-slippers Mrs. Dene had mentioned were lying one at one end of the room and one at the other, as if in a spasm of the toothache they had been kicked as far apart as possible. On one of them was lying, having apparently fallen from the shelf above, where two or three others were piled up, a mouse-trap of the old-fashioned kind that caught its victim alive.

'Eh, the worry mice are here,' Mrs. Dene observed, seeing Bobby had picked up one of these traps from the shelf and was looking at it. 'Sometimes I say they'll have us out of our beds. It's the sugar and the flour and suchlike brings them. We have to use bins with tin linings.'

Privately Bobby hoped that that was so, and that the 'tin linings' were kept in good repair. Mrs. Dene went on to explain that the traps were put there for boiling—they had to be boiled after use, or else the mice would not go near them again. Bobby listened absently, making no comment, but staring round the room and trying, as Superintendent Mitchell had taught him, to let the full meaning of all he saw sink into his mind. He walked over to the window and looked out. As he had more than half expected, the roof of an outhouse was close below, and exit and entry would be easy enough for any active young man. But of such exit or entry he could see no trace, nor was the rough surface of the window-sill, or the roof—a leaden one—of the outhouse, very likely to have preserved such traces.

'Oh, well,' he said at last, 'I must be getting on. I hope your son will be back soon. His keeping out of the way like this is making people begin to talk.'

'People never begin, because they never stop,' retorted Mrs. Dene.

CHAPTER TWELVE

EDDY DENE'S THREAT

FROST FIELD, WHERE EDDY DENE WAS CARRYING OUT his archæological researches, was some distance from the village, on the other side of Cambers House, and Bobby, who had had so long a morning, was feeling more than a little tired. But in such an investigation a detective has little time to rest; indefatigable legs are even more important than high intelligence, since a member of the C.I.D. has to seek not merely knowledge for himself, but facts that he may, so to say, slam down before an anxious jury leaving them no alternative of interpretation.

So to Frost Field now Bobby turned his steps, for he was eager to have another look at the scene of these archæological researches that appeared to have a certain bearing on this recent tangle of circumstance and character of which the outcome had been so grim a tragedy. But where the long village street faded into the open country he found he was not sure which path to continue by. An old labourer who was passing directed him, and, plainly aware of his identity, wanted to know if they had found out yet 'who done it'. Bobby shook his head, and said it was early days yet, and the old man expressed a strong opinion that Mr. Jones, the stranger from London, probably knew something about it, or what did he want to ask such a mort of questions for? Londoners were a queer lot at the best, and Mr. Jones no better than the worst, besides having a knack at throwing darts that was most unfair. It seemed he had not only won sixpence from the old gentleman, but had also taken care to collect it, nor returned any in the shape of a round of beer. The incident rankled, and a glimpse of Mr. Sterling near Cambers House the previous evening, just before the rain came down, had induced a hope that Mr. Sterling had arrived from London 'to see about it'.

Bobby, who, slightly impatient, had been making efforts to get away, grew suddenly interested. If Sterling had been seen in the vicinity of Cambers House at that time, how did that agree with his own statement that he had been delayed by losing his way, by breakdowns of his motor-cycle, by other accidents to such an extent that he had been forced to put up at the inn of which he had given the address, and at which he had admittedly arrived in the small hours of Monday morning, long after the commission of the murder?

It began to look as though young Sterling might be the unknown visitor who had been given, that night, late refreshment in Lady Cambers's sitting-room. She might have been willing to admit her nephew, if somehow he had managed to let her know of his arrival, whereas, of course, in the case of a stranger such a possibility hardly existed. And Sterling might have invented some plausible story to induce her to accompany him to Frost Field. Perhaps that her husband was waiting there for her! But her obvious retort would have been that Sir Albert could come to the house if he wanted to see her. Indeed the whole train of thought seemed far removed from probability; but still, if Sterling had been seen in the neighbourhood at a time when his own story denied his presence there, then that was certainly a point that badly required clearing up.

Further questioning showed that the old labourer was none too certain of his identification. He had had merely a passing glimpse of someone on a motor-cycle, and as he associated motor-cycles with young Mr. Sterling, and he had the impression that the rider resembled Mr. Sterling but no one else he could think of, he had concluded that Mr. Sterling it was. No, he had not mentioned the incident to anyone else, and if the police gentleman didn't wish him to, and if that wish were fortified by half a crown, why, then, he would promise to hold his tongue about it until further orders.

A good deal interested by this chance piece of information, Bobby continued on his way. Only if Sterling were guilty, why was young Eddy Dene keeping out of the way? That had a bad look about it, even though there was always the reflection that Lady Cambers was Eddy's chief financial support, and that men do not kick down the ladder by which they are climbing.

Then, too, as regarded Eddy, there was further the alibi his mother's evidence seemed to establish. Not but that an alibi is always a tricky thing. The question of the clothing, for instance. Clothes, though usual, are not an absolute necessity. At a pinch a night-shirt, or less, might serve, or, indeed, clothing could have been provided by that accomplice who might possibly have taken Eddy's place in his bedroom, but whose very existence had yet to be proved. It was a point, however, that would have to be dealt with, for defending counsel would certainly make great play with it, as, indeed, he would with the attack of toothache Eddy was said to have suffered from as a result of his drenching in the rain. Not a very serious argument, perhaps, but one that would draw a smile from any jury, and put it in a good humour, when told that an attack of toothache was enough to keep any man too fully occupied to leave him any time to think of murder!

But on one detail of the puzzle this business of the clothing had a bearing of some significance. There had to be explained how Lady Cambers had been induced to leave the house in secrecy so late at night. Any theory that Eddy had returned after the butler had let him out by the front-door, that it was for him Lady Cambers had provided the brandy, meant perhaps to ward off a chill if he had come back wet through, had to assume that he was dressed normally. A visitor in a night-shirt, or less, would hardly have been received by her with complete equanimity!

Deep in thought, letting his mind dwell on Eddy's room, trying to let the significance of every object it contained sink into his mind, Bobby came to the shed in the middle of Frost Field that Eddy Dene used in connection with his work.

By Colonel Lawson's orders it had been carefully locked, though with so much to do, so many errands to be run, such a variety of lines of inquiry to be followed up, he had not been able to spare an officer to remain on guard. Now the door was wide open, and Bobby, walking in, found there Eddy himself, contemplating with a certain satisfaction his neatly re-arranged collection of stone implements and fossils that had been so ruthlessly disturbed earlier in the day.

'Hullo,' he said amiably, over his shoulder, as Bobby, somewhat taken aback, gave an exclamation of surprise at seeing him.

'You are being looked for everywhere,' Bobby told him, in his most severe, official tone.

'I rather thought as much,' observed Eddy, quite undisturbed. 'Someone came banging at the door. Couldn't open it, couldn't get the key to turn. I had fixed the lock so it shouldn't. I expect they thought they had the wrong key, and, anyhow, no one could be inside, so they went off again. Had to get my stuff straight, you know.'

Bobby regarded him wrathfully.

'Do you mean,' he demanded, 'that when you knew quite well any information you had to give us might be a help, you were deliberately keeping out of the way?'

'That's right,' said Eddy, as placidly as ever.

He turned towards Bobby, chubby-faced and smiling as ever, but with vivid, eager eyes that seemed to tell of a hasty and imperious will, and nervous, mobile lips where a certain occasional twitching suggested a self-control and composure less complete than they seemed. And on one chubby cheek a plainly visible swelling seemed to prove that as regards toothache his mother's story was fully accurate.

'How did you get in? The place was locked,' Bobby said. 'Had you another key?'

'That's right,' agreed Eddy.

'You are hardly going the way, you know, to make a good impression,' Bobby pointed out, with some heat.

'Do I want to make a good impression?' Eddy wondered. 'But I'll put you right on one point. There's nothing of any value I can tell you. All I know is that after I left last night I got caught in the rain, drenched, gave my things to mother to dry for me, and spent most of the night walking about the room with a bad attack of toothache.' He paused to light a cigarette. He went on: 'I suppose what you mean is that I'm under suspicion. I half thought I should be. But I was jolly well going to see I had my specimens right before anything else happened—before I got marched off to gaol, if that's what's next on the programme.'

'We haven't got as far as that yet,' Bobby answered, not much liking, and not quite understanding either, the young man's attitude.

He looked carefully and slowly all round the room, and with special attention at the fossils and so on that earlier he had noticed thrown together in a confused heap, but that now were all neatly arranged and ticketed again. Eddy certainly had not been wasting his time. The task was one that must have kept him busy all morning. On the floor, where it had fallen behind a packing-case that partly hid it, was the suit-case Lady Cambers had apparently brought out with her.

'That oughtn't to have been left here,' Bobby said.

'Suppose it got forgotten,' Eddy remarked. 'There's nothing in it.'

'We are wondering a good deal what made her bring it out with her,' Bobby observed.

'If you knew that, you would know it all, perhaps,' Eddy said slowly, and almost as if to himself.

He was still holding in one hand the match with which he had lighted the cigarette he had begun to smoke. He put it down on the table, in an ash-tray standing there, and Bobby picked the stalk up and saw that printed thereon were the words: 'Hotel Henry VIII'.

Looking at it meditatively, and wondering what it meant, Bobby went on: 'They didn't know at your home where you were?'

'I didn't tell them,' Eddy answered briefly.

'I understand,' Bobby persisted, 'you are engaged to Miss Amy Emmers?'

'What about it?' Eddy asked sharply. 'It's been arranged for years—since we were kids. My people are set on it. Amy's one of the best, too. She's a darn good sort. What's it got to do with your lot?'

'We have to know who people are to know where we are ourselves,' Bobby answered, in his most conciliatory tones. 'I take it all this must have been a great shock to you?'

'If blue ruin's what you call a shock,' Eddy answered grimly, 'it is. Because, that's what it means, most likely. Perhaps that's what's preventing me thinking so much about the poor old girl herself. It was her money was running the show here, and who is going to take it on now? Not Sir Albert, anyway; he hated to see her spend a penny on it. Looks like it's back to the shop for me, weighing tea and sugar all day long.' As always when he spoke of the shop, there sounded in his voice a veritable passion of hatred and of loathing. Whatever else was doubtful, that he hated the shop, and everything connected with it, beyond all reasonable measure, was perfectly clear. Bobby felt that had Lady Cambers been pushing him back into the shop instead of providing him with probably his only hope of escape from it, then, indeed, a motive for the murder might be guessed at. 'Sorry,' Eddy went on, with a little apologetic laugh as if he noticed how Bobby was looking at him and felt he had unnecessarily betrayed his feelings, 'but it's all rather a wash-out for me. Even the introduction to Mr. Tyler I was to have had has gone down the drain now, I suppose.'

'Who is Mr. Tyler?'

'Some johnny she knew. American millionaire; dabbles in archæology. Don't expect he knows anything about it. Millionaires never know anything. I suppose they spend all their time acquiring money and ignorance—very successfully.'

Bobby put down in his mind another trait of Eddy's character as arrogance. Sure of himself, and contempt for others, Bobby thought. He asked: 'Was Lady Cambers thinking of withdrawing her support?'

'Eh?' asked Eddy. 'First I've heard of it. She was keen enough last night, if only to show that interfering old ass of a parson where he got off.'

'I was told she was worried about a sermon he preached. He excommunicated you, I understand?'

'You heard about that?' asked Eddy, smiling broadly. 'He would hardly have dared try that on Lady Cambers, would he?'

Bobby did not answer the question. He was still looking at the match-stalk he had picked up.

'Do you mind telling me where you got these matches?' he asked.

'Why? Are they the fatal clue?' Eddy asked lightly enough, though he looked a little startled. 'As a matter of fact I believe that chap who has been messing about the village lately left them here. He trotted up here one afternoon, asking a lot of fool questions. Tried to let on he was interested, and seemed to think what I was doing had some connection with cathedrals—Lord knows why!'

'Have you any idea what he wanted here?'

'No. I never worried. Why should I?'

'Or who he was?'

'Just plain fool, if you ask me. Poor old Lady Cambers got it into her head he was a burglar after her jewels. Nonsense, of course. A burglar wouldn't make himself conspicuous hanging about and asking a lot of fool questions.'

'He seems to have disappeared as soon as he heard of the murder,' Bobby remarked.

'The devil he has,' said Eddy, looking a little surprised. 'Got cold feet perhaps. Wonder if my fountain-pen has disappeared with him. Shouldn't be surprised.'

'Your fountain-pen?'

'Yes, one Lady Cambers gave me last Christmas—a jolly good one, too. Gold-mounted and all that. Since that johnny was here I've missed it. I may have dropped it somewhere. I sent an advert. to the *Hirlpool Gazette* on Saturday—no, Friday. Ten bob reward. It'll be in this morning. Lady Cambers wouldn't have liked it if she had known I had lost it—that won't worry her now, poor soul.'

'No, no,' agreed Bobby absently.

It seemed as if the two clues so far discovered had now turned to point away from Eddy and towards the vanished Mr. Jones. But then, as Eddy himself had remarked, would anyone planning a criminal enterprise have begun by drawing attention to himself by endless questioning? Could it have been Jones who had been the unknown guest at Cambers House, or the unknown watcher in the rhododendron-bushes? But then it seemed that for him, too, a firm alibi was established by the evidence of the people at the inn.

'Why not take Jones at his face-value?' demanded Eddy, after a pause. 'Retired gent looking for a bargain in the way of cottage and garden, and wanting to know all about everything before deciding.'

'We can't take anything for granted in our work,' Bobby answered gravely. 'We've got to test it all. You were the last person, except for those in the house itself, who saw Lady Cambers last night?'

'Except, also,' retorted Eddy, 'whoever it was came along afterwards and she treated to a swig of brandy.'

'You've heard about that?' Bobby said, slightly disconcerted.

'Of course. All the village has,' Eddy assured him. 'Someone hid in the rhododendrons for a while, and then went into the house and had a drink with Lady Cambers before he and she went out together. *Ergo*, there's your murderer. Only, who was it, eh?'

Bobby did not point out, as a weak point in this theory, that apparently the man concealed in the rhododendrons had been there a good part of the night, till long after the murder had been committed. And it was quite incredible that a man who had just committed a murder would hang about his victim's house, hiding and waiting in rhododendron-bushes.

'During which time,' Eddy added, 'I was having the devil of a time with my tooth. Anything like a chill or a draught sets it off at once. Not,' he added thoughtfully, 'that toothache doesn't make me feel like murder, especially when people won't leave you alone and come banging at the door, wanting to do things for you you know perfectly well will only make the pain worse, having had some. Mother's like that, what she really wants is to relieve herself, by fussing round, feeling she's doing something. So now I just lock my door, don't answer, and wait till it's through. It's a help, too, if you keep on the move. But then you jolly well can't keep still while it's giving you fair gyp.'

So he knew his mother had been knocking at his door during the night. But then too, if an accomplice had taken his place, he would have been told that that had happened. So the point really did not go for much. Bobby harked back to an earlier point.

'Was there any special reason for your visiting Lady Cambers last night?'

'Only to tell her how things were going.'

'Did you notice anything unusual in her manner?'

'Absolutely no. She was just the same as usual.'

'There was no difference of opinion between you?'

'No. What?' asked Eddy, staring. 'Why, there was no-

thing else. I was always having to put her right—she had
the weirdest ideas. Not that that mattered so long as she
stumped up.'

'The opposition to your work you are carrying on here
had affected her, then?' Bobby insisted, for the point seemed
to him of some importance.

'She worried a bit—not much,' Eddy agreed. 'You know,
I've been thinking about that myself. Our parson here is
a bit crazy. Dotty. He came messing round here once, and
I told him I was going to prove the Bible all wrong. He
took it seriously—more seriously than anyone takes the
Bible, I should say. He talked quite a lot about the judgement of the Lord—jolly excited. Lady Cambers smoothed
him down a bit when he went to see her, but he was soon
up on his hind-legs again.'

'Do you mean, you think Mr. Andrews may have had
something to do with the murder?'

'If it had been me murdered,' Eddy answered, 'I would
have put it down to him without thinking twice. He looked
like it, and a religious fanatic is capable of anything. Of
course, it's a bit different with Lady Cambers. You would
have to explain how he got her to come out alone so late.
That's what beats me. She wasn't so fond of midnight excursions as all that.'

'You've never known anything of the kind before?'

'Good Lord, no! I say, you ask lots of questions, don't
you? Nearly as many as that Jones chap. Perhaps he was
a detective, too?'

Bobby gave a little jump. It was a simple obvious idea
that from its very simplicity had never occurred to him
before.

'Hit the bull's-eye, have I?' Eddy asked, grinning broadly.

'There's another thing,' Bobby said, ignoring this. 'I expect it's all over the village by now. Lady Cambers's jewellery is missing, and we think most likely it's been stolen.'

'What? It hasn't!' Eddy almost shouted, his light indifference dropping from him like a discarded cloak. 'Her jewellery? Good God, it hasn't!'

For some reason he seemed more affected now than ever previously.

He had become quite pale. He was evidently profoundly shocked, profoundly shaken. It seemed as if this story of the theft of the jewellery held for him some staggering significance as well as being an overwhelming surprise. Bobby watched him intently, curiously, doubtfully, but did not speak.

'You are sure? No mistake about it?' Eddy asked, as it were snarling the words through half-closed teeth; and then, when Bobby nodded, he muttered as if to himself: 'Some swine's pinched the stuff, then—he'll find he's pinched more than he bargained for.'

CHAPTER THIRTEEN

EVOLUTIONARY THEORY

BOBBY WAITED, PATIENT AND INTENT. HE KNEW THAT in moments of surprise and agitation people often speak with greater frankness than they intend. But Eddy, though plainly shaken, relapsed into a silence he showed no sign of breaking. After a time Bobby asked: 'Why do you say that? What do you think it means?'

'Burglary,' Eddy answered, almost too promptly, as if he had had that answer ready and prepared.

Then he was silent again, and again Bobby waited, wondering very much what was in the other's mind and convinced that this news of the lost jewellery had started in Eddy a new train of thought, and one in which so obvious and so simple an idea as burglary played but a small part.

So for a time they remained, each standing there as silent as the other, and gradually Bobby grew convinced that Eddy, too, was patient and watchful as himself, waiting what next might come. And either Eddy's patience was the greater, or else this silent waiting suited best his play, for he still showed no sign of speaking or of moving, and it was Bobby who was forced to break the silence first.

'Mr. Dene,' he said gravely, 'I can't help feeling you know something that would help us if you told it.'

'Eh?' said Eddy, looking surprised. 'Why? What makes you think that?'

Bobby did not answer—at least, not in words, but his body stiffened almost automatically, and Eddy gave a little abrupt laugh that had not much merriment in it.

'You look just like our cat when it's getting ready to spring,' he said with more than a touch of mockery in his voice. 'The huntsman whose quarry's man, eh?'

'No, the truth,' Bobby answered quietly; 'and there I think you could help.'

'I'm afraid I don't see how, myself,' Eddy retorted. 'When you say "truth", you mean the facts, I suppose, though that's a different thing sometimes. Well, about the safe. The jewellery was kept in the safe, wasn't it? Has the safe been forced?'

'No; the key was used.'

'Well, now, then,' Eddy muttered; 'well, that's queer.' He looked uneasy and troubled, and busied himself lighting another cigarette, offering at the same time one to Bobby, who declined it. 'Quick work,' he said, 'unless it was done before—was it done before?'

'Before the murder? That has to be decided.'

'Yes—well, no, I don't see how I can help. I don't know anything. You're sure the things have been stolen?'

'They are not in the safe. We understand they were always kept there. The assumption is they've been stolen. That may be the motive for the murder. We can't say for certain yet.'

'No. No, it's soon yet,' Eddy agreed. 'I suppose you know Lady Cambers's husband claimed that legally it was all his—the jewellery, I mean? He said it all passed to him, once the entail was broken. He had raked up some old deed he said showed that. Lady Cambers told me. She said her lawyer said it was rubbish.'

'Do you mean Sir Albert Cambers may have taken possession of the jewellery?' Bobby asked.

'Better ask him,' Eddy retorted. 'I don't mean anything because I don't know anything. If the things are missing, someone's got them.' He stared and frowned and flung down his unsmoked cigarette. 'Well, there you are,' he said. 'I don't know. I suppose there's just the chance it may turn up. She might have sent it to the bank for safety?'

'She didn't say anything about the jewellery to you last night?'

'Good Lord, no. She wouldn't have been likely to, would she? We talked about how the work was getting on, and about the fuss Andrews was making, and that's all.'

'She said nothing about going out?'

'That night? Good Lord, no; not at that time of night.'

'You can't suggest any reason—any possibility . . .?'

'No. At least . . .'

'Yes?'

'Well, it's nothing much, only I do remember . . . you know what sort of a woman Lady Cambers was?'

'I knew her very slightly. I thought she seemed very pleasant and friendly.'

Eddy grinned again—so wide a grin it seemed he became little else but grin incarnate.

'Some people would tell you she always was—to good-looking, presentable young men like you and me.' He paused to let his grin grow wider still, little possible as that had seemed before. 'Not that I claim to be in the Public Attraction No. 1 class and don't go and imagine I mean anything more than I say. I don't. If anyone tells you anything of the sort, you can wash it out. She was always ready to take an interest in any deserving cause, and if the deserving cause happened to be young and male, with bright blue eyes and a damask cheek, she didn't object. But it never went beyond friendly interest. I'm telling you because some people may drop you hints that was why she spent rather a lot of coin on helping me establish my theories—not that there's much bright blue eye or damask cheek about me, but you see the idea? Well, perhaps if I had had a beard a foot long and a bald head, the old girl mightn't have been so willing to part. But that's all.'

Bobby wondered if that was all or if this confidence meant more than appeared on the surface. But all he said was: 'You were saying you thought there might be some reason why she wanted to go out.'

'Not quite that. Only there is this. You know she always thought you ought to do just what she said. Of course, always because it was best for you. But she knew, and she let you know she knew. That's why hubby got out.'

'Sir Albert?'

'Yes, I expect he found it a bit trying to be with someone who was always right—especially when she wasn't. And not only right for herself, but for you, too. She always— knew. For your own good, of course. Why, she would even start in to tell me things about my work! Well, one of her pet fads was about traps for rabbits—she thought the sort that are used about here are cruel. She was right enough there. She often was—right, I mean. I hate the things myself. They are worse even than those new mouse-traps— break-back, they call them. All right when they work, but sometimes they catch the poor little beast by one paw or the tail or something. It's all right to keep mice and rabbits down. I know that. But I always use the old-fashioned trap that catches them alive, and then you can give them a whiff of gas that does them in without their knowing it. Lady Cambers was rather keen about all that; she was a big subscriber to the Anti-trap Society or whatever they call it, and she wanted all the tenants on the estate to use the new trap. Well, they all promised all right, but promising's one thing and doing's another, and I know she wasn't too sure they all kept to it. The parson—Andrews, you know—was as keen about it as she was, and he told her things he had heard. I heard her say once she would see for herself one night, and it's just possible that's what she was after, and that she took the suit-case with her to bring back any of the steel traps she happened to find. Of course, that's only an idea of my own. Very likely there's nothing in it. I don't suppose I should ever have thought of it, if you hadn't worried on about my being able to tell you something to help. Well, if that's a help, there it is.'

'It's an idea that may be worth following up,' Bobby agreed. 'Only it's murder that's happened, and it seems a long way from a steel trap for rabbits to—murder.'

'Yes, I know,' agreed Eddy. 'Wash it out, then.'

Bobby asked one or two more questions. But Eddy seemed to have exhausted all he had to say, and Bobby asked presently: 'If Mr. Andrews supported Lady Cambers about this and talked to her about it, they were on good terms except . . .'

'Except about me,' interposed Eddy. 'That's right. They backed each other up in lots of ways. She was quite bucked when he preached that divorce was a mortal sin. Not that she believed it herself. But she wanted everyone else to, because what she wanted was to get Sir Albert back. And she would have, too, in the long run.'

'How?'

'Don't know, so can't say. But she would have managed it somehow. She was that sort. Fair means or foul, she would have had him again, and, if you ask me, Sir Albert knew it and was dead-scared. That's my idea.'

'She seems to have been a woman of strong character.'

'She meant to go her way. If it was your way, too, well and good and all O.K. If it wasn't, then there were squalls. Mind you, it was always your own good she was thinking of, only she knew it such a darn sight better than you did. I had some myself, but not much, because she backed me up all right in what really mattered. She spent a lot to help what I'm doing here, and she told me she had put aside enough to see me through three years. That was what I put as the outside limit. Now I suppose all that's washed out. Sir Albert won't take any bally notice of what she said—nor would anyone else, I suppose. She never put anything in writing—and then there'll be Andrews doing his best to double-cross me.'

'What is it exactly you're doing?' Bobby asked. 'I've heard some vague sort of talk about the Missing Link, and that's all.'

'They've all got hold of the Missing Link,' observed Eddy. 'They have no idea what it means, though, and it happens that's just exactly what I'm not after.'

'Not?'

'No. I mean to prove there never was a link, missing or not. People seem to think evolution means inch by inch and little by little, like Eric.'

'Eric?' repeated Bobby, into whose ambit that master-piece had never penetrated.

'School prize,' explained Eddy briefly. 'Most people think evolution means a slow, gradual change of fish into land animal, for instance. It doesn't. It just happens—sudden, dramatic, a jump. A fish is hatched with gills that don't function properly—in water. Probably it suffocates, can't breathe. But one freak fish of that kind discovers through some accident that it can breathe all right in air. In other words, it's got lungs instead of gills. But there was never a link, never a gill changing slowly into a lung. A link would have meant equally faulty functioning in both air and water, and why quit uncomfortable water for equally unsuitable air? Why give up accustomed water for unaccustomed air unless there was some advantage? There had to be some-thing dramatic, something forcible and sudden, to chuck the fish, quite content in the water, out on dry land that must have been uncomfortable and difficult at first. Think of leaving cool, flowing water you could dodge about in, up or down, any way you wanted, for dry ground you could only crawl on slowly and painfully. No fish in its senses would have dreamed of it unless it had been obliged to. Same with man. Man was originally one of the apes, one of the less successful species. That's plain enough. Well, you know what the difference is now between ape and man?'

'A good many, aren't there?'

'I mean the fundamental difference. It isn't the tail. Man has that, or the rudiments of it. It isn't mind. The ape has the rudiments of that all right. It's the hand. Man can turn it, pronate it, grasp with it, as the ape can't. There's the difference. Man is the creature, not of his mind, but of his hand.'

'Do you mean that Mr. Andrews . . .?'

'Yes. That's what it's all about. That's why he shouts blasphemy. That's why he does all he jolly well can to stop me going on with my work. He wants us to believe man is all mind. I mean to show that man is all hand. Man is just an ape who has learnt to use his hand, that's all. So Andrews bawls blasphemy—because he's afraid. He daren't face the truth. He knows he would have to change all his ways of thinking, all his beliefs and so on, and he just can't face up to it. And when you're afraid like that, well, you're capable of anything, aren't you?'

CHAPTER FOURTEEN

ON THE ORIGIN OF MAN

BOBBY LOOKED AT HIS WATCH. HE KNEW HE OUGHT to be getting back to Cambers House, where his shorthand notes were awaiting transcription, and yet he felt this conversation was throwing a certain amount of light on the psychological outlook of at least some of the actors in the tragedy. Eddy, talking eagerly and excitedly, as if he wished Bobby to understand his position, went on quickly.

'That's my theory. Man was just an ape, like others of the species. Then one day a little ape was born with the ability to turn his hand right round. We've still a slight difficulty about that. We don't pronate our hands quite easily. But this special little ape, half a million years ago, found he could use tools better than the others could. All apes use elementary tools—a stone or a stick. But this ability to turn the hand gave this one little ape an advantage. He became the boss of the tribe. He chose the females he fancied; he founded a family; he handed on his special ability to his offspring; and there starts Man, no more an ape, beginning his long career that leads to Shakespeare and to our own time.'

'It's very interesting,' agreed Bobby. 'What did Lady Cambers think of it?'

'She was keen on it. I'm not sure how far she saw what it meant. I didn't press that side so long as she paid up. You see, my theory means that mind is the creature of the machine. The machine—the hand—came first. Then came mind, as its product. That knocks out the bishops when they tell you mind can only have come from mind. I show that mind comes from the use of the tool. When you use a tool you have to think, or it's no good. First you do a thing. Then you think about it. Knocks out superstitious fancy about special creation and so on. That's what Andrews saw. I'll give him credit for that. He saw clearly enough what it meant. He couldn't argue, so he excommunicated, as he called it, and, if he could, he would have had me burnt alive. I can tell you he looked murder, and the Spanish Inquisition and the fires of Smithfield, all right, when he came here once and wanted to preach. I cut him short, though. I told him to wait a bit and I would have proof he could rub his nose against if he liked, it would be so plain.'

'Is that what all this digging outside is about?' Bobby asked.

'You mean my pot-holes?'

'Pot-holes?'

'Technical term,' explained Eddy lightly. 'I take it you don't know anything about archæology?'

'Nothing at all.'

'I thought you wouldn't,' Eddy observed. 'Few do—especially archæologists. What I'm working on is the origin of man. That's what I'll call my book when it comes out —*The Origin of Man*. It'll be as big a thing as Darwin's *Origin of Species*—bigger.'

Bobby looked at him sharply. For a moment he thought the other was joking, but it was perfectly plain that what had been said had been meant literally, that Eddy Dene really saw himself as the pupil, the successor, of Darwin, the carrier-on of the Darwinian torch to heights the earlier master never dreamed of.

'My book,' Eddy added, very simply, 'will be a landmark in human thought—after it has been published mental processes will never be quite the same again.'

'Oh,' said Bobby, slightly overwhelmed at this claim, and by the calm manner in which it was put forward. 'Well, of course. I don't know anything about all that.'

'No, of course not,' agreed Eddy, as one might say to a toddling child that as yet it knew nothing of some subject it had heard discussed by its elders.

'Have you always been interested in that sort of thing?' Bobby asked.

'I'll tell you about that. When my people took over the —the shop'—Bobby noticed that he hesitated for a fraction of a second over the word, as though he found it unpleasant to pronounce—'there was an old sketch-book lying about. It had belonged to a man named Winders, an old chap in the village. He had got interested in archæology picking up eoliths. There are plenty lying about here, you know. You can fill your pockets with them any day, as well as with flints of a later period.'

'What are—eoliths, did you call them?'

Eddy went across to one of the shelves running round the walls of the shed, and took up three or four roughly shaped stones.

'Dawn stones,' he said. 'The first step man took when he stopped being an ape and started to become a man.'

Bobby looked at them with interest. To him they did not seem to show much sign of human handiwork. But Eddy handled them with reverence.

'It may be half a million years since they were worked,' he said slowly. 'How many generations does that mean? All in their turn, all passing away again. Four generations to a century—how many individuals to a century? Think of all that long slow interminable procession through the ages—years and centuries and millenniums—while the ape was struggling to be primæval man, and primæval man to be man barbarian, and the barbarian to be man as we know him to-day; and think of the years and the centuries and millenniums before us till man can call himself civilized— and when you think of it all, can you believe that one life, one little life in all that, counts for as much as we seem to think it does, to judge by the fuss we make when one goes out?'

'Yes,' said Bobby simply, 'every brick in a building counts, every soldier in an army. One brick out of place, one soldier sleepy or cowardly, may ruin everything.'

Eddy shrugged his shoulders.

'That's the sentimental view,' he pronounced. 'I find it a little hard to suppose any one ordinary individual counts against the enormous background of the past.' He put down on the table the eolith he had been holding. 'There's a theory they aren't human work at all,' he went on, 'but they are all right. You have only to hold them to feel the human touch. It's how we began. Now we've got to the aeroplane and the wireless—and the daily Press. To-morrow —but ask the daily Press about that. And all comes from the accident that a few odd hundreds of thousands of years ago a freak ape was born with the power to pronate his hand. That was what I found in that sketch-book I told you about. There were sketches that showed both the ape formation and the human quite plainly. The difference was picked out by the use of different colours. Winders, the man it belonged to, was a wheelwright about here. Then he took to digging wells—and to bone-setting. He had quite a reputation for treating sprains and so on. And for finding water. There's lots of water here, but it runs underground and wants finding—even the stream at the bottom of the field dries up at times, for no known reason. A bit awkward for a farmer who wants a permanent water-supply. Apparently old Winders always knew where you could sink a well. It was when he was digging one for Mr. Hardy, the man who rents Mounts Farm, that he came across some fossil bones, dating from back in the tertiary period, I should think. Perhaps the pliocene, perhaps the eocene. That's a difference, but in this business you need a wide margin. Anything within a hundred thousand years is getting warm. Winders couldn't read or write, but he had eyes in his head, which is more than most have, and he could draw. He spotted the different formation in the wrist-bones—he saw some were purely human and some purely ape, yet they came from the same spot. Well, you see what that means?'

'Not very clearly,' Bobby confessed.

'It means we can put our finger, if I'm right, here and now on the very spot where man became man. Not in any mythical Garden of Eden early one morning, but right here at that one moment—and there's the fossil to show. No special creation, but just a freak—a sport. Proves that mind is only a function of the body—a result of the accident of a freak ape baby being born with a slightly different formation of the bones of the wrist, so he could use tools, and in order to do so had to think. Well, that's how thought came into the world.'

Eddy was speaking now with an intensity of belief that seemed, as it were, to light up his personality with a kind of inner fire. He looked taller even; his eyes were bright and fervent. Bobby reflected that when Eddy called the vicar a 'fanatic' he was making use of a word that could with equal justice have been applied to himself. But then science, just as much as religion, has always had its fanatics and its bigots; it has more than once tried to establish something like an inquisition. If it had the power, even to-day it would probably have its *autos-da-fé* for those who refused to subscribe to the true faith—for the osteopath, the scoffer at vaccines, the supporter of any theory not yet generally accepted.

Why, only that week-end Bobby remembered he had been reading an article in which a very learned professor traced the Œdipus complex and the castration motive as implicit all through the study of Esperanto!

But then, after all, that is only to say that the scientist, like the priest, is human, and that humanity has always found it less trouble to stone its prophets than to change its way of thinking.

And Bobby found himself wondering to what the clash of these two fanaticisms—the scientific and the religious—might not in this affair have given birth. Yet, even so, what bearing could there be upon the tragedy it was his business to investigate? Eddy was going on talking. He said: 'Well, now, then, you can see for yourself, when I get my book out, it means the whole current of contemporary thought has got to change. All superstition will be ended for good. People will see the truth of things—see them as they are. There'll be no more putting up with slums and starvation here and now in the hope of golden crowns and harps here-after. Man will be himself at last, standing on his own legs, putting his trust in himself, and not in flopping down on his knees to ask an old man with a beard to do conjuring-tricks.'

'And these proofs you speak of?' Bobby asked.

'Yes, I know, it all hangs on that,' Eddy admitted, his fervour slightly diminished. 'Proof's no good unless it's the sort of proof you can rub people's noses on. Pure reason gets you nowhere. Well, that's what I've been spending Lady Cambers's money trying to find. It's a fight for the freedom of the human mind that's been going on between vicar and me, and now it looks like vicar coming out on top, unless I can find someone to take poor Lady Cambers's place and cash up like her. Not too easy.'

He went to the window of the shed and stood there in silence, staring out intently, and Bobby divined that what he saw was no such common pasture-field as every parish in England could display, but a battlefield where knowledge and ignorance, science and superstition, tremendously fought for dominion over the soul of man.

'All the same,' Bobby said, half to himself, 'I don't see why your ape's wrist becoming human in type shouldn't have been a special creation.'

Eddy was not listening. He said from the window, still staring from it at the quiet, empty field where to his fevered imagination was being fought the ultimate battle, the Ar-mageddon of the soul: 'The proof's there, and I'll get it if I have to dig up the whole field with my bare hands.'

Then he laughed a little, as if there were no more to be said and he was glad. He turned away, and Bobby said: 'If you've got it all in this sketch-book you speak of, isn't that enough?'

'Standing by themselves the sketches can't prove any-thing,' Eddy replied. 'I showed them once to a man who is supposed to have some reputation. He does know a lot, too. But he wasn't interested. I think sometimes a man gets to know so much he simply can't take anything more in—no room. But then people are like that. If a thing's new, they just can't grasp it. He couldn't see what it meant; he wanted to know how I could tell the sketches weren't pure fancy. As if an old illiterate man like Winders could have had an idea like that. I saw, then, I had to find the actual fossils and show them.'

'Winders must have had them in his possession if he drew them?'

'That's right,' Eddy agreed. 'And do you know what became of them? They were thrown away at his death. Used for road-metal, most likely, or perhaps burnt for manure.'

His voice was tragic; he drooped as he stood there, almost one expected to see him fall flat—crushed beneath the weight of such a thought.

'It's happened often enough,' he said. 'Another hour or two, and most likely the Piltdown skull would have gone that way. Over and over again that must have happened. Just think of it. The key to open the door to a new humanity, freed for ever from all the dead old soul-destroying superstitions, used to mend a road for the carts of country bumpkins. That's tragedy!'

'You are expecting to find other fossil bones of the same sort?' Bobby asked.

'Yes. I managed to get a talk with old Mrs. Winders. She was very feeble; she didn't live much longer. I don't think Winders quite understood the importance of his discovery. But he did understand that once there had been a big river here. Of course, that's plain enough when you know, but not many men in his position would have seen it—or cared if they had. It was along the banks of this river the ape community lived when was born the little freak ape that was the dawn man. Apparently some catastrophe happened. Possibly an earthquake. We had them in England in those days, before we were separated from Europe. Perhaps it was a sudden flood. Whatever it was Winders found, it can't have been a burying-place, because, of course, apes don't have them. But there were a number of these fossil bones, all miraculously preserved. It may be the only spot in the world where that's happened. Anyhow, there it is. Winders had dug down to the "floor". I don't suppose he knew what a "floor" is, but his instinct told him it was something that counted. And there was this collection of fossil bones. He drove out small longitudinal galleries in each direction. Always more bones. Evidently a whole community had been destroyed at once and all their bodies heaped together. Then water was found—lots of it—in another well he was sinking not far away, so there was no need to go on with this one. He made a collection of a few of the bones, and then the shaft he had sunk was filled in. You see the significance of their provenance? The fossils all came from the same spot at the same level—all part of one and the same lot. And most of them were pure ape, and one or two were of the human type. That means the human type and the ape type were living together—*in the same community.*'

He had been speaking quickly and with a growing excitement. Bobby watched him curiously, realizing that to Eddy these speculations on the remote past, on the origin of man, seemed the most important thing in the world. But he did not offer any comment, and Eddy, who had apparently expected him to speak, went on more quietly after waiting for a moment or two: 'That means differentiation had not yet begun. The ape was still the ape; the human type had not yet begun to think itself out of apehood into humanity. Well, what I'm out for is to trace the old river-banks that lie thirty feet deep under the present-day surface, find again the bones Winders found and sketched—and find more perhaps. And what I'm up against now,' he added abruptly, 'is, where's the coin coming from?'

Bobby had no answer. He looked at his watch again,

and said he must go on. Colonel Lawson would be waiting.

'He wants to see you, too,' Bobby added. 'Will you come with me?'

'I'll go home first,' Eddy said. 'Then I'll come on.'

Bobby repeated that the authorities were anxious to interview him, and Eddy retorted impatiently that they could very well wait another half-hour.

'I must go home first,' he said again. 'I'll come straight on, but there's the shop—after all, we live by the beastly thing.' He paused, contemplating the 'beastly thing' with evident disgust. 'Just think of it,' he burst out fiercely, 'just because an old woman's dead I may have to chuck the whole thing and spend all the rest of my life weighing tea and cutting bacon for any fool who happens to want them, while there's knowledge waiting to be found—knowledge that would set man free from all the old errors and superstitions, and would make me famous as well. My name would rank with Darwin's. I might get a university post offered me. Your Colonel Lawson wouldn't be so handy with his "Dene" then; he would remember to put a "mister" before it. I nearly told him so just now.'

Bobby remembered noticing how Eddy had appeared to resent the somewhat cavalier manner in which Colonel Lawson addressed him. It was childish to notice it, for certainly no rudeness had been intended. It was more childish still to remember and resent it, as Eddy was evidently doing. Probably it was the contrast between the work in the shop that was forced upon him, and that he despised, and his belief in the high intellectual value of his theories that made him so absurdly sensitive. But the insight thus given into the touchy vanity of his character was not without interest.

'Oh, well,' Bobby said, 'what's a "mister" matter? You ought to go through the police and hear a sergeant talk to a recruit.'

'That's different,' Eddy answered. 'Recruits grow into

sergeants, but colonels don't think other colonels grow behind counters.'

'Oh, well, I must be getting on,' Bobby said. 'I can say you are following. It's necessary, you know.'

'That's all right,' Eddy answered. 'I'm not going to bolt, if that's what you're afraid of. Why should I?'

CHAPTER FIFTEEN

TRAPPED RABBITS

'BUT SUPPOSE,' BOBBY THOUGHT TO HIMSELF, AS HE made his way back across the fields to Cambers House and his shorthand notes there awaiting transcription, 'suppose the vicar had actually got hold of Lady Cambers, and she warned Dene she was going to stop supplies? But then her death wouldn't have helped him. If she's left her money to Sir Albert, then Dene says himself there would be no chance of getting any more help; and if it goes to young Sterling, he's hardly likely to be so interested in archæology as to go on paying out some hundreds every year.'

Besides there was this question of the lost fountain-pen, a clue that seemed now clearly to point away from the young man.

Still deep in thought, Bobby came to the path that ran from the village by Cambers House past the gate admitting to the grounds of the house, and here he saw coming along towards him, though still at a distance, the odd, unmistakable figure of the vicar himself; his long arms swinging; his long legs striding over the ground almost as though he were perched upon stilts; his big bald head pushed forward as if oppressed by a weight of thought or trouble.

Bobby was in a hurry to get back, for he was not sure what Colonel Lawson would be thinking of so prolonged an absence, but the opportunity seemed too good to be lost.

He waited accordingly, and the vicar, recognizing him,

nodded a greeting, and said, without further preamble: 'They tell me in the village, the young man, Eddy Dene, can't be found, and that Lady Cambers's jewellery is missing, too.'

'The jewellery can't be found,' Bobby answered, with professional caution. 'It may be in the bank or . . .'

'It was always kept in the safe in the house,' the vicar interrupted. 'It was a weakness of Lady Cambers to think too much of it. If it's not in the safe, it's been stolen. She liked to have it there to take out to look at when she wanted. Is it true about young Dene?'

'No,' answered Bobby. 'He's at the shed in the field over there. He's been busy putting his things straight and didn't want to be interrupted. That's all.'

'I'm very glad to hear it,' said the vicar quickly, but with an accent in his voice that Bobby thought was more like disappointment than pleasure.

'He is coming along in a few minutes,' Bobby continued. 'I'm on my way to tell Colonel Lawson to expect him. I expect the Colonel would be glad to hear anything you have to say.'

'I know. I've had a note from him,' the vicar answered. 'You might tell him I should have been in to see him before only I've had much to attend to. A terrible affair,' he added gravely. 'A great shock to us all, as you can imagine.'

'Yes,' agreed Bobby. 'I'm sure everyone feels that.'

'Colonel Lawson is still at Cambers House, I suppose? I can see him there?'

'Yes,' Bobby answered again. 'I expect he will be there some time. The whole thing is such a complete mystery at present. I think you disapproved of Dene's work, and had asked Lady Cambers not to support it?'

'That is so,' the vicar answered. 'I naturally disapprove of blasphemy.'

'I gathered as much from what Mr. Dene told me,' Bobby said. 'Only he calls it searching for the truth.'

'I know he does. He twists my words. That is characteristic. He pretends I am afraid of the truth. That is not so. How can one who serves the truth fear the truth?' The vicar lifted his great head and raised one hand high in the air, so that Bobby had a swift vision of him in the pulpit, a dominating, formidable figure. 'No,' he went on, 'it is not the truth a servant of the truth fears, but the way in which presumptuous and foolish man may twist it. Dene, in his insolence, talks of proving not only that man came from the ape, but that he is ape still—"an ape that has learnt the use of the hand", I think he says. He actually went so far as to give a public lecture with some such title. Fortunately, I understand, very few attended. But you can see the harm that sort of thing does—where it leads? Teach the young they are all ape, and as ape they will behave.'

He spoke with a fervour, even a fierceness, of conviction that reminded Bobby almost comically of the equal fervour and fierceness of conviction with which Dene had delivered himself, and he had again a moment of sympathy for the dead woman caught between two such strong opposing faiths.

But though fanaticism sometimes causes, excuses, explains bloodshed, there was also the disappearance of the jewels, and there intensity of belief in the mischief of another's views and theories could play no part.

He did for a moment think of suggesting to Mr. Andrews that Eddy did not want to prove that man was ape, but only that man was an ape that had learnt; this last a word that has much virtue—none more, indeed. But the point was hardly one he felt competent to discuss and, except for the clash of personalities and interests it revealed, it had no bearing on the investigation. Abruptly the vicar added: 'A soul is more easily lost through a twisted truth than a downright lie.'

'Did Lady Cambers make any promise to stop her help to Dene?'

'She did not,' answered the vicar sternly. 'I told her that on her lay the ultimate responsibility for those who might be led astray. Apparently she had consulted the diocesan chancellor. He said he considered I took exaggerated views.' Mr. Andrews paused, plainly remembering his former description of that official as Antichrist, and equally plainly regretting the Christian charity that had made him withdraw it. 'Later on, I spoke as plainly as I could from the pulpit,' he continued.

'Without effect.'

'Without the least effect,' agreed the vicar. 'But now judgement has been given,' he added passionately.

'You don't surely mean . . .' began Bobby, a little shocked.

'I mean no more than the facts,' the vicar interrupted. 'Don't misunderstand me. I have suffered so much from misunderstanding—wilful, very often. But there are the facts. There was a work going on in this parish more than likely to lead the ignorant into error—soul-destroying error. Now it has been put an end to—tragically, dreadfully ended. Is not that a judgement?'

Bobby looked at the pale, emaciated face of the priest— the emaciation all the more noticeable for the unusual size of the head with which somehow one rather expected a great round full-fleshed countenance—and he experienced a sudden touch of fear. He felt in the presence of that tremendous force which comes from complete surrender to one belief. He said: 'One thing that's bothering us is to understand why Lady Cambers went out alone so late at night without saying a word to anyone, apparently without even asking that the house shouldn't be locked up before her return. I suppose you can't suggest anything?'

Mr. Andrews shook his head.

'No,' he said. 'If she had refused to continue her help to Dene, I should almost have been inclined to suspect him. Why shouldn't an ape strangle? But her death deprives him of the money help he depended on. I don't think I can suggest anything.'

'You had no other differences of opinion with Lady Cambers?' Bobby asked. 'There was some question of divorce. She agreed with you about that?'

'Entirely,' declared Mr. Andrews. 'She fully appreciated the Church's standpoint. I don't know if it's of any importance, but she expressed herself as being very grateful for the explanation I was able to give her. She was grateful that my teaching had perhaps prevented her from acting too quickly. I have some reason for thinking she hoped her husband might return to her. She even destroyed, the other day, a will she had made in her first distress and anger when Sir Albert left her. By it everything went to her nephew, Mr. Sterling.'

'Did Mr. Sterling know that?' Bobby asked quickly, for this was a piece of information that seemed of significance.

'No one knew except myself,' the vicar answered. 'I don't think even her lawyers knew.'

'You are quite certain the will was actually destroyed?'

'I saw her burn it. That was last Monday—a week ago. I approved. In a way, it was by my advice. Her husband remained her husband, however grievously at fault, and between husband and wife there should be complete community of goods.'

'Would you say Lady Cambers was ready to take advice as a general rule?'

The vicar permitted himself to smile. It was not a thing that often happened to him, and the effect was to soften and to humanize his expression to an extraordinary degree.

'As a general rule she was more ready to give it,' he answered. 'Even as regards purely Church matters. Fortunately her advice was generally good, and her extreme generosity gave her, in a way, a right to express her opinion. I didn't always agree, but I am always ready to give way in the non-essentials. I think I may say we never differed seriously, except in this matter of her most unfortunate support of Dene. And there she had engaged herself deeply before she understood fully what was intended—before I did myself, for that matter. It was a weakness in her character that she never wished to draw back. She prided herself on not changing—it was pride, too, the sin of pride. Now it is too late.'

'There was some argument about rabbit-traps you supported her in, wasn't there?'

'You mean about the cruelty of using steel traps? I confess I had little idea of what was going on till she told me. We met with a good deal of opposition from some of the farmers. There was reason to fear some who had promised to give up steel traps continued to use them all the same. Lady Cambers felt very strongly about it; she even said publicly she would refuse to renew the lease of any of her tenants who continued to use the steel trap. But surely there is no connection . . .?'

'Oh, I don't suppose so,' Bobby answered. 'Rabbit-traps can hardly lead to murder. Only in such a difficult case every fresh angle of approach may be useful. There's so little to go on. A dead woman at night in a lonely field. We want a starting-point.'

'I hardly think you will find one there,' observed the vicar, 'even though, certainly, Lady Cambers felt very strongly—very strongly indeed. And I fear she was right about the steel trap being still in use. Last night I was certain I heard a rabbit crying, as they do when they are caught—a most pitiful sound, almost like a child. I went out to see if I could find it, so as at least to put it out of its pain.'

'Did you succeed?'

'No. The rainstorm we had last night burst almost at once, and I had to take shelter. It was lucky there was an old hut near that saved me from a drenching. After the rain stopped I looked round a little, but I found nothing.

Possibly the rain had drowned the poor little thing. I hope so.'

'Whereabouts was this?'

'Over there,' the vicar answered, with a wave of one long arm towards the rising ground known as The Mounts. 'The vicarage is at the foot of the slope on the other side. The night was so calm and still before the rain came that one could hear sounds a long way. I thought the cry I heard came from up there somewhere, and I knew it was Mr. Hardy's land, and that Lady Cambers suspected young Ray Hardy was still using spring-traps. The young are often cruel; they have not yet suffered enough themselves. That comes after. It was Mr. Hardy Lady Cambers had specially in mind when she talked about refusing to renew leases of tenants who persisted in using the steel trap. She knew Ray Hardy had been boasting he wouldn't give them up for her.'

'Then you came down this way looking for the trapped rabbit after the rain stopped?' Bobby remarked slowly. 'You must have been quite near when the murder took place. I take it you didn't see or hear anything, either of Lady Cambers or of anyone else?'

'If I had, I should have said so at once,' the vicar answered severely. Then he added: 'I had a glimpse of a motor-cyclist on the road going towards the village. It was dark, of course. I could not see who it was.'

But to Bobby this seemed important, since here was apparently some confirmation of the old labourer's story.

'About what time was that?' he asked.

'Soon after the rain stopped. I only had a glimpse,' the vicar repeated. 'I could not say who it was.'

That was the second time he had said this. Bobby asked: 'At the moment, did you think it might be anyone you knew?'

'It did just strike me,' the vicar answered, with evident reluctance, 'that it was young Sterling. He frequently came to see Lady Cambers, and generally on a motor-cycle. I just thought it might be . . . it was far too dark to be sure.'

'Yes, quite so,' Bobby said, looking at the other thought-fully; and perhaps there was something in his voice or manner of which he was himself unaware, but that Mr. Andrews thought he noticed.

'I presume,' he said, very stiffly, 'you do not intend to suggest . . . to hint . . . in any case be good enough to inform your superiors I will be with them shortly.'

He walked on quickly—indeed he always walked quickly, as if those long legs of his made speed a necessity—and Bobby, looking after him doubtfully, was again conscious of that quaint impression he gave of an enormous bird flapping its way along the ground.

CHAPTER SIXTEEN

THE CIPHERS

THE DOOR OF CAMBERS HOUSE STOOD OPEN, AS IT HAD done all the day, since the constant traffic had never yet allowed it time to close. A constable was on duty, for by now the help summoned by Colonel Lawson had arrived and he had his men at his disposal. Bobby, at first taken for a newspaper-man—for already reporters had made their appearance on the scene—had to explain his identity before he was allowed to enter, and in the hall, as he went through, he met Farman, grumbling at all the extra work involved but secretly finding so much bustle and excitement quite amusing.

'Might be an hotel,' he complained, and then, noticing Bobby, and with an odd mixture of official respect for one who had been a guest in the house and of dignified condescension as from a butler to a common policeman, he said to him: 'Oh, it's you, sir. The Colonel has been inquiring for you. Better pull up your socks before you go in; he was getting a bit hot under the collar about you not being back.'

'Is he in the same room?' Bobby asked.

'No; that's locked, and no one's to go in on any account. They're in the library now. But you'll have to wait. Sir Albert's in there now.'

'Oh, he's arrived, then?'

'Yes. The garage kept him waiting for a car or he would have been here before. And then he was in bed when he heard—influenza—and looks a wreck all right.'

'It must have been a terrible shock to him,' Bobby observed.

'Yes,' agreed Farman. 'So it must. All the same, I wouldn't mind betting it won't be a month of Sundays before we have a new missus here. At least, unless he's been cut out of her will.'

'Is that likely?'

'Well, perhaps she said more than she meant. But she had the lawyer here, and some seemed to think as young Mr. Sterling would come in for it all. But that was just gossip, which of course I put my foot on soon as I heard it.'

'Quite right, too,' approved Bobby.

'But you couldn't go for to expect her ladyship to leave everything to the guv'nor, just for him to go and enjoy himself with someone else.'

'Miss Bowman?' Bobby asked.

'Oh, you've heard about that,' exclaimed Farman, slightly surprised. 'Had any lunch?' he added. 'I've no orders, and no one to give them, but I thought as it was up to the house to do as much as possible in the way of refreshments, and Lady Hirlpool thought so, too.'

'I'm sure it's very good of you,' said Bobby. 'I got something to eat in the village, thanks all the same. I expect all this means a lot of work and upset for you.'

'It does that,' agreed Farman gloomily; 'but I will say for the staff they're doing their best—all except cook, and with her it's hysterics along of expecting it may be her next. Only, as I said to her, even if Sir Albert spoke free about her sauces—free and frequent he spoke—who'll strangle when they can sack?'

'Very true,' murmured Bobby, impressed by the wisdom of this aphorism.

'And I must say,' admitted Farman, 'Amy Emmers is taking on the cooking very smart like. Of course, nothing high-class, but turning out eggs and bacon very competent; very competent indeed.'

'Oh, yes, there was something I wanted to ask,' Bobby put in, quick to seize the opening offered. 'You told us there had been some sort of scene between Miss Emmers and Lady Cambers. You can't tell us anything more definite? You've not been able to think of any reason for it?'

Farman shook his head regretfully.

'None of us could,' he said, with more than a suggestion in his manner that the question was one that had already been very thoroughly debated. 'Amy Emmers is a close one,' he added resentfully. 'She'll listen; she'll stand and look as if you wasn't there; but open her mouth—not she. An oyster,' said Farman, rising in his emotion to an unusual height of poetic imagery, 'is a babbling brook along of her.'

'She and Eddy Dene are engaged, I believe,' Bobby observed.

'Brought up to it. That's why she went to service, Mrs. Dene not thinking it proper the two of 'em should go on living together in the same house and them as good as wed; and there was some as thought,' added Farman, in his capacity of treader upon gossip, 'as Mrs. Dene had her reasons for acting so.'

Bobby disregarded the insinuation, but wondered if this reason Mrs. Dene had apparently put forward had been her real one, or if it had been—to use the current highbrow slang—a 'rationalization' of a decision of Amy's that had in fact disappointed her good aunt. It was the second alternative Bobby was inclined to accept, from his memory of his talk with Mrs. Dene.

'We all heard 'em,' Farman went on reminiscently, 'though not the words spoke, but both of 'em talking loud and frequent. And, when I went in afterwards, there was the morning paper lying on the floor, tore nearly in half as if they had been having a tug-of-war, and her ladyship sitting and looking so you knew you only had to open your mouth to get your notice before you had time to close it again.'

'What paper was that?'

'The *Announcer*.'

'Could there have been anything in it to upset Lady Cambers—something about Miss Emmers, for instance?'

'About Amy Emmers? In the paper? What could there be?'

Farman evidently thought the suggestion very absurd, but under pressure agreed to see if he could find that issue of the *Announcer*, though of opinion that almost certainly it had been destroyed. However, he succeeded in discovering it—torn across, as he had said, as if snatched between the two women. Carefully and swiftly Bobby ran his finger up and down the columns, searching for some item that might account for the quarrel but finding none. In the 'agony' column, however, were two advertisements, one a 'figure' cipher and the other so odd and confused a jumble of words, thrown together in so confused a fashion and apparently so utterly without meaning or coherence, that Bobby was inclined to think it, too, must be some kind of concealed cipher. A curious thing about it was that in some odd way it seemed to suggest to him some kind of literary association, though of what kind or nature he could not for the life of him imagine. He proceeded to cut it out. It ran:

'MMMM: They don't carved at the worry if aunt meal with suspects gloves must of fix steel and things once they drank for all the red wine expect me through late the Sunday helmet evening barred shall wait they

carved rhododendrons till at the coast
meal clear. MIT.'

'Don't seem to make much sense,' observed Farman, who
had been reading it over Bobby's shoulder, as the young
man carefully cut the thing out.

'No,' agreed Bobby. 'Only it does seem somehow to hint
at something I've read somewhere.'

'No one, in a manner of speaking,' commented Farman
thoughtfully, 'could read it.'

Bobby did not answer, but proceeded to cut out the
second cipher, the one in figures. It ran:

'AAA. 504 : 634 : 346 : 51 : 394 : 303 : 25 : 66 : 259 :
    21 : 465 : 734 : 33 : 925 : 77 : 652 : 14 : 284 :
    634 : 88 : 285 : 148 : 146 : 99 : 381 : 12 : 291 :
    54 : 645 : 51 : 66 : 259 : 194 : 66 : 493 : 14 :
    181 : 34 : 77 : 23 : 394 : 13 : 205 : 88 : 565 : 34 :
    394 : 15 : 99 : 23 : 934 : 834 : 54 : 66 : 42 :
    292 : 24 : 304 : 21 : 66 : 12 : 205 : 77 : 52 :
    3049 : 12 : 3930 : 25 : 88 : 54 : 34 : 0012 : 256 :
    371 : 562 : 304 : 363 : 6363 : 99 : 6564 : 03047 :
    24 : 914 : 925 : 22 : 914 : 6623 : 77 : 5555 : 14 :
    59910 : 33 : 50306.'

'But that's all figures, not letters,' Farman pointed out
indignantly. 'Figures don't make words.'

'Figures can be used instead of letters,' Bobby explained.
'As a rule, figure ciphers are simple enough, given a little
time and patience. The other looks more difficult. Most
likely every fourth or fifth word makes up the message, or
something like that. Anyhow, I haven't time to bother
about them just now; they may have nothing to do with
what's happened. Miss Emmers never said anything in explanation afterwards?'

'Not so much as a grunt or a groan, and, when asked,

only looked as if you was a thousand miles away and sorry it wasn't further. Cook did up and ask her straight out about her eyes, and why they was so red and swollen, and she said it was a cold and she must remember not to let any of us kiss her for fear of infection. Sarcastic, that was,' explained the butler darkly.

'Evidently a young woman you have to be careful with,' agreed Bobby, who in fact had already arrived at that conclusion.

Farman contrived, without uttering a word, to express complete agreement.

'Robins did think it might be about Ray Hardy and his spring-traps,' he added after a moment's pause. 'Lady Cambers was very hot about spring-traps, very hot indeed.'

'But where's the connection?' Bobby asked. 'Was Miss Emmers interested in spring-traps too?'

'Well, it was more Ray Hardy being interested in her,' Farman answered, 'or so Robins thought. Gone on her, he was, like half the rest of the village lads—all except Eddy Dene himself, and very likely he was only slack because he was sure of her.'

'But was he?'

'Well, it was an understood thing,' Farman answered; 'but Robins has a sort of kind of natural gift for twigging love-affairs. Tells you who's going to fall for who long before they know themselves. It's a gift,' said Farman thoughtfully, 'but it's study and thought and practice as well. Trained herself to it, as you might say, and it was her said at once that Eddy Dene and Amy Emmers never thought a thing of each other. As Robins said herself, that wasn't to say they wouldn't marry, and get on the better for is, too, maybe, but you could say "Eddy" to Amy and she wouldn't even hear, and you could say "Amy" to Eddy and he would answer "Yes" and go on talking about his bones and stones and suchlike. So you can see we all thought Robins was right again when she came back from Hirlpool one night and said as how, walking up from the station, first she saw Ray Hardy dodging in among the trees by Middle Copse and then Emmers coming out from the same copse. So of course she teased her about it, if you call it teasing what might be the Marble Arch for all the notice took.'

To Bobby all this seemed interesting, though what bearing it might have upon the investigation, if indeed it had any at all, he could not make up his mind. But he felt it would be necessary to try to get to know more of this enigmatical Amy Emmers whose quarrel with her mistress had so impressed the rest of the household staff and had been by her so simply explained.

Bobby had an impression that behind that gentle and controlled appearance volcanic fires might lurk. But one could not be sure. There were, too, these hints of indifference on Eddy Dene's side, but was that indifference genuine, and, if it were, was it reciprocated or resented? Was there anything in this talk about Ray Hardy? Or was there some other hidden love-affair? The thought flashed into Bobby's mind that the suspicions Lady Cambers had entertained of her husband had perhaps taken a wrong direction. Was it possible that not Miss Bowman, but Amy Emmers, had been the object of Sir Albert's wandering affections? Or was there some other explanation altogether? And, in any case, what bearing had all this upon the murder he was investigating? None that he could see, and yet from so confused a situation of conflicting interests and desires he felt that at any moment the compelling motive might emerge. *Cherchez la femme*, the old French tag warns us, but 'Seek the motive' Bobby's teaching and experience told him was a better motto for the detective.

Because simple sexual jealousy nearly always leaves traces too plain for misconception or mistake. It is Iago who is subtle and hidden, not Othello. He was trying to think as quickly as he could, but there was no connecting thread he could see to lay hold upon. He said presently: 'Miss Emmers seems to have plenty of admirers. Any more on the list?'

'Oh, well,' answered Farman, pursing his lips and looking as if he knew them all, 'half the village lads, as I said before, and others too, though I could never see any more in her than in another.'

The idea had been lurking in Bobby's mind that perhaps Farman might hint or say something to show he thought his master was of the number. But no suspicion of that kind seemed to have been entertained by the butler, who added: 'Well, there's one thing I must say for the girl, and cook says so, too. She never takes notice; never seems to know even, as you might say. Only she's a deep one, and what she's thinking to herself she gives you no notion ever. And there it is that Robins saw both her and Ray Hardy hanging about Middle Copse—and Ray's swore it's him she'll marry in the end. But, then, Ray Hardy shoots off his tongue a deal too much, especially when the beer is in.' Farman hesitated. 'I don't know if I did ought to tell you, but if I don't you'll hear from others, for there's them in this village would talk from now to Doomsday if you let them. Only there it is; and it's what he told me once himself, being one over the nine at the time—meaning him and not me, for such as that my worst enemy could never say of me.'

'I'm sure he couldn't,' agreed Bobby warmly. 'What was it Ray said?'

'Well, it was this way,' Farman answered uncomfortably, 'and others heard as well, but we took no heed, knowing he never meant it and as it was the beer spoke and not him, but what he called to me as I was going was to mind and tell my old girl—meaning,' explained Farman in a slightly shocked parenthesis, 'not my wife, which I haven't got, but Lady Cambers herself—that if she didn't mind her own business he would wring her neck for her, like any other clucking old hen.'

'Was that on account of these traps?' Bobby asked.

'Yes. You see, her ladyship had Ray's father in a sort of a trap himself, so to speak. In a bit of a hell of a hole, he was, in a manner of speaking, along of owning some of his land himself and renting some from her as well. He works 'em together, and if he lost the lease of what he rents it would knock the value of what he owns by half, or two-thirds even. In a manner of speaking the landlord knuckles in to the tenant these days, the tenant knowing he can have a farm any day, anywhere, for the asking. But if Mr. Hardy moved away, what is to become of the land he owns? He couldn't take it with him; he couldn't sell it, for it's worth little by itself; you see how her ladyship had him between finger and thumb, in a manner of speaking. That was why Mr. Hardy was the first to promise not to use spring-traps. But Ray didn't promise, and he makes his pocket-money trapping and selling the skins for the seal and ermine and mink coats you see in town.'

Bobby made up his mind that some attention would have to be given to Ray Hardy. A little odd, he thought, that this young man, whose name had so unexpectedly surged into the affair, should have been the one to give him first news of the tragedy. But was that entirely coincidence?

'Don't go for to think,' Farman said earnestly, 'that I mean I think Ray Hardy did it. A most respectable young man, and never would.'

'Not even when the beer was in?' Bobby asked.

Farman looked a little startled, but was saved from answering by the sound of voices and of an opening door.

'There's Sir Albert coming,' he said in a quick whisper.

CHAPTER SEVENTEEN

BOBBY REPORTS RESULTS

BOBBY TURNED QUICKLY TO LOOK WITH INTENT IN-terest at this new-comer whose personality and character might have played, might still be playing, so great a part in the drama it was his own business to unfold—or try to. He saw a small, round, bustling man, a little bald, a little stout, a little red in the face, a little watery about the eyes, the mouth permanently a little open—a little, indeed, it seemed, of everything, though not very much of anything; altogether, an indeterminate sort of person. Such at least was the impression Bobby received from the one swift, concentrated glance that was all he had time to give—though, too, he had a vague impression of a kind of latent nervousness that might at times transform itself into a capacity for swift and sudden action—and then Sir Albert announced his appearance in the hall by one loud, sudden, shattering sneeze.

'Farman,' he called, ignoring Bobby, whom probably he guessed to be one of the numerous police scattered about the house, 'Farman, I'm going to bed. My head's splitting. A touch of flu, I think. Tell them to get me a room ready —one of the spare-rooms.'

'Very good, Sir Albert,' Farman answered. 'Shall I send for the doctor, sir? Advisable, sir, in a manner of speaking, if I may say so.'

Sir Albert answered with another out-size in sneezes.

'Doctors are all humbugs,' he declared petulantly. 'Tell Marshall he can come along if he likes. Fact is, I oughtn't to have got up this morning—and I wouldn't, either, only for this awful thing happening. And then I had to wait hours for their beastly car, feeling worse all the time. You had better be looking out for a new place, Farman.'

'Sir?' said Farman, a good deal startled.

'Have to sell up, most likely,' Sir Albert told him gloomily between two more resounding sneezes. 'Nothing much left now the jewellery's gone—not insured either. I always wanted that done, and it never was. Rotten look-out altogether.'

He vanished upstairs as he spoke in a crescendo of

sneezes; they heard one final effort that sounded like the Platonic 'form' of sneeze made manifest on earth; then a door banged, and all was peace once more. Farman, who had been gazing after his master open-mouthed, turned disconsolately to Bobby: 'Well, in a manner of speaking, that's a nice thing to shoot off at a man,' he complained, 'and me at my age and the competition getting fiercer every day.'

He wandered away with a very depressed and melancholy air, and Bobby proceeded to the library, where he was received but coldly by Colonel Lawson, who was busy with Moulland and two or three other assistants.

'Oh, there you are at last,' Lawson said. 'I'm waiting for those notes of yours—tried to get them read, but the man I gave them to said it was impossible to make them out.'

'Indeed, sir,' said Bobby, stung in a tender spot, for he really was proud of his shorthand. 'I use Pitman's, sir. It's generally considered very legible, sir.'

'Oh, it is Pitman's, then,' observed the Colonel. 'They seemed to think it was most likely some private system of your own. Well, get to work; the sooner I have them in longhand the better.' He turned to one of his newly arrived subordinates. 'We've got to find this young Dene,' he declared. 'Get out a description of him at once. Looks pretty bad, his disappearing like this, especially when there was his pen found on the spot.'

'Beg pardon, sir,' said Bobby, bending sulkily over his insulted script, where every line and curve and angle seemed to him as plain as any print. 'I've had a talk with Dene. He promised to come straight on. He should be here any minute.'

One of the county police appeared at the door.

'Young man of the name of Dene, sir,' he reported. 'Says he's been told you want to see him, sir.'

'Oh, yes, quite right, quite right,' answered Lawson. 'Ask Mr. Dene if he would mind waiting a minute or two

—explain what a lot one has to attend to in these affairs; and—er—see that he does.'

'Very good, sir,' said the policeman, and vanished, and Lawson turned to Bobby.

'I was informed Dene could not be found—that he had probably left the village,' he said severely, evidently holding Bobby much to blame.

'Yes, sir, that's what I heard,' Bobby agreed. 'I inquired at his home, but they didn't seem to know anything there, so I went on to the field where he works. I thought it a likely place, and he was in the shed there. He said he had locked himself in to avoid interruption while he was putting his things straight. They all had been very much upset this morning.'

'Very extraordinary,' commented Lawson. 'At a time like this, too. Locked himself in, you say? H'm! On pretence of work?'

'Yes, sir, though I shouldn't think it was altogether pretence,' Bobby ventured to say. 'I think he is very keen. I think he thinks it's very important. He has scientific theories he hopes to get accepted—about evolution and the origin of man. He is writing a book he thinks will prove very important.'

'More important than getting to the bottom of a thing like this?' demanded Lawson sarcastically.

'The impression he gave me, sir,' Bobby answered, 'was that he was entirely wrapped up in his work, and took very little interest in, and cared very little about, anything else. He mentioned his fountain-pen. He says he lost it last Thursday. He said that before I said anything about it. He has advertised in the *Hirlpool Gazette* for its return, offering ten shillings reward. The advertisement was sent so that they would get it some time Saturday, he says. I haven't checked it, but that can easily be done by phone. I noticed also that when he lighted a cigarette he used a match of the type of the one found near the body. He said it had been left in the shed by Jones, the stranger staying in the village Lady Cambers thought might be a burglar. It seems he went off in a hurry this morning, as soon as he heard the news of the murder. Dene said, too, that it was after Jones had been to see him that he missed his pen.'

'Queer story altogether,' commented Lawson. 'Have to look into it. Can the pen have been left there to throw suspicion on Dene? Or . . .? Odd, very odd. Find out anything else?'

'Yes, sir. I had a talk with an old labourer who thinks he saw Mr. Sterling in the neighbourhood on his motor-cycle about half-past ten last night, before the rain began. And Mr. Andrews, the vicar, thinks he saw Sterling, too, after the rain, about half-past eleven. But neither of them could swear to his identity.'

'Very odd,' commented Lawson, beginning to look a little worried and to breathe a little hard, as he was apt to do in moments of mental stress. 'Didn't Sterling tell us he had a breakdown on the way, and, instead of coming on here, put up at an inn because he was afraid of arriving too late? And he didn't explain very clearly why he was coming down late on a Sunday when he would have to be back at work first thing Monday morning. Curious altogether. Did Mr. Andrews explain how it was he happened to see him?'

'He says he went out to look for a trapped rabbit he thought he heard crying. Then the rain came on and he had to take shelter. Afterwards he saw the motor-cyclist he took for Sterling.'

'That means,' commented the colonel, 'he was in the neighbourhood himself at the time the murder was committed?'

'Yes, sir,' agreed Bobby, his voice as non-committal as had been that of the colonel. 'I asked if he had seen or heard anything else in any way suspicious. He said he hadn't.'

'Does he often go out late at night looking for trapped rabbits?' demanded Lawson.

'I understand there's been some feeling locally about the use of spring-traps,' Bobby answered. 'Both Lady Cambers and the vicar objected strongly. They want the farmers to promise to give them up. It seems Lady Cambers had gone so far as to threaten one farmer, a man named Hardy—he rents the land where her body was found—that she wouldn't renew his lease unless he promised not to use spring-traps any longer. That would have meant a heavy loss for him as he owns some land himself, which he works with what he rents. It's not enough to work by itself but it's enough to prevent him from wanting to move. So he was rather tied up, and apparently Lady Cambers took advantage of it to make him give in about the traps. His son, a young man called Ray, resented it a good deal, and Farman, the butler here, says he heard him one night threatening to wring Lady Cambers's neck if she went on interfering. But he was drunk at the time and no one took him seriously.'

'Perhaps it's a pity they didn't,' observed Lawson moodily.

'I'm told also he professes to be violently in love with Amy Emmers, one of the maids here—the one who found out that Lady Cambers was missing. She is engaged to Eddy Dene.'

Colonel Lawson gave a little jump.

'Well, now, there we're back at Eddy Dene,' he said.

'Yes, sir,' agreed Bobby. 'He appears to have an alibi that would have to be broken down before he could be suspected. His mother says he was in his room all night. He came home wet through, having been caught in the storm, and toothache came on. She says she heard him moving about all night. She says he kept her awake, shuffling up and down in his slippers, as the pain prevented him from sleeping. There is no doubt about the toothache, for his face is quite badly swollen. I am sure Mrs. Dene believes what she told me, but of course she didn't actually see him and it might have been someone else she heard. There's an out-house just under his bedroom window that would make it quite easy to climb in or out.'

'Engaged to the Amy Emmers girl?' mused Lawson. 'If they were both in it, she might have taken his place. Anything more?'

'Only that, as he had got wet through, all his things were in the kitchen all night, drying before the fire. All his other clothing Mrs. Dene has put away, so if he went out he must have gone in a sack or something like that—or in nothing at all.'

'Any accomplice taking his place,' Lawson observed, 'might have brought a change of clothing—this Emmers girl, for instance.'

'I suppose that's possible,' agreed Bobby, though doubt-fully.

'In any case,' decided Lawson, 'I think we had better have a chat with young Mr. Sterling and hear what he has to say. It looks bad, only then how to explain the rest?' He paused, hesitating, staring, doubtful. 'Find Sterling, some-one,' he ordered, 'and bring him along—Oh, and tell Dene how sorry I am to keep him waiting. I suppose Sterling is still here?'

'Yes, sir, I think so,' Moulland answered. 'He rang up where he works to say he was detained. I saw him in the garden a few minutes ago.'

'Well, send someone to find him,' Lawson ordered, and added to Bobby: 'You heard Sir Albert Cambers had arrived?'

'Yes, sir,' Bobby answered. 'I heard him tell Farman he felt poorly and thought he had a touch of flu. He's gone to bed and they've sent for the doctor. I understand he says Lady Cambers has left very little money?'

'Yes, that is so,' agreed Lawson. 'It seems he has been mixed up in speculation on the Stock Exchange, and has lost so much it will take all his wife's fortune to clear him.

But what's interesting is that he admits she did not know how heavy his liabilities were when she took them over.'

'Hell of a row when she found out,' observed Moulland suddenly from the background, where he was busy with a large and heavy note-book.

'Yes, but had she found out,' mused Lawson, 'or was he afraid of her finding out? We've got to know that. He seemed genuinely upset about the disappearance of the jewellery.'

'That's a point I ought to mention, sir,' Bobby put in. 'Dene gave me the idea he was very surprised and disturbed when he heard about that. I thought it seemed there was something behind, though I can't be sure. But I do feel fairly certain his surprise was genuine.'

'Put on, perhaps,' suggested Moulland. 'Never know.'

'Well, there it is,' Bobby said. 'That's my impression. And Mr. Andrews says he saw Lady Cambers burn her will. She had made one leaving everything to Mr. Sterling and then changed her mind and burnt it, partly because she hoped her husband would return. Mr. Andrews says he thinks no one knew except himself.'

'Difficult to be sure,' commented Lawson. 'There's that maid of hers, the Amy Emmers girl. Maids get to know a lot. I've an idea that girl has played a bigger part in what's been going on than she pretends. There's that story of her quarrel with her mistress, for example—undarned stockings, she said, didn't she? A bit thin. She'll have to be questioned again, too, after we've heard what Sterling has to say.'

As he spoke, the door opened and there entered young Tim Sterling, more pale, more thin, more eager-looking even than before.

'You want to ask me some more questions?' he said quietly.

CHAPTER EIGHTEEN

TIM STERLING'S EXPLANATIONS

'YES, THAT'S SO,' COLONEL LAWSON ANSWERED. 'SOME new facts have come to our knowledge we should like to ask you about. If you'll sit down a minute, I'll look at our note of what you told us before.'

There had not been time for Bobby to transcribe in full his shorthand notes of Sterling's previous examination, so, a little pleased to show how easily he himself at least could read his shorthand, he fluttered over the pages of his notebook and hurriedly jotted down what he thought were the salient points. He put the result before Colonel Lawson, who concentrated on it with frowning and deep-breathed attention, and Sterling, who was evidently beginning to feel a little nervous, said: 'May I smoke? Is that allowed?'

Moulland frowned. He thought the suggestion showed a lack of proper respect. Colonel Lawson, who thought so too, was about to refuse, when he saw Bobby looking at him, and, without quite knowing why, changed his intended refusal into consent. At once Bobby was offering his petrol-lighter.

'Oh, thanks,' Sterling said, accepting the offer, and then, noticing how hard Bobby was looking at his cigarette-case, offered it to him. 'Have one?' he said.

'Oh, thanks awfully,' Bobby said, instantly taking one; and Moulland, almost unable to believe his eyes and ears at such slack ideas of discipline, looked at the chief constable in mute appeal to be allowed to launch the thunderbolt he had all ready. No less displeased at such slackness, the colonel was about to let go one of the largest size on his own account, when Bobby meekly came across and put the cigarette down on the table before him.

'I suppose I must wait till the investigation is over. This is duty for us, you know,' he said to Sterling as he did so, and Colonel Lawson frowned and breathed more deeply than ever as he saw it was a Bulgarian Tempo, that expensive and not too common brand whereof the stumps had been so frequent in the rhododendron-bushes before the front-door of the house.

'What's up?' Sterling asked, vaguely aware of by-play, of an increase of tension.

'I used to smoke Balkan cigarettes myself,' Lawson observed. 'Found them a bit expensive, though.'

Sterling made no answer. Apparently he saw no reason for discussing his choice of cigarettes. Lawson went on: 'Do you always smoke the same brand?'

'No. Generally the cheapest gasper I can get hold of,' Sterling replied then. 'Why? You didn't ask me to come in here to chat about cigarettes, did you?'

'No, no,' Lawson answered. 'There are some new facts that have been mentioned. Can you say what was the exact time you started last night to come here?'

'I didn't notice particularly,' Sterling answered. 'I suppose it would be somewhere about eight.'

'It was dark?'

'Practically.'

'The distance is about forty miles—say, about an hour's run.'

'Rather more—built-up area a good part of the way. I'm not a speed merchant.'

'You expected to arrive between nine and half-past?'

'Yes, I suppose so. But I think I told you I had a breakdown. I had to stop to adjust . . .' He gave brief technical details. 'And I got caught in that storm, lost my way—the rain was like a wall; you couldn't see an inch before your nose. Then I had another breakdown—jolly awkward at that time of night. Finally I got to Hirlpool in the small hours. I got a bed at the Red Lion. They might be able to tell you the exact time I got there. I didn't notice. I was only too glad to get to bed.'

'I suppose you got thoroughly drenched?'

'Well, I had my waterproof cape and leggings,' Sterling answered. 'Rain like that will go through pretty nearly everything, though—it splashed up from the ground a good eight or ten inches. Soaked my shoes and socks all right.'

'As a matter of form,' Colonel Lawson went on, poking distastefully at that cigarette of Balkan brand that lay upon the table before him, 'we want to establish the whereabouts of everyone at the time when the murder, so far as we can calculate, was committed. That would be, we think, a little before midnight.'

'I understand,' Sterling answered gravely. 'Well, I'm afraid I can't help you very much. A little before midnight I suppose I was scooting round trying to find my way to Hirlpool—or anywhere else where I could get a bed.'

'You had definitely given up all idea of trying to reach Cambers?'

'Yes. I didn't want to fetch everyone out of bed. Aunt wouldn't have been awfully pleased.'

'I think I ought to tell you,' Lawson said slowly, 'that two witnesses state that they saw you in this neighbourhood, one quite early in the evening—about half-past ten—and one later on, after the rain had stopped.'

'I am suspected of the murder, then?' Sterling asked, quietly enough but a little more pale than usual.

'I have not said so,' Lawson retorted. 'In point of fact, we don't suspect anyone yet. We are merely making preliminary inquiries on which to proceed. But it does seem that what these two witnesses tell us is inconsistent with your own story.'

'Why?' asked Sterling. 'In the first place, they may easily be mistaken. It was a dark night. I was travelling at a fair pace. Certainly no one stopped me or spoke to me. Everyone about here knows I often run down on my motorbike. Any motor-cyclist seen near here would very likely be taken for me. Secondly, I told you I lost my way and had two breakdowns.'

'If you come so often, surely you know the way well enough?' interposed Lawson.

'Oh, yes,' agreed Sterling; 'that is, when I can see it. After I got the bus running again, I tried a short-cut. That was pretty fatal. Short-cuts generally are. I got completely fogged. And then the rain came till I didn't know south from north. It is quite possible I buzzed right by here without knowing it.'

Lawson said nothing for a time. He was staring at the ceiling, scowling and breathing harder than ever. Moulland had, as usual, an air of listening with a kind of stolid official attention. Bobby was busy again with his shorthand, in an aggrieved mood taking special care with his loops and angles as he put them down.

'Any ass will be able to read this,' he thought, and then: 'Pretty thin yarn. Something behind it. Only what?'

Lawson brought down his eyes from the ceiling, gave the cigarette another dissatisfied poke with his finger, and said: 'I suppose you didn't often choose late on Sunday evening to visit your aunt? You would have had to leave again first thing Monday morning, I take it?'

Sterling hesitated. They all waited. Lawson seemed unable to keep himself from fidgeting with that incriminating cigarette before him, and Moulland's air of attention grew more stolid, more official, every moment. Bobby found himself thinking: 'Is he making up his mind to tell the truth? Or is he taking time to invent a plausible lie? But, then, he ought to have had one ready.'

'I don't see that my private affairs come in,' Sterling said at last, 'but it's like this. I've got a dodge for improving short-length reception. I used to be with Ballantyne & Watson, the big wireless-manufacturers. I expect you know their advertisements—Ballantyne and Watson as two handsome, earnest young men talking to each other confidentially over big pipes about how good their stuff is. As a matter of fact, Ballantyne's seventy and Watson's a widow. Well, when I hit on this dodge of mine, Aunt lent me a bit to start a small show of my own. It's been going pretty well. Developments and all that. Only getting going fairly eats capital. There's an overdraft at the bank. If Aunt had wanted her money back, it would rather have put the lid on.'

'You mean you were expecting she might do that? You had some reason for thinking so?' demanded Lawson, while Moulland, wakening from his attitude of profound attention, an attention so profound indeed it might have seemed somnolent, proceeded to make another entry in that formidable pocket-book of his.

'Only that she had this idea of wanting me to marry. Aunt was a bit like that. She would do anything for anyone, but afterwards she rather felt she had bought you, body and soul. Of course, she didn't mean it. I suppose she felt she had helped you once and so she was jolly well going on helping you, whether you liked it or whether you didn't. What I wanted was to rub into her that the girl herself wasn't keen, for the jolly good reason that she was sweet on another chap—good luck to him. I hoped when Aunt knew that she would let up worrying me.'

'It still seems a late hour to choose for your visit,' Lawson persisted, and Moulland startled them all by not exactly speaking, but by uttering a grunt that sounded as if it were meant for strong agreement with this view.

'I had been busy all day with accounts, and making plans and all that,' Sterling explained. 'You haven't much time to spare when you're starting for yourself.' He was perspiring gently. He took out his handkerchief and wiped his forehead, while they still all watched him in grave scrutiny. He said with a certain desperation: 'Oh, I dare say it looks rotten, but it was either then or waiting goodness knows how long.'

'I wish you had told us all this before,' Colonel Lawson observed severely. 'I don't feel you were altogether frank with us in the first place, Mr. Sterling.'

Sterling got to his feet and threw his cigarette-stump into the fire-place.

'There you are,' he said remorsefully. 'If I had done that before, poor old Aunt would have been down on me like a ton of bricks. Sorry and all that if you think I was keeping anything back, but how was I to tell you wanted to know all about my private business affairs? I don't suppose you'll believe me, but I'm just as keen as any of you on spotting who did Aunt in.' He paused and faced them, upright and tall, very pale, little drops of perspiration again on his forehead. For a moment Bobby had an impression of a bull tied to the stake and awaiting the onslaught of the straining dogs soon to be loosed. Abruptly Sterling said: 'Well, there it is. I didn't know I was suspected myself.'

'Nothing has been said about suspicions,' Lawson protested once more. 'We are seeking explanations.'

'No,' retorted Sterling, though a little more quietly, 'you don't say suspicion because, if you did, you would have to caution me, instead of all this third-degree business.'

'There has been no third-degree, whatever that may be,' declared Lawson angrily, in his best 'marked for punishment' voice. 'We have information, too, that after a young man named Dene left Lady Cambers someone else visited her room, and that she gave him refreshment there. Also that apparently someone was in hiding in the rhododendron-bushes in front of the house, as if he were on watch there.'

'Yes, I know,' Sterling interposed.

'Oh, you do?' snapped Lawson. 'May I ask how?'

'It's common knowledge,' Sterling retorted impatiently. 'Everyone knows. They are all talking about it here, and most likely it's all over the village by now. I should have thought you could have guessed that much.'

'It doesn't do any good to adopt that tone, Mr. Sterling,' said Lawson, looking angrier than ever. He gave the cigarette on the table before him another poke, and then went on: 'About these Balkan cigarettes? You say you don't often smoke them?'

'No, I don't. We buy them to offer clients. We keep several different kinds. People like it if you remember and offer them the sort they fancy. It may mean bringing off a deal. That's all.'

'I suppose,' suggested Lawson, 'you have a supply in your office, then, at the moment?'

'As a matter of fact,' Sterling admitted, 'we've run out'; and Colonel Lawson looked as if he had only just stopped himself from saying 'Ah' very significantly. 'Is that important? There were only a few left at the bottom of the box when I looked the other day, so I put them in my case. I didn't mean to get any more. They're expensive, and no one seemed keen on them. You can find out from Sanders, the tobacconist near our place, that he did supply a box, if that's what you're after.'

'The point is not in doubt,' Lawson answered dryly, 'since we can see you're smoking them. There's one thing more. Had you any knowledge of the state of Lady Cambers's finances?'

'No; only that she had taken over Uncle Bert's liabilities, and they were pretty heavy. I gathered she was a bit worried. If it's true someone's gone off with her jewellery, there mayn't be an awful lot left. It was jolly valuable—the jewellery, I mean.' He added: 'That's common gossip, too. Everyone knows the jewellery's missing, and everyone knew before that Uncle Bert had let Aunt in pretty badly.'

Colonel Lawson consulted his notes, frowned and scowled, and pursued his customary deep-breathing exercise, and then told Sterling that was all for the present and he could go, but would he please remain in the vicinity for the present.

'It looks bad,' declared the chief constable when the door had closed upon the young man, though he spoke with reluctance, for he did not wish to abandon his first belief that Eddy Dene was the guilty man. 'It sounded to me as if he knew perfectly well he had been close by here last night.'

'He might have known that and not wished to admit it, without being actually guilty,' Bobby pointed out. 'He may have realized it would look bad, and have hoped he hadn't been noticed and needn't say anything. I suppose he might think it wouldn't do a young business any good to have its owner suspected of murder.'

'Then it looks as if he were afraid Lady Cambers meant to claim back the money she had advanced him,' Colonel Lawson continued, 'though that hardly seems a motive for murder. There's the stolen jewellery, of course. We have to remember that. And he was on the spot and denied it; and then there's this business of the cigarettes.'

'Yes, sir,' agreed Bobby, 'only what was the idea of this hiding in the rhododendrons? Apparently that happened after the murder.'

'But not after the burglary, perhaps,' Lawson remarked. He went on: 'I think we must make a few inquiries about the rabbit-trap business. Not that I think there's likely to be much in it. Still, if this Ray Hardy used threats we had better see him.'

'Shall I send for him, sir?' Moulland asked.

'I think we'll take a stroll that far,' Lawson said. 'It might be as well to have a look at the place and the people—and I'm tired sitting so long.'

'There's Eddy Dene,' Bobby ventured to remind them. 'I expect he is waiting.'

'Yes, yes,' agreed Lawson, vexed at having forgotten Dene for the moment and looking sternly and rebukingly at all in the room. 'Certainly. We must hear what he has to say. Tell them to send him in.'

CHAPTER NINETEEN

EDDY DENE GIVES ADVICE

THERE CAME, AS THE CHIEF CONSTABLE WAS SPEAKING, a knock at the door, and one of the maids appeared. Would the gentlemen like tea? she asked. The gentlemen accepted the suggestion with alacrity, and the girl at once brought in a tray with the tea, cakes, scones and so on she had in readiness.

A smart, good-looking girl, Bobby thought, as he watched her with the concentrated interest he felt should be directed upon all the inmates of this house till the mystery was solved. A little better-looking she might have been, though, had her nose been a trifle less long, her chin a trifle less pointed. Her eyes, a light grey, were small, alert, and bright, and on her side she was evidently very much interested in them all, and greatly impressed. It was, Bobby supposed, the first time she had ever seen real live detectives actually at work, and he reflected that the dull slow stolid routine he knew so well had somehow got invested in the popular mind with an extraordinary halo of romance.

He smiled ruefully as he turned from his tea to his shorthand notes. Not much romance in writing those cabalistic signs, fit product in their lines and angles of a utilitarian age, and he remembered that this girl was the Miss Robins described by Farman as such an expert in the psychology of love. It might, he told himself, be worth while to try to find an opportunity for a chat with her. She might have something interesting to say on the characters and the motives of the people engaged in this complicated and confused drama.

Again the door opened, and Eddy Dene came in. On the threshold he paused and stood looking at them. They were all relaxing over their tea. Moulland was thoughtfully chewing scone as though beyond chewing scone he hadn't a thought in the world. Colonel Lawson was lying back in his chair, lazily making smoke-rings from the cigarette he had just lighted. It was a pastime in which he had much skill. Behind, his two or three expert assistants had their heads together, chuckling over a faintly improper story one of them had just related. It was a peaceful, friendly scene that merited in no way the extraordinary—indeed, magnificent—disdain wherewith Dene regarded it. To Bobby there came a ridiculous memory of his school-days, when his housemaster had intruded upon a surreptitious dormitory supper.

Colonel Lawson straightened himself, letting his last and most successful smoke-ring float unheeded ceilingward. Moulland put down the piece of scone he was conveying to his mouth, and looked as if he and scone were strangers for evermore. The experts in the background hurriedly resumed their usual air of grave authority, and the little chubby-faced youngster in the doorway, with that odd air of arrogant authority with which he seemed to be able to clothe at will his at first sight unimpressive physique, Bobby almost expected to hear him ordering them all to bring him five hundred lines by next Wednesday evening. Instead he said: 'Oh, sorry. If I had known you were so busy I wouldn't have interrupted.'

'Mr. Dene, I believe,' said Colonel Lawson, visibly deciding to ignore this as a piece of impudence beneath notice.

'There's one thing I want to ask you,' Dene went on, ignoring this in his turn. 'I thought it might be as well to have a look round Lady Cambers's room—the one she used to call her den, so she could feel she had one, too. Some fathead in uniform out there told me no one was allowed in.'

'The room was locked by my orders,' said Colonel Lawson, in his most severe voice—a voice calculated, indeed, to make most tremble in their shoes, so instinct was it with 'shot at dawn' and 'confined to barracks' and 'pay docked' and other similar dooms. He went on: 'When you refer to members of the force I have the honour to command, I will ask you to choose your words more carefully.'

'I do—jolly carefully,' retorted Eddy, quite unabashed. 'I won't ask you what authority you have to lock doors in other people's houses. But it meant I had to get in by the window.'

'You—you—what?' gasped Lawson, his gasp echoed all round the room, except by Bobby, who was so startled he knocked his note-book over and had to stoop to pick it up, thus being able to indulge in a quick little smile all to himself.

'Get in by the window,' repeated Eddy, with a touch of impatience in his voice, and apparently quite unaware of the sensation he had caused. 'Luckily it was open. Easy enough to hop in.'

'Against my strict orders,' interposed Lawson, heavy menace in every inflexion of his voice.

'My dear sir,' retorted Eddy. 'Your orders don't affect me. I'm not one of your policemen. I take orders from no one.' And lounging there in the doorway, from which he had not yet moved, his whole body seemed again instinct with that strange, deep, almost involuntary arrogance of his. 'Have you people any idea what Lady Cambers's jewellery was worth?'

'Sir Albert is getting us the inventory,' Lawson replied, almost meekly.

'Thirty thousand,' Dene said. 'That counts. She showed it me once or twice. She liked to play with it. And when I say thirty thousand, I mean selling price. What you could pick up for it anywhere, any day.'

Colonel Lawson had recovered himself slightly by now.

'We are fully aware of the value of the missing jewellery . . .' he began, and once more Eddy interrupted him.

'Stolen jewellery,' he corrected sharply. 'Are you fully aware, too, that if the stuff's gone, then it was the murderer took it, and, once you've found it, then you can bet your last copper the murderer won't be far off.'

'Mr. Dene,' Colonel Lawson tried again, but still Eddy was not listening.

'What's more,' he said, 'it's a darn sight more important. Death's death, and nothing to be done about it. Common enough, too.' He pointed from the window towards Frost Field. 'I can show you there the bones of men and women who died half a million years ago. I dare say it seemed important at the time. Personal prejudice. But thirty thousand pounds—that means life; that means power. And life and power they count—not death.'

He seemed to dismiss death with a shrug of the shoulders —an incident in the cosmic process, no more. The others watched him in silence, puzzled and impressed, too, by a kind of force that seemed to emanate from him. With his round chubby face, his slight stooping figure, his staring eyes, he looked insignificant enough, and yet there was this power about him, too. The first to break the brief silence, he said: 'That's what you want to concentrate on—finding the jewellery. And when you've found that, you'll have found the murderer, too.'

'Mr. Dene,' said the chief constable, rallying somewhat, 'when I want your advice, I'll ask for it . . .' and once more Dene interrupted.

'Yes, I know. When it's too late,' he said. 'That's why I wanted to have a look round that room you've locked before everything was messed up. Of course, I knew you people had had a look round, but I expect you thought of nothing but finger-prints and clues of that sort. As if to-day every two-year-old starting out to raid the jam-cupboard doesn't put on gloves first.'

There was enough truth in this remark about the finger-prints to make Colonel Lawson angrier still.

'Mr. Dene,' he thundered, so loud and so fast that this time you could no more have interrupted him than you could have an express train, 'your attitude is most improper, and is making a most unfavourable impression on me.'

'My good sir,' retorted Dene, 'I always make an un-favourable impression—one can't help it except when one is talking to one's intellectual equals.'

'I don't want,' pursued Lawson, 'to be forced to take extreme steps . . .'

'Extreme steps sometimes mean actions for damages,' retorted Eddy; and the poor Colonel winced, for that shot went home, since one was at the moment pending against him. 'By the way, what's this about that pen of mine?'

'Your—pen?' repeated Lawson, rather helplessly, so much again was he taken aback.

'Well, I've lost mine, and I heard you've found it,' answered Eddy. 'Isn't that right?'

'How did you know we had found it?' interrupted Moul-land this time, so anxious to make what he thought a good point he forgot to wait for his superior officer to ask the question.

Eddy surveyed him with an almost infinite pity. He gave the impression of bending gently, quietly, a little sadly, over the cradle of a new-born babe, regretting all it had yet to learn.

'There isn't a thing,' Eddy explained very gently, 'you people have done or said, or thought even, that isn't known and gossiped about all through the village. Everyone knows about that pen. Some people seem to think I choked the poor old girl with it. What about it? Can I have it back? It happens to be my property, you know.'

'It has been sent to Scotland Yard for examination,' said Lawson briefly.

'To find finger-prints?' asked Eddy, looking very amused. 'I don't believe there's a thing in all the world but finger-prints that you people can think of. Well, I suppose that's your idea of your job, and anyhow I don't want to row with you. Why should I? I want to help. I'm as anxious as you are to get to the bottom of all this. I don't know if it's occurred to you that my apple-cart is pretty thoroughly upset. And what I say is—that when you've got the stolen jewellery, you'll have got the murderer, too. That's why I wanted to look round in there. Sorry if it's upset you—my going in, I mean. I don't see why. After all, if you wanted to keep people out, you should have shut the window.'

This was a statement so incontrovertible that no one had anything to say. Colonel Lawson realized that to pursue the subject would mean having that point raised quite frequently. He contented himself, therefore, with turning in his chair and fixing on Superintendent Moulland a baleful glare, full of the promise of things to come. Moulland looked pitifully at his superior officer and very fiercely at the door. Plainly someone out there was in for a hot time. Dene said: 'Well, go ahead. Anything I can tell . . . I'll make it as plain and simple as I can. Not so easy to tell a plain simple story, either. But you can trust me. I'll help you along.'

'Very good of you, I'm sure,' said Lawson, with a sarcasm Eddy showed no sign of noticing.

He repeated the story he had already told Bobby. Evidently his memory was good, for he often used almost the same words. The only difference was that several times he referred to the stolen jewellery, and repeated again that the important thing was to recover it at the earliest moment.

'Thirty thousand pounds,' he insisted. 'That's life, that's power, that counts. The other's only death, and death's—well, dead, isn't it?'

He told again how he had spent the night, shuffling up and down his room, since his aching tooth had not allowed him to sleep and movement had seemed to alleviate the pain; and Bobby, remembering those old carpet-slippers he had seen, wondered if even they were capable of transforming Dene's quick, decided tread into a shuffle. But then, if someone else had taken his place, who could that have been?

When the chief constable went on to question him about

rabbit-traps, Dene, when he understood the reference, was a trifle scornful. It was a silly business all round, he thought. Rabbits had got to be kept down, and what was the sense of making a fuss about the means used.

'Like mice,' he said, 'you've got to use traps, and what's the good of getting sentimental because they squeal when they're caught? I know Ray Hardy was wild about Lady Cambers interfering. He told me so. He thought her a confounded old nuisance. And I shouldn't wonder if she didn't have a prowl round at nights, just to see who was using what traps; and I dare say Ray Hardy would have liked to wring her old neck for her if he caught her doing it. But liking's not doing. If we all did what we liked . . .' He paused and smiled, the phrase and the idea evidently pleasing him. 'Ray wouldn't,' he repeated, 'and, if he had, he would never even have thought of the jewellery. If he had done a thing like that, he would just have panicked, not gone on to burglary. Stick to looking for the jewellery, that's my advice.'

The colonel consulted his notes, whispered to Moulland, asked a question or two of Bobby, and then turned back to Eddy.

'I think that's all we require to ask you for the present, Mr. Dene,' he said. 'But I must warn you we shall perhaps wish to question you again.'

He tried to make his voice ominous with unexpressed threat, but Eddy was quite unaffected.

'That's all right,' he said graciously. 'Any time you want a tip and you think I can give it you, just let me know.'

With that for a parting promise he retired, and Lawson said darkly: 'A deliberately defiant attitude—most suspicious, to my mind.'

He subsided into an outraged silence, and Bobby reflected that Eddy had never been asked if he had noticed anything in the locked room into which he had so audaciously penetrated. He decided to repair the omission as soon as he could find opportunity.

CHAPTER TWENTY
A PSYCHOLOGIST ON LOVE

THE ATMOSPHERE IN THE CAMBERS LIBRARY REMAINED sultry. Colonel Lawson was magnificently retaining his self-control, but no one cared to risk breaking it down by so much as moving a finger. One felt a conductor for the lightning of his wrath would have been accepted with gratitude—and alacrity.

'For two pins,' he said suddenly, 'I'd arrest the fellow.'

'Yes, sir,' agreed Moulland, and Lawson turned fiercely upon him.

'Then get the evidence,' he commanded.

'Yes, sir,' repeated Moulland, rising from his chair as if intending instantly to bustle away on the errand, and then rather helplessly sitting down again.

'Shall I clear away the tea-cups, sir?' asked Bobby.

'Nothing better to do?' demanded Lawson. 'That your idea of your work, is it?'

'Yes, sir—no, sir,' answered Bobby confusedly; and, as if supposing he had been given permission, proceeded to collect the crockery, securing thus an excuse for escaping from a room where he felt the temperature was too high for calm concentration on the problems to be solved.

In the hall he found, as he had hoped he might, Eddy Dene, standing idly with his hands in his jacket-pockets, apparently deep in thought.

'I say,' he said to him confidentially, 'you've rather put their backs up in there.'

'Have I?' Eddy asked indifferently.

'Makes them feel they'd rather like to bring it home to you,' Bobby went on.

'Very likely; but then they can't,' Eddy answered, as indifferently as before.

'Well, of course, that's all right,' agreed Bobby, 'but there is such a thing as obstructing the police in the execution of their duty.'

'Run me in, eh?' Eddy asked. 'Rather cramp their style, wouldn't it? Obvious bias from the start—unfair prejudice, un-English methods used—first-class line for defending counsel to take. Besides, as a matter of fact, I'm out to help.'

'About the murder, or about the theft of the jewellery?' Bobby asked.

Eddy turned and stared at him.

'You talk like a fool,' he said thoughtfully, 'you act like a fool, you look like a fool—you can't see what's lying there right under your nose—and yet I'm damned if I believe you are a fool.'

'Thank you,' said Bobby meekly. 'Quite a nice school-leaving certificate, so to speak. By the way, you didn't answer my question.'

'The answer's both.'

'But the theft rather than the murder?'

'More important, isn't it? Murder is only a name for one kind of death—hanging by law of the land, cancer by act of God, run down by car in a hurry, shot by burglar about his business—is there any real difference, apart from convention and convenience? You might think, from all the excitement, death was a rarity that hadn't been happening every day for the last million years and won't go on just the same for the next million. But the jewellery means money, and money means a lot.'

'I suppose it does,' agreed Bobby, 'if it's yours.'

'You mean the jewellery isn't mine?' Eddy asked sharply. 'Yes, I know. But it means a lot to me, all the same. I want money to carry on with, if I'm not to be held up just as I'm getting there.'

'About establishing that theory of yours on the origin of man?' Bobby asked.

'Which happens to mean revolutionizing human thought,' Eddy told him. 'That's big, you know—and it may be held up just for the want of a little money, and because one old woman's dead. Can you wonder I'm interested?'

'Not if you put it that way,' Bobby answered cautiously, and added: 'Did you notice anything in Lady Cambers's room when you were looking round?'

'No. I didn't expect to. But I left something there for you to notice—a tear in the curtain where I put my foot through it, though I was being as careful as I could, and it was broad daylight, too.'

'Yes. Yes. I see,' Bobby said thoughtfully, and Eddy gave him another sharp look, as if wondering whether he did in fact 'see', and then abruptly turned and walked out through the front-door into the grounds.

'I wonder,' Bobby thought, a little ashamed of the idea, and yet feeling forced to consider it, 'if this means he's got hold of the jewellery himself somehow, and means to keep it to finance himself with—or perhaps he's so keen because if he can find it he would be entitled to a reward big enough to keep him going. Anyhow, that's the second useful tip he's given me.'

He picked up his cups and saucers and penetrated through the service-door into the back-regions, where his luck for once was good, since the first person he met was that psychologist of love, Miss Robins, by whose insight into affairs of the heart Farman had been so much impressed. It was, in fact, in the hope of meeting her that he had made his offer to clear away the used crockery.

She seemed a little surprised by his appearance there, and even a little disappointed, as if she had been hoping in secret for another glimpse of that rare spectacle, detectives at work. But a few compliments on the excellence of the tea provided, and a few added, less impersonal perhaps in their general tenor, soon resulted in the establishment of friendly relations. When Bobby ventured to wonder if she could help their investigation in any way, she showed herself at once gravely eager to oblige.

'Not that there's so much I can tell you,' she admitted regretfully.

'There are things you may have noticed,' he suggested. 'Observation is a gift with some people. Most of us in the police have to be trained to it, but some seem to possess it by nature—especially ladies.' He paused to assure himself that this had been well and thoroughly lapped up. Convinced by evident signs that was the case, he went on: 'Now, there's a story going about that young Ray Hardy is head-over-heels in love with Miss Emmers. Do you think that's true?'

'He's crazy about her,' Miss Robins asserted at once. 'Anyone can see that with half an eye. But she won't look at him. I will say that for her, though if she lifted a finger he would be down on his knees.'

'You are sure that's so?'

'You can always tell,' the psychologist asserted. 'When a boy's really soft about a girl, there's a sort of look in his eyes—I don't quite know how to put it. . . .'

'Sort of imbecile?' Bobby suggested hopefully.

'Well, silly like,' she corrected him. 'But that's not what I meant. Every fellow looks that way when he looks at a girl. You can see it oozing out.'

'And when it's a girl looking at a boy?'

'More dripping and running than oozing,' the lady answered promptly. 'What I mean is . . . well, more a "lost for ever if you don't find me" sort of air. You can always tell it. Except,' she added thoughtfully, 'with Amy herself. I believe if she was going to cut her heart out for a man, or wish him "good afternoon", she would look just the same. It makes them ever so much worse. There's nothing pays like treading them under your foot. I wish I could. But someways I can't. It's them that treads on me,' she said, sighing.

'Then you think Ray Hardy is in love with her, but you don't know about her?'

'I don't even know,' declared Miss Robins, in a burst of candour, 'if there's anything to know. She's like a box with the lid shut, and what's inside there's no way of telling.'

'She is engaged to Mr. Eddy Dene, isn't she?'

'Yes. And they might be stock and stone for all the notice they take of each other. The old people fixed it up. You see, they took Amy out of the workhouse. She was sent there when her father and mother died, and then Mr. and Mrs. Dene heard and took her out, and she's so grateful still there isn't anything she wouldn't do for them. No wonder, either; it's something to be taken out of a workhouse, as you'll know if you've ever been in one. But, all the same, Eddy and her don't mix, no more than oil and vinegar do they mix. Perhaps if they marry they'll get on all the better for that—not mixing, they won't separate.'

Bobby found this rather subtle. He thought it over, and then said: 'You know Mr. Sterling?'

'Oh, yes. A very nice young gentleman. Always the gentleman, and never gave any more trouble than he could help.'

'Do the people in the village like Mr. Dene?'

'Eddy Dene? No one likes him. He always seems to think he's God Almighty, and you're a blackbeetle. You can't,' observed Miss Robins, with some force, 'like anyone like that. Of course, he's very clever. He can pick a stone up out of the road and tell you just who made it, and what for and when—he says there was a time when there was elephants and such hereabout, not in a Zoo, he don't mean, but running loose. Now Lady Cambers isn't there to give him any more money he'll have to look after the shop more, and mind more if he loses custom. Why, there's some stop away just because they can't bear to see the way he despises them. Asking him for a quarter of butter or a half of tea is like asking the King of England to come and black your boots. You don't know how you dare.'

'I suppose that does hardly attract people,' Bobby

168

agreed. 'Lady Cambers's death will mean a big loss to him, then?'

'It'll put him back where he belongs,' she answered. 'They're saying that already, down in the village.'

'Hard luck,' Bobby commented. 'There's something else I would like to ask you. It's not curiosity, remember. Every bit of information may help. Do you think Lady Cambers was still fond of her husband, and wanted him to come back to her?'

Miss Robins appeared to consider this.

'Well,' she said finally, 'she wasn't soft about him. You aren't once you're married, are you? No need to be. But she wanted him back all right. Wouldn't you? I mean, if you had a man and another woman came along and took him—well, you wouldn't feel like putting up with it, would you?'

'I suppose it depends . . .' began Bobby cautiously, but she interrupted him with scorn.

'It doesn't depend at all,' she said. 'It's just like that. If you've a man and he gets away, you're out to fetch him back. Insulted, you feel. Of course,' she admitted, 'there's many such a good riddance it almost makes up for the insult.'

'How do you think Sir Albert felt about it?'

'Puffed up, same as a man always does when two's after him. Of course,' she again admitted, though this time reluctantly, 'a man's always a man, otherwise what Miss Bowman saw in the master, few could tell.'

'He was attracted by Miss Bowman, then?'

'She made it so,' Miss Robins answered simply. 'And now, if you ask me, she'll be Lady Cambers as soon as decency and law permits. I don't know whether I'll stop, though a good place up till now, as places go these days, but plenty better to choose from.'

'Well, thank you very much for telling me all this,' Bobby said.

'Welcome, I'm sure,' answered Miss Robins, and a voice in the distance became audible, calling Bobby by name.

'There's Colonel Lawson. I must go. Thanks awfully,' Bobby exclaimed, and hurried back into the hall.

'Oh, there you are,' said the chief constable, who seemed now in a slightly milder mood. 'You know the way to Mr. Hardy's farm?' he asked. 'I think I'll take a stroll that way. I don't suppose there's anything in this rabbit-trap business, but if he used threats we had better see him, and hear what he has to say.'

They started off accordingly, Colonel Lawson, Superintendent Moulland, Bobby in attendance. No one spoke, for the chief constable was evidently deep in thought, and neither of the other two ventured to interrupt the current of his heavy meditations.

'Possible, I suppose,' he said suddenly, 'that Lady Cambers wanted to see for herself whether spring-traps were still being used, and preferred to slip out quietly at night without letting anyone know. That would explain why she took the attaché-case with her, and why it was empty. She may have wanted to bring back the traps, if she found any of the kind she objected to. And it's possible she met young Hardy and there was some sort of quarrel, and he—well, carried out what he had threatened. Only, then, who was hiding in the rhododendrons, and why? And what about the jewellery? We must try first to establish where he was that night.'

'He mentioned specially, when he was telling me the body had been found, that he was in bed early,' Bobby said. 'He told me the rain woke him, and he was glad he wasn't out in it.'

Turning a corner, they came in sight of the farm and of the yard behind it, where they saw, hung out to dry in the sun, coat, trousers, a set of men's underclothing, down even to the socks.

'Someone at the farm seems to have been out in the rain last night,' Bobby observed.

CHAPTER TWENTY-ONE

NEAR ARREST

COLONEL LAWSON MADE NO COMMENT, BUT HE STOOD still for a moment or two, looking his hardest at those dangling garments, and then, with a very intent and resolute air, resumed his forward march, a little as though he were leading a forlorn hope. Moulland followed him determinedly. Bobby had to hurry to keep pace with them, and he told himself he was growing fanciful, so oddly, so ominously, did that dangling clothing remind him of a human body, swinging, it also, unsupported from a rope.

Strange, indeed, he thought, if a thing so simple, so harmless, so ordinary as a rabbit-trap, was to be proved the cause and origin of so grim a tragedy, though, indeed, in the tangled, complicated, unreasoning web of human emotions and beliefs, there is no cause so great or small but it may lead to consequences immeasurably huge or tiny, and the fall of an empire mean the release of a mouse from a trap, and the cackling of geese the changing of the destiny of man.

Crossly Bobby told himself that a detective's business is truth; and that of proof there was as yet no shred, since a man may be out in the rain for many reasons besides murder, and the talk of an ill-balanced youth too fond of strong ale must not be taken too seriously. All the same, he found it hard to keep his eyes away from those hanging garments with their grim suggestiveness accentuated by the shifting shadows the declining sun cast from them upon the walls of the old barn behind.

A certain movement and agitation was becoming apparent about the farm. Evidently the approach of Colonel Lawson and his companions had been observed. A tall, thin, worried-looking man came down to the gate admitting to the yard, and stood there waiting. He was wearing blue overalls, and was fidgeting with an oil-can he held, for he was a farmer of the new type, put his faith in petrol, and, like mankind in general, had solved the problem of production but not of distribution, so that his ancestors would have been equally amazed at the amount of food he produced from the ground, and at his difficulty in disposing of it except at actual loss. Behind him hovered an elderly woman, see-sawing, as it were, between gate and house, and then suddenly, as if at last making up her mind, running full speed into the house and banging the door behind her. In the yard itself two or three of the farm-workers found occasion to busy themselves eagerly about unimportant jobs that permitted them to give their whole and undivided attention to the approaching trio.

'Good evening. Mr. Hardy, I think?' Colonel Lawson greeted the worried-looking man in blue overalls, who, still leaning on the farm gate, made no effort to move at their approach.

'Aye, that's me,' he answered. 'You're police. About the murder. There's nothing anyone can tell you here.'

'That's what we've come to inquire about,' Colonel Lawson began, and was interrupted by the brief retort: 'That's what I'm telling you.'

'Then you can tell me this as well,' the chief constable retorted sharply. 'Lady Cambers has been brutally murdered, and her body found in one of the fields of your farm. Is it true you and your son resented certain ideas she had about spring-traps; that she had spoken of refusing to renew your lease; that your son is known to have made violent threats against her?'

He paused. There was no reply. The farmer gaped and stared, and became very pale. He was holding the oil-can he carried at an angle that allowed the contents to drip slowly out, but he paid no attention. It seemed as if the violence of this direct assault of the chief constable's words upon his mind had served to stun him. Bobby felt very sorry for him, and yet felt that the colonel's direct methods very often had much to recommend them. Lawson went on, evidently satisfied with the impression he had made: 'I am here as chief of the county police, in pursuance of my duty, to ask your son what explanation he has to give, and to account for his whereabouts last night.'

'So that's it, is it?' Hardy mumbled.

'Yes, it is,' Lawson snapped angrily. 'I must ask you to stand aside.'

'Where's your warrant?' Hardy demanded.

'None is needed,' Lawson told him. 'Now, Mr. Hardy, you had better be reasonable. I don't want to have to put you under arrest for wilful obstruction of the police in the execution of their duty, but I will remind you that your attitude is highly suspicious.'

'Wait here,' Hardy told them, and began to walk back towards the house.

Disregarding this injunction, they followed him closely. He gave them an angry look over his shoulder, but made no comment. He even slackened his pace and began to dawdle a little till he was quite near the house, when he suddenly broke into a run and dashed inside, banging the door behind him.

'The man's a fool,' said Lawson, frowning heavily.

'Looks bad,' Moulland pronounced. 'Very bad.'

'Panicking, that's what it is,' Bobby observed.

Lawson lifted the knocker on the door, and smashed it down two or three times with vigour, so relieving, a trifle, his feelings.

'We'll wait a moment or two,' he said. 'I don't want to have to take extreme measures'; and on a sudden impulse Bobby slipped round the corner of the house just in time to see a side-door open and Ray Hardy, pale, wild-eyed, panic-stricken, come slipping out.

'Hello, Ray,' Bobby hailed him cheerfully. 'Colonel Lawson wants to ask you something. Now, don't go playing the silly goat. Running away is open confession, and if you tried to hide you would be spotted in no time.'

Ray, who was evidently in a highly nervous state, still seemed more than half inclined to run. But Bobby slipped an arm through his and spoke again.

'Whatever you do, don't run,' he repeated. 'If you are innocent, it's merely putting in a plea of guilty. If you are guilty, then it's the final proof needed. And innocent or guilty, you're soon caught. There's no hiding-place in all England for a man we know, and know we want.'

Talking thus, he propelled Ray gently back to the front of the house, and the young man made no resistance.

'They're saying, in the village, I did it,' he muttered, 'but I never did.'

'That's all right,' Bobby said. 'But I'll give you one tip—tell the truth and nothing else. If you're innocent, it's safest, and if you're guilty, it's quickest.'

'I never did it,' Ray repeated. 'I never meant . . .'

They came round the corner of the house. Colonel Lawson, his patience exhausted, had just begun to ply the knocker with all the downright, straightforward energy of his nature; nor had the resultant reverberations died away when the door opened, and Mr. Hardy showed himself, so thin, so tall, so pale, so spectral, in a word, he had the appearance of a ghost.

'You can come in, if you want to,' he said. 'You can search the house from top to bottom. You can search every building on the farm. You can . . . Oh God!' He broke off in a sudden anguished cry as he caught sight of Bobby and Ray approaching, arm-in-arm.

'This is Ray Hardy, sir,' Bobby said to the colonel. 'He was in the yard just behind the house. He says he is quite prepared to give all the information he can.'

'Very good,' said Colonel Lawson severely, and regarded Bobby with equal severity. 'What were you doing behind the house?' he demanded. 'I don't remember your asking permission.'

'No, sir. Very sorry, sir,' Bobby answered meekly. 'I acted on impulse, sir. It just struck me he might be there.'

'Well, as he was there, as it happened, we'll say no more about it,' promised the chief constable, 'but I would like you to remember, for the future, that I prefer my men to follow instructions.'

'Yes, sir,' said Bobby, still more meekly.

'You had better come inside,' said the farmer, eyeing with dislike sundry peeping heads and staring eyes now growing visible in convenient positions near-by.

They all went indoors accordingly, and in the seldom-used front sitting-room the examination began. Ray admitted the use of threats, but protested vehemently that he had never intended to carry them out. Pressed, he admitted, too, that if Lady Cambers had implemented her threat of refusing to renew their lease, the result would have been something like ruin. Nor did he deny that he had continued the use of the spring-traps Lady Cambers so strongly objected to.

'Just foolishness, what her and vicar and the others said,' Ray protested. 'All very well for them. They didn't want to sell the skins; they didn't have their sowings eaten down as soon as up. Ask Eddy Dene. He's brain's hasn't he? And he said it was all fuss and foolishness. Quickest best, he said. He said you might as well talk about not sticking pigs because it hurts when the knife's put in. Pigs have to be slaughtered, and rabbits has to be trapped, and that's all there's to it.'

Bobby thought this interesting, and looked to see if Colonel Lawson thought so, too. But apparently the colonel had noticed nothing, and went on hammering away with question after question.

Soon Ray admitted, too, that he had been out when the rain began that night. With some hesitation he came at last to admit, as well, that he always made the round of his traps at night, because occasionally they strayed on other people's land—most frequently, somehow, on that belonging to Lady Cambers herself.

'The fat would have been in the fire, all right, if the old girl had found that out,' he confessed, 'so I reckoned it was better like to go round while it was dark.'

Bobby, taking all this down, thought that with every word the case looked blacker. The young farmer, slow of mind, badgered, confused by the ceaseless hail of questions, evidently did not realize how grave were the admissions he was making. Colonel Lawson's method of direct and simple frontal assault was succeeding well this time. Probably, indeed, it was the method best suited for breaking down the young man's defences. How easy for a jury to believe, to accept it as proved, that on this midnight expedition he and Lady Cambers had chanced to meet, she, on her side, having come out to see for herself if her wishes had been observed, and perhaps already suspecting that they had been ignored. If things had happened like that, what more probable than that Lady Cambers had repeated threats about the lease, and that thereon, in rage and desperation, Ray had carried out the threats that he, on his side, had undoubtedly made?

'Why didn't you tell the truth at once instead of denying you had been out that night?' demanded Colonel Lawson finally.

'Well, I didn't do it,' Ray answered sulkily, 'but I didn't want to give folk the chance to say I had—same as I knew they would if they could.'

He stuck firmly to his story to the end. He had neither seen nor heard Lady Cambers. He didn't believe she had come out to look for the traps because for one thing he didn't believe she would have had the least idea where to begin looking. He had been caught in the rain and drenched to the skin almost instantly, so heavy was the downpour. He had gone back home after it stopped. And that was all he knew, he insisted.

Moulland was so far stirred by all this as to take, for

once, independent action. He got up and muttered something in his chief's ear. Bobby was sure he was advising immediate arrest. Lawson looked doubtful, hesitated, but finally told Ray that was all they wanted to ask him for the moment, but that he must remain at hand in case he was again required. The young man stumbled unhappily away, dazed as if with drink under the mental bludgeoning he had received, and Bobby was aware of an impression that very shortly he would have been ready to confess, though probably only to retract it again soon enough. When the door had closed behind him, Lawson said: 'Looks about as bad as it can. Looks as if we were on the right track. Only what about Dene? Deliberately defiant and insolent he was, and why, unless there's a reason?'

Neither of the other two ventured to attempt this conundrum. But it was evident that Lawson's prejudice against Eddy was still strong, nor perhaps, considering the attitude Eddy had chosen to adopt, was that much to be wondered at. After a pause, when Lawson seemed to be breathing and thinking a little less vigorously, Bobby ventured to say: 'I think myself, sir, there are several points that ought to be cleared up before any action is taken. We don't know yet who hid in the rhododendrons, or why.'

'If the case is complete, we can safely ignore that as a side-issue,' pronounced the chief constable, and to Bobby that seemed dangerous doctrine.

'Might have been young Hardy himself, hiding in a panic, wondering what to do next,' Lawson added, after a pause.

'He doesn't smoke Balkan cigarettes,' Bobby observed. 'Then we don't know who had the refreshment, brandy and so on, we've heard was taken in Lady Cambers's room that night.'

'Young Hardy again,' Lawson said. 'It appears there's

something between him and that Amy Emmers girl. Suppose he went back to the house and told her what had happened? She lets him in. They talk a little, and she gets him brandy to help him steady himself. Afterwards she lets him out and locks up behind him. That's why the butler found all the doors and windows fastened. Afterwards Hardy hung about in the rhododendrons for a time, wondering whether to stay and face it out or bolt, and possibly smoking cigarettes he's got hold of somehow.'

'Plenty been hanged on less than that,' declared Moulland suddenly.

'There is still the jewellery,' Bobby said. 'Would he go on from murder in a passion to cold-blooded theft?'

'Why not? The Emmers girl knew all about the jewellery, and quite likely had the keys, or knew where they were. They took the jewellery because they meant to go abroad together when they thought it safe.'

He paused. He was plainly thinking deeply. His heavy breathing seemed laden with Ray Hardy's fate. To Bobby, too, it seemed just then that arrest must mean condemnation, so neatly did opportunity and motive appear to fit together.

'There's Dene's pen,' he said, half to himself.

Lawson turned and looked at him.

'If it wasn't for that,' he said slowly, 'I think we could take action, but perhaps that should be cleared up first. If we can trace it to Hardy, though, I shall think it conclusive.'

CHAPTER TWENTY-TWO

THE JUBILEE GARAGE GRIEVANCE

EVEN COLONEL LAWSON, BY NO MEANS INCLINED, either by temperament or training, to expect small things from his subordinates, showed a touch of surprise when Bobby presented him next morning with all the statements that had been taken from the persons interviewed the previous day, all carefully and neatly transcribed, ready to be submitted to those concerned for their approval and signature.

'Um . . . ah,' the chief constable said, as he received them, going thus about as far as he ever thought prudent in the way of a commendation he was always afraid might afterwards turn out undeserved. 'Yes . . . you've put in a little overtime?'

'A little, sir,' agreed Bobby gravely, not choosing to explain he had been sitting up the greater part of the night to get the job done.

Lawson referred to some notes at his side.

'Oh, yes,' he said. 'London rang up last night. They want you to clear up details of a case you were engaged on —complaint about street bookmakers operating somewhere near the Jockey Club.'

'Yes, sir. Do they want me to ring up?' Bobby asked, afraid this might mean he was going to be withdrawn from a case that interested him, both from a professional point of view and from a personal standpoint, since he had been the victim's guest at the time of her murder.

'No, they want you to report in person,' Lawson answered. 'At the same time you can report on this case. I have asked for help on two or three points, and you can explain any details required. Further, I should like you to see what information you can gather about Sir Albert Cambers and his recent movements—whether he has been in touch with Miss Bowman, for instance. You had better interview Miss Bowman, too, and see if she has anything pertinent to say. Then, too, there is the man Jones. The Record Office will be getting this morning the finger-prints we found in his room. If they are known, you had better report by phone at once.'

'Very good, sir. Are they following up the clue Eddy Dene suggested?'

'Yes. It was mentioned. They undertook to inquire.'

'There's the match-stalk, too,' Bobby suggested.

'The one marked with the name of that hotel?' the colonel asked. 'I don't think they attach much importance to that. I don't either. There must be tens of thousands of those matches knocking about.'

'Yes, sir,' said Bobby. 'I will inquire at the hotel, though, if I may. There's just a chance.'

If Colonel Lawson had not been put in a specially good humour by the sight of all those nicely written transcripts Bobby had spent so large a share of the small hours copying out, he would probably have refused the required permission. As it was he contented himself with telling Bobby not to waste his time on wild-goose-chases, and Bobby said, 'No, sir,' very meekly, and decided that was all the permission he wanted, and so presently found himself in the train for London, making good use of the opportunity thus given him to secure some of the sleep he had missed during the night, and incidentally providing a nice old gentleman who was a fellow-traveller with opportunity for a letter to *The Times* on the decadence of modern youth, racketing through the small hours of the night and then wasting in slumber the golden morning made for Work (with a capital letter).

At the Yard he handed over his street-bookmaking case to the man who was to carry on in his place, and discovered from the Record Office that no finger-prints corresponding to those found in the vanished Mr. Jones's room were filed there.

'Doesn't look as though there were much in the "burglar prospecting for a job" theory,' Bobby observed, 'unless he is quite a beginner.'

'Burglars never begin,' answered the man he was talking to, an officer of vast experience. 'They grow. Burglary's never a first offence. No other clue to your bird's identity?'

'A match-stalk,' Bobby said.

'Well, that's better than none,' opined the other.

But not much better, Bobby thought. On the whole he was inclined to attach more importance to the hint that Eddy had dropped, wittingly or unwittingly. Of course, the Yard was already hard at work, testing it, and the upshot must be awaited.

Leaving the Yard, Bobby proceeded to the Jubilee Garage, meaning to check there Sir Albert's repeated and rather curiously insisted-on complaint that he had been hindered in answering the summons to Cambers by delay at the garage in supplying the car ordered. From the carriage department he had already learned that the concern in question was well conducted and flourishing, doing a big business with, as a rule, society people, wealthy visitors to London, and others who for one reason or another found it more convenient to hire than to purchase.

'People with small service-flats and no garage,' the carriage department said. 'The Jubilee gives long credit, and charges high to make up. They're always willing to help our people—when they see they've got to. Of course, they don't give away their customers if they can help it.'

Bobby nodded, understanding well how torn a garage doing a 'west-end' business might often be between its need to stand well with the police authorities and its fear of offending influential customers.

A motor-bus put him down near his destination, and when he entered the garage and began by mentioning the name of Sir Albert Cambers he was at once interrupted.

'Come to pay his bill, have you?' he was asked. 'Time, too.'

Bobby dashed this optimism by producing his official card, and the garage-manager said, with unwonted zeal, that he would be only too glad to give Bobby any help he could.

'Does he owe as much as that?' Bobby asked, impressed by such unnatural willingness to assist.

'It isn't what he owes,' said the manager darkly. 'We don't mind how much a gentleman owes so long as he's got a rich wife behind him. But when we're doing our best to oblige a client, and then he takes his cash custom somewhere else—wouldn't you call that a bit thick?'

Bobby agreed warmly that he would—that, indeed, in his opinion, 'bit thick' was an expression altogether too mild. Encouraged by such a warmth of sympathy the garage-manager went into details. Only a week or two ago, Sir Albert Cambers had paid down two hundred pounds in cash to a neighbouring and rival establishment for a smart little coupé—a good enough bargain, no doubt, though the Jubilee would have been happy to supply one of the same make for ten per cent. less.

'Owes what he does,' said the manager disgustedly, 'and then takes his cash down to those blighters.'

Bobby gathered that there was considerable rivalry between the two establishments, that a liaison existed through the chauffeurs each employed, and that the securing by the one of two hundred cash from a client heavily in debt to the other had been a tremendous triumph and the subject of much banter and leg-pulling.

'If it had been me,' said the manager, whose feelings had been deeply hurt, 'I should have shut down on his account, and next time he sent round for a car I should have told him to take his "credit please" to where his "cash down" went. But our chairman said that would only mean doing in any chance of getting our money, but, anyhow, I did see he had to cool his heels a bit next time he wanted a car out. Of course, I didn't know then what it was for, or anything about the murder the papers are so full of. If he comes in for her money, he ought to be able to settle soon.'

'Perhaps,' agreed Bobby, half inclined to wonder if this remark indicated any vague, subconscious suspicions floating in the other's mind. 'If Sir Albert had just bought a car,' he asked, 'why did he want to hire one?'

'It wasn't for himself he got it. He wanted it to give a little lady,' the manager explained; and added, as one admitting extenuating circumstances: 'Most likely that's why he didn't come here—afraid of her finding out how much he owed.'

'Do you know her address?' Bobby asked.

The manager didn't. Under pressure, he admitted that one or other of the garage chauffeurs might know it. One was soon found, in fact, who remembered having driven Sir Albert more than once to a block of service-flats in Bayswater.

So Bobby thanked them, bought three sausage-rolls and a bunch of bananas to eat on the way, since it did not look as though there was going to be much time for luncheon, and caught another motor-bus for Bayswater. Without too much trouble he found the block of flats indicated, and, at a venture, knocked at one door and asked for Miss Bowman.

But they had never heard of her, and knew no one of the name; and so he sought out the porter, and explained he must have made a mistake in the number, as Miss Bowman, whom he had come to see, did not live at the flat at which he had just knocked.

'Oh, that's the next block—No. 32,' the porter told him.

Bobby thanked him and remarked what admirable flats they were, and how well kept, and were any vacant? But then, what about a garage if a tenant wished to keep a car?

Regretfully the porter admitted that the flats, though replete with every modern necessity, such as telephones, wireless, cocktail-bar, and so on, did lack garage-accommodation.

'Generally,' said the porter, 'they hire a car when

wanted. But some have their own, and garage round about. There's a lock-up garage just behind as several go to.'

Bobby thanked him, and walked round to the indicated garage, a small, not very busy or prosperous-looking place.

'Miss Bowman keeps her car here, doesn't she?' he asked.

'Does she want it out?' asked in return the man he had spoken to, and glanced as he spoke at a smart new coupé standing near-by.

Bobby strolled over to look at it, and then came back and once more drew a bow at a venture.

'Had a bit of a job getting it clean and dry again, hadn't you?'

'I don't think,' answered the other emphatically. 'A day's work, pretty near. You remember that rain Sunday night? Splashed up to the roof, she was, and inside—it was almost like she had sprung a leak and had to be bailed out.'

Bobby asked a few more questions, but the garage-hand had no more to tell. All he knew was that someone—he didn't know who; Miss Bowman he supposed, but he didn't know—had rung him up on the Monday afternoon, and had asked him to clean the car. When he unlocked the compartment Miss Bowman rented, he found the car in a state suggesting, as he put it, that it had been doing the Channel-swim stunt. But he knew nothing more. There was no one there on night duty. Clients were provided with keys of the separate garages they rented, and took their own cars in and out—late or early, or neither —as they wished. Obviously they could have duplicate keys made for the use of friends, or when a car was owned jointly. Why not? The garage-management didn't object. Why should they?

Thoughtfully Bobby went away, and outside the garage, near the entrance to the second block of service-flats, he noticed a tobacconist. He went in and asked if they kept Balkan cigarettes, and as they did, he purchased a packet of Bulgarian Tempo.

'Sell many of these?' he asked; and when the tobacconist answered that he only stocked that brand because of one customer who sometimes came in and asked for it, Bobby declared that it must be a friend of his, and gave a description of Sir Albert Cambers that was at once recognized.

CHAPTER TWENTY-THREE

SIR ALBERT'S LETTER

THOUGHTFULLY BOBBY TURNED AWAY, AND, CROSSING the street, entered the block of flats opposite to knock at the door of that occupied by Miss Bowman.

An evident 'charlady' appeared, untidy and rather sullen-looking, and admitted reluctantly that Miss Bowman lived there. She softened a little, however, under the influence of Bobby's smile, and perhaps that of his age and sex, since he was, after all, better-looking than some, and consented to allow him to wait within while she informed Miss Bowman of his presence. In a tiny room, furnished, 'as per schedule submitted' by a big Tottenham Court Road firm, in the very latest style of chromium and right-angles, Bobby accordingly waited till there entered a pale, plump, fair little lady—one who had the air of having probably existed in a previous avatar as an eiderdown cushion, so completely did it seem that her function in life was just that of offering a passive repose and comfort to the weary.

That Bobby's visit had both disturbed and frightened her was evident, not only from such symptoms as the dab of powder that had missed the nose and found the left cheekbone, but from a look in the pale-blue eyes that seemed not far removed from panic. Indeed, she appeared in a highly nervous condition, and that perhaps was not greatly to be wondered at.

As gently as he could, Bobby set himself to explain his errand. She listened vaguely—Bobby suspected she always listened vaguely—and wept a little—Bobby suspected she wept freely and often—and told him presently that she had in fact been expecting all day that the police would call, but was so grateful he hadn't come in uniform, because, even if it was only 'motors', people did talk so. Not that there was anything she knew, or could tell anyone, though it was simply all too dreadful for words, and never, never could anyone have dreamed that such a thing could ever happen to dear, dear Lady Cambers.

Bobby agreed gravely that it was in fact dreadful, noted that the 'dear' in 'dear Lady Cambers', had a certain subtle feminine accent that made one think at once of another word in one syllable also beginning with a 'd', expressed his complete conviction that Miss Bowman would do all in her power to help the course of justice, and started his questioning by asking if it were not true that Sir Albert Cambers was a great friend of Miss Bowman's.

At once there came back into her eyes that look of startled terror he had noticed there before, but that his gentle manner had a little soothed away. She hesitated, stammered, then as he patiently waited, but with an air of being prepared to wait as long as might be necessary, she seemed to make a sudden decision, and launched out into a long account of her friendship with Sir Albert, of how Lady Cambers had quite misunderstood it—and in her references to Lady Cambers the adjectival 'dear' soon dropped out. Bobby listened silently, helping only now and again by a sympathetic murmur. He made no attempt to produce his note-book, judging that the sight of pencil and paper would check instantly the free emotional flow of her recollections, which, indeed, were so far chiefly of value for the insight they gave into the characters of herself and of Sir Albert and Lady Cambers, as well as of the relations between husband and wife. Indeed, as the flow of talk went on and on, Bobby found himself wondering a little at the clearness of the picture that evolved.

'Nobody ever thought more of anyone than he did of her when they married first,' Miss Bowman said, 'and he used to think it fun, then, to be ordered about and told just what to do. But she kept it up. Like a little boy she treated him, and what made it so bad was that she was nearly always right. It was very trying. A man,' Miss Bowman pointed out with profound truth, 'does like to be looked up to, and I think it's quite right and only natural. But Lady Cambers never looked up to poor Bertie—never. She just told him what to do till he could hardly bear it any longer. And he found it so restful to come to me. Lady Cambers misunderstood dreadfully. It was nothing but the merest friendship—at first. He felt he needed a true woman's sympathy. Ours was a beautiful friendship, and everything might have gone on just the same only for Lady Cambers herself, and never shall I forget the things she said.'

'To whom?' Bobby asked.

'To me—one afternoon when she happened to call just as I was bathing his poor head. The things she said— even now she's gone I can't help remembering them— lump of putty, half a pound of Russian butter. Russian,' she repeated bitterly, 'and me a member of the Primrose League and hardly able to sleep at times for thinking of those dreadful Bolsheviks.'

'I gather Lady Cambers was a rather authoritative lady,' Bobby observed.

Miss Bowman burst into a fresh flood of talk, from the hazy intricacies of which emerged once more the picture of Lady Cambers as a strong, resolute, managing woman, well-meaning and kindly, determined, indeed, to do good to others whether they liked it or not. Not that this picture of the dead woman was a new one, but Miss Bowman provided fresh and convincing touches, made it, in fact, clear that only by accepting Lady Cambers's benevolent dictatorship could you retain her friendship. On her active, and, indeed, eager help you could fully rely so long as she approved your aim, but if she did not, then she expected you to change it for one that did meet with her approval.

'She was the same with everyone,' Miss Bowman said. 'There's that nice Mr. Sterling, her nephew. She simply told him who he was to marry, and she quite thought that was settled. But I happen to know it wasn't.'

'She did a good deal for young Mr. Dene, didn't she?' Bobby asked.

'Oh, yes, everyone talked about it,' Miss Bowman answered. 'Hundreds of pounds she spent to help him. No wonder he knuckled under the way he did. Everyone else he looked at as if they were dirt, even when serving behind the counter and handing you a pound of tea like spurning you for wanting it, but with Lady Cambers it was always. "Just what you think best." Of course,' she added thoughtfully, 'he had always taken care to tell her first what was best.'

'He knew how to manage her?' Bobby suggested.

'So as to get money out of her,' said Miss Bowman.

This had, indeed, been apparently a minor cause of the breach between husband and wife. He had resented an expenditure for objects he had no sympathy with, and she had persisted in her patronage of a young man whose talents she believed she had been the first to appreciate. Apparently too, Sir Albert's business dealings had been entered into chiefly in the hope of securing a greater measure of independence than his wife's stronger personality allowed him at home.

'You know,' Miss Bowman said, in a sudden burst of candour and of insight, 'Lady Cambers could make people very fond of her. I used to adore her. I thought she was—wonderful. And she would always go to any trouble to help you. It was through that Bertie and I got friendly at first—because I admired his wife so tremendously. And then somehow . . . it was always being told just what to do. Golf,' she added abruptly, after a moment's pause.

'Golf,' repeated Bobby, puzzled.

'The last straw,' she explained, 'that made the cup overturn. She said he must take up golf for his health. She said he was getting fat. Really, as I told him, it was only a dignified filling-out. He joined a golf-club to please her. Only it's such a tiny ball they use, so different from the one they have when they're playing football. Dear Bertie found it so difficult always to hit it, and then a stupid man got in the way of Bertie's club when he was trying and Bertie had to pay for his false teeth and his spectacles, and I don't know what else, and everybody seemed to think that that was so funny. People have such funny ideas of what's funny, haven't they? Lady Cambers wanted him to go on playing, all the same. But I said: "It's beneath your notice, don't have anything more to do with them," because I saw that's what he wanted me to say. It was just about then business went all stupid, just as business always does, doesn't it? And what made everything worse was when Lady Cambers walked right into our drawing-room without knocking, while I was bathing his poor head. So rude of her. And the things she said. I told you about that. Bertie was splendid. He asserted himself just as a man ought to. He gave her one look, and walked straight out of the house. And, of course, it was all over the village at once—the servants having heard it all as well as the butcher's boy bringing the chops.'

'What happened after that?'

'He was splendid still. He came to live in Town. So did I. Not together, of course,' she explained hurriedly, going very red. 'Only I couldn't stay there with all the things people were saying. So horrid of them. Besides, Oscar said it was upsetting for his business; and it was bad enough already. But then business always is, isn't it? And I don't think he need have been so horrid about it.'

'Thank you,' Bobby said. 'I think you've made all that quite clear.'

'You know,' she said timidly, blushing harder than ever, 'Bertie and I—we, we mean everything to each other now. Everything.'

'I realize that,' Bobby answered gravely, very sorry for the poor little feeble, futile woman to whom dreams of romance had come so late in life only to find themselves at once face to face with such tragic realities. 'Have you ever heard Sir Albert mention his wife's jewellery?'

Miss Bowman gave a little gasp, like that you may sometimes hear from a boxer when a blow has got home. She hesitated, and that odd, lurking terror she had shown before was once more plain in her eyes. She stammered, hesitated, said nothing very coherent.

'I think Sir Albert claimed it as his own property, didn't he?' Bobby asked.

'He never took them, if that's what you mean,' the little woman cried, fierce as a kitten defying a mastiff. 'I don't know how you dare . . .'

'But I don't dare, because I didn't say he had,' Bobby pointed out, for, indeed, to him the disappearance of the jewellery seemed to suggest the innocence rather than the guilt of Lady Cambers's husband.

However, Miss Bowman collapsed into a flood of tears and a state so near hysteria that it was almost impossible to get anything more out of her. He did try to ask one or two questions about her car, and she insisted that it hadn't been used for several days, that certainly she had given no orders to have it cleaned—why should she, when it hadn't been used?—and that naturally Sir Albert had a key to the separate lock-up garage in which it was kept.

Why not? Most certainly, though, he would not take out the car without letting her know, and still more certainly he had not had it out on Sunday. He had had tea with her that day. He had been suffering from a very bad cold; on her advice he had gone home early to bed, and now the cold had turned to influenza, just as she feared, and very likely pneumonia next—and how cruel, cruel it was that she couldn't go to Cambers to nurse him.

Perhaps Bobby did not look as if he thought a bad cold a perfect alibi, for now, desperately and palpably lying, she announced that she had paid a visit to the garage at midnight, and had assured herself the car was there.

'Was there any special reason for your visiting the garage so late?' Bobby asked.

'Only to make sure it was safe,' she answered, after what was evidently a pause for reflection, and Bobby thought it unnecessary to pursue the subject further.

He took his leave then, quite convinced that Miss Bowman at least more than half believed in Sir Albert's guilt.

'If they got her in the box, they would make her say what they liked,' he thought. 'Her evidence alone would be nearly enough to hang Sir Albert.' And as he slowly and thoughtfully walked away down the street, there sidled up to him an elderly woman in whom he recognized the 'charlady' who had admitted him to Miss Bowman's flat.

It seemed she had a grievance against her employer. She hinted darkly that Miss Bowman was not all she seemed, not the 'class' that she, the 'charlady', was accustomed to. There was a gentleman, she said, and left the rest to be understood. Also, there had apparently been trouble about a bottle of whisky, of which the contents tended mysteriously to diminish, though no lady as was a lady would ever have thought so low as to use her tape-measure, and the 'charlady' herself a teetotaller from her earliest days, and ready to take her dying oath she never tasted anything except a glass of port at the King's Arms, and very cheap, too, with just a drop of gin, perhaps, at times, to give it a flavour.

Bobby hinted gently that all this was very interesting, but hardly any business of his, and the woman looked at him sideways, and said: 'You're police?'

'I expect you saw my card when I gave it you for Miss Bowman,' Bobby reminded her.

'There's a Lady Cambers been murdered,' she said. 'It's on all the placards.'

'Yes,' said Bobby. 'Well?'

'Sir Albert Cambers what's her husband—isn't he?—visits—her,' the woman went on.

'You mean Miss Bowman? Yes. I know.'

'Stays all hours he does, as the porter will tell you if you ask, and me always most particular them I obliges is respectable same as me.'

Bobby made no comment, but waited for what he felt was coming.

'There, you read that,' she said, and thrust a letter into his hand.

'Where did you get it?' he asked.

'Found it,' she answered; and, when Bobby still looked at her, she added: 'In her desk. Why not? She hadn't locked it.'

Bobby looked at the letter. It was addressed to Miss Bowman, signed by Sir Albert. It was long. It was couched in affectionate, if hardly passionate, terms. Certainly it testified to a considerable degree of intimacy. There were references to marriage and a future to be spent together. One passage ran, and Bobby read it twice: 'I won't go into details. It would be more prudent for you not to know them. But I have made up my mind things can't go on like this, unbearable for both you and me. I shall go through with it, no matter at what risk or cost. My dearest, I give you my solemn word. By Monday morning next, the obstacle that keeps us apart will no longer exist.'

Once again Bobby read this passage that seemed as though it stood out in blood-red letters, and the thick voice of the charwoman said, by his side: 'We've all got our duty to do, and now I've done mine.'

CHAPTER TWENTY-FOUR

'GREAT SCOTT!'

FROM THE LOCAL POLICE-STATION, WHITHER BOBBY had conducted the charwoman, there to deposit her letter and to repeat her statement before the C.I.D. officer for the district, Bobby took another bus to Fleet Street, to the office of the *Daily Announcer*, his next destination.

That incriminating letter was almost enough in itself, he thought, to bind the rope about Sir Albert Cambers's throat. An ugly meaning it had seemed to bear, and one only too easy for a jury to understand, and yet how completely this new re-marriage motive, as it might be called, seemed to clash with the rabbit-trap theory they had previously been working on, and how entirely left to one side were such odd incidents as Amy Emmers's prompt washing-up of the plate and glass found in Lady Cambers's den, or the discovery of Eddy Dene's pen on the scene of the murder.

To Bobby, as he sat and brooded, the general pattern of the case seemed more puzzling and confused than ever till there broke upon his troubled thoughts the voice of the conductor.

'Penny more if you're going on,' said the conductor, and Bobby apologized and hurriedly scrambled down as the bus began to climb the slope towards St. Paul's.

He had a few yards to walk back to where a gilded figure with a brazen trumpet presided over the magnificent portal of the imposing building whence the editor of the *Announcer* directed the world each day on the course the proprietor of the *Announcer* wished it to take—not that the world took any overwhelming notice.

A file was available, and once more Bobby studied intently the issue for that day on which there had occurred the quarrel between Amy Emmers and Lady Cambers that had so startled the rest of the household staff, had seemed to have no visible result, and had been so simply explained by the Emmers girl as due to neglected darning.

The tearing of the morning's newspaper Farman had mentioned might of course have been the merest incident, with no real connection either with the actual quarrel or its underlying cause. A newspaper is easily torn when tempers rise. Once again Bobby scanned it with care, noting every paragraph, examining even the advertisements. It was a long and tedious task, and in the end he was left with nothing but the two advertisements he had already noticed in the agony-column, the one a figure cipher, the other apparently a mere meaningless jumble of words.

He inquired what was known of the circumstances of their insertion, but they had attracted no special attention at the time, and such routine information as had been supplied was soon found to be false. So that line of inquiry was blocked, as Bobby had fully expected it to be; and with the two agony-column advertisements in his pocket he adjourned to a small restaurant near-by, where he ordered dinner, for it was now late in the day. While he was waiting for his meal and eating it, he would have, he thought, good opportunity to see what he could make of the two ciphers.

There are, of course, those at the Foreign Office to whom the darkest, most involved cipher is clear as sunlight at noon, but the hour was late, the Foreign Office would be seeking repose after its customary heavy labours of the day, and Bobby had a fancy, too, to try his own luck.

First of all he turned his attention to the combination of numbers, each set of which would probably represent either a letter or a word.

Carefully, intently, Bobby studied the thing.

'AAA. 504 : 634 : 346 : 51 : 394 : 303 : 25 : 66 : 259 :
21 : 465 : 734 : 33 : 925 : 77 : 652 : 14 : 284 :
634 : 88 : 285 : 148 : 146 : 99 : 381 : 12 : 291 :
54 : 645 : 51 : 66 : 259 : 194 : 66 : 493 : 14 :
181 : 34 : 77 : 23 : 394 : 13 : 205 : 88 : 565 : 34 :
394 : 15 : 99 : 23 : 934 : 834 : 54 : 66 : 42 :
292 : 24 : 304 : 21 : 66 : 12 : 205 : 77 : 52 :
3049 : 12 : 3930 : 25 : 88 : 54 : 34 : 0012 : 256 :
371 : 562 : 304 : 363 : 6363 : 99 : 6564 : 03047 :
24 : 914 : 925 : 22 : 914 : 6623 : 77 : 5555 : 14 :
59910 : 33 : 50306.'

It looked discouraging, but Bobby knew enough of ciphers to be aware that they are seldom so formidable as they appear at first sight.

To begin with, he counted that there were about eighty-five of the separate combinations. If each stood for a word, then that would make a somewhat lengthy message, and cipher messages in agony-columns are generally brief. Moreover, if a numerical combination representing words is used, it probably means that the system of reference to a previously chosen book by number of page and of word thereon has been adopted. Now some of these combinations of figures were in the thousands, and one or two began with a nought. But there are few books with over six thousand pages and none where the numbering starts with a nought.

Bobby made up his mind, therefore, to begin on the assumption that each set of figures stood for one letter.

Again he set himself to a careful examination of the cipher, so that a grieved waiter had to ask him if the soup was not to his taste since he was letting it go cold.

'Oh, no, very nice, very nice indeed,' answered Bobby, pushing it away untasted, for he had noticed suddenly that every now and then there occurred single sets of doubled figures that were always above five—though once the doubled nought appeared—that they occurred in regular progression from 66 to 99, and that such doubled figures seemed to occur nowhere else. It struck him that perhaps this doubling was for some special purpose, as perhaps to mark the division between words. He noticed, too, that towards the end of the cipher some of the sets of numbers were in four and even five figures, though at its start none exceeded three.

What reason, he asked himself, could there be in the nature of any scientifically constructed cipher for this sudden increase in the number of figures in each combination?

It seemed to him unlikely there could be any such necessary cause for so abrupt an increase. But if not, if there were no such reason, then this increase in the number of digits used must be arbitrary, impelled perhaps by an uneasy desire for finding greater security in greater variety. And if the number of the figures used had been increased arbitrarily, then it followed that some of them must be meaningless—merely inserted to confuse.

'Mirabeau's cipher,' he said to himself excitedly. 'I'll bet anything that's it.'

The waiter brought him his fish. He disposed of it in about two mouthfuls, so great a hurry was he in to pursue his idea.

The distinguishing feature of the familiar cipher known as Mirabeau's, from the legend that it was invented by that statesman, is precisely the abundance it provides of 'non-values', as they are called—of signs, that is, that can be inserted merely to confuse, being instantly so recognizable by the recipient of the message. As in this system each letter is represented by two figures, neither of which is ever above five, the higher figures—six, seven, eight, nine—as well as the nought, are available for this purpose, to be used merely to baffle those not in the secret.

The idea of the Mirabeau cipher is the simple one of breaking up the alphabet into five groups of five letters each, the selection of letters for each group, and their order in it, being entirely arbitrary. To each letter is then assigned, first the number of the group, from one to five, in which it occurs, and then the number of the order in which it occurs in that group. If, for example, 'e' is the fourth letter in the third group as arranged, then it will appear in the cipher as '34', and this can be varied by adding any of the 'non-values' as fancy dictates, since the recipient of the message will know that only the figures 3 and 4 possess any significance.

Calmer now that he felt himself on the trail, Bobby devoted almost equal attention to the chicken that had followed the fish and to writing out and musing on the cipher with every figure above five and every nought eliminated, and on the supposition that every doubled figure meant the ending of a word.

He knew that much the commonest letters in the English language are 'e' and 't'; 'a' 'o' 'n' 'i' following as bad seconds. Now the 'non-values' had been removed, a glance told him 34 was the most frequent combination, occurring about thirteen or fourteen times. At once he wrote down 34 as 'e'. The next most frequent combination seemed to be 25, so he put that down as 't'. Then he noticed that each of the first two words ended in 'e–t', and, since 'est' is a common termination, and agony-columns tend to superlatives, he wrote down the 33 sign as meaning 's'. So now the first two words stood '-ee-est, t—est', and it was little trouble to guess they were 'deepest, truest', thus giving the signs for four more letters. But what in agony-columns is likely to be truest and deepest but love?—especially as the last sign in the next word was again that convenient 34. The following word was in three letters beginning with a 't'. 'The' suggested itself, but there was no 34, and the second and third letters

were the same. 'Too' was Bobby's guess, and so was 'o'
added to the growing alphabet.

Working on these lines, Bobby soon had the key to the
cipher jotted down, thus:

I	II	III	IV	V
m a x o k	r i n v t	h b s e q	g f c z u	p l y d w
1 2 3 4 5	1 2 3 4 5	1 2 3 4 5	1 2 3 4 5	1 2 3 4 5

Thus 'm', for example, in this arrangement would
always be represented by 11, as the first letter of the first
group, 'e' by 34, as the fourth letter of the third group,
and so on, the message now standing revealed as:

'Deepest, truest love. Too hard up to come next week.
Need fiver at least. Deathless devotion. Wopsy.'

Bobby stared at it thoughtfully and disgustedly, and
inded with a certain heat.

'Well, of all the beastly waste of time and trouble,' he
said to himself ruefully, 'to think of all the time and trouble
and energy I've given to making out some ne'er-do-well's
attempt to borrow a fiver from the fool of a woman he's
got in tow.'

Bobby felt almost too sad and dispirited to tackle the
other cipher—if, that is, the meaningless jumble of words
he had copied out was in fact one. And if it were, and if it
turned out to be the same sort of thing as that he had just
read, he felt as though it would be unbearable.

However, he supposed stern duty compelled him to the
attempt. He read it over again:

'MMMM: They don't carved at the worry if aunt
meal with suspects gloves must of fix steel
and things once they drank for all the red
wine expect me through late the Sunday
helmet evening barred shall wait they
carved rhododendrons till at the coast
meal clear. MIT.'

Bobby had arrived at the coffee and cigarette stage now, and, after he had read this twice over, he felt that a liqueur was indicated as well, so he ordered one. Then he read the paragraph over again, and decided it might have been better to stick to soda-water. Could even the F.O., to whom ciphers are as the sun at noon, make head or tail of this gibberish? 'Suspects gloves' and 'Sunday helmet', for instance. 'Carved rhododendrons' too! What a phrase! Who wanted to carve rhododendrons, anyway? Yet if it had not been for that word 'rhododendrons' he would have been inclined to give the thing up as wasting time. But it was a rhododendron-clump in which some unknown person had certainly been concealed that tragic Sunday night, and was it only coincidence that a reference to rhododendrons appeared in this mad medley of meaningless words about which there seemed to Bobby to hang in some vague way a kind of literary flavour, somehow reminiscent of something he had once seen or heard or read? And idea struck him. At Oxford he had been friendly with a man who now held a position on the staff of that well-known weekly, *The New Prophet*, and had the job of explaining week by week how poor, how thin, how dull, was the literature of the day. He had, indeed, a widespread reputation through parts of Chelsea, and even into the outlying districts of Bloomsbury, for the way in which he could express that bored disdain wherewith the mere sight of a new novel afflicted him. Bobby found him on the point of setting out to join a midnight literary party, where reputations would be made and marred—chiefly the latter —and showed him the cutting from the *Announcer*. He read it with interest.

'A very fine bit of prose,' he declared. 'Gertrude Stein, I should think. I can't place it exactly, but it has the touch that only she can give. Notice the rhythm; notice with what care each word has been chosen to make its own effect. Oh, very fine indeed. Observe how splendidly, with what cunning art, that many-syllabled word "rhodo-dendrons" comes rolling in at the end.'

'Yes,' agreed Bobby, with a mingling of doubt and respect in his voice, 'yes—that word is what specially interested me.'

'Good,' said his friend heartily. 'Style always tells—wonderful how surely the most subtle effects appeal to the most primitive mind. Great Scott, there's my bus. Glad to have been a help,' he said as he fled.

'Great Scott!' repeated Bobby dazedly. 'Why, of course, why on earth didn't I think of that before? Makes it plain at once,' he said, with a grateful glance after the bus that was bearing his friend away.

CHAPTER TWENTY-FIFE

CHASE THROUGH LONDON

FULL OF HIS DISCOVERY OF THE MEANING OF THAT ODD jumble of words printed in the *Announcer* agony-column, convinced that it was the origin of the quarrel between Amy Emmers and her mistress, positive that it was proof of secret communication between Amy and Tim Sterling, but by no means sure what its exact bearing was upon the murder, Bobby hurried back to headquarters to report. There he was kept till late, writing out his report and submitting it, explaining how he had discovered the meaning hidden in those jumbled words, communicating by phone this new information to Colonel Lawson, who so far qualified his habitual disapproval of anything his sub-ordinates might do as to agree to Bobby staying in London to pursue other inquiries, and in especial to try to trace the missing Jones.

'Not,' pronounced the chief constable, 'that he's likely to be able to tell us anything useful. Probably he is what he said—a retired business man on the look-out for a country home, and when he heard about the murder he thought that didn't seem much like a peaceful rural retreat so he took himself off back to Town.'

'Yes, sir. Very likely indeed, sir,' agreed Bobby dutifully. 'But I always feel a little worried about that fountain-pen. If Dene's story is true, it seems possible the thing was last in Jones's possession.'

'Oh, for that,' answered the chief constable, and Bobby could almost see the gesture with which at the other end of the line Eddy Dene's fountain-pen was relegated to the realm of the unimportant, 'there may be fifty explanations.'

Again Bobby dutifully agreed, though reflecting to himself that it was certain only one of the fifty explanations could be the right one, and possibly it might have its significance. However, by now Colonel Lawson had rung off, so Bobby finished what he had to do, and then retired to seek his rooms and his bed.

In the morning he was up early, and went first to headquarters to see if any fresh instructions were awaiting him. None were. But reports had now been received from all the private detective—agencies known, and none of them admitted to any knowledge of anyone answering to the name or description of the elusive Mr. Jones.

So it seemed the hint, intended or not intended, Bobby had derived from Eddy Dene's remark that Jones asked as many questions as a detective, was proved valueless; and that the idea that he was a private detective employed to watch Lady Cambers had to be given up.

'Of course,' the official Bobby was talking to remarked presently, 'there are plenty of bright lads who mix a dash of private detection with a spot of blackmail, and who take care we never hear of them if they can help it, but this letter you got hold of from Miss Bowman's charwoman does not seem to tune in very well. If you're employing a private detective to watch your wife in the hope of getting a divorce because she's carrying on with someone—Eddy Dene, probably, in this case—you would hardly switch on to murder while your private detective was still on the spot, would you?'

'It seems a weak point in the case,' Bobby agreed. 'I suppose the prosecution would argue impatience and disappointment at lack of results leading to other methods —the method someone did adopt with Lady Cambers. It might be the private detective developed into the accomplice. There's always that fountain-pen to account for. I suppose it's been examined here?'

'Goes back with full report to Colonel Lawson to-day, I believe,' the other answered. 'Nothing significant discovered, though. What do you propose now?'

'To get hold of Jones.'

'How?'

'There's the match-stalk from the Hotel Henry VIII. I thought of trying there first.'

'Rather an off chance,' observed the other. 'If you draw blank there . . .?'

'I'll ask Colonel Lawson if we hadn't better call in the Press and the B.B.C.'

The official nodded agreement, and Bobby went on to the Hotel Henry VIII, where the manager, aware of the advantages of being on good terms with the police, received him amiably, and promised at once to do all he could to help.

But he looked blank when Bobby produced his precious clue—the burnt match-stalk with on it the name of the hotel.

'But, inspector,' he protested—he knew perfectly well Bobby was a sergeant, but thought a little temporary promotion might be acceptable, 'we order those things by the hundred gross. People come in for a cocktail and go out with a book of matches. It is wonderful,' he mused, 'how those who pay willingly our price for a cocktail love to feel they are getting their matches for nothing. It is, I suppose, as it were, a consolation.'

'I expect so,' said Bobby. 'I was thinking more of your staff,' he added.

'Oh, the staff,' repeated the manager, darkly brooding as on a word that to him, represented all that is incomprehensible, bewildering, dangerous, liable at any moment to offend a client, spoil a dinner, cork the best bottle of wine in the cellar—in a word, to let red ruin loose with cheerful unconcern. 'A staff,' he said bitterly, 'is capable of all—nor do I suppose there is one of them, from my secretary down to the man who washes the silver, who ever dreams of buying a match. I know I never do, superintendent,' he admitted candidly.

'What I thought,' explained Bobby, hopefully wondering if presently he would find himself 'commissioner', 'is that if we questioned your heads of departments, or whatever you call them, one of them might be able to tell us something useful. I know how carefully you pick your staff,' he added, in his most conciliatory tones, 'but you know, too, that waiters...'

'Oh, waiters,' repeated the manager, and again his voice expressed an even darker, stranger significance, so that one seemed to see in the waiter no longer a simple, shuffling, subservient figure, tray in hand, napkin under arm, but rather an immense and brooding form stooping from immeasurable heights to take cognizance of the follies and the weaknesses of man. 'Waiters,' repeated the manager, as one who pronounced a word of power. 'It is true. They see. They hear. They know. And sometimes they tell.'

'That's just it,' agreed Bobby.

'It is not, of course,' the manager pointed out earnestly, 'professional for them to tell. But occasionally it happens that they do. Then,' said the manager simply, 'the fat burns.'

'Exactly,' said Bobby.

'We will inquire. Any help that we can give, it is yours

'—we will do our utmost. One thing only we ask in return, inspector—that the name of the Hotel Henry VIII is not mentioned.'

Bobby, though a little disappointed that not further promotion, but a reversion in rank, had been his fate, promised no avoidable mention of the hotel should be made, and expressed his gratitude for the promise of help.

Well he knew how many are the opportunities the waiter has of acquiring knowledge; well he knew, too, the uses to which that knowledge may at times be put—as, for instance, when the dashing, middle-aged cavalier, or perhaps some lovely lady, does not very much wish it known with whom they dined that night of the supposed pressure of office work or the imagined visit to the aunt in the country. Or when business men, a strangely simple-minded, even innocent, race, not wishing their City friends to know what negotiations are in progress, avoid each other's offices, and meet instead in West-End restaurants, where they are almost equally well known, and then are surprised to find a paragraph in the financial columns that has been worth a fiver or even more to the observant waiter.

Now in long procession Bobby interviewed the banqueting-manager, his assistant, the head waiter, the deputy head waiters, the senior service waiters, the wine waiter, and none could help till at the last one remembered that about two weeks previously Lady Cambers had dined there. He remembered the name because a phone-message had come for her during the meal, and it had been his duty to identify her—no easy task in a crowded restaurant. He remembered her companion, too.

'Wasn't class,' the waiter explained. 'Anyone could see he wasn't—cut from the joint, two veg. and sweet, one shilling, was his usual. She paid, too; and when he got his hat and coat afterwards he asked if there was any charge!'

'Did he, though?' said the manager, impressed.

'So Peters—it was him there at the time—Peters said gentlemen gave what they liked, and he'—the waiter paused and drew a long breath—'he handed Peters twopence.'

'My God!' said the manager, appalled.

'Peters thanked him very grateful,' the waiter added, 'and gave him an extra brush-down, and said how much he hoped they would see him again. You see,' he explained, 'Peters knew it wasn't intended, only ignorance.'

'Would Peters know him again?' Bobby asked.

The waiter answered that Peters said he often dreamed of it still; and Peters, being produced, gave a description of the young man of the twopence that made it abundantly clear he was Eddy Dene.

It seemed a fact significant of much to Bobby. If Sir Albert had heard that his wife had been dining in a West-End restaurant with young Dene, it was quite possible he had entertained suspicions. Inquiries as to who had been the waiter serving Lady Cambers and her guest produced evidence presently that it was a man who had now left.

'Said he had been offered a good job in the country,' the staff-manager explained, 'and went off to it. Name of Jones—Sammy Jones.'

Bobby got Mr. Samuel Jones's address, and proceeded thither, only to draw blank once again. Mr. Jones had, in fact, lodged there, but had left on securing work in the country, and his present address was not known. Patient inquiry revealed, however, that he had been wont to 'use' a certain public-house in the neighbourhood. But there nothing had been seen of him for some time; nothing was known of his present whereabouts. One of the barmen, however, remembered that he had boasted sometimes of an interest he had in a small eating-house in Islington. To Islington Bobby accordingly proceeded, found, with some difficulty, the eating-house indicated, and discovered that Mr. Jones's interest in it consisted in the fact that he owed its proprietor nearly three pounds for meals there partaken of, so that the proprietor was nearly as anxious as Bobby himself to get in touch with Mr. Jones.

'Not that I suppose I shall ever see him again,' he opined pessimistically.

Persistent questioning by Bobby brought presently to mind that Mr. Jones had on one occasion mentioned that he knew the young lady who presided over the tobacco-kiosk at Hammersmith in the Square—a slender clue, but one Bobby felt he must do his best to follow up.

So he thanked the eating-house proprietor warmly, retired, paused a moment or two outside to relieve his feelings by a few appropriate words, reflected moodily that a detective needs a stout leg as much as, indeed more than, a strong head; thanked heaven that whatever might be said of his brains no one could deny the highly satisfactory measurement of his calves—no less an authority than John Ridd himself declares them the true test of a man—and made his way to Hammersmith, pessimistically persuaded that he would next hear of Mr. Jones in connection with Palmer's Green or Greenwich.

There is no need to follow the unfortunate Bobby through the rest of his perambulations as he raced and chased all that day through—and under—the streets of London, till he loathed the very thought of a tube, and felt positively sick at the mere sight of a motor-bus. It was evening when at last he discovered, within three or four hundred yards of the Hotel Henry VIII where he had started, the back-room above a greengrocer's which Mr. Jones had rented on his return the previous Monday from a holiday in the country.

'Says he'll be leaving for Canada soon,' the greengrocer remarked. He added enviously: 'An aunt left him a tidy bit of money the other day.'

'Did she, though?' said Bobby, interested. 'How jolly!'

And the greengrocer said it was—for them as had aunts.

It appeared Mr. Jones was out at present, but was expected back soon, and Bobby was shown into an ordinary shabby back-bedroom, very poorly furnished. And on the mantelpiece was a letter, stamped, sealed, ready for the post, addressed to Sir Albert Cambers. Bobby's look was grim as he took possession of this and put it in his pocket.

Then he set himself to wait, occupying himself jotting down in a new note-book, with which he had provided himself, since his other was full, the points in the case that seemed to him the most significant.

Fortunately it was not long before Mr. Jones returned, a little the worse for drink, but with apparently his legs more than his mental faculties affected, for the moment he saw Bobby he pointed an accusing finger at him.

'You're police,' he said. 'I know you.'

'Quite right,' agreed Bobby. 'There's my card.'

'About the murder, is it?' Jones asked.

'Right again,' said Bobby. 'What can you tell us about it?'

'I can tell you who did it,' Jones answered simply. 'Sir Albert Cambers.'

CHAPTER TWENTY-SIX

STORY OF AN EYEWITNESS

SUCH SIMPLICITY AND DIRECTNESS OF STATEMENT— made, too, with such evident sincerity—startled Bobby considerably. Jones had certainly had more beer than was good for him, and possibly it had loosened his tongue to some degree, but he was beyond doubt fully aware of what he was saying. There had even come a certain gravity into his manner.

'You know what you are saying?' Bobby asked him.

'I'm saying he did it, and so he did,' Jones answered as simply as before.

Bobby took from his pocket the letter to Sir Albert of which he had taken possession.

'Is that what you were writing to him about?' he asked.

'Here, I say,' Jones cried excitedly. 'Where did you get that?'

'It was on the mantelpiece,' Bobby said. 'Have you any objection to my reading it?'

'It wasn't posted,' Jones protested. 'I take you to witness. You can't say it was. There's no postmark. That's proof.'

'I've just told you I found it on the mantelpiece,' Bobby reminded him.

'It wasn't going to be posted, either,' declared Jones. 'See? You had better read it now you've got it. Tell you all about it, it will. But you can't bring it up against me when it wasn't posted. I don't deny as I was tempted, same as anyone would be—and me a poor man and all. Besides, it was him I was working for, and you've got to stand for them as pays you—or where's your reputation? you've got to think of your reputation when you've your living to earn.'

'So you have,' agreed Bobby. 'Sir Albert Cambers employed you, did he?'

'To find out what his old woman was up to. If I wasn't paid for it, you wouldn't catch me in a god-forsaken hole like that there where she hung out. And when I knew she was done in, I knew at once who had done it. What are you doing?'

'I'm taking down what you tell me,' answered Bobby, who had produced pencil and note-book. 'Afterwards it will be written out for you to sign. You understand, of course, it's pretty serious, what you're saying?'

'You can't bring it up against me when it was never posted,' Jones retorted defiantly. 'It ain't blackmail or nothing till it's posted. Mind, I don't deny as I was tempted same as anyone else—same as you in my place. "Let him that taketh a stone, take heed who it hits." That's Bible, that is. And I thought better of it. What I came back here for was to burn the letter, and go straight on to you chaps and tell you what I saw.'

Bobby thought it equally likely Mr. Jones had been out to re-enforce his resolution at the nearest public-house, and had returned to carry out an intention much beer had helped him to decide was best.

'What did you see?' he asked.

'You read that letter, and you'll know,' Jones answered. 'But you can't bring it up against me. It wasn't posted. I was going to tear it up, so I was. There hasn't been any overt act,' he declared, a little proud of a phrase that he felt put him on a level with his questioner. 'You read it, and you'll see.'

Slowly Bobby slit the envelope and extracted the contents—two sheets of closely written notepaper. It ran thus:

'To Sir A. Cambers, Esq., Bart.

'SIR,

'This is to say I saw all that happened Sunday night and now hasten to assure you my sympathies are all yours, besides which it isn't for me to judge others, never having been convicted myself through the jury saying there was no evidence, and there wasn't, either.

'I wish to state, sir, that acting on your honoured instructions to keep out and leave you by yourself to spot your good lady come out to meet the young gentleman, I did so, but being uneasy in my mind, re developments, I got out again by the window to avoid attracting attention as before.

'Sir, I saw it all, just what you did.

'I beg to respectfully say my sympathies are all yours as I fully understand and appreciate how you felt, being married myself and knowing well how often you feel the only thing to do is to out them.

'But for understanding so well and knowing just how you felt and how it happened, through having been married myself, not to mention the others, I should have gone immediate to the police if it had been an ordinary case, just as duty demands.

'Only then there's my duty to my employer I always remember just the same as my duty to King and Country.

'There's this, too, I've got to think of and suppose the police which is slow and stupid enough as all know and can read in the papers every day, and especial the young fellow they've got messing about there, only suppose they do come asking questions same as they may any moment almost.

'Done in, both of us, sir, if you ask me.

'I beg to respectfully suggest for both our sakes it would be best for all concerned if I went abroad, having friends in Canada and same speak well of it with my fare paid and adequate compensation for risk run and loss of situation and prospects (both first-class) at home.

'I beg to respectfully suggest one thousand pounds in one pound and ten shilling notes, in a brown-paper parcel, delivered to above address, same being moderate enough when you come in for all her money.

'I beg to respectfully suggest an early reply by return will oblige, same being necessary on account of me not knowing if I am acting right and feeling all the time I ought to split, being so troubled sometimes I feel I must though fully sympathizing as a married man and knowing well what it's like.

> 'I am,
>> 'Honoured sir,
>>> 'Your obedient servant,
>>>> 'SAMUEL JONES.

'Ps. What I mean is, the sooner I'm out of it, the safer for you.'

Bobby folded the letter again, and replaced it in its envelope.

'Quite plain,' he said. 'I take it Sir Albert had employed you to watch his wife?'

'That's right.'

'How did you get in touch with him?'

'Saw the old girl at the Henry VIII one night having dinner. They were at my table. You could see the young chap with her wasn't her class, and when you see an old girl like her standing treat to young fellows like him, you know what's up. I made a few inquiries on my own, because there's times when a gent will come down handsome for a tip about what his wife's been up to—worth a lot sometimes. I found out easy enough there had been a split, and Sir Albert was living in London on his own and sweet on a bit of skirt himself, and wanting a divorce she wouldn't agree to, aggravation being woman's nature all along. So I rung him up, and sounded him cautious what he would give to know how his wife was carrying on. He bit at once. Recognized the young man the moment I said what he was like, been suspicious of him before, seemingly. So he engaged me at five quid a week, my ex's, and a hundred bonus if it came off, fifty when the divorce suit was entered, twenty-five when the decree nisi was pronounced, and the rest of it when made absolute. He wasn't taking any risks. At first it seemed a wash-out. They had put it across so well down there where they lived it was only digging for bones and suchlike they was interested in; no one spotted what was behind. Lapped it all up at face-value,' said Mr. Jones, with a superior smile. 'Called the young fellow her ladyship's tame cat, and left it at that. Innocent lot down there—comes of watching the flowers grow and hearing the birds sing, but it takes more than a tale like that to kid you when you've lived in London all your life. But they covered careful—remarkable careful—I will say that for them, and I was getting a bit worried till I got the tip I wanted.'

'Who from?'

'I didn't know; I didn't ask; I didn't care,' answered Mr. Jones. 'The tip was all that I wanted. Never drag in others if you can help it, or most like they'll want a share of the coin. So I just said, "Thank you," and acted according to my own judgement.'

'But surely you knew who had told you?'

'I was rung up,' Jones explained. 'First time I was told to be in a call-box named at a certain time. So I did, and what was said was that Eddy Dene and Lady Cambers used the shed in the field where he did his digging to meet in, and if Sir Albert waited in the rhododendrons on Sunday night, then, somewhere about twelve or soon after, he would see Lady Cambers slipping out on the q.t. by the front-door, and if he followed her he would find Eddy Dene waiting for her in the shed. And that's what happened—only they fell out on the way,' concluded Jones, his voice a little shaken now, as if some sense of the tragedy of which he told had penetrated even his dull consciousness.

Nor did Bobby speak for a moment or two, so plainly did he seem to see visualized before him that dreadful deed in the darkness of the night. Presently he asked: 'Had you no idea who was speaking to you?'

'If you ask me—then, from internal evidence alone, it was Eddy Dene himself.'

'But why should he . . .?'

'Lummy, ain't that plain to anyone but a blessed dick?' demanded Jones impatiently. 'If there was an open scandal and a divorce through them being caught out that way, wouldn't she have had to marry him afterwards, and isn't a rich wife like her, even if a bit old, a catch for a grocer's assistant? Smart, I call it, real smart.'

'Yes, I see,' agreed Bobby thoughtfully. 'You told Sir Albert to be there that evening?'

'That's right. He told me to keep out of the way—wanted

it private, I thought at the time, but now I wonder if perhaps he had it in his mind all the while what he meant to do. But when the rain come down the way it did, I wasn't so sorry to get along back to the pub where I was stopping.'

'You mean,' Bobby asked, 'that Sir Albert had instructed you to keep out of the way, but you had intended to be on the spot all the same?'

'That's right. You never know what you mayn't pick up; though never once, I take my Bible oath, did I dream what he might be up to—a row, yes, and just as well to know the details in case of same coming in handy later on. But strangling is what never once I thought of.'

'It was the rain drove you back to your room?'

'That's right. Only it wasn't rain so much as buckets—buckets it was all right, and me never the same since laid up with rheumatic fever, and not wanting same any more, thank you. So I changed my things, being drenched, and waited a bit, and, soon as the rain stopped, I slipped out of the window same as I had before when I wanted to keep an eye on Lady Cambers and the young man without causing talk or notice took. But never any luck as far as that goes.' He paused and hesitated. 'It was a shock all right,' he said. 'Uneasy, I was, in a manner of speaking, and that's what took me out after changing to my dry things and being snug and dry in my room at the pub. But I never thought of—of that. Most like he didn't either; most like it just began with words, and then he got her by the throat and squeezed a bit harder than he meant, and there you are! Easy done. So then I thought I had best get out. You can see for yourself how awkward I was placed—with my duty being to go straight to the police and tell 'em all, and my duty to my employer, remembering how the Bible says who was their neighbour when the disciples fell among thieves, and what right had I to send my neighbour to the gallows? Torn I was—just torn this way and that—but in the end I come to it I must face my duty to the bitter end. I said to myself: "Samuel, split you ought and split you must, painful as such must be." So my mind being made up and peaceful, I come back to tear up that letter you've got; and blackmail you can't bring it in nor nothing else, when same wasn't ever posted nor going to be.'

'I'll have to ask you to come along with me to Scotland Yard and tell them your story there,' Bobby remarked.

'I thought that was coming,' Mr. Jones sighed dispiritedly. 'It's a place I never could abide. But duty's duty, though hard.'

'There's just one little point,' Bobby remarked. 'About Eddy Dene's fountain-pen.'

'Eddy Dene's fountain-pen,' repeated Jones, evidently puzzled. 'What about it? What are you getting at? I never even knew he had one. Why should I?'

CHAPTER TWENTY-SEVEN

THE CLEOPATRA PEARL AGAIN

TO SCOTLAND YARD, THEREFORE, BOBBY ESCORTED MR. Jones, and there Mr. Jones was somewhat pressingly invited to remain till his story could be further investigated, and till it could be decided whether a charge, if not of attempted blackmail, then of having been an 'accessory after the fact,' should be laid against him, or whether he should be accepted as a witness of fact for the Crown.

'And if you don't,' Mr. Jones pointed out, 'where's your case, for there's nobody saw but me?'

He was told in official language that all relevant facts would receive careful consideration, and then was shown to his room, a small, plainly furnished, but quite comfortable apartment, provided, too, with a bell within sound of which, he was assured, would be an attendant all night long, so that every want of his would be certain to receive prompt attention—and there are quite expensive hotels where a bell rung in the small hours has small notice taken of it.

While Mr. Jones was thus being so carefully looked after, Inspector Ferris was instructed to return in Bobby's company to Mr. Jones's lodging, where careful examination was made of all his personal belongings.

'May turn out,' said Ferris, 'this bird didn't only look on—he may have helped as well.'

The task was not very arduous, for Jones's personal possessions were scanty enough. They were contained in a large, old, and exceedingly shabby trunk, and a small, very smart, brand-new suit-case. The brand-new suit-case contained equally new underclothing, night-wear, and so on, all of good quality and recent purchase, some of the articles, indeed, with the price-tab still upon them. And in the old and shabby trunk all the contents were equally old and shabby. There was an ancient dress-suit—a necessity, of course, to a man who worked as a waiter—an old and threadbare lounge-suit in tweed, and other clothing, all very much patched and worn. To the aged tweed lounge-suit Bobby drew Inspector Ferris's attention, and explained why it seemed important, since at first the inspector did not seem to grasp its significance. But when he did he nodded in agreement.

'Yes, I see what you mean,' he agreed. 'It does look a bit fishy. We'll rub that in all right.'

'In the same way,' Bobby went on, 'if he was pretending at the Cambers Arms to be a well-to-do man, retired on what he had made in business, he had to have luggage to fit the part. That explains the suit-case being brand-new, and its contents all nice and new, too.'

'"Ex's",' pronounced Ferris, 'paid for by Sir Albert. And his tumbledown old trunk, and all the old junk in it that looks as if it came out of the Ark, he would just store somewhere. Hullo, what's this?'

Fumbling at the bottom of the trunk he had discovered a pile of manuscripts, the first scrap of paper they had found so far, since Sir Albert Cambers himself was apparently Mr. Jones's only correspondent. Examination showed the manuscripts to include a play, of which it seemed only the first half of the first act had been completed, the author having apparently not been quite sure how to go on after the Duke had fallen dead beneath the avenging pistol of the fiancé—a waiter at the Savoy—of the girl he had betrayed. There was also a novel, which, however, had more nearly reached its appointed end; an essay entitled 'Customers I have Known', but whereof only the title had been set down, the writer's feelings having apparently been too strong to allow him to continue, and, finally, a poem on the Jubilee, whereto had been carefully pinned a printed rejection-slip from *The Times*.

'Quite the literary man,' observed Ferris.

'Yes,' agreed Bobby. 'Yes. You know, that has its interesting side, too.'

'Nothing to do with us, anyhow,' declared Ferris, beginning to put the manuscripts back again.

'Only as a sidelight on character,' observed Bobby.

'Oh, well,' answered Ferris, not quite understanding this, 'I wouldn't say writing plays and poems and stuff proves a bad character—suspicious, of course, but some of them as does so is quite respectable.'

'Anyhow, there's nothing to show Jones ever tried his hand at any other blackmailing stunts,' Bobby observed.

'Never had such a chance before; dropped right into his lap, so to say,' Ferris pointed out. 'Must have thought it as good as an income for life. Nothing else here, I think.'

Bobby agreed, so they locked the room, warned the landlord that his tenant would not be back for a day or two, and that the room must not be entered or its contents interfered with in any way, gave him a receipt for the suitcase of which they had taken possession, and then separated,

Inspector Ferris returning to headquarters with the suitcase, and Bobby deciding that before he caught the last train back to Cambers there was time to look in at the Hotel Henry VIII and find out if anything was known there of Mr. Jones's literary ambitions.

He found they were well known, and had earned for him much respect, so that his aid was often sought in solving crossword-puzzles and other competitions in the papers. The rejection-note from *The Times* had, for example, been shown to many admiring fellow-workers, though one or two, suspicious or envious, had pointed out that it bore no name, and might quite easily have been sent to some other poet. Most of the staff, however, had been disposed to accept it as perfectly genuine—as, in fact, it was.

Even the manager had heard, apparently, but had not been pleased, for he distrusted literary men and thought his hotel the better without them, either as guests or staff.

'You never know where you are with them,' he complained. 'You may see two of 'em hobnobbing thick as thieves, and one of 'em perhaps selling neckties at one of the big shops, and the other with an income in five figures; and, what's more, the five-figure-income man listening humble and respectful while the necktie-seller tells him all about it—not natural, to my mind. You don't know where you are with 'em.'

'I've only known one,' Bobby observed. 'He came to a bad end. They gave him the Hawthornden Prize.'

'Pity,' said the manager vaguely. 'There's an American gentleman here—a Mr. Tyler. He's been talking about the murder—it seems he knew Lady Cambers.'

Bobby was a little startled. He knew the Yard had been trying, at the request of Colonel Lawson, to get into touch with Mr. Tyler, but so far without success, as he had been said to be motoring or visiting friends in France. Of course, if Jones's explicit statement could be accepted at its face-value, the case was at an end. And certainly, while it remained on record, there would be no possibility of bringing the crime home to anyone else. The statement of an eyewitness seems conclusive enough. Nevertheless Bobby had learnt to take nothing for granted, and never to be satisfied while any of the pieces of the puzzle refused to fit in the completed pattern. So he thought it might be as well to try to find if Mr. Tyler had anything interesting to say; and, when he sent up his card, he received, late as the hour was, a prompt invitation to join Mr. Tyler in his private room.

There Bobby was greeted warmly and with liberal offers of liquid refreshment, and of a cigar of incredible length, aroma, and cost. To his host's sad disappointment he declined these with many thanks and the explanation that he was on duty, and that duty forbade. It was 'the inside dope', as he called it, that Mr. Tyler had been hoping to hear, and Bobby satisfied him by giving him in strict confidence a few pieces of information he knew would shortly appear in the papers. Then discreetly he began to endeavour to discover if Mr. Tyler knew anything of interest, and Mr. Tyler explained that he was an old friend, both of Sir Albert and of Lady Cambers.

'She bossed him pretty badly,' Tyler remarked. 'But then she did that to everyone—only, always wanting to help. Always the philanthropist. Never let up on the job for an hour.'

'Your knew them before their marriage?' Bobby asked.

'Him, not her. Of course, he never had a chance once she made up her mind he needed her. Timid, nervous sort of bird, he was, didn't mind being told not to do things, but just hated being pushed. And her nature was to push—hard.'

'Seems the general idea most people have of them,' Bobby observed. 'There's an Eddy Dene, Lady Cambers was interested in. Do you know anything of him?'

'Oh, yes. Lady Cambers mentioned him once or twice

—spoke very highly of him. Sure you won't try a cigar? Made specially for me in our own factory in Cuba. No? Well, you Britishers are whales for duty, I will say that.'

'Had Lady Cambers any reason for speaking about him to you?'

'Yes. I'm interested in the old Maya culture. If I don't miss my guess—and my guessing hasn't been so bad, Wall Street way—there was a culture there calculated to knock spots off any you knew in Europe, whether Greek or Roman or Egyptian or any other. Yes, sir, that's my notion. I'm planning to investigate on the spot. Mrs. Tyler's coming—she's more interested 'most than me—and Professor Hawkins, from our new State University, and I've been looking out for suitable help. Last week—Wednesday it was; Wednesday afternoon—Lady Cambers rang up to say she had just what was wanted—this Eddy Dene and the girl he's to marry. Lady Cambers argued a young married couple like them would be more content and restful, and less likely to quit in the middle of the show, leaving us high and dry.'

'I don't quite see why,' observed Bobby.

'I don't know that I do,' admitted Mr. Tyler, 'but she put it very strong, and said if I hired them she would come in on the expense side. As a business proposition, it appealed. But I don't deny I rather got the idea she had some reason of her own for having those young people out of the way quick as she knew how. Mrs. Tyler thought so, too. But nothing to do with us.'

'Have you any idea why?'

'Tired of helping him maybe,' answered Mr. Tyler. 'Not that that was like her; in the ordinary way it was the others got tired first, not her. Anyway, it didn't worry me. Mrs. Tyler said maybe it was the girl had been the cause of the upset between Sir Albert and her. You never know. I didn't mind one little bit what it was so long as they seemed suitable. The girl had been Lady Cambers's own maid, and was willing and useful, she said. Quiet and well-behaved. And she said Dene would be much more useful than any ordinary valet. He hadn't done any of that kind of work but he could soon pick up all that was necessary out there in the jungle; he was naturally handy at fixing things, she said, and he knew a bit about archæology, having made a sort of hobby of it in his spare time from his pa's grocery-store. According to her, he would have been useful as a kind of secretary at times when he wasn't valeting me.'

'Dene was to come with you on this expedition as a valet-secretary?' Bobby asked. 'And his wife as maid to Mrs. Tyler?'

'That was the notion. Lady Cambers had it all planned out—doing good to them by finding them a job, and good to me and Mrs. Tyler by finding us thoroughly good honest capable British servants. I tell you, she was a whale for doing good.'

'Was it settled? Had you seen Dene?'

'No, but I guess it was settled all right. Lady Cambers knew how to put the "p" in "push", when she wanted a thing. It went or you bust—that was her motto. She had the money to back it, too. You see, this expedition is going to cost me money—real money, and I had no objection whatsoever to counting in her cheque. It did worry me some why she was so keen, so quick and sudden on us hiring those two young people, but they seemed suitable, and likely she thought it was for their good. And when,' he added thoughtfully, 'Lady Cambers made up her mind a thing was for your good, then she saw you got it.'

'Everyone I've talked to about her, says that,' Bobby remarked. 'A formidable lady,' he added musingly. 'Oh, by the way, Mr. Tyler, there was something about a pearl she had you wanted to buy—"Cleopatra's pearl", it was called.'

Mr. Tyler looked slightly disconcerted.

'Oh, you've heard about that,' he said. 'I suppose they told you down there at Cambers House?'

'We understood you wished to buy it—that you offered more than its market value...?'

'Double,' interposed Mr. Tyler, with feeling. 'Double, and the cheque written out and in my hand, and she wouldn't even look at it.'

'You were anxious to have it if you offered so much more than it was actually worth?' Bobby remarked.

'Mrs. Tyler set her heart on it,' the other answered. 'Cleopatra wore them as ear-rings, and Mrs. Tyler wants to do the same. I've one of the pair, you know, that's why I wanted the other. I don't deny I was real peeved she was so mulish about it. I saw in the papers it was stolen along with the rest of what she had. I told her myself it was a fool trick to keep it there in that room the way she did.'

'It was a little rash,' agreed Bobby, and though he made his voice as flat and non-committal as he could, Mr. Tyler began suddenly to go first a little red and then a little white.

'See here,' he said fiercely, 'you've got nothing on me. I can prove an alibi, for one thing. I can tell you just where I was in France the night it happened.'

'Yes, we know that,' Bobby answered, a little rashly, for Mr. Tyler's face went simultaneously, though in different patches, both more red and more white.

'Trailing me, are you?' he demanded. 'I'll...I'll...I'll...'

'Mr. Tyler, really,' Bobby protested. 'It's our business to trail, as you call it, to get in touch with, as we say, everyone in any way connected with this business. We knew you were interested in the Cleopatra pearl; we knew it had disappeared with the rest of the jewellery. It was possible you might have some information to give us. The thief may, for instance, offer it to you for sale. In that case we should, of course, expect you to communicate at once with us.'

'Oh, yeah,' said Mr. Tyler thoughtfully, dropping into pure American. 'I've had no such offer,' he added briskly. 'I don't mind telling you, though, I was specially willing to oblige Lady Cambers about this Dene boy and his young woman, so as to have her in a favourable mood next time I mentioned the Cleopatra pearl. Mrs. Tyler has just naturally set her heart on it, and when she has set her heart on a thing, then I don't hear the last of it till she's got it. See?'

Bobby said with sympathy that he did, and asked if Mr. Tyler had ever met Eddy Dene.

'Once,' answered Mr. Tyler. 'He was there, at Cambers House, once when I was there. Oh, and I saw him in his pa's store, too, when I went in to get some ink for my fountain-pen. I remember him because he seemed to be looking at you through the small end of the biggest telescope ever made. But Lady Cambers said that was only his way, and really he was always willing and eager to oblige. See here, young fellow, don't let any of your Scotland Yard smarties get it into their heads I know anything about that pearl, or I tell you straight—I'll go right away quick to the American Ambassador.'

'I am sure, sir,' Bobby answered formally, 'you will find you have nothing to complain of in the way the investigation is conducted.'

Mr. Tyler grunted fiercely, and looked fiercer still, and Bobby thanked him for all he had told him, and regretted that most likely he would have to be asked to repeat his statement later on, and might even be called as a witness at the adjourned inquest, and so took his leave.

To himself he thought, not without a certain grave exultation: 'At last it really looks as if the pattern were beginning to take form and shape.'

CHAPTER TWENTY-EIGHT

THE LOST HORACE

BUT NEXT MORNING, WHEN BOBBY PRESENTED HIMSELF at the headquarters of the county police, it was to find that Colonel Lawson had already, early as it was, departed for

London. He had been informed over the phone of the statement made by Jones, and, greatly excited by the news, had departed in his car at the earliest possible moment for Town, so as to interview Jones in person, and to hear further details on the spot.

'I expect he'll bring this Jones bird back with him,' Superintendent Moulland told Bobby. 'He said, before he went, he thought we ought to have charge of him. Anyhow, the case seems over if Jones was an eyewitness of what happened, and I can't say I'm sorry, either. Give me a schedule to work to—times, names, hours of duty—and I'll handle it as well as the next man. Give me straightforward instructions to clear the streets when there's a row on, and I do it. But all this guessing in the dark who was where, when, and why, and if they weren't, then where were they, and because of that then it follows that this isn't so but something else is—well, I tell you straight, young fellow, it has me beat, and, what's more, it isn't my idea of police work, either. Guess, guess, guess all the time, and if you're right you're right, and if you aren't you're wrong, and all of it the same game as buying a ticket in a sweepstakes and hoping you've got the right number.'

'Well,' Bobby protested, 'I don't think it's quite like that, because, after all, there's no guessing about it, only the facts. Get your facts, and if you've got them right so they fit without contradicting each other, then you've got the truth, too.' Very slowly he added: 'I've got so many facts now, I feel almost sure I've got the truth as well.'

'Not so difficult,' observed Moulland, smiling a little, 'when you've had the luck to be told who did it by someone who saw. Simple then to know who it was. But look here.' He fumbled in a drawer of his desk and produced a packet containing Eddy Dene's fountain-pen Bobby had discovered on the scene of the murder, and a long report on it from the new police laboratory. He put it down on his desk in front of him and poked at it disdainfully with his finger, and the longer he looked and poked, the broader grew his smile. 'There isn't a thing about it,' he said finally, 'they haven't found out up there. It's a wonder they didn't add a history of rubber, and a report on the character and record of the factory-manager. And what's it all amount to? Just nothing at all. Look at it yourself. The weight and length of the barrel and the cap, together and apart, put down to a decimal. The make of ink used— the "Perennial" they're pushing so much just now I dare say they would give a fiver to be able to say so in their advertisements. There was one of their chaps in here trying to sell it us so hard I had to get a sergeant in to throw him out before he would go. The amount of the ink in the barrel is noted—full up it was—and the very clever, useful deduction drawn that it hadn't been used much since filled. Very valuable to know that,' said Moulland, with heavy sarcasm. 'And they've found out the nib isn't eighteen-carat gold, as advertised, not by a long chalk, and there are no finger-prints, and the nib is unusually broad. Fat lot of good knowing all that. If you ask me,' said Moulland, putting pen, report, and packet back in his drawer, 'a sheer waste of time and of the taxpayer's money.'

'I was always interested in that pen,' Bobby observed thoughtfully; 'and more than ever now you know so much about it, it seems like an old friend. How did it get where I found it?' he asked abruptly.

'All the scientific laboratory reports in the world won't help you to know that,' retorted Moulland. 'Most likely one of the crowd dropped it. I've got some work to do,' he added meaningly. 'Real work, too, not guessing-competitions.'

'Yes, sir,' said Bobby, getting to his feet in obedience to this hint. 'Are there any instructions for me?'

'Only to wait here till the chief returns.'

'I suppose I can mooch round a bit till he comes,' Bobby asked. 'I'll keep in touch of course.'

'You can do what you like,' Moulland informed him, 'so long as you're on hand when wanted.'

'Thank you, sir,' said Bobby and withdrew, and first took himself to Cambers and the Cambers Arms, where he bought a soft drink, and then wandered round behind the building, where he found the landlord proudly surveying a placid-looking cow.

Bobby was not altogether sure what part of the cow the milk comes from, but the proud looks of the landlord warned him this could be no ordinary animal, and so he proceeded to praise it in terms of cautious vagueness that could have applied equally well to a motor-bus. And the landlord, a simple soul, responded bravely.

'She's all you say, and more, sir,' he assured Bobby. 'You wouldn't think, either, that last Sunday night I was sitting up with her expecting her to die on my hands. The whole blessed night I spent in the stable there, watching her, and look at her now.'

'That was the night of the murder, wasn't it?' Bobby remarked.

'That's right. Bad affair that is, too; never known the like before in these parts—though it's been good for business I would rather have been without. Crowds of people there've been, prying and staring, and wanting to know just where it happened and who did we think did it. I suppose you haven't found out anything yet for certain?'

'As a matter of fact,' Bobby answered slowly, 'I am fairly certain I know who is guilty, but there's always getting proof. Isn't the window just opposite that of the room Mr. Jones occupied while he was here?'

'Why, you don't think it was him, do you?' the landlord asked excitedly. 'He went off in a mighty hurry the very next morning after it happened.'

'Well, if we do suspect him,' Bobby observed, 'you can prove an alibi, can't you? He couldn't have left his room by the door and gone down the stairs and out by the back way without being seen or heard. If you were sitting up with your sick cow all night, he could hardly have climbed out by the window without your knowing. And there's no doubt he was in his room before the murder was committed?'

'That's so,' agreed the landlord, looking quite relieved. 'I'm glad of it, too. I wouldn't care to think we had had a murderer stopping with us.'

Bobby agreed that would have been an unpleasant thought, and took his empty glass back indoors, where he spoke to the maid who attended to the bedrooms.

'You remember Mr. Jones who left last Monday rather in a hurry?' he said to her. 'Can you tell me what luggage he had?'

The girl's lower jaw dropped.

'Oh, was it him did the murder?' she asked breathlessly.

'I believe,' sighed Bobby, 'if I asked who had the measles last, you would all think I meant that was who did it. Do you remember what luggage Mr. Jones had?'

'A small suit-case, that's all,' the maid answered, in a slightly aggrieved tone. 'It only held his shirt and drawers and his things to wash with, so missis told us to keep an eye on him in case he skipped off without paying; they try it on sometimes when they've so little with them as he had.'

'Thank you. That may be important,' Bobby said.

'He could easy have hid the rope in his pockets that was used to strangle the poor lady,' the girl pointed out, her eyes round at the thought.

'So he could,' Bobby agreed. 'Could you tell me what time he got back here that Sunday night?'

'It was after the rain began, because he was wet through with being in it; and it was before it stopped, I know that,' she answered. 'Somewhere about eleven, it would be. He went to bed, and he asked us to put his things in the kitchen to dry, and he had a hot drink—whisky, lemon, sugar.'

'After he had gone to his room?'

'Yes, about half-past eleven. I remember that because the clock struck the half-hour just as I was taking it to him, and I minded it was just the same time when I took the American gentleman an iced drink the night he stayed here. Only that was a hot, close night.'

'Do you mean Mr. Tyler?' Bobby asked, a little surprised. 'I thought he stayed with Lady Cambers.'

'They had words,' she explained, 'because he wanted to buy her big pearl they say's ever so large, and she wouldn't part, so he went off in a tear. That was why we were all surprised to see him back so soon. We thought he was going to have another try for it, but he never went near her that time. He was motoring to London from where he had been staying, and it got late, so he stopped here, that was all.'

'I see,' said Bobby. 'You say he didn't go near her that time. Did he any other, do you know?'

'Well,' the girl answered slowly, 'it was my day off week before last, and coming home a bit late I saw him sort of hesitating at the turning that leads to Cambers House, first going up it and then coming back. I watched him, it seemed so funny like, but then he got back in the car and drove off. I suppose he thought it wasn't any good —if she wouldn't sell it, she wouldn't, and no good worrying.'

'I dare say that was it,' agreed Bobby thoughtfully. 'One never knows. By the way, are you bothered with mice here?'

The girl, though slightly bewildered by this abrupt change of subject, admitted that they were. She also promised to communicate Bobby's offer—of half a crown for eight or nine live mice—to the potman, who would no doubt, she thought, be able to fill the order. She also promised, with giggles, to say nothing about it, and to persuade the potman to similar silence. Bobby's explanation

—that he wished to train performing mice for exhibition at the next police sports—she accepted as fully adequate.

'Tell him to take them as soon as possible to Station-Sergeant Weatherby, at the Hirlpool police-station, will you?' Bobby asked. 'I'll ring him up and tell him to expect them—that'll be half a crown for the mice, alive and in good condition, a shilling for the fare to Hirlpool, a shilling for delivery. That all right?'

The girl thought it would be, and Bobby thanked her for her assistance and the information she had given him, and, though a little worried over the unexpected references to Mr. Tyler, which he felt might, or might not, prove of significance, he went to the telephone-box and rang up the Hirlpool police-station to give his message for Station-Sergeant Weatherby—already warned to expect it. He took the opportunity, too, to ring up the Hirlpool dentist who had attended Eddy Dene, and received a prompt reply that Eddy had in fact visited him and had a tooth extracted on the day following the murder.

'Exposed nerve,' the dentist said. 'Sort of thing anything might set off—a chill, or biting on a crust or almost anything.'

Bobby thanked him, said that was interesting, and, ringing off, went on to find Ray Hardy, whom he discovered walking home from work in the fields. Bobby was really shocked at the young man's appearance; he looked so changed, years older, with red, inflamed, and sleepless eyes, and a pale, drawn expression.

'He's having a bad time of it,' Bobby thought. 'Dreams of being hanged every night. He'll have a nervous break-down soon.'

He called to Ray, who had not seen him yet, and when the lad turned and recognized him, he started violently, and looked more than half inclined to run. But he stood his ground, though plainly on the verge of panic.

'What's it now?' he asked, in a high, uncertain voice.

'Have you come . . . do you want . . . My God, if you're going to arrest me, do it and get it over. I can't stand it much longer.'

'No, because you've been drinking too much,' Bobby retorted; and to himself he thought: 'The poor devil is in such a state of nerves I believe I could get a confession out of him if I tried.'

'Well, a chap must do something to keep up,' Ray muttered. 'They all think it was me. It wasn't, but I can see them—pointing and thinking.'

'You ought to have more sense,' Bobby told him roughly, 'than to take to drinking at a time like this.'

'I've got to,' Ray repeated, in the same sullen undertone. 'I won't touch another drop when it's over.'

Bobby produced his note-book and a pencil, and presented a blank page.

'Write that there and sign it,' he ordered. 'Date it, too.'

Ray stared, hesitated, but then obeyed the order given with such confidence.

'What's that for?' he asked.

'So you won't forget,' Bobby answered. 'You're the sort that's best T.T.'

'How do you know I've been drinking? Been watching, have you?'

'Good heavens, no! I know because I can see; the same way I know you've been having bad dreams. I've got eyes in my head.'

'You're right enough about the dreams,' Ray admitted, shivering a little. 'What do you want, anyhow?'

'I want you to tell me all over again, from the very start down to the smallest detail, everything you did or thought or said that Sunday night, down even to the colour of the tails of the rabbits you trapped.'

Ray considered this.

'Rabbits' tails are always white,' he announced.

'Then don't forget to say so,' Bobby snapped. 'Wire

in.' And Ray, controlled by the other's stronger will, proceeded to repeat his story, amplifying the details, and admitting that in these midnight excursions of his he had made a practice of trespassing pretty widely on Lady Cambers's land.

'There was more rabbits there,' he explained simply.

'You never saw anyone else that night?'

'I kept out of folks' way,' Ray explained. 'I didn't want any talk about what I was doing out so late. I saw vicar, though.'

'Where was he?'

'Coming out of the old shed beyond Low Copse. He had been taking shelter there against the rain. It was where I was making for when it came on so hard, like a solid wall almost, so I was soaked through pretty well before I knew it had begun. I stood against a tree, and the water ran down it like a gutter-pipe. When it let up, and I moved, I saw vicar coming out of the shed.'

'You are sure it was Mr. Andrews?'

'Yes. It was dark, but he struck a match to light his pipe, and I saw him plain. He didn't see me. When he had gone, I went inside the shed, to wring the wet out of my things a bit, and there was a book of his on the ground. So I'd have known who it was even if I hadn't seen him.'

'What book was it? Have you got it still? Besides, how do you know it was his?'

'It has his name in it,' Ray explained. 'It's in foreign language—German perhaps; not French anyhow, I know that.'

He produced a small copy of Horace as he spoke, and Bobby examined it with interest.

'It ought to be returned to Mr. Andrews,' he said. 'I'll do that for you, shall I?'

'He'll want to know what I was doing round about there,' Ray protested.

'Then you can jolly well explain,' Bobby retorted, putting the book in his pocket. 'If you don't want it known where you've been, you shouldn't go there. It was Solon said that, or else Socrates.'

'Who're they?' Ray asked.

'Dead,' explained Bobby briefly, and Ray lost interest at once. 'I'll give you some advice on my own, though—keep off the drink, and if you must dream, dream of something jolly.'

With that he nodded a farewell and went off towards the vicarage, leaving behind him a puzzled, but relieved, Ray, and thinking to himself that things were really beginning to clear a bit.

'Though there's one pretty bad hurdle to get over,' he reflected, and grew lost in thought and deep contemplation thereof.

CHAPTER TWENTY-NINE

A QUESTION OF CIGARS

FORTUNATELY FOR THOSE LEGS OF HIS BOBBY HAD HAD to work so hard during his investigations into this case, he was lucky enough to meet the vicar almost immediately, so saving himself the journey back to the vicarage. Mr. Andrews knew him again at once, and paused of his own accord to speak, and when Bobby produced the little pocket Horace he claimed it immediately.

'Why, yes, that's mine,' he said. 'Where did you find it?'

'Have you any idea where you lost it?' Bobby countered cautiously.

'I've been wondering,' the vicar answered. 'I was reading it on Sunday night when I heard the rabbit crying I told you about.' He paused and blushed slightly. 'I amuse myself in odd moments,' he explained, 'by attempting a fresh translation of the Odes. Purely for my own amusement, you understand. After the intense strain of

Sunday, with its very strong emotional experiences, I—I don't know that I should like some of my brethren of the church to hear me say so, but I find something calm, cooling, even refreshing, in what is I am afraid Horace's very earthly philosophy. It seems to call one back from what is at times perhaps a somewhat dangerous exaltation of spirit. While we remain in the flesh we are not meant, I think, entirely to forget the flesh—and Horace certainly reminds one of it very effectively and even agreeably, in a way. So I have got into the way of often reading him on a Sunday evening. One feels, somehow, less risk of being—well, carried away. One relaxes the tension—loosens the bow.'

'Yes, I understand,' said Bobby, though in fact he found it a little difficult to take in this view of Horace as a kind of cold-water bandage to be applied to a head too fevered by strong religious emotion. But he supposed it might be effective. 'You can't remember what you did with the book when you went out?'

'I can't be sure. I didn't miss it till the next day. Then I thought perhaps I had put it in my pocket and it had dropped out. I remember when I was sheltering in the old hut by the Low Copse I took my coat off to give it a shake, as some raindrops had fallen on it before I got inside. I thought perhaps the book dropped out then, but when I went back to the hut to look, it wasn't there.'

'It had been picked up,' Bobby explained. 'The finder gave it me; that's how I got it. There's one little point—I think I've heard you don't smoke on Sundays?'

'It's a busy day; there is not time,' Mr. Andrews answered. 'That's all. Over Horace I often do indulge myself with a pipe.'

'Were you smoking when you went out to look for the rabbit?'

'No, I don't think so. Why? I remember lighting my pipe, though, as I was leaving the hut after the rain stopped.'

Bobby thanked him for what he had said, asked him to regard their conversation as confidential for the present, returned him the book, thanked him again for information he astonished the vicar by saying might prove of value, and then made his way to Cambers House, where Farman admitted him, and informed him that Sir Albert was still in bed, though making a good recovery.

'Nasty turn it's been,' Farman said. 'Touch of pleurisy. Might easily have turned to pneumonia, the doctor says; and that's always touch-and-go.'

'I should like to have a little talk with him,' Bobby explained. 'There are one or two points he might be able to clear up.'

Farman said he would inquire, and came back presently to show Bobby to the room where Sir Albert was still in bed, though he had been promised permission to get up that afternoon.

'Got any news? Found out anything yet?' he greeted Bobby, as soon as the young detective entered the room.

'Well, sir, there have been some very remarkable developments,' Bobby answered, 'and at present I am trying to clear away the accessories, so to say. If we can only get to the bare facts, we shall know where we are.' He paused for a moment, wondering to himself what the other would say if he knew that these developments included a statement of an eyewitness who claimed to have seen Sir Albert himself commit the murder. 'There are one or two points I should like to put to you,' he went on.

'Wish I had been able to get about,' Sir Albert remarked. 'Rotten luck being tied up like this.'

'If I may say so,' Bobby observed, 'it was only to be expected after spending a few hours in wet clothes in the midst of dripping rhododendrons.'

Sir Albert jerked to a sitting position as if under the impulse of sudden physical pressure. His eyes had fear in them, and he moistened with his tongue his lips that had become suddenly very dry. Bobby made no comment, but watched him steadily. After a time, Sir Albert muttered: 'I was going to tell you . . . of course . . . I was a fool not to at first . . . how did you find out?'

'It would have been better to be open about it,' Bobby said, ignoring this last question. 'Why weren't you?'

Sir Albert lay back in the bed and stared at the ceiling.

'Makes it worse I didn't, I suppose,' he said. 'There was a kind of choking feeling round the throat I had that stopped me when I thought of telling you. Besides, why should I? And then my head was going like a traffic roundabout, and I could hardly think. If you ask them, they'll tell you I was a bit delirious that Monday evening. But I was going to explain the whole thing as soon as I felt up to it.'

It was a statement concerning whose accuracy Bobby felt some doubt. Still, he supposed the sharp attack of influenza Sir Albert had suffered did to some extent excuse his silence. He had certainly been in no condition to consider calmly his course of action.

'If you care to tell me all you can now, it may be useful,' Bobby said slowly. 'But I must warn you first that you will most likely be asked soon to make a formal statement. Certain of the developments I spoke of just now are very grave, and, I think you ought to know, seem to point to your own guilt.'

Sir Albert nodded gloomily.

'Just my luck,' he said. 'Things always happen like that for me. The only time I've ever tried to catch anyone out in my life, and of course I get caught out myself. I know I was a fool to try to keep things quiet. I've been thinking that all the time I've been lying here. God knows, poor Lotty was enough to drive anyone mad with her, "Just think it over and you'll see I'm right," and her, "Of course, that's what you must do, so you had better start at once," but I would never have thought of hurting a hair of her head. Then there's the jewellery that's been stolen. I am not likely to have stolen my own property, am I? Of course, you'll say I was trying to make it look like a burglary. And then, what the blazes was Lotty doing out at that time of night, unless it was to meet young Dene? And I'm told now, there's proof he was in his room at home when it happened.'

'You suspected there was something between Lady Cambers and Eddy Dene?' Bobby asked. 'I haven't come across anything to make me think that was so. Had you any reason?'

'It was Oscar Bowman put me up, first, to what was going on,' Sir Albert replied. 'When Lotty took Dene up, I thought it was just one of her fads—just someone else to boss; someone else's life to manage and arrange.' He said this with a certain bitterness, and then, after a short pause, went on: 'She spent money on him like water. If I wanted a pound or two it was: "Why? What for? What have you done with what you had?"—as if I were at school still, and had spent too much at the tuck-shop. But when Dene wanted anything, she drew whacking big cheques without a murmur. Oscar Bowman told me right out there was more to it than I thought. Then one day . . .' Again Sir Albert hesitated, looked embarrassed, finally made up his mind, and continued with a rush: 'I dare say you've heard about Miss Bowman. She always understood me much better than Lotty did. When she wanted help and advice, she got into the way of turning to me quite naturally—Lotty never did that. Oscar felt he ought to tell me certain things he had heard, and then there was an open breach—a scene, in fact—when Lotty had the bad taste to walk right into the Bowmans' drawing-room without a by-your-leave, or with-your-leave, or anything —just walked straight in. That made me feel things had become intolerable, and I decided to take a flat in London, and then I got more information backing up what Oscar said—that Lotty and this grocer's assistant she was infatuated with were being seen together in West-End restaurants. I felt that had to be looked into—after all, Lotty bore my name still—and I made up my mind if I got the evidence I would go into the divorce-court with it. Oscar said it was my duty, and I felt he was right. I sent an agent down here, and he told me there was no doubt about it, and he had reliable information that they would be meeting late on Sunday night in the sort of hut she put up for him on the pretence it was needed for what he called his pot-holes. It was settled I was to see for myself. I was to wait outside the house, and, when she came out to keep the appointment, I was to follow her. I felt I had a right to know the truth, and I wrote to Miss Bowman to tell her I hoped we should be free to marry soon, and I borrowed her car—one I had given her myself only just before. I had the key to the garage where she kept it. On the way I took a wrong turning in the dark, and that delayed me, and then there was the rain. It came down in sheets. I drew in to the side of the road to wait till it was over. You could hardly see a yard before you, it was so thick—like a curtain. Where I had drawn up there was a dip in the road—at the West Leigh cross-roads. It was flooded in no time, and a big Rolls-Royce went by, making such a wave, the water came right over the footboard. I moved on and sheltered again, and it must have been close on midnight before I got here.'

'When you arrived, you hid in the rhododendrons near the front-door of the house?' Bobby asked.

'I took shelter there,' Sir Albert answered coldly, evidently not approving of the word 'hid'. 'It was extremely wet, but there was nowhere else where I could be sure of not being seen and yet be positive of seeing myself if Lotty went out to keep her appointment—or came back from it, for that matter. I waited till nearly three, and then I gave it up and drove back home, and I had hardly got to bed when I heard what had happened. I saw at once it was a very awkward position for me. But I had had nothing to do with it. I had seen and heard nothing all night, so what was the good of drawing attention to myself by saying anything?'

It was in character, Bobby thought, for Sir Albert Cambers to adopt always what seemed at the moment the line of least resistance.

'Have you any suspicion yourself who is guilty?' he asked presently.

'I made sure at first it was young Dene,' Sir Albert answered, 'but I couldn't think why. Besides, it seems he was in his room at home at the time. Rather looks as if there hadn't been any appointment, after all. Only, my agent said he was sure of his facts—reliable information, he said. In the village, Farman tells me they think it was very likely young Ray Hardy. Apparently he had used threats about Lotty. That wasn't through her doing good to him; it was her doing good to the rabbits—always doing good, Lotty. Then, I know it sounds fantastic, but when you're lying in bed with nothing to do but think, you think a lot, and I've been wondering if it could be Andrews —the vicar, you know. He told me himself Lotty was helping Dene to destroy men's faith, and couldn't I stop it, and I told him to stop it himself, only to try stopping the earth going round the sun first, by way of practice. And he said any means would be justified in the sight of Heaven, for men's souls were in danger. The fellow's a fanatic, and a fanatic can work himself up to any pitch.'

'I suppose,' asked Bobby, 'while you were—er—waiting in the rhododendrons, you didn't see or hear anything or anyone, did you?'

'Farman, smoking my Cabanas,' said Sir Albert, looking very black indeed. 'Cigars that work out at three and nine each, buying them by the hundred. I keep them for a special treat, and there was Farman, if you please, leaning out of his window where he sleeps in the little room next the pantry and enjoying them as calm as you please— seven-and-six gone up.'

'To make a butler's holiday,' sympathized Bobby. 'Too bad; though I wouldn't grudge him them this time. It may be useful. I take it, you are sure they were your Cabanas?'

'I could tell one whiff a mile away,' declared Sir Albert, with emphasis, 'and then, besides, I got Emmers to bring me the box. I happen to know there were fourteen left. I make it a rule to order a fresh box when they get down to a dozen, and the day before I went away from here to London I counted them to see, and there were fourteen. Now there are ten left. That means four gone—two that evening while I was watching with nothing better to smoke myself than some Bulgarian Tempo cigarettes, and two some other time when Mr. Farman wanted to enjoy himself. I'll have a word or two with him when I feel a bit stronger.'

'If you don't mind,' Bobby said seriously and gravely, 'I will ask you very specially to say nothing to him at present.'

Sir Albert, who was really still a little weak, had been lying down in his bed during almost all this conversation, but now, again, he jerked himself abruptly to a sitting position, exactly as if someone had suddenly pulled the string that actuated him: 'Do you mean you think Farman did it?' he asked eagerly.

CHAPTER THIRTY
APPROPRIATE PENALTY

ON LEAVING SIR ALBERT, BOBBY ASKED IF HE MIGHT use the library for a few minutes, and there he made notes of their talk, and put his mind to the problem of how far the fresh facts he had learned confirmed, contradicted, or illumined those he had so laboriously collected.

To him his case seemed now fairly complete, and yet

he could not feel certain how others would regard it, or whether the logical structure he had built up in his mind might not seem to them to have but shaky foundations. And no erection, mental or physical, is stronger than that whereon it stands. Then, too, he had to admit that in his theory there were two weak points that might be considered fatal to it—one of them being that he had as yet no explanation to offer of the missing jewellery.

He put his note-book away, and, turning to examine the book-lined shelves, soon found a complete set of Walter Scott's novels. There was no copy of the poems, however, though a gap at the end of the long line of novels suggested one volume might be missing. Bobby went into the hall, and, finding Farman there, said to him: 'Didn't Mr. Sterling bring back that copy of Walter Scott's poems he borrowed?'

'Not that I know of. He didn't tell me if he did,' Farman answered, and then began to think, marking the operation by slowly opening eyes and mouth to their widest. 'How did you know he had it?' he asked.

'In the same way,' Bobby answered severely, 'that I know you were not telling the whole and exact truth when you said you were smoking your pipe at your bedroom window on Sunday night.'

'But I was. I don't know what you mean. Who says I wasn't?' demanded Farman, but with a certain uneasiness.

'I do,' Bobby retorted. He went on with authority: 'Now you just listen to me. There are small breaches of duty and discipline that don't matter very much. Murder is different. You get that?'

'I don't know what you mean,' Farman muttered. 'I don't know what you're after. Anyhow, I've my work to see to,' and he made as if to walk away.

'Just as you like,' said Bobby grimly. 'Only I warn you if you don't talk to me now, you'll probably have to talk to someone else later on.'

Farman was beginning to perspire gently. He hesitated. He made a fresh movement to go. Bobby took no notice. Farman came back.

'I suppose it's about those damn cigars,' he burst out.

'What cigars were those?' Bobby asked, looking full at him.

'Oh, you know,' Farman answered sulkily. 'Two of Sir Albert's own I pinched from his box.'

'Yes, I know,' Bobby said slowly. 'But I'm not worrying about them. Pinching your employer's cigars is one thing. Murder is another. What I'm trying to do is to find out who murdered Lady Cambers, and for that every little detail is important. One item that doesn't, or does, correspond with another may make all the difference to the theories we are working on.'

'I don't see what my wanting to try those cigars has to do with it,' Farman muttered sulkily. 'Get me the sack if it was known. I never done such a thing before. It just came to me Sir Albert was away and not likely to come back, and it seemed a shame them lying there wasting, as you might say. Her ladyship told me to offer them to Mr. Tyler when he was here, only he wouldn't have one, preferring his own, so I thought it would be easy to tell Sir Albert, if asked, Mr. Tyler had had them by her ladyship's orders.'

'That's all right,' Bobby said. 'I don't care anything about that. What I want to establish is that you were at your window that night for some considerable time after the rain stopped, long enough to smoke two cigars.'

'That's right,' admitted Farman sulkily.

'Did you see or hear anything?'

'No, no-o, nothing, only that I thought I heard a sound of something moving coming from the rhododendrons—I just thought it was a cat or something. I didn't bother.'

'When you saw the cigarette-ends in the rhododendrons next morning, you knew quite well it must have been Sir Albert who had been there?'

'I didn't know ... I just thought ... I wondered ... it wasn't my business to say anything.'

'It's always wisest to tell the truth,' Bobby said dryly. 'It generally comes out in the end.'

'I didn't see it was up to me to say anything about what I didn't know,' Farman protested. 'I had nothing against Sir Albert, and it was him I had to look to to keep me on or give me a good reference if he was giving up the place. You don't know what it's like these days looking for a new place at my time of life, especial if ...'

He paused, and Bobby guessed that what was in his mind was a fear that the old blot on his character—the term he had once served in prison—might be brought up against him. Probably that was the perpetual terror of his life, but Bobby saw no reason to refer to it at present, and waited patiently, as if he had no idea of what that 'especial' meant —though it helped to explain why Farman had jumped so quickly at the chance of keeping Sir Albert's secret, and so establishing a hold upon him. Farman went on: 'I reckoned if I stood by him, then he would stand by me. You aren't going to bring up those cigars against me, are you? If that gets out, it'll be all up with me getting another place. You wouldn't believe how particular people are about your character when applying—it's my belief,' said Farman bitterly, 'the Archbishop of Canterbury wouldn't stand a chance of placing himself if he had to show a character like us—archangels from Heaven is expected, seemingly, for thirty bob a week, all found.'

'Sounds cheap for an archangel,' Bobby admitted.

'If it comes out public about those cigars, I'm done in,' declared Farman.

'Sir Albert knows already,' Bobby pointed out. 'It depends on him. If I were you, I should get some others and put them in the box to make up the right number. That might smooth Sir Albert down a bit, perhaps.'

'Yes, but,' Farman said, though brightening a little,

'I can't get them except buying them, and they cost four bob each by themselves.'

'People with a taste for expensive cigars have got to pay for it,' retorted Bobby callously, and Farman looked gloomy again as he reflected on the hard path that, at any rate at times, the transgressor is forced to tread. Bobby went on: 'Miss Emmers is still here?'

'Yes. She's been down to the village for something. She's just come back,' Farman answered distrustfully, by no means sure this new question did not herald some fresh bombshell about to explode under his feet.

'I should like a few moments' talk with her, if she can spare the time,' Bobby said. 'Could you find her for me, and let us have the library to ourselves for a quarter of an hour or so?'

'Certainly, certainly,' Farman said, and went off in a hurry, very relieved to escape from Bobby's vicinity. 'Two at four bob each,' he muttered to himself, as he hurried to find Amy. 'That makes eight bob—eight bob, and two-penn'orth of shag would have done me just as well; more flavour, too—more bite.'

He shook his head in genuine self-reproach, and then found Amy, who, receiving his message without comment or visible emotion, took her quiet way at once to the library, without even stopping to remove her outdoor things.

She entered very quietly, her manner aloof as ever, and, without speaking, paused by the table, waiting for Bobby to speak. He looked up at her, and again found himself wondering what this cold restraint of hers might hide—whether there was inner fire or whether it was ice all through. He hoped she would speak first, and waited, but she stood silently, a little as though she had forgotten, or was unaware of, his presence, or else found it entirely negligible.

'Won't you sit down?' Bobby said at last.

She turned her gaze upon him then, thoughtfully, as if

considering either him or his suggestion with a wholly detached interest—or lack of it. But somehow he became aware of an impression that she considered his invitation slightly presumptuous. It was as if she had conveyed to him a reminder that this was not his room or his house, that he had not even the permission of the owner, but only of a servant, to be there. He found himself flushing slightly, and it was almost as if to defend himself that he said: 'I am an officer of police.' And then: 'Your mistress has been murdered. Brutally murdered. Murder is a dreadful . . .'

She interrupted him then.

'Is that what you wanted to say to me?' she asked, and quiet as was her voice, and few and simple her words, he knew now that it was fire hidden beneath the surface of her icy restraint—fire of the fiercest. Somehow, too, she made him feel that those banal words of his merely mocked the truth—that murder was a thing to darken the sun at noon and rend the firmament itself.

'Well,' he muttered, 'now, then, it gets like routine with us, just a problem to be solved, the day's work.'

She had an air of listening to his excuse, of considering it, of dismissing it as worthless. He told himself it was unfair, and that he, a sergeant of the Metropolitan Police, wasn't going to be browbeaten and intimidated by any girl with a gift for silence and immobility. He said, a little more loudly and harshly than was his custom: 'Why were you and Mr. Sterling communicating by cipher advertisement in the *Announcer* agony-column?'

'Because,' she answered, without a trace of emotion or surprise, or even hesitation, 'it was our right to communicate, and if he had written to me here, or at home, his handwriting would have been recognized.'

'How do you mean, it was your right to communicate?'

'He is my husband. We were married three weeks ago.'

Bobby gave a little jump, for this was something he had not expected.

'Oh,' he said, trying to consider the implications of this fresh piece of information. 'Did Lady Cambers know?' he asked.

'No.'

'It was kept secret from her?'

'Yes. She would have been very angry. It was not what she wanted. She liked people to do as she wished.'

'Her anger might have had uncomfortable results,' Bobby suggested. 'She had lent money to Mr. Sterling. Eddy Dene depended on her help.'

'That is so,' she agreed gravely.

'Did anyone know of your marriage?'

'Eddy knew.'

'Not his parents?'

'No. Eddy was very anxious they shouldn't know just yet. He wanted to bring them round to the idea by degrees.'

'Lady Cambers didn't suspect anything?'

'Yes. I felt she did. I wrote and told my husband. He replied by a message in cipher in the *Announcer*. Lady Cambers saw it. She showed it me. She was very angry. She tore the paper in half nearly. Afterwards she got quieter. I don't think she had any idea we were married; she thought we were friendly, and making appointments with each other. She calmed down, and said Eddy and I must marry at once.'

'What did you say?'

'Nothing. I thought I would wait till Sunday and I could ask Mr. Sterling what he thought we ought to do.'

'Did Lady Cambers read the cipher?'

'No, she tried, but couldn't. But she saw it was signed "Mit", and that that was "Tim", spelt backwards. And she guessed the four "M's" at the beginning meant me. She tried to make me tell her what it meant and how to read it, and I wouldn't. It was quite simple, really.'

'The key was a quotation from Scott's "Lay of the Last Minstrel", wasn't it?' Bobby asked, and quoted:

> 'They carved at the meal,
> With gloves of steel,
> And they drank the red wine through the helmet
>   barred.'

He went on: 'What was done was to jumble all the words together—those of the quotation and those of the message—so it looked like a lot of gibberish. But when you struck out the words of the quotation, those making up the message were left. Original dodge, as far as I know. Only he chose rather a well-known passage—as soon as I read the thing I thought there was some sort of literary flavour about it, though it took me a long time to spot what it was.'

Amy was not listening. Abruptly, and even a little fiercely, she turned on him, almost as if giving him her full attention for the first time.

'Is it true what they are saying in the village,' she demanded, 'that someone has told he saw Sir Albert kill Lady Cambers—that he was watching while it happened and saw it all?'

'Oh, has that got about already?' Bobby asked, slightly disconcerted.

'Everything gets about in Cambers,' she answered, not with any contempt or condemnation, both of which, indeed, were alien to her, but simply as mentioning a recognized fact. She added, after a long pause: 'It doesn't seem possible; it's like a sheep turning into a wolf.'

Bobby, watching her closely, felt that for once her imperturbable reserve was shaken. For the first time it seemed to him that, in their duel of wills, he had her at a disadvantage; he felt as the bowler feels in cricket when he senses a hesitation, an indecision, in the batsman's play. But he had no idea how to continue, how to take advantage of this weakness—if weakness indeed it were. Only, he felt he must not let the moment pass, and he understood that already she was once more wrapping herself in her cloak of silence and reserve that for the moment she had seemed inclined to let fall. He realized he must go on questioning her, even at random.

'Mr. Sterling kept his appointment on Sunday?' he asked.

But when she answered, it was her own train of thought she followed: 'How could a sheep turn into a wolf?' she asked.

'The most unexpected people do the most unexpected things,' he reminded her. 'We see that often in our work. A man holds the ape or the tiger by the ears, and no one dreams it's there, till one day his grip loosens and it takes full control.' He went on: 'It is the private detective Sir Albert himself employed to watch Lady Cambers who says he saw what happened.' Bobby's voice took on a very hurt official tone. Moulland had evidently been talking. Most irregular to have let the contents of Jones's statement leak out in this casual fashion. 'Nothing ought to have been said about it just yet,' he insisted; and then repeated his question: 'Did Mr. Sterling keep the appointment on Sunday?'

'Yes.'

'He rode down on his motor-cycle, didn't he? What time did he arrive?'

'I don't know exactly. He waited in the rhododendron-bush till I turned up the light in my room. That was the signal to let him know I was ready. It was twelve o'clock. I waited till then to be sure everyone was asleep. He had had a breakdown on the way, and been caught in the rain. He was wet through.'

'You let him in by the garden door?'

'Yes, It was unlocked. I noticed that. I thought Farman had forgotten to lock it. He did sometimes. But I suppose, now, Lady Cambers went out that way. I fastened it after Mr. Sterling left.'

'He saw nothing of Lady Cambers?'

'No. She must have started out as soon as the rain stopped—before Mr. Sterling got here. Besides, if she was going to Frost Field, she would go round by the back of the house. Mr. Sterling used to wait at the front, so he could see my window. I turned my light up and down twice, as a signal, and when he saw it he went round to the garden door and waited for me to let him in.'

'You gave him some brandy?'

'He was so wet, I was afraid he would get a chill. I had some in my room. I got it when we were going to Paris—for the crossing.'

'Afterwards you took away the glass and plate he had used, and washed them up?'

'Yes. I had read about finger-prints in the papers.'

'How long did Mr. Sterling stop?'

'It was just three when he left.'

'Do you know if he saw or heard anything?'

'He came back and told me he had seen someone near the rhododendrons. He thought it was Sir Albert, but he wasn't sure. It was dark. Afterwards we heard a car starting up.'

'Farman sleeps on the ground floor. Do you think he heard anything?'

'No. I told Mr. Sterling to be careful when he passed Farman's window. He told me, afterwards, he heard him snoring.'

'That was three on the Monday morning?'

'Yes.'

'You should have told us all this before.' Bobby said severely. 'Do you realize you've been making yourself uncommonly like an accessory after the fact?'

She appeared to be considering both this and him with her usual detached interest. In her quiet voice, she said presently: 'Have I? I should not have told you now, only I suppose if what happened was seen by someone, there can be no more doubt.'

He was watching her intently, trying to follow the workings of her mind. He still had the impression that she was allowing more of herself to be seen than often happened. He said abruptly, and rather loudly: 'I think at first you thought that it was Eddy Dene, didn't you?'

CHAPTER THIRTY-ONE

DUEL OF WILLS

FOR A MOMENT HE THOUGHT SHE HAD NOT HEARD, AND then, to his immense surprise, he saw there were tears in her eyes. He would have been no less surprised if, standing before the statue of the Venus of Milo, he had seen the same thing happen. He understood, however, that it was this news of the statement made by one claiming to have been an eyewitness of the deed that had so shaken her, both in itself and by the relief from doubts and fears that it had brought her. She said in a voice so low he could hardly catch the murmured words: 'Yes, that is quite true. I did think it might have been Eddy. It was very wicked of me.'

'But now you believe he is innocent?'

'If it is true an eyewitness has come forward,' she said; and, when Bobby made a slight gesture to confirm, she went on: 'Well, then, he must be, mustn't he? Only even now I can't understand how Sir Albert . . . I would never have believed it . . . I thought perhaps he might want . . . I never thought he would dare . . . he was so awfully afraid of her, for one thing, I am sure if she had only looked at him he would have run. But before I heard what Mr. Jones had told you, I knew it couldn't be Eddy. He had an attack of toothache that night with being wet. He went to the dentist to have the tooth pulled out the very next day. But Aunt heard him walking about his room all night. So did Mr. Norris.'

'Who is Mr. Norris?'

'He is the policeman in the village; there is Sergeant Jordan and Mr. Norris.'

'What does he know about it?' Bobby asked quickly, a good deal interested. 'Has he any reason? Did he see Mr. Dene?'

'He was specially watching the back of uncle's shop and the butcher's next to it, because of boys taking away the empty packing-cases for firewood. He noticed there was a light in Eddy's room, and he wondered why Eddy was up so late and if it was all right. They're so stupid about Eddy in the village, very likely he thought Eddy was taking the packing-cases himself. So he listened under the window and he heard him moving about. That was soon after the rain stopped. He kept on watching all the time he was on duty, and at three he saw the light go out and everything was quiet after that. Aunt says it was about three when Eddy told her it was better and he was going to try to get some sleep'.

'Was Norris standing watching there all the time?' Bobby asked.

'Oh, no. I don't think so. He had to walk about as usual, but he kept coming back and watching for a little again.'

'He ought to have reported it,' said Bobby severely. 'Perhaps he did, though, and I was never told. I think it comes to this: you were very much afraid Mr. Sterling might be suspected; you were even more afraid Mr. Dene might be guilty. So you made up your mind to hold your tongue and say nothing—and that,' observed Bobby bitterly, 'is the way the public helps us.'

She let this pass without comment or attempting to defend herself, and Bobby continued: 'Lady Cambers intended to make sure that you married Mr. Dene and that you and he entered Mr. Tyler's service. That was to get you both out of the country—two birds with one stone, in a way. She meant to put a stopper on anything between you and Mr. Sterling, and she was getting uneasy about the results and objects of Dene's work.'

'Mr. Andrews had been talking to her,' Amy agreed.
'Did Mr. Dene know?'

'Oh, yes. He was very angry about it. He said how intolerable it was work like his should depend on the whims of a rich old woman and a parson's superstitions. I think Lady Cambers was a good deal upset by what Mr. Andrews said, only of course she wouldn't admit it.'

'I gather,' Bobby commented, 'from what people say about her, that she was never very fond of admitting she was mistaken. Plenty like that. But if Mr. Dene went abroad with Mr. Tyler, his work here would come to an end quite naturally and simply. That Sunday evening he had a long talk with Lady Cambers. Do you know what it was about?'

Amy hesitated.

'I think he was teasing her,' she said at last.

'Teasing her?' Bobby repeated, astonished.

'Yes. It wasn't like him, but I think that's what it was. She seemed very quiet and worried after he left, but she wouldn't tell me what he had been saying. She seemed frightened, and I think it was because he had been telling her he had succeeded, and now he had all the material he wanted to write his book and prove he was right and all religion was superstition. I think she believed him.'

'He told me once,' Bobby said, 'he was intending to prove human development came through the hand first, and that mind was a by-product. He was looking for evidence of that in those "pot-holes" of his, wasn't he? You mean he was frightening her by letting her believe he had found what he wanted at last?'

'I think it was like that perhaps,' Amy answered, though reluctantly. 'He told me once she hadn't the least idea what his theories were or what his success would mean. He told me he had a good mind to scare her out of her life by showing her. I suppose it would have been quite easy for him to fake one of his fossils so that it looked as if it proved what he said and no one but an expert could have told. He talked about doing that some day so as to make her believe she had subsidized work that had ended by destroying the Christian Church. It would have made her understand he wasn't quite a tame cat, he said. They called him that in the village, and he hated it.'

Bobby was thinking quickly. Suppose Eddy had told Lady Cambers some such story late that Sunday night—how at last he had discovered evidence to prove his theories; that he had the fossils there; perhaps even he might have hinted obscurely that he intended to help their evidence a little to make the proof more plain. With Eddy's boasts and Mr. Andrews's warnings working together in her mind, it was at least conceivable that she had decided to go to the shed in Frost Field and secure the fossils for herself, to see that they were subjected to independent examination—or perhaps quite simply to suppress them. That would be why she had taken the empty suit-case with her—to bring them back in.

Was that, then, the simple trap into which she had fallen that fatal night, and had Eddy Dene been waiting there in the darkness, a noosed cord in his hand? Her death would have meant for him security for the continuance of his work; the avenging of the insult that was to have turned a scientific genius into a rich man's valet; safety for Amy, the one person he had ever expressed any feeling for, threatened with disaster to her husband if her secret became known.

It might be like that, Bobby thought, a tangle not wholly hid, yet leading through arrogance and egotism to a cold-blooded murder. He sighed a little, and said presently: 'This idea of taking on a job with Mr. Tyler as a kind of valet-secretary-maid-of-all-work, did that appeal to him at all?'

It was a question at which she smiled with a mingled tenderness and sadness, as of one sorry about something that she could yet well understand.

'You can't think how furious he was,' she said gently. 'He was too angry even to show it—it was like being insulted in his most tender spot. He really is very, very clever, and he has worked tremendously, and then to be told all he was fit for was to be a rich man's servant, and that was what he was to be in the future, upset him terribly. Lady Cambers never quite understood Eddy. I told her Eddy wouldn't want to go as a valet like that, but she only said, "Why not?" She said it would be such a good opening for him, and Mr. Tyler was interested in the same sort of thing. That made Eddy more cross than ever; he said it was like supposing that playing the violin and playing bridge were the same sort of thing. Going out to Central America would have meant his giving up all work here—all his ambitions, everything—in order to become a rich man's valet. And he thought Mr. Tyler rather an ignoramus.'

'Lady Cambers didn't understand that?'

'Oh, no; she thought she was doing it for Eddy's good; she always thought anything she did was for your good, and she had always been interested in Eddy. When he was leaving school, she offered to pay for him to stop on and perhaps go to the university afterwards. But Uncle and Aunt wanted him to help in the shop. They thought he had all the education necessary, and a university is only waste of time when you're going to be a grocer. They always hoped he would keep on the shop after them. They are very proud of it. Aunt told him how much they depended on him, and he let her refuse. It meant a lot to him then. It meant more later on, when he came to understand better what he had missed. He didn't blame Aunt or Uncle; he thought Lady Cambers ought to have insisted.'

'I suppose help offered and withdrawn is worse than no help at all,' Bobby observed. 'And there's a saying, too, that everything can be forgiven—except a too great benefit. That counted afterwards.'

'I think perhaps,' she mused. 'Eddy might feel like that.'

'You and he were engaged, weren't you?'

'Aunt and Uncle wanted us to be.'

'Didn't you?'

'I wanted anything that pleased them,' she answered. She turned again her full gaze upon him with that effect of shock her sudden glance seemed always capable of giving. 'They took me from the workhouse when I was a child,' she said. 'The workhouse,' she repeated; and, more clearly than ever before, she showed the full force of her rich and passionate nature in the terrible emotion with which she pronounced that word. 'If they had wanted, I would have married the first tramp passing in the street,' she said simply; and then, her look intent like fire: 'And you expected me to tell you things that might have sent their son to be hanged. Why, I would not have said one word if I had known that he had murdered half the village.'

'You would have been wrong,' he said, 'wrong legally and morally.'

With a gesture of her lifted hand, she swept that consideration aside as immaterial.

'But, in spite of that, you married someone else,' Bobby added.

She considered the point gravely.

'You do things you never meant to do,' she said after a time. 'It is more strong than you. Eddy didn't want to marry me. I told him he ought to because Uncle and Aunt wanted it so. He said they had let him down once when they did him out of school and university, and he would take care they didn't again, tying a wife on his back. He said he had no time for women anyhow. I said whenever he had half an hour to spare, if he would let me know beforehand, I would see to the banns and everything; and he said not much, he wouldn't. But after that it wasn't very comfortable at home, because Aunt and Uncle thought it was my fault, and I came here to work when Lady Cambers asked me. I thought perhaps I could help about Eddy, because I knew sometimes he was difficult—she thought he ought to be more grateful and he thought she was lucky to have the chance of helping his work. And then I met Mr. Sterling. I don't mean for the first time. Only it was the first time because it was so different. We had seen each other several times, and I had waited on him at tea and so on. That day a telegram came for him, and I took it to him in the room where he was. It was on a tray, and I held it out to him, and we looked at each other, and it was like a great light shining all around. It was as if all the world were new again. I never even thought of Eddy or of Uncle and Aunt. I was still holding out the tray. I said: "This is for you, sir." He said: "I am going to marry you." It sounded quite natural, like, "I want you to put this letter in the post." He said again: "I shall marry you." I said: "I shall be ready when you want me. Will you please take your telegram?" He took it and I went away. He didn't try to stop me and he never opened the telegram. I found it next day, unopened. I have it still, still unopened.' She paused and flashed her fiery and tremendous glance at Bobby. 'And do you think,' she asked, 'if my man had murdered half the village, I would have said a word to help you?'

'You have your own notion of morality,' Bobby mumbled.

She did not answer this. She had flung, as it were, her whole personality open to him in the reaction from the secret doubts and fears she had experienced, and already he fancied he could see her beginning again to fold her reserve once more about her. She went to the window, and over her shoulder she said to him: 'Sergeant Jordan and Mr. Norris are coming up the drive. What for? Have they come to take Sir Albert away?'

'If they have, you can do nothing,' Bobby warned her,

for her tone had seemed to suggest she contemplated some sort of action. He added: 'I don't suppose so; it may be nothing. Or they may be here to make sure he doesn't try to get away.'

'Well, he's in bed, isn't he?' she said with impatience.

'Most likely Colonel Lawson will come himself when he's ready,' Bobby said. 'I must thank you for what you've told me. You've helped a good deal to making things clear. I'm afraid poor Lady Cambers was playing with fire between the two of you—the three of you, rather.'

'It was when I heard about Eddy's pen being found near her body, I was most troubled,' she said. 'But I suppose Sir Albert might easily have picked it up and kept it. He was angry over her giving him such a present. I hope he didn't leave it there to make people think it was Eddy.'

'I don't think so,' Bobby said. 'The important thing about that pen is not the pen but the ink it was filled with.'

'Why? What does the ink matter?' she asked.

'All details have their importance,' Bobby explained. 'Details of fact and details of character, they all confirm or contradict each other. If they contradict, you know there's something wrong. If they confirm, you may be right—or not. Did Mr. Dene know you were communicating with Mr. Sterling in cipher through the *Announcer?*'

'Yes, I told him.'

'Could he read the cipher?'

'No; he told me he had tried and couldn't. He asked me what it was, but I didn't tell him. I said he must ask Mr. Sterling.'

'If Mr. Sterling had inherited all Lady Cambers's money by the will she made after the breach with her husband, you would have been a rich man's wife. You would have been the mistress here. And you would have asked your husband to continue the help Lady Cambers had been giving Mr. Dene?'

'I suppose so. Yes. Why?' she asked hesitatingly.

'Only an idea,' he answered. 'The statement Jones made about what he says he saw on Sunday left a good many points a bit doubtful. I think after what you've told me I see my way to clear them up.'

He rose to his feet as he spoke, and she came back from the window and faced him. Without speaking, she bent on him the full force of her fiery and challenging gaze, and he met it with one as deep and strange as her own. For an appreciable moment they remained so, staring, silent, gazing into each other's eyes, matching their wills like two duellists of the old days trying and measuring their swords.

'I think I'm afraid of you,' she said at last.

'There has been the life of a man between us,' he said, and went away quickly.

CHAPTER THIRTY-TWO
AN ANALYSIS

AS SPEEDILY AS HE MIGHT, BOBBY, LEAVING CAMBERS, made his way to the headquarters of the county police in Hirlpool, where, when he entered, he found himself the centre of interested, excited, and somewhat scared glances.

'It's about all the old man could do,' the station-sergeant told Bobby confidentially, 'not to have you put on the wanted list. Hopping he's been about you stopping away so long—fair hopping.' He paused, and a vision rose before Bobby's eyes of the stout and dignified Colonel Lawson hopping up and down, to and fro, hopping endlessly, persistently, tirelessly. Gratified to observe how impressed the young Londoner looked, the station-sergeant went on: 'Rang up London to ask if you had gone back there, and spoke sarcastic about our discipline in the country being no doubt different from London ideas. Hope you've got something to smooth him down with, because at the moment he's—well, hopping.'

'I think I've got my case complete at last, if that'll do,' Bobby said.

'Well, we all know that already, don't we?' asked the station-sergeant. 'When a bird comes along and says he saw it all—well, there you are, aren't you? They've been putting him through it good and hard and he hasn't varied his story one scrap. Didn't you see the cars waiting out in front? The old man's just starting to take in Sir Albert Cambers, Esq., Baronet. Something for the papers, eh? "Baronet Arrested on Murder Charge. Sensation of the Century". Some headlines, heh?'

'Colonel Lawson must let me see him first.' Bobby said, speaking with authority. 'I have some facts to put before him.'

The station-sergeant stared, hesitated, and then said: 'Well, they're just off, but he's certainly been wanting to see you pretty bad all afternoon—ever since he brought Jones back from London.'

He got up from his desk as he spoke, disappeared, and then came back.

'Says he'll give you just two minutes,' he announced, grinning. 'I'll warn you—when the old man gets going, he can say a lot in two minutes.'

To the chief constable's private office Bobby was now accordingly conducted, and there was greeted by Colonel Lawson with a restrained and ominous politeness.

'I understood you were instructed to keep in touch,' he said coldly.

'Yes, sir,' answered Bobby. 'There are some points I'm anxious to put before you, before you proceed to the arrest of Sir Albert. It does look so bad, sir, doesn't it, when a man is arrested and then has to be released again immediately?'

'Released?' thundered the colonel. 'What do you mean? You reported Jones's statement yourself. It's been thoroughly tested. Why, there's hardly ever yet been a murder case when an eyewitness could be produced.'

'No, sir, and this isn't one,' Bobby answered. 'Jones's statement won't hold water for a moment.'

'You mean he's lying?'

'It's a nice point,' said Bobby. 'I should put it he is letting his imagination convince him he saw something he is quite certain actually happened—he's so sure of it he now almost feels as if he did see it. But he didn't.'

'What do you mean?'

'I mean he thoroughly and sincerely and honestly believes, and has done from the first, that Sir Albert is guilty. The moment he heard what had happened he felt certain it was Sir Albert; he got into a panic and ran for it for fear of being brought in as an accomplice. That's why he disappeared in such a hurry. Back in London he began to wonder what he ought to do. Probably his first idea was to lie low. I dare say he thought of coming to us. And then he had the idea of blackmailing Sir Albert. Remember, he was quite sure Sir Albert was guilty. But to make it sound more convincing, and Sir Albert more willing to pay up, he put in that bit about having seen it all. What he really meant was that he would have been an eyewitness if he had been there to see what he was so sure had happened. Very likely by now he has thought about it so long, and imagined every detail so vividly, he has almost convinced himself he did see it. Imagination. He has,' said Bobby musingly, 'the making of a first-class novelist in him—he can imagine things so clearly he can persuade himself he saw them and describe them as if he had.'

'First-class lying I should call that,' said the colonel distrustfully, and paused, and Bobby went on: 'Jones states he climbed out of his window that night after he had got back to the inn without anyone seeing him.'

'He explains how in detail, all correct,' interposed the colonel. 'I checked them with him on the spot. He showed me just how. Quite practicable, though it doesn't look so at first.'

'I think his details apply to other occasions,' Bobby said. 'I think there's no doubt he did get out that way sometimes without the people of the inn knowing anything about it. But not that night. On Sunday night the landlord was sitting up with a sick cow in the shed just opposite Jones's window. He is prepared to swear Jones could not possibly have got out that night without his seeing him. Again, Jones says in his statement he changed his clothes. I have evidence he had no spare suit with him to change into. Thirdly, the times don't agree. Lady Cambers was murdered before midnight—probably somewhere about half-past eleven. The rain started about a quarter to eleven and lasted about half an hour. There is a small margin of error in all these times, of course, since no one used a stopwatch. Jones was back at the inn somewhere about eleven —after the rain had started, for he was wet through, and before it stopped. He went straight to bed and asked for a glass of hot whisky-and-water, which was served him about half-past eleven, and for his wet things to be put in the kitchen to dry. But his statement says that he was suspicious of Sir Albert's intentions, waited for his arrival, followed him, and that that is how he came to see the murder committed. Obviously he can't have been watching Sir Albert from before eleven till after midnight and yet been back at the Cambers Arms about eleven and drinking hot whisky-and-water in bed at the half-hour. Treasury counsel wouldn't even put him in the box to tell a tale so full of holes. I think Sir Albert is telling the truth when he says he told Jones to keep out of the way. I think Jones didn't intend to at first, but when the rain came on—he has had a bout of rheumatic fever and is scared of another attack— he gave up his first idea of watching to see what happened, scuttled back to the inn, and had no idea there was anything wrong till morning. And when he heard he got into a panic and ran for it, quite convinced Sir Albert was guilty and afraid of being thought an accomplice.'

Colonel Lawson was thinking deeply, breathing more deeply still. Presently he said: 'Well, even if you're right about all that and Jones's story can't stand, there's plenty more to suggest he was right in his guess.'

'May I go over the case with you, sir?' Bobby asked. 'I've come to a conclusion I would like to put to you, if I may. Even if you don't agree, and still decide to arrest Sir Albert, I shan't keep you long and he can't get away. He is still in bed for one thing, and then your two men are on watch.'

'Eh?' said Lawson, surprised.

'Thought it best, sir,' explained Moulland, lifting his blue, puzzled eyes from the papers he was diligently examining at a desk behind, 'to take all precautions. The officers have strict instructions not to say what they are there for.'

'Oh,' said the colonel, a little doubtfully. 'Go on,' he said to Bobby.

'I think we can all agree,' Bobby went on, consulting his notes now, 'the murder must have been committed by one of the people connected with Lady Cambers. The burglar idea is consistent with the disappearance of the jewellery but quite inconsistent with the murder having happened a mile or so from the house. All our investigations have failed to show any sign of any unknown person being concerned. Those we know of surrounding her, one of whom is certainly the murderer, include her husband, Sir Albert; her nephew, Tim Sterling; her butler, Farman; her maid, Amy Emmers; her protégé, Eddy Dene; her tenant's son, Ray Hardy; the vicar, Mr. Andrews; her neighbours, Mr. Bowman and his sister, Miss Bowman; and her rival jewellery-connoisseur, Mr. Tyler. As it happens, there seems adequate motive for murder in nearly each case. She had managed to make a good many enemies. The picture I have built up of her in my mind is that of a strong-willed, not very intelligent woman, very fond of interfering in other people's lives, confident that she always knew what was best for everyone else, not too scrupulous how she used the power her wealth gave her to enforce her will on others. And thoroughly well-meaning with it all. She was fond of her husband, anxious to keep him with her, and had behaved very generously to him in money matters when he got into some sort of financial tangle. But she probably meant to use her generosity to give her still more completely the upper hand. There was also a dispute about the ownership of the jewellery.

'I think we must remember her personality, strong and narrow, as both the background and the explanation of the tragedy.

'With Sir Albert, then, it stands that he wanted a divorce to marry Miss Bowman and that there was a good deal of feeling between him and his wife, especially over money matters.

'Tim Sterling was her heir and her debtor, and stood in danger of being disinherited and of having his loan called in, if she found out that he could not marry the girl she had chosen for him as he was already married to her maid, Amy Emmers.'

'What? What's that? That's something new,' interposed the chief constable. 'Are you sure of that?'

'I have date and place,' Bobby answered. 'If Miss Emmers herself is in any way guilty, her motive would be to protect her husband. Farman's motive would be the vulgar one of robbery. His character is not too good; he knew all about the Cleopatra pearl; he knew there would be a good market for it with Mr. Tyler. Mr. Tyler himself is said to have shown an unreasonable anxiety to secure the pearl, and to have been seen twice in the vicinity of the house when he had no obvious reason for his presence. Mr. Andrews and Ray Hardy had both uttered threats, and Mr. Andrews is accused of a fanaticism that would stop at nothing. Mr. Bowman, again, had a strong interest in seeing his sister become Lady Cambers. The scandal hadn't done him any good in his business, which wasn't very flourishing anyhow. If his sister had become Lady Cambers, both his business and his social position would have been much improved—and very likely he would have come in for the estate business as well. Eddy Dene . . .'

'I suspected him from the first,' put in Lawson, 'but you can't get away from two things—first, he lost in Lady Cambers his chief financial support; and, secondly, there is a very strong alibi. His mother swears she knocked at his door at about half-past eleven that night. She didn't see him, but she heard him moving about, and when she knocked and asked what was the matter he told her through the door that he had the toothache and she wasn't to worry him. She says—it's a homely touch—he was always ready to bite her head off when he had toothache, and we know that next day he had a tooth pulled out by a Hirlpool dentist. Also our own man, Constable Norris, confirms that he heard Dene moving about in his room till about three, when he saw him put his light out. And he can't very well have been prowling about his room with an attack of toothache and murdering Lady Cambers at the same time. You see,' added the chief constable with a touch of complacence, 'we've been doing a bit of investigating ourselves down here—and, by the way, we have found out something rather curious about Mr. Bowman.'

'Indeed, sir. May I ask what it is?' Bobby asked.

'There's an unexplained time-gap between his discovery of the body and leaving the shed in Frost Field about a quarter to eight or so and his return to his house at nine. The actual hour—nine—is fixed by the evidence of his cook. What was he doing during that hour? It may mean something.'

'Yes, sir,' agreed Bobby, 'but I understood from the cook that she sat up till midnight, doing some sewing, and is certain Mr. Bowman could not have left the house without her knowing.'

'Can't be sure of that,' declared Lawson. 'He might have managed it somehow. Anyhow, what do you want us to do? Arrest the lot? You seem to have proved they all had good reasons for wanting to be rid of the poor soul.'

'Strong reasons, sir, not good ones,' Bobby ventured to say. 'If you will allow me, I'll take one by one the people I've mentioned. If I can show we must, by force of fact and logic, rule them all out but one, then I submit that one must be guilty. And some can be ruled out easily enough. Farman's story is that he was smoking at his window at the time of the murder. There is corroboration by a witness, and further corroboration in that he was smoking his employer's cigars, a fact he tried to keep to himself. Mr. Andrews and Ray Hardy provide each other with an alibi; they saw each other some considerable distance from Frost Field at the time of the murder. Their evidence is independent, and is corroborated by details about a book Mr. Andrews lost and about his lighting his pipe. Besides, Ray Hardy is a sloppy, weak-willed youngster not at all likely to commit a murder of this kind, and Mr. Andrews may be fanatical, but would hardly push fanaticism as far as murder. In any case, their joint alibi is a good one. There is proof Mr. Tyler was nowhere near Cambers the night of the murder—he was in Paris, in fact. Miss Bowman was in London. The time unaccounted for in Mr. Bowman's case is the next morning, several hours after the murder. Besides, why should he commit murder to get rid of Lady Cambers when Sir Albert was talking about getting a divorce? Mr. Sterling and Amy Emmers must be considered together. Their story is that they were in Lady Cambers's "den", as she called it, at the time of the murder. Their story depends on each other's evidence, and is so far unsatisfactory, but it is consistent and is corroborated by small details. It agrees with what in the cipher advertisement Sterling suggested they should do. It explains why the garden door was locked after Lady Cambers had gone out. They had knowledge of Sir Albert Cambers's presence at three Monday morning, and it is difficult to suppose that, if Sterling had committed the murder at half-past twelve, he would hang about till three. It explains why Miss Emmers left the glass and plate Sterling had used on the table without troubling about them, since she expected to have plenty of time to see to them in the morning. It was only when news of the murder arrived that she seems to have thought of finger-prints, seen they might be dangerous, and washed the things. If she had known of the murder before, surely she would have carried out such a simple precaution much earlier?'

Bobby paused, and the chief constable looked at him.

'You haven't said anything about Sir Albert Cambers or about Eddy Dene yet,' he remarked.

'No, sir, I am coming to them now,' Bobby answered, closing his note-book, for now he had come to a part of his narrative that he knew by heart.

CHAPTER THIRTY-THREE

ANALYSIS CONTINUED

'IN A CASE OF THIS KIND,' BOBBY WENT ON, TALKING now nearly as much to himself as to the others, 'there are three lines of approach: motive, material clues, personal character. They all have their difficulties. Motive may not produce action. Material clues may be absent—not every murderer is kind enough to leave his card, or even the usual laundry-mark he can be traced by, and the saying that every murderer makes a mistake only means that every murderer who is caught has made one. Those who don't make mistakes get away with it—as in the Croydon poisoning case. As for character, only God knows our real character, or what opportunity and circumstance may bring out in any one of us.

'All the same, I don't see Sir Albert Cambers as the murderer type. He is neither violent enough nor cunning enough, and he is far too conventional—convention is a greater safeguard than fear of God or fear of the consequences.

'It is true he wished for a divorce, and that he believed there was an intrigue between his wife and Dene entitling him to one. But I don't think there's anything to show he either believed or wished with passion enough to lead to murder; and his private detective, Jones, entirely failed to find any evidence to justify his belief—largely because there was none, since nothing of the kind existed. Jones believed that it did, however, because he was the kind of person always ready to believe in any story like that, and when he got an anonymous message to say Lady Cambers and Dene were meeting secretly in the Frost Field shed late Sunday night, he never thought of doubting. It was what he had expected. I think there's no doubt the message came from Dene himself, and I know Jones thought he recognized Dene's voice, and thought Dene was arranging the exposure in order to force a scandal and a marriage with Lady Cambers. Jones always interpreted everything that happened in the light of his own mentality. He let Sir Albert know he could provide the required evidence, and Sir Albert borrowed Miss Bowman's car and came along accordingly, having first written to Miss Bowman what might seem a rather compromising note. On his way he was caught in the rainstorm, drew up for shelter in a dip of the road, at the West Leigh turning, that was soon flooded, and was badly splashed by a passing Rolls-Royce car. As that was late at night, there was a good chance the Rolls-Royce belonged to someone living near—and to some wealthy person, as it was a Rolls-Royce. I asked the Yard to try to trace it, and Lord Lynton's chauffeur remembers passing a small car at that time, in that spot, and thinking it would soon get flooded out. Sir Albert says that then he drove on to Cambers, left his car parked by the roadside, waited in, or by, the rhododendron-bushes till three, and then gave it up and went home. His story is corroborated by the fact that he knew it was his own pet cigars Farman was smoking, while Farman says he heard sounds coming from the rhododendrons, and Sterling saw someone he thought was like Sir Albert going away about three a.m. Even the number of cigarette-ends picked up by the rhododendrons suggest a fairly long time spent there—and Sir Albert has developed the bad cold and touch of pleurisy you would expect if his story was correct.

'On the whole, it seems to me he is fairly well cleared.'

'Jones was ready to swear he was an eyewitness,' growled Colonel Lawson. 'I'll prosecute for—for—attempted perjury?'

'Public mischief,' suggested Moulland hopefully.

'It's more than that,' said Colonel Lawson sternly. 'He very nearly—very nearly indeed—made me make a public fool of myself!'

Moulland looked shocked, and was evidently trying to think, though without much success, of an appropriate penalty. Bobby continued: 'That leaves Eddy Dene. He has a strong alibi. I'll ignore that for the moment, if I may. Take character first. The most marked feature of his is an extreme arrogance, partly natural, partly a morbid growth in defence against his poverty and surroundings, his daily work behind the counter, his resentment against what he was weak enough and silly enough to consider his inferior social position. Even when his work attracted attention at Oxford, and people came along from the University to see what he was doing, most likely only anxious to help him, he seems to have snubbed them. He was so self-confident he did not want help, only admiration; and probably he thought the Oxford dons wanted to steal his facts and theories he intended for his book he thought was going to startle the world. Also he had a very strong, resolute will—he knew what he wanted, and he meant to have it.

'That is where he clashed with Lady Cambers. She was equally determined on having her own way, equally persuaded her way was the only right way. But she had nothing like Dene's clear-sighted intelligence, and I think it is easy to understand Dene's secret resentment at finding himself and his work, and all his future hopes, entirely dependent on her good-will. I think that resentment festered within him till it turned to hate.

'One could call that the psychological position—Lady Cambers blandly heaping benefits on Dene, but exacting the payment of an implicit obedience. She seems to have made a rule, for instance, that there was to be no work of any kind done by him on Sundays—a trifle, but it made Dene as angry as trifles often do. He got to be like a tin of petrol, ready to explode at any spark.

'That came—though it was more than a spark—when Lady Cambers informed him he was to take a job as valet practically, with Mr. Tyler, and was to marry Miss Emmers. He had never wanted to marry her, for one thing, and, for another, he knew she was married already, and that when Lady Cambers found out, she was likely to make things pretty warm all round and without too much discrimination. I expect, too, he felt Lady Cambers's suggestion as a mortal insult—it showed her real understanding and appreciation of him and his work. Most likely, to her one archæological investigation was just like another; but Dene cared nothing, and knew less, about the Maya question, and was giving his whole knowledge and experience to the question of the emergence of man from the animal—he believed his book about that would make as big a sensation as Darwin's *Origin of Species*, he had already settled his was to be *The Origin of Man*. Obviously the Tyler idea and the Maya expedition would have meant abandoning that and all his hopes of speedy fame and recognition.

'He knew, also, that Lady Cambers had made a will making Sterling her heir, and I've no doubt myself he was quite right in calculating that if Sterling inherited, Mrs. Sterling—Amy Emmers, that is—would see that the help he had been receiving from the Cambers estate would be continued. She seems to have promised him as much, quite innocently. To him, Lady Cambers had come to seem a useless, dictatorial old woman, full of whims and crotchets, it would be an advantage all round to replace by the Sterlings. Further, I think he was really fond of Amy in a brotherly kind of way, and genuinely distressed at the thought of her having to stand the brunt of Lady Cambers's anger—her foolish and unreasonable anger, he thought, and possibly he liked, too, the idea of a cousin reigning at Cambers House.

'As regards motive, then, it seems he had everything to gain and disaster to avoid, both for himself and for his cousin, Amy.

'As regards character, he had worked himself into a mood of mingled arrogance, contempt, resentment, that would make good rich breeding-ground for thoughts of murder.

'Now to come to facts, the actual physical clues.

'Jones states that the voice over the phone, telling him of the imaginary appointment with Dene in the Frost Field shed, was that of Dene himself. I suggest that was really part of a plan to get Sir Albert on the spot that night, and so confuse investigation. I am inclined to think it was Dene, again, who confirmed Lady Cambers's suspicions that Amy Emmers and Tim Sterling were attracted to each other. He knew they were communicating by cipher, and it is fairly certain he would be able to make it out if he tried. It was simple enough, and he went out of his way to tell Miss Emmers he had tried and failed, which I don't believe. I think he planned, too, to get Sterling on the spot that Sunday night, to confuse things still more.

'In his arrogance and self-confidence, I don't suppose he thought it would be very difficult to baffle police investigation.

'But he had to consider how to carry out the murder he most likely thought of merely as the removal of another obstacle, as he had already removed many in winning opportunity to devote himself to his chosen work. To carry out his intention inside the house would have been both dangerous and difficult. But suppose he could induce her to come out alone late at night? It must have seemed difficult, at first, to think how to manage that, but he knew she was much disturbed by the denunciations and protests made by the vicar, Mr. Andrews. He had warned her, for instance, that she would be responsible for souls led astray. I think Dene hit on this plan. He told Lady Cambers he had found fossils that proved his theories, but that to make this proof more obvious and convincing he intended to improve it a little by making a few alterations and additions—faking in fact—before showing the fossils to the world. And I think he pretended to be very excited—that would not be difficult—he would be excited by his secret intentions—and that he managed to convey to Lady Cambers that the only way of preventing him from producing this faked evidence was for her to go herself to take possession of the fossils for independent examination.'

'But this is all theory,' interposed Colonel Lawson. 'You can't put theory in the witness-box.'

'I am trying to outline the probable course of events, sir,' Bobby answered. 'And it is hardly all theory, for I am depending on what Miss Emmers told me when she thought that Jones's claim to have been an eyewitness of the murder proved Sir Albert's guilt and exonerated

Dene, and so left her free to tell me what she knew. What I have just said, Dene outlined to her as a sort of joke he intended to play on Lady Cambers—possibly that was how the idea first occurred to him—to show up her ignorance, and make her less anxious to interfere with him. It got to be serious. He calculated that if she did visit the hut she would do so without saying anything to anyone, because, for one thing, she wouldn't want gossip about her visiting Frost Field alone and late at night, and then there was no one she could take with her except Amy, who was Dene's cousin, or the butler, Farman, whom I don't suppose she much wanted. She was a strikingly self-reliant woman, but if she did take a companion, or if she didn't go at all, it would only have meant thinking out another plan. Nothing would have been lost.'

'Dene has his alibi still. And the pen found near her body, Dene lost some days before,' Lawson remarked.

'It was the pen that finally convinced me of Dene's guilt,' Bobby said. 'Or rather the ink in it.'

'The ink?' repeated Lawson. 'Why? How?'

'The ink was identified at the laboratory as being the "Perennial" brand. Dene claims he missed the pen on Wednesday, and he sent in his advertisement about its loss on Friday. But all that may only prove careful preparation. As it happens the "Perennial" brand of ink is entirely new—it was only on public sale last Monday, and there was none of it in the village till a traveller left a sample at Mr. Dene's shop on the Friday and urged him to try it himself. Mr. Dene took it into his little private office with that idea. It follows, therefore, that the pen must have been filled with "Perennial" ink on or after the Friday, and no one but Eddy Dene and old Mr. Dene had access to the ink. Old Mr. Dene may be safely left out of the question, and there seems, therefore, a clear inference that Eddy Dene was using the pen two days after he claims to have missed it. I think it is fairly certain he hit on the idea of leaving the pen on the spot to draw on himself the instant suspicion he knew he could not wholly avoid, with the idea that when he could show he had missed the pen three days earlier, suspicion would be turned away, and therefore be all the slower, once proved unfounded, to attach itself to him again.'

'There's still the alibi—the proof he was in his room at the time,' Colonel Lawson said.

'Yes, sir,' agreed Bobby. 'I've asked Station-Sergeant Weatherby to help me there, and I think there's a room used for stores at the top of the building, but otherwise empty. If you could come up there with me, sir, I think I could show you how that might have been worked. Only I would like to point out one thing first. Both Norris and Mrs. Dene confirm Dene's alibi and support each other. But neither actually saw Dene, and Mrs. Dene's statement that he spoke to her through the closed door is an afterthought. In her original statement she signed she says clearly and plainly that he made no answer when she knocked the first time. It was on the second occasion, a couple of hours later, when he responded.'

With that he led the way to the top of the building, where Sergeant Weatherby was waiting outside a closed door.

'Busy as bees, sir,' he announced, with a grin as his chief appeared.

'What are?' Colonel Lawson asked.

'Shall we listen, sir?' Bobby asked; and when they were all silent they heard coming from within the room a curious indeterminate kind of shuffling, jerking noise, very much as if someone or something were moving to and fro.

'What's that?' Colonel Lawson demanded. 'Who's there?'

'No one, sir,' answered Weatherby, evidently enjoying a joke to himself.

'Mrs. Dene,' Bobby said slowly, 'hearing sounds like

these coming in the middle of the night from her son's room would naturally conclude they were caused by him. She would think it could be nothing else, and so would be certain that was what it was. Her belief would be quite honest and sincere, and her getting no answer to her knock she would put down to his state of nerves over his supposed toothache—perhaps the toothache was genuine, though; the dentist said there was an exposed nerve anything could start. Dene may have started it himself, with a pin or something, so as to make his face swell, or the swelling I saw may have been a bit of cotton-wool. Norris, too, hearing sounds coming from the room, and hearing afterwards that Dene had had an attack of toothache that night, would be ready to believe just in the same way that he had heard him walking up and down the room.'

'What is causing it?' Lawson asked impatiently.

Sergeant Weatherby opened the door. In the middle of the floor were two old carpet-slippers, and attached to the toe of each, by a short piece of string, was a kind of open wire framework or cage, each enclosing a captive mouse. In their efforts to escape from their confinement, their legs having been left a certain freedom of movement, the mice were dragging the slippers to and fro. The effect was one that could easily with the aid of a little imagination and suggestion, be mistaken for that of a person shuffling up and down a room.

'What the devil . . . ?' began Lawson.

'If you remember, sir,' Bobby went on, 'Eddy Dene's room had a new linoleum, very highly polished. Mrs. Dene remarked on it. That was to let the slippers move more easily and naturally, and this is how Dene produced the effect of sounds coming from his room that his mother and Norris heard and interpreted as proof of his presence, since they could imagine no other cause.'

'You know, I suspected Dene from the first,' declared the chief constable.

'Yes, sir,' said Bobby.

'What made you guess he had played a fantastic trick like this?' Lawson asked, and a mouse that had managed to wriggle its way through wire put together with less care than perhaps Dene had used scampered across the floor and disappeared.

'Now we shall be overrun with mice,' said Moulland severely.

'I wondered why Dene had put so much energy into polishing his lino,' Bobby answered. 'And then I noticed that he was using the old-fashioned kind of mouse-trap that catches the little beasts alive. Apparently he had gone to some trouble to explain that was because he thought the break-back kind were cruel. I thought that was a little surprising, too, and then I found he had been telling Ray Hardy that it was only a silly sentimental fad to object to the use of spring-traps for rabbits. It seemed contradictory —a contradiction always wants explaining—and I thought about it till I seemed to see how he could have brought off his fake. His trick had the great advantage of using life to imitate life, as mechanism never does. Life is always variable and spontaneous, mechanism just the opposite. Reproduction of the human voice by gramophone or wireless can always be told at once—it's mechanical and unvarying. Dene used life itself to give the illusion of the presence of a living creature—himself.'

A constable appeared on the stairs.

'Beg pardon, sir,' he said. 'There's a gentleman just come in—name of Dene, Eddy Dene, and it's very pressing and important—about the Cambers murder, sir. He has important information.'

Behind the speaker appeared Eddy himself.

'I've just come to tell you,' he said, 'I've found out where the stolen Cambers jewellery is hidden, and if you come along with me you can see the murderer coming to fetch it from its hiding-place.'

CHAPTER THIRTY-FOUR

EDDY DENE ACCUSES

THE ABRUPT APPEARANCE OF EDDY DENE AND THIS announcement that he made were alike so unexpected and so startling, none of them could do anything but gape bewilderedly. It was Station-Sergeant Weatherby who had presence of mind enough to close the door of the store-room so that Dene might not grasp the nature of the experiment they had been making, and the constable who had come to announce his arrival said to him severely: 'You did ought to have waited down below, sir, same as I told you.'

Eddy took no notice. From where he stood on the stairs he smiled up at the chief constable and his companions, and though he was thus below them he somehow gave the impression of looking down from some superior height. He showed himself amused, even a little flattered, by their evident disarray, and the arrogance of his dark and haughty glance seemed more than ever emphasized by the smile lurking in it as he looked from one to the other.

'Well?' he said at last, much in the manner of the indulgent parent who has given his children a new toy to play with and is waiting to see what they will do with it.

They made no answer still, only stood and watched, finding, indeed, the situation a little overpowering, a little beyond them, now the man whose guilt had just been demonstrated was come, smiling and confident, lightly to denounce another.

'Bowled you over a bit?' Eddy suggested, still with that lofty smile of his.

'Yes, yes,' agreed Colonel Lawson nervously. 'Yes ... we were examining stores.' He paused to turn and look at Bobby, and his look said as plainly as words: 'Well, now, are you sure you aren't mistaken? If Dene were really guilty, he couldn't surely come swaggering here like this.' Bobby remained impassive. The colonel turned back to

Dene. 'Yes, examining stores, you know,' he repeated.

'Very necessary work, I'm sure,' agreed Dene, scarcely troubling to hide his scorn. 'More necessary than pressing, perhaps. But then everything always depends on a proper routine—we all know that.' And now it was almost an open sneer that played across his small and chubby features that contrasted so oddly with the breadth of his forehead and the dark lightning of his eyes. 'Hampers original work, perhaps, but it has to be done, of course.'

'Mr. Dene,' Lawson said, beginning to recover himself to some degree. 'You say . . . I understand . . . very serious,' he mumbled, looking helplessly at Bobby, as if wondering what ought to be done and what Bobby was thinking. 'Very serious what you say,' he concluded. 'You have serious grounds for your statement?'

'I shouldn't be here if I hadn't,' Dene retorted.

'You have found out where the stolen jewellery is?' Bobby interposed.

'That's what I'm telling you, if you could try to take it in,' retorted Dene again.

'You know also, you say,' Bobby went on, and into his voice crept now, against his will, a strange and sombre note, 'who murdered Lady Cambers last Sunday night?'

For the fraction of a second Dene hesitated, as though for just that one fleeting moment he recognized a warning. But the next moment he could almost be seen pushing it aside, recovering his self-confidence, too sure of his superiority to others to trouble himself about them, so that all his habitual insolence was in his voice and manner again as he said: 'You're the London man, aren't you? Teaching the clodhoppers their business, I suppose. Well, I've found out one or two things very likely you've all been too busy to notice, but that may interest you. I can show you where the jewellery stolen from Lady Cambers's safe is hidden. It's just—there. And I know who put it there, and I know he is coming in an hour or two to remove it. I know that because I know he has booked his passage by air from Croydon to Paris, and I take it as certain the jewels will go with him, especially as the place where they are hidden is evidently only temporary. I am ready to show you where it is; if you like you can watch for yourselves and see who comes to fetch them. You can draw your own deductions—if you can, that is. Anyhow, here's a sequence. Murder. Jewels stolen. Jewels hidden. Who hides, can find. Who steals, hides. Who murders . . . You can go on for yourselves. I don't see myself that it matters much, though. The murder's done and can't be undone; it belongs to the past. But the jewels are there still—they do matter.'

'You mean that whoever committed the murder, stole the jewellery?' suggested Lawson.

'As an exercise in logic,' Dene retorted, and shrugged his shoulders. 'You must work it out for yourselves—none of my business.'

'It's our business,' agreed Bobby softly, and again Dene looked at him, and again dismissed him as evidently counting for little.

'How do you come to know all this?' demanded Colonel Lawson.

'By using my brains,' Eddy answered, with rather too evident an implication that those to whom he spoke had none. 'I don't think the process would interest you. I gave you a broad hint once, if you had chosen to follow it up.'

'What was that?' asked the colonel sharply.

'Mr. Dene means, I think,' interposed Bobby, 'that when he entered Lady Cambers's locked room by the window he tore the curtain.'

'That showed,' Dene pointed out tolerantly, 'that no one could have entered the room by the window without leaving traces. That showed the key had been used to open the garden door to get into the house. That proved the murderer was the thief as well, didn't it, since how could he have got the keys except from her dead body?'

He paused for a moment, as if expecting an answer. But no one spoke, and Bobby wondered to himself if Dene really expected reasoning with so obvious a gap in it to be accepted. If he did, his opinion of their intelligence must be poor indeed—as it was, in fact. Dene went on: 'But it's results you want, not intellectual processes. Well, it's results I'm giving you. Well, what do you say? Are you coming along to see for yourselves? There's not too much time.'

'Oh, yes, we'll come along,' Lawson answered.

They moved down the stairs. At the door the cars were still waiting. The chief constable gave the necessary instructions to the chauffeurs. They all took their places—Lawson, Moulland, Bobby, and Dene himself in the first car, and three uniformed constables in the second. Dene had suddenly grown silent. It was as though his supreme self-confidence, hitherto so unshakable, was now at last a little troubled. At any rate he was very silent, and, as the others did not speak, no word was uttered during that brief and sombre journey. When Dene, who had already indicated the direction, gave the signal to stop, Bobby jumped to the ground first, and, when Dene moved a few steps away, Bobby followed him.

'You needn't keep so close,' Eddy said to him. 'I'm not going to run away, you know.'

'Mr. Dene,' Bobby answered formally, 'the position is that you have made a very serious accusation against some person you have not yet named. Unless you show good and sufficient reason, it may be our duty to take proceedings against you.'

'Oh, it's public mischief, as they call it, you're afraid of,' Eddy said, and laughed, as if relieved. 'Oh, that's all right, if that's what you've got in your head.' And he made no further objection to Bobby's keeping close by him as he led them through some close undergrowth, by a grove of young oaks recently planted, to a spot where ash and beech grew more closely round a hollow in the ground, the bottom of it thick with high bracken. As the little procession moved along, Dene said to Bobby: 'They say in the village Lady Cambers wouldn't have had anything by the time she had paid off what her husband lost in the City.'

'Well, I don't know for certain,' Bobby answered, 'but I've a strong idea this jewellery is about all she had left. Unless it is recovered, I don't imagine there will be anything to speak of for her heirs.'

'Yes, that's what I thought,' Dene answered; and added, half to himself: 'The dirty swine who took it wants all he'll get—and that'll be more than he bargained for.'

They had reached now the hollow round which the trees grew so thickly, and there Dene arranged them about it, making sure they were well hidden and no part left unguarded.

While he was so occupied Colonel Lawson took the opportunity of drawing Bobby aside, and saying to him in a very troubled voice: 'How does all this go with your theory? Dene seems very sure of himself—and really anxious the jewellery should be recovered. How does that go with the idea that he's guilty?'

'Well, sir,' Bobby answered, 'I think myself he probably is quite keen on the jewellery being recovered.'

'If he's guilty, why doesn't he keep it himself, if he knows where it's hidden?' Lawson asked.

'He has sense enough to see he would find it difficult to dispose of,' Bobby answered. 'And probably impossible while he was still going on with his work and his book. It's always that he thinks of first. I gather he doesn't know Lady Cambers destroyed the will making Sterling her heir. His calculation, as I see it, is that his being responsible for the recovery of the jewellery would go a long way to discount any suspicion that he was concerned in the murder—

here's no logical connection, but the fact is, people would very likely feel like that. And he calculates, too, that as the jewellery would, as he thinks, go to Sterling, Miss Emmers, as Mrs. Sterling, would see he got enough to carry on his work. He could reasonably claim ten per cent. as due to him for recovering it. Then, on the strength of that, he could finish his book.'

Eddy Dene came hurrying back to them, contemptuous that they should be chatting together in what seemed so casual and indifferent a manner while he was arranging the positions of their men.

'We were only just in time,' he said. 'Our man's coming.'

He pointed as he spoke, and they saw approaching through the trees the round squat figure of Oscar Bowman, coming furtively and cautiously and slowly, as though dreading each tree or bush might hide an enemy.

'Mr. Bowman,' Colonel Lawson exclaimed.

'Never thought of him, did you?' smiled Dene, with even more arrogance in his tone than usual. 'You never spotted there was an odd little time-lag. I saw it at once. Bowman vanished from the shed in Frost Field before eight. He said he felt too sick and upset to go on to his office and was going home instead. Well, it's not far, but it took him an hour and a quarter. Proof—his cook remembers it was exactly nine when he did get there, because she was grumbling at the milkman for being late and pointed to the clock to show him what the time was. Now, what was Bowman doing during that hour and a quarter? I suppose you might say that perhaps he was sitting under a hedge holding his head in his hands?'

Colonel Lawson was beginning an indignant outburst when Bobby, throwing all thoughts of discipline to the winds, and daring greatly, trod upon his superior officer's toe. As it was a toe provided with a corn the device was successful, and the interval prolonged and stormy before Dene went on: 'So I thought I would nose around a bit, and I can give you the name of a woman in a cottage—Mrs. Jenks—who remembers seeing Mr. Bowman hurrying along a bypath that morning, from Cambers House towards his own home, carrying a brown-paper parcel. She is fairly sure of the time, because of having got the children off to school. I should say that what happened was this. Bowman was pressed for money; he knew all about Lady Cambers's jewels; and he knew there wasn't going to be any divorce, because Lady Cambers meant to get her Albert back, and in any case wasn't meaning to let anyone else have him. Bowman got her to come out that night by telling her some yarn about his sister and Sir Albert.'

'What made her take a suit-case with her?' Bobby interposed.

Dene looked slightly discomposed.

'How should I know?' he snapped. 'Some idea of her own, most likely. But Bowman was waiting, and he polished her off, very neatly. Once the cord was round her neck she wouldn't even know what was happening. An easy death.'

'Did she struggle much?' Bobby asked.

'No; all over in no time,' Dene answered, too absorbed in his story—perhaps in his memories, too—to notice the look of stricken horror that Colonel Lawson gave him, or the grim tightening of Bobby's mouth. 'Like that,' Dene said, with a gesture of one hand, and they who were listening knew a murderer was showing them unconsciously just how his crime had been committed. 'No struggle even. But then,' Dene went on, in a slightly different tone, though he himself was not aware of the change, 'Bowman found himself up against a snag. He knew Lady Cambers always had her keys with her. That was all right. She had, and he took them. But he had reckoned on the door she had come out by being open for her return. Unluckily for him someone had found it open, thought it had been forgotten, and locked and bolted it. So there was Bowman with his keys that were no good to open a door bolted on the inside. That did him. He was no burglar, and had no idea how to force an entry. He must have thought it over, and finally planned to be on hand in the morning, when the body was discovered, so he would be able to take advantage of the confusion and the excitement to slip into the house and Lady Cambers's room and open the safe and clear off with the jewellery. It would only take a moment or two, and in the general excitement he could reasonably hope to escape notice.'

Colonel Lawson was just about to remark there was satisfactory evidence that as a matter of fact Bowman had spent the night asleep in his bed as usual when Bobby made a sudden movement, and the chief constable, whose toe was still painful, moved hurriedly away and was silent, and Dene, who had not noticed this by-play, said: 'Look out, he's nearly here. You can see for yourselves now . . . and you can decide for yourselves whether you think the man who took the jewels had anything to do with the murder. Not my business.'

'Oh, you've made it your business, Mr. Dene,' Bobby could not help answering, and Dene looked at him and said nothing; and soon Bowman came out from the trees into the comparatively open border round the rim of the little hollow.

He was plainly nervous and excited, constantly stopping to look and listen, and yet too restless and uneasy to take note of what it was or the significance of what he saw and heard. For a little he stood or moved to and fro uneasily, and then he came to a standstill beneath an ancient elm. Into it he climbed, drawing himself up by an overhanging branch and when he let himself down again he was carrying a brown-paper parcel.

This he opened, and showed, all piled together, a great heap of those glittering toys for which, from time immemorial, men and women have been so apt to barter their immortal souls, though dewdrops on a spider's web in the dawn are lovelier by far, and their possession scarce less transitory.

So there they lay, on their brown paper, on the green grass, while Bowman bowed himself above them in a kind of ecstasy; and in his excitement one of the watching constables moved, letting his helmet become visible. Bowman heard the movement, saw the helmet. With a loud cry, all the terror latent in him unloosed and rampant, he turned and ran, and, as it chanced, ran straight towards where Eddy Dene lay hid.

Seeing him coming, Eddy sprang to his feet from the bracken that had kept him concealed.

'Oh, no, you don't,' he called, mocking the fugitive. 'No getting away this side, Bowman.' And Bowman snatched a pistol out and fired.

Eddy screamed, a shrill and dreadful scream, and his expression was that of a man who had received some gross and unexpected insult; nor was the arrogance in his dark eyes one whit diminished. Bowman was rushing on. They met, they grappled, they rolled together, over and over in the bracken that grew red where their writhing bodies passed, and three times more the pistol snarled. When the others came to separate them, Eddy had been shot three times—once in the chest, twice through the stomach—and Bowman had the tiny bullet of his own small automatic buried deep in his heart.

CHAPTER THIRTY-FIVE

CONCLUSION

THAT OSCAR BOWMAN WAS PAST ALL AID WAS PLAIN, for as evident as strange is the difference between the body wherefrom the soul has fled and the body wherein the soul lingers still. But Eddy lived and was conscious, lifting himself on one hand and coughing a little, blood and froth gathering on his lips that he kept wiping with his other hand, the gesture with which he did so one of anger and impatience.

Later on, a doctor who examined his body denied the possibility of this, and asserted that a man shot at point-blank range through the chest, the stomach, and the lungs could not possibly have had the strength to think or talk consecutively.

But this doctor was a man of science, trained on scientific lines, and had no knowledge of the fierce, prideful will of Eddy Dene's that could bend to itself most things, though not all. None the less, though his will was passionate still, and it was that alone held him, body controlled and mind clear, he well knew and well understood; and when Bobby came and knelt beside him, he said aloud: 'Of all the luck, of all the crossway ends . . . there's no one left to carry on my work.'

'I wouldn't talk,' Bobby said to him. 'They've sent for a doctor.'

'You'll never hang Bowman now,' Eddy said; and Bobby answered sternly, for the words offended him: 'We never should have. We knew the truth.'

Eddy stared at him, and one could almost see his grasp upon his life slackening, as though that stern reply had loosened it.

'What do you mean? . . . You knew?' he asked; and then: 'That chap at Hirlpool said something about mice . . . you knew about that?'

Colonel Lawson came up in time to hear this, and it was he who answered.

'We do,' he said. 'Also we have reason to believe that the fountain-pen you say you lost on Wednesday you filled with ink not available till the following Friday. I think you had better say nothing more at present, Dene. There are other questions you will have to answer.'

'Not I—not one,' Eddy answered, in a loud, unnatural

voice; and, a little startled, the chief constable said to Bobby: 'Is it serious? There's not much bleeding.'

'That's why it's more than serious, you fool,' Eddy retorted, and, with that last characteristic word upon his lips, he sighed deeply, twice over, and was dead.

Only a day later the adjourned inquest on Lady Cambers was to be held. So now two more were conducted at the same time and the whole story made clear.

There could be no certain knowledge, since both concerned were dead, how Lady Cambers had been tempted out alone that tragic Sunday night, but there could be little reasonable doubt that Eddy Dene had played upon her fears of the consequences flowing from his pretended discovery of a fossil or fossils proving his contention. Almost certainly—as he had hinted to Amy he would do—he had added a suggestion that he might reinforce this supposed evidence by a little judicious faking; and Lady Cambers, simple-minded, direct, authoritative, had fallen headlong into the trap, and had determined to secure the fossils for herself.

Dene had laid his plans carefully and well, and the complications he had so astutely introduced had done much to confuse and mislead the investigation, aided to an unexpected degree by the imaginative exercises of Mr. Samuel Jones.

It was sufficiently plain, too, that Bowman, on discovering the body, had seen his opportunity to secure the keys of the safe in which the jewellery was kept. Nor had it been difficult, in the excitement and confusion of the morning, to slip unperceived into the house by the garden door—the key for that, too, was one of those he had obtained—rifle the safe, leave the keys in a convenient drawer, and slip off again, still unseen by any of the inmates of the house all gathered together in panic in the hall.

From the first, Dene, alone in his knowledge that since he himself had not touched the keys they must have been taken by who first found the body, must have been certain Bowman had the jewellery. That meant Bowman was attempting to secure for himself the whole of the material gain from the crime, and Eddy was as determined to prevent that as he was to take his revenge upon the man thus crossing his careful plans.

Unless Amy Emmers, as Mrs. Sterling, was put in a position to carry out her promise to continue to assist his work till there was completed his book he fondly dreamed was to bring him fame and fortune, all he had done was wasted, except, indeed, as removing one whom he had come to regard as intolerable meddler and tyrant.

And with his private knowledge that it must be Bowman who had taken the keys, and therefore the missing jewellery, it was easy for him to see that a scapegoat lay ready to his hand, amiably offering himself.

A careful, steady watch on Bowman's movements would soon tell Eddy where the stolen jewellery was hidden, and it was quite reasonable to suppose that the possession of it would be taken as proof of guilt of the murder as well. Even if Bowman were acquitted, for lack of sufficient proof, of the charge of murder, no one would be likely to think that the real murderer was the clever disinterested tracker-down of the thief.

In the end these calculations had proved vain, and, though it was plain Bowman had yielded to the sudden temptation to secure the jewellery, it was equally clear that Eddy was the murderer. The verdicts were given after but brief deliberation—in the case of Lady Cambers, 'wilful murder' against Eddy Dene; in the case of Dene himself, and of Bowman, 'death by shooting'.

Of the others who had played their part in these events there is little to be told. The Cambers estate had to be sold. The jewellery had to go, too. Mr. Tyler seized his opportunity, and Mrs. Tyler now proudly appears, with her 'Cleopatra pearl ear-rings', on the front page of nearly every issue of the *Pictorial Babbler*, so that she is almost as famous as the last divorced film-star. After all the liabilities resulting from Sir Albert Cambers's violent assault upon the City had been cleared, there was no very large sum left. But on the four or five hundred a year remaining, Sir Albert and the new Lady Cambers (*née* Bowman) live very happily and comfortably in a Cheltenham villa, golf by day and contract by night filling their simple, peaceful, yet colourful days, since at golf no hole, at contract no bidding, is ever the same.

They have made many friends, too, for they are an amiable and reasonable couple, and quite content to leave the money Lady Cambers lent to her nephew as an investment in his wireless business, which is developing very satisfactorily. He has had several offers already from larger firms prepared, and even anxious, to take it over, but so far has preferred to remain independent, largely through the influence of his wife, for Amy is taking a very keen, efficient, and increasingly important share in the development of the commercial side of the business.

By her advice, too, Mr. and Mrs. Dene sold their shop and retired to a small seaside bungalow. With their own small savings supplemented by the allowance she makes, they live their days as peaceful as their tragic memories permit—for in the end it was they who suffered most, and at nights they still whisper to each other of the strange misguided lad, talented, arrogant, and lost, whom it was their lot to have brought into the world. And, though there is not a word of it they can understand, they still read over, at times, pages of the disjointed, fragmentary manuscript notes, all that is left of the great book he planned.

As for Sammy Jones, he, released with what he graphically described as a 'flea in the ear', and stern warnings about keeping his imaginative faculties in rein for the future, may be found any day working in a fairly good job he has obtained in a fairly good restaurant fairly near the West End of London. And Bobby, returning to duty, was told off at once to track down the headquarters of a band of miscreants reported to be endangering the morals of the country by carrying on raffles for boxes of chocolates at country fairs.

THE END

Printed in Great Britain
by Amazon

37670076R00165